I looked out over the balcony. The chant of "Heretic" was as loud as before. I could hear the bronze gates being drummed by angry fists, and the palace guards warning the people to stand back. "No," I said firmly. "I will confront them. There is no way to stop them from believing the unbelievable except to face them myself."

"They will kill you, Highness!" one of the soldiers exclaimed.

But Ramesses looked at me with rash admiration. "I will come with you."

Merit pleaded, "My lady, no! Don't do this!" But we rushed through the halls while Merit simpered behind us. I turned and told her to wait in my chamber. Her eyes were wide with fear, and I knew that what we were doing was unwise. It was the kind of foolish thing that Pharaoh Seti had warned me against.

We hurried along the corridors, while on either side courtiers were locking themselves in their chambers for fear of what was to come. Unless the army was roused quickly, thousands of commoners could break the gates and loot the palace. When we reached the courtyard, the two soldiers who accompanied us stood back in fear, their eyes focused warily on the gates, which shook with the pounding fists of the mob. At the top of the ramparts, archers watched the angry crowd with their bows at the ready. Ramesses held on to my hand as tightly as he could without crushing it, and the sound of my heartbeat was even louder in my ears than the chanting or the wind.

Also by Michelle Moran

Nefertiti

The Heretic Queen

MICHELLE MORAN

Quercus

First published in Great Britain in 2008 by Quercus
This paperback edition published in 2009 by

Quercus
21 Bloomsbury Square
London
WC1A 2NS

A CIP catalogue reference for this book is available
from the British Library

ISBN 978 1 84724 722 3

This book is a work of fiction. Names, characters,
businesses, organizations, places and events are
either the product of the author's imagination

Printed and bound in Great Britain by Clays Ltd, St Ives Plc.

To my mother, Carol Moran
Without you, this would never have been possible.

NINETEENTH DYNASTY

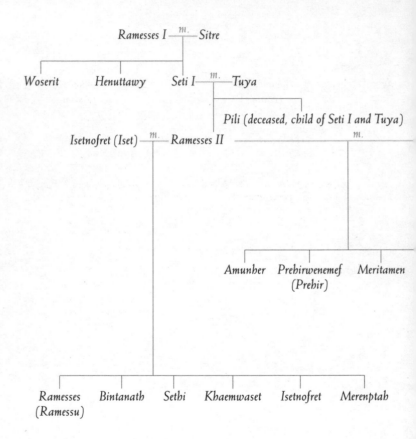

Ramesses I —m.— Sitre

Woserit   Henuttawy   Seti I —m.— Tuya

Pili (deceased, child of Seti I and Tuya)

Isetnofret (Iset) —m.— Ramesses II —m.—

Amunher   Prebirwenemef   Meritamen
(Prehir)

Ramesses   Bintanath   Sethi   Khaemwaset   Isetnofret   Merenptah
(Ramessu)

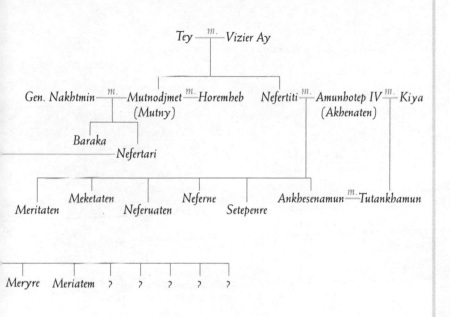

Tey —m.— Vizier Ay

Gen. Nakhtmin —m.— Mutnodjmet —m.— Horemheb   Nefertiti —m.— Amunhotep IV —m.— Kiya
                    (Mutny)   (Akhenaten)

        Baraka
              Nefertari

Meritaten   Meketaten   Neferuaten   Neferne   Setepenre   Ankhesenamun —m.— Tutankhamun

Meryre   Meriatem   ?   ?   ?   ?   ?

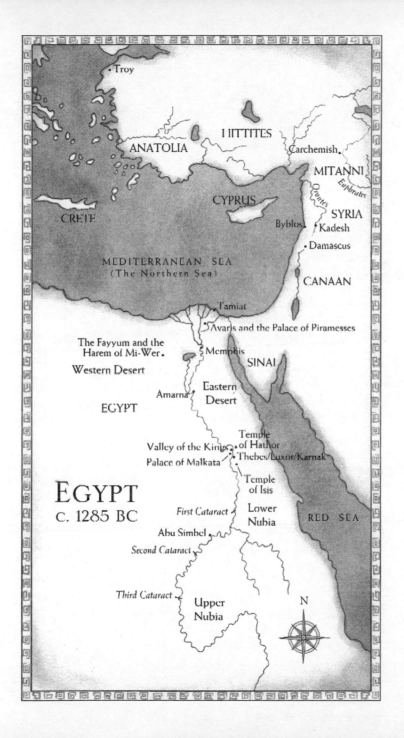

Author's Note

THERE WAS A time in the Eighteenth Dynasty when Nefertiti's family reigned supreme over Egypt. She and her husband, Akhenaten, removed Egypt's gods and raised the mysterious sun deity Aten in their place. Even after Nefertiti died and her policies were deemed heretical, it was still her daughter Ankhesenamun and her stepson, Tutankhamun, who reigned. When Tutankhamun died of an infection at around nineteen years of age, Nefertiti's father, Ay, took the throne. With his death only a few years later, the last link to the royal family was Nefertiti's younger sister, Mutnodjmet.

Knowing that Mutnodjmet would never take the crown for herself, the general Horemheb took her as his wife by force, in order to legitimize his own claim to Egypt's throne. It was the end of an era when Mutnodjmet died in childbirth, and the Nineteenth Dynasty began when Horemheb passed the throne to his general, Ramesses I. But Ramesses was an old man at the start of his rule, and when he died, the crown passed to his son, Pharaoh Seti.

Now, the year is 1283 BC. Nefertiti's family has passed on, and all that remains of her line is Mutnodjmet's daughter, Nefertari, an orphan in the court of Seti I.

PROLOGUE

I AM SURE that if I sat in a quiet place, away from the palace and the bustle of the court, I could remember scenes from my childhood much earlier than six years old. As it is, I have vague impressions of low tables with lion's paw feet crouched on polished tiles. I can still smell the scents of cedar and acacia from the open chests where my nurse stored my favorite playthings. And I am sure that if I sat in the sycamore groves for a day with nothing but the wind to disturb me, I could put an image to the sound of sistrums being shaken in a courtyard where frankincense was being burned. But all of those are hazy impressions, as difficult to see through as heavy linen, and my first real memory is of Ramesses weeping in the dark Temple of Amun.

I must have begged to go with him that night, or perhaps my nurse had been too busy at Princess Pili's bedside to realize that I was gone. But I can recall our passage through the silent halls of Amun's temple, and how Ramesses's face looked like a painting I had seen of women begging the goddess Isis for favor. I was six years old and always talking, but I knew enough to be quiet that night. I peered up

1

at the painted images of the gods as they passed through the glow of our flickering torchlight, and when we reached the inner sanctum, Ramesses spoke his first words to me.

"Stay here."

I obeyed his command and drew deeper into the shadows as he approached the towering statue of Amun. The god was illuminated by a circle of lamplight, and Ramesses knelt before the creator of life. My heart was beating so loudly in my ears that I couldn't hear what he was whispering, but his final words rang out. "Help her, Amun. She's only six. *Please* don't let Anubis take her away. Not yet!"

There was movement from the opposite door of the sanctum, and the whisper of sandaled feet warned Ramesses that he wasn't alone. He stood, wiping tears from his eyes, and I held my breath as a man emerged like a leopard from the darkness. The spotted pelt of a priest draped from his shoulders, and his left eye was as red as a pool of blood.

"Where is the king?" the High Priest demanded.

Ramesses, summoning all the courage of his nine years, stepped into the circle of lamplight and spoke. "In the palace, Your Holiness. My father won't leave my sister's side."

"Then where is your mother?"

"She . . . she's with her as well. The physicians say my sister is going to die!"

"So your father sent *children* to intervene with the gods?"

I understood for the first time why we had come. "But I've promised Amun whatever he wants," Ramesses cried. "Whatever shall be mine in my future."

"And your father never thought to call on me?"

"He has! He's asked that you come to the palace." His voice broke. "But do you think that Amun will heal her?"

The High Priest moved across the tiles. "Who can say?"

2

"But I came on my knees and offered him anything. I did as I was told."

"*You* may have," the High Priest snapped, "but Pharaoh himself has not visited my temple."

Ramesses took my hand, and we followed the hem of the High Priest's robes into the courtyard. A trumpet shattered the stillness of the night, and when priests appeared in long white cloaks, I thought of the mummified god Osiris. In the darkness, it was impossible to make out their features, but when enough had assembled, the High Priest shouted, "To the palace of Malkata!"

With torchlights before us we swept into the darkness. Our chariots raced through the chill Mechyr night to the River Nile. And when we'd crossed the waters to the steps of the palace, guards ushered our retinue into the hall.

"Where is the royal family?" the High Priest demanded.

"Inside the princess's bedchamber, Your Holiness."

The High Priest made for the stairs. "Is she alive?"

When no guard answered, Ramesses broke into a run, and I hurried after him, afraid of being left in the dark halls of the palace.

"Pili!" he cried. "Pili, *no! Wait!*" He took the stairs two at a time and at the entrance to Pili's chamber two armed guards parted for him. Ramesses swung open the heavy wooden doors and stopped. I peered into the gloom. The air was thick with incense, and the queen was bent in mourning. Pharaoh stood by himself in the shadows, away from the single oil lamp that lit the room.

"Pili," Ramesses whispered. "*Pili!*" he cried. He didn't care that it was unbecoming of a prince to weep. He ran to the bed and grasped his sister's hand. Her eyes were shut, and her small chest no longer shook with the cold. From beside her on the bed, the Queen of Egypt let out a violent sob.

"Ramesses, you must instruct them to ring the bells."

3

Ramesses looked to his father, as if the Pharaoh of Egypt might reverse death itself.

Pharaoh Seti nodded. "Go."

"But I tried!" Ramesses cried. "I begged Amun."

Seti moved across the room and placed his arm around Ramesses's shoulders. "I know. And now you must tell them to ring the bells. Anubis has taken her."

But I could see that Ramesses couldn't bear to leave Pili alone. She had been fearful of the dark, like I was, and she would be afraid of so much weeping. He hesitated, but his father's voice was firm.

"Go."

Ramesses looked down at me, and it was understood that I would accompany him.

In the courtyard, an old priestess sat beneath the twisted limbs of an acacia, holding a small bronze bell in her withered hands. "Anubis will come for us all one day," she said, her breath fogging the cold night.

"Not at six years old!" Ramesses shouted. "Not when I begged for her life from Amun."

The old priestess laughed harshly. "The gods do not listen to children! What great things have you accomplished that Amun should hear you speak? What wars have you won? What monuments have you erected?"

I hid behind Ramesses's cloak, and neither of us moved.

"Where will Amun have heard your name," she demanded, "to recognize it among so many thousands begging for aid?"

"Nowhere," I heard Ramesses whisper, and the old priestess nodded firmly.

"If the gods cannot recognize your names," she warned, "they will never hear your prayers."

CHAPTER ONE

PHARAOH OF UPPER EGYPT

Thebes, 1283 BC

"STAY STILL," Paser admonished firmly. Although Paser was my tutor and couldn't tell a princess what to do, there would be extra lines to copy if I didn't obey. I stopped shifting in my beaded dress and stood obediently with the other children of Pharaoh Seti's harem. But at thirteen years old, I was always impatient. Besides, all I could see was the gilded belt of the woman in front of me. Heavy sweat stained her white linen, trickling down her neck from beneath her wig. As soon as Ramesses passed in the royal procession, the court would be able to escape the heat and follow him into the cool shade of the temple. But the procession was moving terribly slow. I looked up at Paser, who was searching for an open path to the front of the crowd.

"Will Ramesses stop studying with us now that he's becoming coregent?" I asked.

"Yes," Paser said distractedly. He took my arm and pushed our way through the sea of bodies. "Make way for the princess Nefertari! Make way!" Women with children stepped aside until we were standing at the very edge of the roadway. All along the Avenue of

Sphinxes, tall pots of incense smoked and burned, filling the air with the sacred scent of *kyphi* that would make this, above all days, an auspicious one. The brassy sound of trumpets filled the avenue, and Paser pushed me forward. "The prince is coming!"

"I see the prince every day," I said sullenly. Ramesses was the only son of Pharaoh Seti, and now that he had turned seventeen, he would be leaving his childhood behind. There would be no more studying with him in the edduba, or hunting together in the afternoons. His coronation held no interest for me then, but when he came into view, even I caught my breath. From the wide lapis collar around his neck to the golden cuffs around his ankles and wrists, he was covered in jewels. His red hair shone like copper in the sun, and a heavy sword hung at his waist. Thousands of Egyptians surged forward to see, and as Ramesses strode past in the procession, I reached forward to tug at his hair. Although Paser inhaled sharply, Pharaoh Seti laughed, and the entire procession came to a halt.

"Little Nefertari." Pharaoh patted my head.

"Little?" I puffed out my chest. "I'm not little." I was thirteen, and in a month I'd be fourteen.

Pharaoh Seti chuckled at my obstinacy. "Little only in stature then," he promised. "And where is that determined nurse of yours?"

"Merit? In the palace, preparing for the feast."

"Well, tell Merit I want to see her in the Great Hall tonight. We must teach her to smile as beautifully as you do." He pinched my cheeks, and the procession continued into the cool recesses of the temple.

"Stay close to me," Paser ordered.

"Why? You've never minded where I've gone before."

We were swept into the temple with the rest of the court, and at last, the heavy heat of the day was shut out. In the dimly lit corridors a priest dressed in the long white robes of Amun guided us swiftly to the inner sanctum. I pressed my palm against the cool slabs of stone where images of the gods had been carved and painted. Their faces were frozen in expressions of joy, as if they were happy to see that we'd come.

"Be careful of the paintings," Paser warned sharply.

"Where are we going?"

"To the inner sanctum."

The passage widened into a vaulted chamber, and a murmur of surprise passed through the crowd. Granite columns soared up into the gloom, and the blue tiled roof had been inlaid with silver to imitate the night's glittering sky. On a painted dais, a group of Amun priests were waiting, and I thought with sadness that once Ramesses was coregent, he would never be a carefree prince in the marshes again. But there were still the other children from the edduba, and I searched the crowded room for a friend.

"Asha!" I beckoned, and when he saw me with our tutor, he threaded his way over. As usual, his black hair was bound tightly in a braid; whenever we hunted it trailed behind him like a whip. Although his arrow was often the one that brought down the bull, he was never the first to approach the kill, prompting Pharaoh to call him *Asha the Cautious*. But as Asha was cautious, Ramesses was impulsive. In the hunt, he was always charging ahead, even on the most dangerous roads, and his own father called him *Ramesses the Rash*. Of course, this was a private joke between them, and no one but Pharaoh Seti ever called him that. I smiled a greeting at Asha, but the look Paser gave him was not so welcoming.

"Why aren't you standing with the prince on the dais?"

"But the ceremony won't begin until the call of the trumpets," Asha explained. When Paser sighed, Asha turned to me. "What's the matter? Aren't you excited?"

"How can I be excited," I demanded, "when Ramesses will spend all his time in the Audience Chamber, and in less than a year you'll be leaving for the army?"

Asha shifted uncomfortably in his leather pectoral. "Actually, if I'm to be a general," he explained, "my training must begin this month." The trumpets blared, and when I opened my mouth to protest, he turned. "It's time!" Then his long braid disappeared into the crowd. A great hush fell over the temple, and I looked up at Paser, who avoided my gaze.

"What is *she* doing here?" someone hissed, and I knew without turning that the woman was speaking about me. "She'll bring nothing but bad luck on this day."

Paser looked down at me, and as the priests began their hymns to Amun, I pretended not to have heard the woman's whispers. Instead, I watched as the High Priest Rahotep emerged from the shadows. A leopard's pelt hung from his shoulders, and as he slowly ascended the dais, the children next to me averted their gaze. His face appeared frozen, like a mask that never stops grinning, and his left eye was still red as a carnelian stone. Heavy clouds of incense filled the inner sanctum, but Rahotep appeared immune to the smoke. He lifted the *hedjet* crown in his hands, and without blinking, placed it on top of Ramesses's golden brow. "May the great god Amun embrace Ramesses the Second, for now he is Pharaoh of Upper Egypt."

While the court erupted into wild cheers, I felt my heart sink. I fanned away the acrid scent of perfume from under women's arms, and children with ivory clappers beat them together in a noise that filled the entire chamber. Seti, who was now only ruler of Lower Egypt, smiled widely. Then hundreds of courtiers began to move, crushing me between their belted waists.

"Come. We're leaving for the palace!" Paser shouted.

I glanced behind me. "What about Asha?"

"He will have to find you later."

🔲 🔲 🔲

DIGNITARIES FROM every kingdom in the world came to the palace of Malkata to celebrate Ramesses's coronation. I stood at the entrance to the Great Hall, where the court took its dinner every night, and admired the glow of a thousand oil lamps as they cast their light across the polished tiles. The chamber was filled with men and women dressed in their finest kilts and beaded gowns.

"Have you ever seen so many people?"

I turned. "Asha!" I exclaimed. "Where have you been?"

"My father wanted me in the stables to prepare—"

"For your time in the military?" I crossed my arms, and when Asha saw that I was truly upset, he smiled disarmingly.

"But I'm here with you now." He took my arm and led me into the hall. "Have you seen the emissaries who have arrived? I'll bet you could speak with any one of them."

"I can't speak *Shasu*," I said, to be contrary.

"But every other language! You could be a vizier if you weren't a girl." He glanced across the hall and pointed. *"Look!"*

I followed his gaze to Pharaoh Seti and Queen Tuya on the royal dais. The queen never went anywhere without Adjo, and the black-and-white dog rested his tapered head on her lap. Although her *iwiw* had been bred for hunting hare in the marshes, the farthest he ever walked was from his feathered cushion to the water bowl. Now that Ramesses was Pharaoh of Upper Egypt, a third throne had been placed next to his mother.

"So Ramesses will be seated off with his parents," I said glumly. He had always eaten with me beneath the dais, at the long table filled with the most important members of the court. And now that his chair had been removed, I could see that my own had been placed next to Woserit, the High Priestess of Hathor. Asha saw this as well and shook his head.

"It's too bad you can't sit with me. What will you ever talk about with Woserit?"

"Nothing, I suspect."

"At least they've placed you across from Henuttawy. Do you think she might speak with you now?"

All of Thebes was fascinated with Henuttawy, not because she was one of Pharaoh Seti's two younger sisters, but because there was no one in Egypt with such mesmerizing beauty. Her lips were carefully painted to match the red robes of the goddess Isis, and only the priestesses were allowed to wear that vivid color. As a child of seven I had been fascinated by the way her cloak swirled around her sandals, like water moving gently across the prow of a ship. I had thought at the time that she was the most beautiful woman I would ever see, and tonight I could see that I was still correct. Yet even though we had eaten together at the same table for as long as I could remember, I couldn't recall a single instance when she had spoken to me. I sighed. "I doubt it."

"Don't worry, Nefer." Asha patted my shoulder the way an older brother might have. "I'm sure you'll make friends."

He crossed the hall, and I watched him greet his father at the generals' table. *Soon*, I thought, *he'll be one of those men, wearing his braided hair in a small loop at the back of his neck, never going anywhere without his sword.* When Asha said something to make his father laugh, I thought of my mother, Queen Mutnodjmet. If she had survived, this would have been her court, filled with her friends, and viziers, and laughter. Women would never dare to whisper about me, for instead of being a spare princess, I'd be *the* princess.

I took my place next to Woserit, and a prince from Hatti smiled across at me. The three long braids that only Hittites wore fell down his back, and as the guest of honor, his chair had been placed to the right of Henuttawy. Yet no one had remembered the Hittite custom of offering bread to the most important guest first. I took the untouched bowl and passed it to him.

He was about to thank me when Henuttawy placed her slender hand on his arm and announced, "The court of Egypt is honored to host the prince of Hatti as a guest at my nephew's coronation."

The viziers, along with everyone at the table, raised their cups, and when the prince made a slow reply in Hittite, Henuttawy laughed. But what the prince said hadn't been funny. His eyes searched the table for help, and when no one came to his aid, he looked at me.

"He is saying that although this is a happy day," I translated, "he hopes that Pharaoh Seti will live for many years and not leave the throne of Lower Egypt to Ramesses too soon."

Henuttawy paled, and at once I saw that I was wrong to have spoken.

"Intelligent girl," the prince said in broken Egyptian.

But Henuttawy narrowed her eyes. "*Intelligent?* Even a parrot can learn to imitate."

"Come, Priestess. Nefertari is quite clever," Vizier Anemro offered. "No one else remembered to pass bread to the prince when he came to the table."

"Of course she remembered," Henuttawy said sharply. "She probably learned it from her aunt. If I recall, the Heretic Queen liked the Hittites so much she invited them to Amarna where they brought us the plague. I'm surprised our brother even allows her to sit among us."

Woserit frowned. "That was a long time ago. Nefertari can't help who her aunt was." She turned to me. "It's not important," she said kindly.

"Really?" Henuttawy gloated. "Then why else would Ramesses consider marrying Iset and not our *princess?*" I lowered my cup, and Henuttawy continued. "Of course, I have no idea what Nefertari will do if she's not to become a wife of Ramesses. Maybe you could take her in, Woserit." Henuttawy looked to her younger sister, the High Priestess of the cow goddess Hathor. "I hear that your temple needs some good heifers."

A few of the courtiers at our table snickered, and Henuttawy looked at me the way a snake looks at its dinner.

Woserit cleared her throat. "I don't know why our brother puts up with you."

Henuttawy held out her hand to the Hittite prince, and both of them stood to join the dancing. When the music began, Woserit leaned close to me. "You must be careful around my sister now. Henuttawy has many powerful friends in the palace, and she can ruin you in Thebes if that's what she wishes."

"Because I translated for the prince?"

"Because Henuttawy has an interest in seeing Iset become Chief Wife, and there has been talk that this was a role Ramesses might ask you to fill. Given your past, I should say it's unlikely, but my sister would still be more than happy to see you disappear. If you want to continue to survive in this palace, Nefertari, I suggest you think where your place in it will be. Ramesses's childhood ended tonight, and your friend Asha will enter the military soon. What will you do? You were born a princess and your mother was a queen. But when your mother died, so did your place in this court. You have no one to guide you, and that's why you're allowed to run around wild, hunting with the boys and tugging Ramesses's hair."

I flushed. I had thought Woserit was on my side.

"Oh, Pharaoh Seti thinks it is cute," she admitted. "And you are. But in two years that kind of behavior won't be so charming. And what will you do when you're twenty? Or thirty even? When the gold that you've inherited is spent, who will support you? Hasn't Paser ever spoken about this?"

I steadied my lip with my teeth. "No."

Woserit raised her brows. *"None* of your tutors?"

I shook my head.

"Then you still have much to learn, no matter how fluent your Hittite."

⊥ ⊥ ⊥

THAT EVENING, as I undressed for bed, my nurse remarked on my unusual silence.

"What? Not practicing languages, my lady?" She poured warm water from a pitcher into a bowl, then set out a cloth so I could wash my face.

"What is the point of practicing?" I asked. "When will I use them? Viziers learn languages, not spare princesses. And since a girl can't be a vizier . . ."

Merit scraped a stool across the tiles and sat next to me. She studied my face in the polished bronze, and no nurse could have been more different from her charge. Her bones were large, whereas mine were small, and Ramesses liked to say that whenever she was angry her neck swelled beneath her chin like a fat pelican's pouch. She carried her weight in her hips and her breasts, whereas I had no hips and breasts at all. She had been my nurse from the time my mother had died in childbirth, and I loved her as if she were my own *mawat*. Now, her gaze softened as she guessed at my troubles. "Ah." She sighed deeply. "This is because Ramesses is going to marry Iset."

I glanced at her in the mirror. "Then it's *true?*"

She shrugged. "There's been some talk in the palace." As she shifted her ample bottom on the stool, faience anklets jangled on her feet. "Of course, I had hopes that he was going to marry you."

"Me?" I thought of Woserit's words and stared at her. "But why?"

She took back my cloth and wrung it out in the bowl. "Because you are the daughter of a queen, no matter your relationship to the Heretic and his wife." She was referring to Nefertiti and her husband, Akhenaten, who had banished Egypt's gods and angered Amun. Their names were never spoken in Thebes. They were simply *The Heretics*, and even before I had understood what this meant, I had known that it was bad. Now, I tried to imagine Ramesses looking at me with his wide blue eyes, asking me to become his wife, and a warm flush crept over my body. Merit continued, "Your mother would have expected to see you married to a king."

"And if I don't marry?" After all, what if Ramesses didn't feel the same way about me as I felt about him?

"Then you will become a priestess. But you go every day to the Temple of Amun, and you've seen how the priestesses live," she said warningly, motioning for me to stand with her. "There wouldn't be any fine horses or chariots."

I raised my arms, and Merit took off my beaded dress. "Even if I were a High Priestess?"

Merit laughed. "Are you already planning for Henuttawy's death?"

I flushed. "Of course not."

"Well, you are thirteen. Nearly fourteen. It's time to decide your place in this palace."

"Why does everyone keep telling me this tonight?"

"Because a king's coronation changes everything."

I put on a fresh sheath, and when I climbed into bed, Merit looked down at me.

"You have eyes like Tefer," she said tenderly. "They practically glow in the lamplight." My spotted *miw* curled closer to me, and when Merit saw us together she smiled. "A pair of green-eyed beauties," she said.

"Not as beautiful as Iset."

Merit sat herself on the edge of my bed. "You are the equal of any girl in this palace."

I rolled my eyes and turned my face away. "You don't have to pretend. I know I'm nothing like Iset—"

"Iset is three years older than you. In a year or two, you will be a woman and will have grown into your body."

"Asha says I'll never grow, that I'll still be as short as Seti's dwarfs when I'm twenty."

Merit pushed her chin inward so that the pelican's pouch wagged angrily. "And what does Asha think he knows about dwarfs? You will be as tall and beautiful as Isis one day! And if not as tall," she added cautiously, "then at least as beautiful. What other girl in this palace has eyes like yours? They're as pretty as your mother's. And you have your aunt's smile."

"I'm *nothing* like my aunt," I said angrily.

But then, Merit had been raised in the court of Nefertiti and Akhenaten, so she would know if this were true. Her father had been an important vizier, and Merit had been a nurse to Nefertiti's children. In the terrible plague that swept through Amarna, Merit lost her family and two of Nefertiti's daughters in her care. But she never spoke about it to me, and I knew she wished to forget this time twenty years ago. I was sure, as well, that Paser had taught us that the High Priest Rahotep had also served my aunt once, but I was too afraid to confirm this with Merit. This is what my past was like for me. Narrowed eyes, whispering, and uncertainty. I shook my head and murmured, "I am *nothing* like my aunt."

Merit raised her brows. "She may have been a heretic," she whispered, "but she was the greatest beauty who ever walked in Egypt."

"Prettier than Henuttawy?" I challenged.

"Henuttawy would have been cheap bronze to your aunt's gold."

I tried to imagine a face prettier than Henuttawy's, but couldn't do it. Secretly I wished that there was an image of Nefertiti left in Thebes. "Do you think that Ramesses will choose Iset because I am related to the Heretic Queen?"

Merit pulled the covers over my chest, prompting a cry of protest from Tefer. "I think that Ramesses will choose Iset because you are thirteen and he is seventeen. But soon, my lady, you will be a woman and ready for whatever future you decide."

CHAPTER TWO

THREE LINES
OF CUNEIFORM

EVERY MORNING for the past seven years I had walked from my chamber in the royal courtyard to the small Temple of Amun by the palace. And there, beneath the limestone pillars, I had giggled with other students of the edduba while Tutor Oba shuffled up the path, using his walking stick like a sword to beat back anyone who stood in his way. Inside, the temple priests would scent our clothes with sacred *kyphi*, and we would leave smelling of Amun's daily blessing. Ramesses and Asha would race me to the white-washed schoolhouse beyond the temple, but yesterday's coronation changed everything. Now Ramesses would be gone, and Asha would feel too embarrassed to race. He would tell me he was too old for such things. And soon, he would leave me as well.

When Merit appeared in my chamber, I followed her glumly into my robing room, lifting my arms while she fastened a linen belt around my kilt.

"Myrtle or fenugreek today, my lady?"

I shrugged. "I don't care."

She frowned at me and fetched the myrtle cream. She opened the alabaster jar with a twist, then spread the thick cream over my cheeks. "Stop making that face," she reprimanded.

"What face?"

"The one like Bes."

I suppressed a smile. Bes was the dwarf god of childbirth; his hideous grimace scared Anubis from dragging newborn children away to the Afterlife.

"I don't know what you have to sulk about," Merit said. "You won't be alone. There's an entire edduba full of students."

"And they're only nice to me because of Ramesses. Asha and Ramesses are my only real friends. None of the girls will go hunting or swimming."

"Then it's lucky for you that Asha is still in the edduba."

"For now." I took my schoolbag grudgingly, and as Merit saw me off from my chamber she called, "Scowling like Bes will only scare him away sooner!"

But I wasn't in the mood for her humor. I took the longest path to the edduba, through the eastern passageway into the shadowed courtyards at the rear of the palace, then along the crescent of temples and barracks that separated Malkata from the hills beyond. I have often heard the palace compared to a pearl, perfectly protected within its shell. On one side are the sandstone cliffs, on the other is the lake that had been carved by my *akhu* to allow boats to travel from the River Nile to the very steps of the Audience Chamber. Amunhotep III built it for his wife, Queen Tiye. When his architects had said that such a thing could never be made, he designed it himself. With his legacy before me, I walked slowly around the Arena, past the barracks with their dusty parade grounds, and then beyond the servants' quarters that squatted back into the wadis to the west. When I came to the lakeshore, I approached the water to peer at my reflection.

I don't look anything like Bes, I thought. *For one, he has a much bigger nose than I do.* I made the grimace that all artists carve on statues of Bes, and behind me someone laughed.

"Are you admiring your teeth?" Asha cried. "What kind of face was that?"

I glared at him. "Merit says I have a face like Bes."

Asha stepped back to scrutinize me. "Yes, I can see the resemblance. You both have big cheeks, and you *are* rather short."

"Stop it!"

"I wasn't the one making the face!" We continued our walk to the temple and he asked, "So did Merit tell you the news last night? Ramesses will probably marry Iset."

I looked away and didn't reply. In the heat of Thoth, the sun cast its rays across the lake like a golden fisherman's net. "If Ramesses was going to be married," I said finally, "why wouldn't he tell us about it himself?"

"Perhaps he isn't certain. After all, it's Pharaoh Seti who will ultimately decide."

"But she isn't a match for Ramesses at all! She doesn't hunt, or swim, or play Senet. She can't even read Hittite!"

Tutor Oba glared as we approached the courtyard, and under his breath Asha whispered, "Prepare for it!"

"How nice of the two of you to join us!" Oba exclaimed. Two hundred faces turned in our direction, and Tutor Oba lashed out at Asha with his stick. "Get in line!" He caught Asha on the back of the leg, and we scampered to join the other students. "Do you think that Ra appears in his solar bark when he *feels* like it? Of course not! He's on time. Every sunrise he's on time!"

Asha glanced over his shoulder at me in line as we followed Tutor Oba into the sanctuary. Cloth mats had been spread out for us on the floor, and we took our seats and waited for the priests. I whispered to Asha, "I'll bet Ramesses is sitting in the Audience Chamber right now, wishing he was with us."

"I don't know. He's safe from Tutor Oba."

I snickered as seven priests entered the chamber, swinging incense from bronze holders and intoning the morning hymn to Amun.

Hail to thee, Amun-Ra, Lord of the thrones of the earth, the oldest
existence, ancient of heaven, support of all things.
Chief of the gods, lord of truth; maker of all things above and below.
Hail to thee.

As the incense filled the room, a student coughed. Tutor Oba turned around to look fiercely at him and I elbowed Asha in the side, bent my mouth into a mean, angry line, then imitated Oba's snarling. One of the students laughed out loud, and Tutor Oba twisted around. "Asha and Princess Nefertari!" he snapped.

Asha glared at me and I giggled. But outside the temple, I didn't ask him to race me to the edduba.

"I don't know why the priests don't throw us out," he said.

I grinned. "Because we're royalty."

"*You're* royalty," Asha countered. "I'm the son of a soldier."

"You mean the son of a general."

"Still, I'm not like you. I don't have a chamber in the palace or a body servant. I need to be careful."

"But it was funny," I prompted.

"A little," he admitted as we reached the low white walls of the royal edduba. The schoolhouse squatted like a fat goose on the hillside, and Asha's footsteps slowed as we approached its open doors. "So what do you think it'll be today?" he asked.

"Probably cuneiform."

He sighed heavily. "I can't afford another poor report to my father."

"Take the reed mat next to mine, and I'll write big enough for you to see," I promised.

Inside the halls of the edduba, students called to one another, laughing and exchanging stories until the trumpet sounded for class. Paser stood at the front of our chamber, observing the chaos, but when Iset entered, the room grew silent. She moved through the students, and they parted before her as if a giant hand had pushed them aside. She sat across from me, folding her long legs on her reed mat the way she always did, but this time, when she swept back her dark hair, her fingers seemed fascinating to me. They were long and tapered. At court, only Henuttawy surpassed Iset's skill with the harp. Was that why Pharaoh Seti thought she'd make a good wife?

"We may all stop staring now," Paser announced. "Let us take out our ink. Today, we translate two of the Hittite emperor's letters to Pharaoh Seti. As you know, Hittite is written in cuneiform, which will mean transcribing every word from cuneiform to hieroglyphics."

I took out several reed pens and ink from my bag. When the basket of blank papyrus came to me, I took the smoothest one from the pile. Outside the edduba a trumpet blared again, and the noise from the other classrooms went silent. Paser passed out copies of Emperor Muwatallis's first letter, and in the early morning heat the sound of pens scratching on papyrus settled upon the room. The air felt heavy, and sweat beaded behind my knees where I sat cross-legged. Two fan bearers from the palace cooled the room with their long blades, and as the air stirred, Iset's perfume moved across the chamber to tickle my nose. She told the students she wore it to cover the unbearable smell of the ink, which is made from ash and the fat boiled off a donkey's skin. But I knew this wasn't true. Palace scribes mixed our ink with musk oil to cover the terrible scent. What she really wanted was to attract attention. I wrinkled my nose and refused to be distracted. The important information in the letter had been removed, and what had been left was simple to translate. I wrote several lines in large hieroglyphics on my papyrus, and when I'd finished with the letter, Paser cleared his throat.

"The scribes should be done with the translation of Emperor Muwatallis's second letter. When I return, we will move on," he warned sternly. The students waited until the sound of his sandals had faded before turning to me.

"Do you understand this, Nefer?" Asha pointed to the sixth line.

"And what about this?" Baki, Vizier Anemro's son, couldn't make out the third. He held out his scroll and the class waited.

"*To the Pharaoh of Egypt, who is wealthy in land and great in strength.* It is like all of his other letters." I shrugged. "It begins with flattery and ends with a threat."

"And what about this?" someone else asked. The students gathered around me and I translated the words quickly for them. When I glanced at Iset, I saw that her first line wasn't finished. "Do you need help?"

"Why would I need help?" She pushed aside her scroll. "You haven't heard?"

"You're about to become wife to Pharaoh Ramesses," I said flatly.

Iset stood. "You think that because I wasn't born a princess like you that I'll spend my life weaving linen in the harem?"

She wasn't speaking about the harem of Mi-Wer in the Fayyum, where Pharaoh's least important wives are kept. She was speaking about the harem behind the edduba, where Seti housed the women of

previous kings and those whom he himself had chosen. Iset's grandmother had been one of Pharaoh Horemheb's wives. I had heard that
one day he saw her walking along the riverbank, collecting shells for
her own husband's funeral. She was already pregnant with her only
child, but just as that had not stopped him from taking my mother,
Horemheb wanted her as his bride. So Iset was not related to a
Pharaoh at all, but to a long line of women who had lived, and fished,
and made their work on the River Nile. "I may be an orphan of the
harem," she went on, "but I think everyone here would agree that
being the niece of a heretic is much worse, whatever your fat nurse
likes to pretend. And no one in this edduba likes you," she revealed.
"They smile at you because of Ramesses, and now that he's gone they
only go on smiling and laughing because you help them."

"That's a lie!" Asha stood up angrily. "No one here feels that way."

I looked around, but none of the other students came to my defense, and a shamed heat crept into my cheeks.

Iset smirked. "You may think you're great friends with Ramesses,
hunting and swimming in the lake together, but he's marrying *me.* And
I've already consulted with the priests," she said. "They've given me a
charm for every possible event."

Asha exclaimed, "Do you think Nefertari is going to try and give
you the evil eye?"

The other students in the edduba laughed, and Iset drew herself
up to her fullest height. "She can try! *All* of you can try," she said vi-
ciously. "It won't make any difference. I'm wasting my time in this
edduba now."

"You certainly are." A shadow darkened the doorway, then
Henuttawy appeared in her red robes of Isis. She glanced across the
room at us, and a lion could not have looked at a mouse with any
less interest. "Where is your tutor?" she demanded.

Iset moved quickly to the side of the High Priestess, and I noticed that she had begun to paint her eyes the same way that Henuttawy did, with long sweeps of kohl extending to her temples. "Gone to see the scribes," she answered eagerly.

Henuttawy hesitated. She walked over to my reed mat and looked down. "Princess Nefertari. Still studying your hieroglyphs?"

"No. I'm studying my cuneiform."

Asha laughed, and Henuttawy's gaze flicked to him. But he was taller than the other boys, and there was an intelligence in his glare that unnerved her. She turned back to me. "I don't know why you waste your time, especially when you'll only become a priestess in a run-down temple like Hathor's."

"As always, it is charming to see you, my lady." Our tutor had returned with a handful of scrolls. He laid them on a low table, as Henuttawy turned to face him.

"Ah, Paser. I was just telling Princess Nefertari to be diligent in her studies. Unfortunately, Iset does not have time for that anymore."

"What a shame," Paser replied, looking at Iset's discarded papyrus. "Today, I believe she was going to progress to *three* lines of cuneiform."

The students snickered, and Henuttawy hurried from the edduba with Iset in tow.

"There is no cause for laughing," Paser said sharply, and the room fell silent. "We may all go back to our translations now. When you are finished, come to the front of the room and bring your papyrus. Then you may begin work on Emperor Muwatallis's second letter."

I tried to concentrate, but tears blurred my vision. I didn't want anyone to see how much Iset's words had hurt, so I kept my head low, even when Baki made a hissing noise at me. *He wants help now*, I thought. *But would he even glance at me outside the edduba?*

I finished my translation and approached Paser, handing him my sheet.

He smiled approvingly. "Excellent, as always." I glanced back at the other students and wondered if I detected resentment in their eyes. "I must warn you about this next letter, however. There is an unflattering reference to your aunt."

"Why should I care? I'm nothing like her," I said defensively.

"I wanted to be sure you understood. It seems the scribes forgot to take it out."

"She was a heretic," I said, "and whatever words the emperor has for her, I am sure they are justified."

I returned to my reed mat, then skimmed the letter, searching for familiar names. Nefertiti was mentioned at the bottom of the papyrus, and so was my mother. I held my breath as I read Emperor Muwatallis's words.

> You threaten us with war, but our god
> Teshub has watched over Hatti for a
> thousand years, while your gods were
> banished by Pharaoh Akhenaten. What
> makes you think that they have forgiven his
> heresy? It may be that Sekhmet, your
> goddess of war, has abandoned you
> completely. And what of Mutnodjmet,
> Nefertiti's sister? Your people allowed her
> to become a queen when all of Egypt knows
> she serviced your Heretic King in his temple
> as well as his private chamber. Do you
> really think your gods have forgiven this?
> Will you risk war with us when we have
> treated our own gods with respect?

I glanced up at Paser, and in his expression seemed to flicker a trace of regret. But I would *never* be pitied. Clenching the reed pen in my hand, I wrote as quickly and firmly as I could, and when a tear smeared the ink on my papyrus, I blotted it away with sand.

🏛 🏛 🏛

WHILE COURTIERS filled the Great Hall that evening, Asha and I waited on a corner of the balcony, whispering to each other about what had happened in the edduba. The setting sun crowned his head in a soft glow, and the braid he wore over his shoulder was nearly as long as mine. I sat forward on the limestone balustrade looking at him. "Have you ever heard Iset so angry?"

"No, but I've never heard her say much at all," he admitted.

"She's been with us for seven years!"

"All she does is giggle with those harem girls who wait for her outside."

"She certainly wouldn't like it if she heard you say that," I warned.

Asha shrugged. "It doesn't seem she likes much of anything. And certainly not you—"

"And what have I ever done to her?" I exclaimed.

But Asha was saved from answering when Ramesses burst through the double doors.

"There you are!" he called across to us, and Asha said quickly, "Don't say anything about Iset. Ramesses will only think we're jealous."

Ramesses looked between the two of us. "Where have both of you been?"

"Where have *you* been?" Asha countered. "We haven't seen you since your coronation."

"We thought we might not ever see you again," I added, a little more plaintively than intended.

Ramesses embraced me. "I would never leave my little sister behind."

"How about your charioteer?"

At once, Ramesses let go of me. "It's done then?" he exclaimed, and Asha said smugly, "Just a few hours ago. Tomorrow I begin my training to be an officer of Pharaoh's charioteers."

I inhaled sharply. "And you didn't tell me?"

"I was waiting to tell you both!"

Ramesses gave Asha a congratulatory slap on the back, but I cried, "Now I'll be the only one left at the edduba with Paser!"

"Come," Ramesses said, placating me. "Don't be upset."

"Why not?" I complained. "Asha is going to the army and you're getting married to Iset!"

Asha and I both looked at Ramesses to see if it was true.

"My father is going to announce it tonight. He feels she'll make a good wife."

"But do you?" I asked.

"I worry about her skills," he admitted. "You've seen her in Paser's class. But Henuttawy thinks I should make her Chief Wife."

"Pharaohs don't choose a Chief Wife until they're eighteen!" I blurted.

Ramesses studied me, and I colored at my outburst. "So what is that?" I changed the subject and pointed to the jeweled case he was carrying.

"A sword." He opened the case to produce an arm-length blade.

Asha was impressed. "I've never seen anything like it," he admitted.

"It's Hittite, made of something they call iron. It's said to be even stronger than bronze." The weapon had a sharper curve than anything I had seen before, and from the designs carefully etched onto its hilt, I imagined that its cost had been great.

Ramesses handed the weapon to Asha, who held it up to the light. "Who gave this to you?"

"My father, for my coronation."

Asha handed the iron blade to me, and I gripped the hilt in my palm. "You could use this to decapitate Muwatallis!"

Ramesses laughed. "Or at least his son, Urhi."

Asha looked between us.

"The emperor of the Hittites," I explained. "When he dies, his son, Urhi, will succeed him."

"Asha doesn't care about politics," Ramesses said. "But ask him anything about horses and chariots . . ."

The double doors to the balcony swung open, and Iset fixed us instantly in her gaze. Her beaded wig was adorned with charms, and a talented body servant had dusted the kohl beneath her eyes with small flecks of gold.

"The three inseparables," she said, smiling.

I realized how much she sounded like Henuttawy. She crossed the balcony, and I wondered where she'd gotten the deben to afford sandals with lapis jewels. What gold had been left when Iset's mother died had long since been spent educating her.

"What is this?" She looked down at the sword I had returned to Ramesses.

"For war," Ramesses explained. "Would you like to watch? I'm going to show Asha and Nefer how it cuts."

Iset frowned prettily. "But the cupbearer has already poured your father's wine."

Ramesses hesitated. He breathed in her perfume, and I could see how he was affected by her closeness. Her sheath was tight over her curves and exposed her beautifully hennaed breasts. Then I noticed the gold and carnelian necklace at her throat. She was wearing Queen Tuya's jewels. The queen, who had watched me play with

Ramesses since we were children, had given her favorite necklace to Iset.

Ramesses glanced across at Asha, and then at me.

"Some other time," Asha said helpfully, and Iset took Ramesses's arm. We watched as they left the balcony together, and I turned to Asha.

"Did you see what she was wearing?"

"Queen Tuya's own jewels," he said with resignation.

"But why would Ramesses choose a wife like Iset? So she's pretty. What does that matter when she doesn't speak Hittite or even write cuneiform?"

"It matters because Pharaoh needs a wife," Asha said grimly. "You know, he might have chosen you—if not for your family."

It was as though someone had crushed the air from my chest. I followed him into the Great Hall, and that evening, when the marriage was formerly announced, I felt I was losing something I would never get back. Yet neither of Iset's parents were there to see her triumph. Her father was unknown, and this would have been a great scandal for Iset's mother had she lived through childbirth. So the herald announced her grandmother's name instead, for she had raised Iset and had once been a part of Pharaoh Horemheb's harem. She had been dead for a year, but this was the proper thing to do.

When the feast was finally over, I returned to my chamber off the royal courtyard and sat quietly at my mother's ebony table. Merit wiped the kohl from my eyes and the red ochre from my lips, then she handed me a cone of incense and watched as I knelt before my mother's *naos*. Some *naoi* are large and granite, with an opening in the center to place a statue of a god and a ledge on which to burn incense. My *naos*, however, was small and wooden. It was a shrine my mother had owned as a girl, and perhaps even her mother before her. When I knelt, it only came up to my chest, and inside the wooden doors was a statue of Mut, after whom my mother had been named. While the feline goddess regarded me with her cat eyes, I blinked away tears.

"What would have happened if my mother had lived?" I asked Merit.

My nurse sat on the corner of the bed. "I don't know, my lady. But remember the many hardships that she endured. In the fire your mother lost everyone she loved."

The chambers in Malkata to which the fire had spread had never been rebuilt. The blackened stones and charred remains of wooden tables still stood beyond the royal courtyard, reclaimed by vines and untended weeds. When I was seven, I had insisted that Merit take me there, and when we arrived I'd stood frozen to the spot, trying to imagine where my father had been when the flames broke out. Merit said it was an oil lamp that had fallen, but I had heard the viziers speak of something darker, of a plot to kill my grandfather, the Pharaoh Ay. Behind those walls, my entire family had vanished in the flames: my brother, my father, my grandfather and his queen. Only my mother survived because she had been in the gardens. And when General Horemheb heard that Ay was dead, he came to the palace with the army behind him and forced my mother into marriage. For she had been the last royal link to the throne. I wondered if Horemheb felt any guilt at all when she too embraced Osiris, still crying out my father's name. Sometimes, I thought of her last weeks on earth. Just as my *ka* was being formed by Khnum on his potter's wheel, hers had been flying away.

I looked over my shoulder at Merit, watching me with unhappy eyes. She didn't like when I asked questions about my mother, but she never refused to answer them. "And when she died," I asked, even though I already knew the answer, "who did she cry out for?"

Merit's face grew solemn. "Your father. And—"

I turned, forgetting about the cone of incense. *"And?"*

"And her sister," she admitted.

My eyes widened. "You've never said that before!"

"Because it's nothing you needed to know," Merit said quickly.

"But was she truly a heretic, as they say?"

"My lady—"

I saw that Merit was going to put off my question, and I shook my head firmly. "I was named for Nefertiti. My mother couldn't have believed that her sister was a heretic."

No one spoke the name of Nefertiti in the palace, and Merit pressed her lips together to keep from reprimanding me. She unfolded her hands and her gaze grew distant. "It was not so much the Pharaoh-Queen herself, as her husband."

"Akhenaten?"

Merit shifted uncomfortably. "Yes. He banished the gods. He destroyed the temples of Amun and replaced the statues of Ra with ones of himself."

"And my aunt?"

"She filled the streets with her image."

"In place of the gods?"

"Yes."

"But then where have they gone? I have never even seen a likeness of them."

"Of course not!" Merit stood. "Everything that belonged to your aunt was destroyed."

"Even my mother's name," I said and looked back at the shrine. Incense drifted across the face of the feline goddess. When she died, Horemheb had taken everything. "It's as though I've been born with no *akhu*," I said. "No ancestors at all. Did you know that in the edduba," I confided, "students don't learn about Nefertiti's reign, or the reign of Pharaoh Ay, or Tutankhamun?"

Merit nodded. "Yes. Horemheb erased their names from the scrolls."

"He took their lives. He ruled for four years, but they teach us that he ruled for dozens and dozens. *I* know better. *Ramesses* knows better. But what will my children be taught? For them, my family will never have existed."

Each year, on the Feast of Wag, Egyptians visit the mortuary temples of their ancestors. But there was nowhere for me to honor my own mother's *ka* or the *ka* of my father with incense or a bowl of oil. Even their tombs had been hidden in the hills of Thebes, safe from the Aten priests and Horemheb's vengeance. "Who will remember them, Merit? *Who?*"

Merit placed her palm on my shoulder. "You."

"And when I'm gone?"

"Make sure you are never gone from the people's memory. And those who know of your fame will search out your past and find Pharaoh Ay and Queen Mutnodjmet."

"Otherwise they will be erased."

"And Horemheb will have succeeded."

CHAPTER THREE

THE WAY
A CAT LISTENS

THE HIGH PRIESTS divined that Ramesses should marry on the twelfth of Thoth. They had chosen it as the most auspicious day in the season of Akhet, and when I walked from the palace to the Temple of Amun, the lake was already crowded with vessels bringing food and gifts for the celebration.

Inside the temple I kept to myself, and not even Tutor Oba could find fault with me when the priests were finished. "What's the matter, Princess? No one to entertain now that Pharaoh Ramesses and Asha are gone?"

I looked up into Tutor Oba's wrinkled face. His skin was like papyrus; every part of it was lined. Even around his nose there were creases. I suppose he was only fifty, but he seemed to me to be as old as the cracking paint in my chamber.

"Yes, everybody has left me," I said.

Tutor Oba laughed, but it wasn't a pleasant sound.

"Everybody has left you!" he repeated. *"Everybody."* He looked around him at the two hundred students who were following him to the edduba. "Tutor Paser tells me you are a very good student, and now I wonder if he means in acting or in languages. Perhaps in a few years, we'll be seeing you in one of Pharaoh's performances!"

I walked the rest of the way to the edduba in silence. Behind me, I could still hear Tutor Oba's grating laugh, and inside the class I was too angry to care when Paser announced, "Today, we will begin a new language."

I don't remember what I learned that day, or how Paser began to teach us the language of Shasu. Instead of paying attention, I stared at the girl on the reed mat to my left. She was no more than eight or nine, but she was sitting at the front of the class where Asha should have been. When the time came for our afternoon meal, she ran away with another girl her age, and it occurred to me that I had no longer had anyone to eat with.

"Who's in for dice?" Baki announced, between mouthfuls.

"I'll play," I said.

Baki looked behind him to a group of boys, and their faces were all set against me. "I . . . don't think we allow girls to play."

"You allow girls every other day," I said.

"But . . . but not today."

The other boys nodded, and shame brightened my cheeks. I stepped into the courtyard to find a seat by myself, then recognized Asha on the stone bench where we always ate.

"Asha! What are you doing here?" I exclaimed.

He leaned his yew bow against the bench. "Soldiers get meal-times, too," he said. He searched my face. "What's the matter?"

I shrugged. "The boys won't allow me to play dice with them."

"Which boys?" he demanded.

"It doesn't matter."

"It *does* matter." His voice grew menacing. "Which ones?"

"Baki," I said, and when Asha rose threateningly from the bench, I pulled him back. "It's not just him, it's everyone, Asha. Iset was right. They were friendly to me because of you and Ramesses, and now that you're both gone, I'm just a leftover princess from a dynasty of heretics." I raised my chin and refused to be upset. "So what is it like to be a charioteer?"

Asha sat back and studied my face, but I didn't need his sympathy. "Wonderful," he admitted, and opened his sack. "No cuneiform, no hieroglyphics, no translating Muwatallis's endless threats." He looked to the sky and his smile was genuine. "I've always known I was meant to be in Pharaoh's army. I was never really good at all that." He indicated the edduba with his thumb.

"But your father wants you to be Master of the Charioteers. You have to be educated!"

"And thankfully that's over." He took out a honey cake and gave half to me. "So did you see the number of merchants that have arrived? The palace is filled with them. We couldn't take the horses to the lake because it's crowded with foreign vessels."

"Then let's go to the quay and see what's happening!"

Asha glanced around him, but the other students were rolling knucklebones and playing Senet. "Nefer, we don't have time for that."

"Why not? Paser is always late, and the soldiers don't return until the trumpets call them back. That's long after Paser begins. When will we ever see so many ships? And think of the animals they might be bringing. Horses," I said temptingly. "Maybe from Hatti."

I had said the right words. He stood with me, and when we reached the lake, we saw a dozen ships lying at anchor. Above us on the dock, pennants of every color snapped in the breeze, their rich cloth catching the light like brightly painted jewels. Heavy chests were being unloaded, and just as I had guessed, horses had arrived, gifts from the kingdom of Hatti.

"You were right!" Asha exclaimed. "How did you know?"

"Because every kingdom will send gifts. What else do the Hittites have that we'd want?"

The air filled with the shouts of merchants and the stamps of sea-weary horses skittering down the gang-planks. We picked our way toward them through the bales and bustle. Asha reached out to stroke an ink-black mare, but the man in charge chided him angrily in Hittite.

"You are speaking with Pharaoh's closest friend," I said sharply. "He has come to inspect the gifts."

"You speak Hittite?" the merchant demanded.

I nodded. "Yes," I replied in his language. "And this is Asha, future Master of Pharaoh's Charioteers."

The Hittite merchant narrowed his eyes, trying to determine if he believed me. Finally, he gave a judicious nod. "Good. You may instruct him to lead these horses to Pharaoh's stables."

I smiled widely at Asha.

"What? What is he saying?"

"He wants you to take the horses to Pharaoh Seti's stables."

"Me?" Asha exclaimed. "No! Tell him—"

I smiled at the merchant. "He will be more than happy to deliver Hatti's gifts."

Asha stared at me. "Did you tell him *no*?"

"Of course not! What's the matter with delivering a few horses?"

"Because how will I explain what I'm doing?" Asha cried.

I looked at him. "You were passing by on the way to the palace. You were asked to do this task because you are knowledgeable about horses." I turned back to the merchant. "Before we take these horses from Hatti, we would like to inspect the other gifts."

"What? What did you tell him now?"

"Trust me, Asha! There is such a thing as being *too* cautious."

The merchant frowned, Asha held his breath, and I gave the old man my most impatient look. He sighed heavily, but eventually he led us across the quay, past exquisitely carved chests made from ivory and holding a fortune in cinnamon and myrrh. The rich scents mingled with the muddy tang of the river. Asha pointed ahead to a long leather box. "Ask him what's in there!"

The old man caught Asha's meaning, and he bent down to open the leather case. His long hair spilled over his shoulder; he tossed his three white braids behind him and pulled out a gleaming metal sword.

I glanced at Asha. "Iron," I whispered.

Asha reached out and turned the hilt, so that the long blade caught the summer's light just as it had on the balcony with Ramesses.

"How many are there?" Asha gestured.

The merchant seemed to understand, because he answered, "Two. One for each Pharaoh."

I translated his answer, and as Asha returned the weapon, a pair of ebony oars caught my eye. "And what are those for?" I pointed to the paddles.

For the first time, the old man smiled. "Pharaoh Ramesses himself—for his marriage ceremony."

The tapered paddles had been carved into the heads of sleeping ducks, and he caressed the ebony heads as if the feathers were real. "His Highness will use them to row across the lake while the rest of the court follows behind him in vessels of their own."

I imagined Ramesses using the oars to paddle closer to Iset as she sailed in front of him, her dark hair covered by a beaded net whose lapis stones would catch at the light. Asha and I would have to sail behind them, and there would be no question of my calling out to Ramesses or tugging his hair. Perhaps if I had acted less like a child at Ramesses's coronation, I might have been the one in the boat before him. Then, it would be me he would turn to at night, sharing the day's stories with his irresistible laugh.

I followed Asha to the stables in silence, and that evening, when Merit instructed me to change from my short sheath into a proper kilt for the night, I didn't complain. I let her place a silver pectoral around my neck and sat still while she rubbed myrtle cream into my cheeks.

"How come you're so eager to do as I say?" she asked suspiciously.

I flushed. "Don't I always?"

The pelican's pouch lengthened as Merit pushed in her chin. "A dog does what its master says. *You* listen the way a cat listens."

We both looked at Tefer reclining on the bed, and the untamable *miw* placed his ears against his head as if he knew he was being chastised.

"Now that Pharaoh Ramesses has grown up, have you decided to grow up as well?" Merit challenged.

"Perhaps."

🜚 🜚 🜚

WHEN IT was time to eat in the Great Hall, I took my place beneath the dais and could see that Ramesses was watching Iset. In ten days she would become his wife, and I wondered if he would forget about me entirely.

Pharaoh Seti stood from his throne, and as he raised his arms the hall fell silent. "Shall we have some music?" he asked loudly, and next to him Queen Tuya nodded. As always, her brow appeared damp with sweat, and I wondered how such a large woman could bear living in the terrible heat of Thebes. She didn't bother to stand, and fan bearers with their long ostrich feathers stirred the perfumed air around her so that even from the table beneath the dais it was possible to smell her lavender and lotus blossom.

"Why don't we hear from the future Queen of Egypt?" she suggested, and the entire court looked to Iset, who rose gracefully from her chair.

"As Your Highnesses wish."

Iset made a pretty bow and slowly crossed the chamber. As she approached the harp that had been placed beneath the dais, Ramesses smiled. He watched her arrange herself before the instrument, pressing the carved wooden shoulder between her breasts, and as the lilting notes echoed across the hall, a vizier behind me murmured, "Beautiful. *Exceptionally* beautiful."

"The music or the girl?" Vizier Anemro asked.

The men at the table all snickered.

🎵 🎵 🎵

ON THE eve of Ramesses's marriage to Iset, Tutor Paser called me aside while the other students ran home. He stood at the front of the classroom, surrounded by baskets of papyrus and fresh reed pens. In the soft light of the afternoon, I realized he was not as old as I had often imagined him to be. His dark hair was pulled into a looser braid, and his eyes seemed kinder than they had ever been. But when he motioned for me to sit in the chair across from him, tears of shame blurred my vision before he even said a word.

"Despite the fact that your nurse allows you to run around the palace like a wild child of Set," he began, "you have always been the best student in this edduba. But in the past ten days you've missed six times, and today the translations you completed could have been done by a laborer in one of Pharaoh's tombs."

I lowered my head. "I will do better," I promised.

"Merit tells me you don't practice your languages anymore. That you are distracted. Is this because of Ramesses's marriage to Iset?"

I raised my eyes and wiped away my tears with the back of my hand. "Without Ramesses here, no one wants to be near me! All of the students in the edduba pretended to be kind to me because of Ramesses. Now that he's gone they call me a Heretic Princess."

Paser leaned forward, frowning. "Who has called you this?"

"Iset," I whispered.

"That is only one person."

"But the rest of them think it! I *know* they do. And in the Great Hall, when the High Priest sits at our table beneath the dais . . ."

"I would not concern myself with what Rahotep thinks. You know that his father was the High Priest of Amun—"

"And when my aunt became queen, she and Pharaoh Akhenaten had him killed. I know that. So Iset is against me, and the High Priest is against me, and even Queen Tuya . . ." I choked back a sob. "They are all against me because of my family. Why did my mother name me for a heretic?" I cried.

Paser shifted uncomfortably. "She could never have known the hatred that people would still have for her sister twenty-five years later."

He stood and offered me his hand. "Nefertari, you must continue to study your Hittite and Shasu. Whatever happens with Pharaoh Ramesses and Asha, you must excel in this edduba. It will be the only way to find a place for yourself in the palace."

"As what?" I asked desperately. "A woman can't be a vizier."

"No," Paser said. "But you are a princess. With your command of languages there are a dozen different futures for you. As a High Priestess, or a High Priestess's scribe, possibly even as an emissary." Paser reached into a basket and produced several scrolls. "Letters from King Muwatallis to Pharaoh Seti. Work you missed while you were in the palace pretending to be sick."

I'm sure my cheeks turned a brilliant scarlet, but as I left, I reminded myself of the truth in Paser's words. *I am a princess. I am the daughter and niece and granddaughter of queens. There are many possible futures for me.*

When I returned to the courtyard of the palace, a large pavilion of white cloth had been erected where Ramesses's most important marriage guests would feast. Hundreds of servants scurried like ants, rushing from the Great Hall into the tent with chairs and tables held high above their heads. Beneath a golden sunshade, away from the chaos, Pharaoh Seti's sisters had arrived to oversee the preparations. Iset was there, too, with her friends from the harem.

"Nefer!" Ramesses called from across the courtyard. He left Iset to hurry over to me. He had taken off his *nemes* crown in the heat, and the summer sun set his hair aflame. I imagined Iset running her fingers through the red-gold tresses, whispering in his ear the way Henuttawy whispered to handsome noblemen whenever she was drunk.

"I haven't seen you in days," he said apologetically. "You can't imagine what it's been like in the Audience Chamber. Every day it's another crisis. Do you remember last year how the lake receded?"

I nodded. Ramesses shaded his eyes with his hand. "Well, that's because the Nile didn't overflow its banks. And without an overflow to water the land, very little was harvested this summer. In some cities it's already led to famine."

"Not in Thebes," I protested.

"No, but in the rest of Upper Egypt," he said.

I tried to imagine a famine when tomorrow the palace would feed a thousand people. Cuts of beef, roasted duck, and lamb were already being prepared in the kitchens, and wide barrels of pomegranate wine were waiting in the Great Hall to be rolled into the pavilion.

Ramesses caught my glance and nodded. "I know it's hard to believe," he said, "but the people outside of Thebes are suffering. We've had a little rain, but not cities like Edfu and Aswan."

"So will Thebes share its grain?"

"Only if there's enough. The viziers are angry that the Habiru are growing so plentiful in Egypt. They say there are nearly six hundred thousand of them, and in a time when there's not enough food for Egyptians, some of my father's men are saying that measures must be taken."

"What kind of measures?"

Ramesses looked away.

"What kind of measures?" I repeated.

"Measures to be sure that there are no more Habiru sons—"

I gasped. "*What?* You wouldn't allow—"

"Of course not! But the viziers are talking. They're saying it's not just their numbers," Ramesses explained. "Rahotep believes that if the sons are killed, the Habiru daughters will marry Egyptians to become like us."

"They *are* like us! Tutor Amos is a Habiru and his people have been here for a hundred years. My grandfather brought the Habiru to Thebes when he conquered Canaan—"

"But Rahotep is telling the court that the Habiru worship one god like the Heretic King." Ramesses lowered his voice so that none of the servants who were passing could hear him. "He thinks they're *heretics*, Nefer."

"Of course he would say that! He was a heretic himself—a High Priest of Aten. Now he wants to show the court that he's loyal to Amun."

Ramesses nodded. "That's what I told my father."

"And what does he say?"

"That a sixth of his army is Habiru. Their sons fight alongside Egyptian sons. But the people are growing angrier, Nefer, and every day it's something different. Droughts, or poor trade, or pirates in the Northern Sea. Now everything has to stop while hundreds of dignitaries arrive and you should see the preparations. When an Assyrian prince came this morning, Vizier Anemro gave him a room that faced west."

I covered my mouth. "He didn't know that Assyrians sleep facing the rising sun?"

"No. I had to explain it to him. He moved the prince's chamber, but the Assyrians were already angry. None of this would have happened if Paser had simply agreed to be vizier."

"*Tutor* Paser?"

"My father has already asked him twice. He'd be the youngest vizier in Egypt, but surely the most intelligent."

"And both times he declined?"

Ramesses nodded. "I can't understand it." He looked down at the scrolls I was carrying. "What are these?" There was a glint in Ramesses's eyes, as if he was tired of talking about his wedding and politics. "It looks like several days' worth of *work* to me," he said, and snatched one of the scrolls. "Have you been *missing classes?*"

"Give it back!" I cried. "I was sick."

I made a grab for the papyrus but Ramesses held it higher.

"If you want it," he teased, "you're going to have to catch it!"

He sprinted across the courtyard, and with my arms full of scrolls, I gave chase. Then a shadow loomed across the stones and he stopped.

"What are you doing?" Henuttawy demanded. The red robes of Isis swirled at her feet. She snatched the scroll that Ramesses had taken and shoved it at me. "You are a king of Egypt," she reminded him sharply, and her nephew flushed. "Do you realize that you have left Iset all alone to decide which instruments shall be played at the feast?"

The three of us looked across the courtyard at Iset, who didn't seem *all alone* to me. She and her friends were huddled together, whispering. Ramesses hesitated, and I saw how keenly he felt Henuttawy's disappointment in him. She was his father's sister, after all. He glanced apologetically at me. "I should go and help her," he said.

"But first, your father wants you in the Audience Chamber." Henuttawy watched, waiting until Ramesses was inside the palace before she turned to face me. Her slap was so hard that I staggered, spilling Paser's scrolls across the courtyard floor. "The days when your family ruled in Malkata are over, Princess, and you will *never* chase Ramesses around this courtyard like an animal! He is the King of Egypt, and you are a child who is tolerated in this palace."

Henuttawy turned and strode toward the billowing white pavilions. I bent down to pick up Paser's assignments, and several servants came running.

"My lady, are you all right?" they asked. The entire courtyard had seen what had happened. "Let us help."

One of the cooks from the kitchen bent down to collect the scattered scrolls.

I shook my head firmly. "It's fine. I can do it."

But the cook piled my arms with papyrus. At the entrance to the palace, a woman's hand took me by the shoulder. I braced myself for more of Henuttawy's violence, but it was Henuttawy's younger sister, Woserit.

"Take these scrolls and place them in her room," Woserit ordered one of the guards. Then she turned to me and said, "Come."

I followed the hem of her turquoise cloak as it brushed across the varnished tiles and into the ante-chamber where dignitaries waited

to see the king. It was empty, but Woserit still swung the heavy
wooden doors closed behind us.

"What have you done to anger Henuttawy?"

I still held back tears. "Nothing!"

"Well, she is determined to keep Ramesses away from you."
Woserit watched me for a moment. "Tell me, why do you think
Henuttawy is so invested in Iset's fate?"

I searched Woserit's face. "I . . . I don't know."

"Haven't you wondered whether Henuttawy has promised to help
make Iset a queen in exchange for something?"

I placed two fingers on my lips in a nervous habit I had taken from
Merit. "I don't know. What could Iset have that Henuttawy doesn't?"

"Nothing, yet. There is no status or bloodline that my sister
could offer you. But there is plenty that she can offer Iset. Without
Henuttawy's support, Iset would never have been chosen for a royal
wife."

I wondered why she was telling me this.

"There are a dozen pretty faces Ramesses might have picked,"
Woserit continued. "He named Iset because his father suggested her,
and my brother recommended her due to Henuttawy's insistence.
But *why* is my sister so insistent?" she pressed. "What does she hope
to gain?"

I sensed that Woserit knew exactly what Henuttawy wanted and I
suddenly felt overwhelmed.

"You have never thought of this?" Woserit demanded. "This court
is going to bury you, Nefertari, and you will join your family in
anonymity if you don't understand these politics."

"So what do I do?"

"Decide which path awaits you. Soon, you will no longer be the
only young princess in Thebes. And if Iset becomes Chief Wife
as Henuttawy wishes, you will never survive here. My sister and

Iset will push you from this court and you'll end your dusty days in the harem of Mi-Wer."

Even then I knew there was no worse fate for a woman of the palace than to end up in the harem of Mi-Wer, surrounded by the emptiness of the western desert. Many young girls imagine that marrying a Pharaoh will mean a lifetime of ease spent wandering the gardens, gossiping in the baths, and choosing between sandals beaded with lapis or coral—but nothing could be further from the truth. Certainly, there were some women, like Iset's grandmother, the prettiest or cleverest, who were kept in the harem closest to Pharaoh's palace. But Malkata's harem could only house so many women, and most were sent to distant palaces where they were forced to spin and weave to survive. The halls of Mi-Wer were filled with old women, lonely and bitter.

"Only one person can make sure that Iset never becomes Chief Wife with the power to drive you away," Woserit insisted. "One person close enough to Ramesses to persuade him that Iset should be just another princess. You. By becoming Chief Wife in her place."

I had been holding my breath, but now, it left me. I sat down on a chair and gripped its wooden arms. "And challenge Iset?" I thought of rising against Henuttawy and suddenly felt sick. "I could never do that. Even if I wanted to, I couldn't," I protested. "I'm only thirteen."

"You will not be thirteen forever. But you have to start behaving like a princess of Egypt. You must stop running wild through the palace like some harem girl."

"I'm the niece of a heretic," I whispered. "The viziers would never accept it. Rahotep—"

"There are ways around Rahotep."

"But I thought I would study at the edduba and become an emissary."

"And who appoints the emissaries?" Woserit asked.

"Pharaoh."

"And once my brother is gone? Remember, Pharaoh Seti is twenty years my senior. When he is called by Osiris, who will assign his emissaries then?"

"Ramesses."

"And when Ramesses is off at war?"

"His viziers," I guessed. "Or the High Priest of Amun. Or—"

"Pharaoh's Chief Wife?"

I stared at the river mosaic on the wall. Fish swam across the brightly painted tiles while fishermen lay idly on the river's banks. Their lives were quiet. They were carefree. The fisherman's son didn't have to worry about what he would become when he reached fifteen. His destiny was certain, and his fate rested with the Gods and the seasons. No maze of choices lay before him. "I cannot begin a war with Iset," I resolved.

"You won't have to," Woserit said. "My sister has already begun it. You want to be an emissary, Nefertari, but how will you be able to do that in Iset and Henuttawy's Thebes?"

"I can't challenge Henuttawy," I said with certainty.

"Perhaps not alone. But I could help you. You aren't the only one who suffers if Iset becomes Chief Wife. Henuttawy would love to see me banished to a temple in the Fayyum."

I wanted to ask her why, but her tone had a finality I dared not question. It occurred to me that in the Great Hall, she never spoke with her sister, even though they both sat at the same table beneath the dais.

"She won't succeed," Woserit continued, "but that's only because I am willing to rise up against her to stop it. There are many times when I go to my brother's feasts simply to make sure that Henuttawy isn't destroying my reputation."

"But I don't want to have anything to do with court politics," I protested.

Woserit searched my face to see if I was serious. "Soon, life is going to be very different, Nefertari. You may change your mind about challenging Iset. If you do, you will know where I am."

She offered me her arm in silence, and when I took it, she walked me slowly to the door. Outside, the tiled halls still teemed with bustling servants. They rushed about us, carrying candles and chairs for the wedding feast. All the palace had talked about for ten days was Iset. What if it was always like this, and the excitement of a new princess and possibly a child meant that Ramesses was lost to me forever? Woserit's figure receded down the hallway, as servants polishing the tiles with palm oil stood quickly to bow to her as she passed. Their eager chatter about the feast resumed, until my nurse's voice cut through the noise.

"My lady!"

I turned and saw Merit approaching with a basket of my best sheaths in her arms.

"My lady, where have you been?" she cried. "I sent servants to the edduba looking for you! They are moving your chamber!" She took my arm as Woserit had done, and I struggled to keep up with her as she trotted through the maze of passageways. "Lady Iset is to have your room! Queen Tuya came and said that Iset is moving from the harem."

"But there are plenty of rooms in the royal courtyard," I protested. "And two are empty!"

"Lady Iset insisted that yours was meant for a princess. Now that *she* will be the highest-ranked princess in Malkata, she asked for your chamber."

I stopped in the hall beneath an image of Ma'at holding the scales of truth. "And the queen didn't deny her?"

"No, my lady." Merit looked away. "She's moving in now, and I took what I could. But she's demanded to sleep there tonight."

I stared at Merit. "And where am I to go? I have had that room since I was born. Since my mother—" My eyes welled with tears.

"Oh, no, my lady. Don't cry. Don't cry."

"I'm not crying," I insisted, but the tears rolled fast and hot down my cheeks.

"They have found you a new room that's just as pretty," she promised. "It's also in the royal courtyard." Merit put down her basket and took me in her embrace. "My lady, you will still have me. You will still have Tefer."

I swallowed a sob. "We should go before Iset decides that she wants my ebony chests as well," I said bitterly.

Merit straightened. "Nothing of yours will go missing," she vowed. "I saw her with your mother's gold and lapis mirror and I have ordered the servants to watch *everything*."

"Nefer!"

Ramesses was standing at the end of the hall, and as he strode toward us, Merit took out a small piece of linen and quickly wiped the tears from my face. But Ramesses could see that I had been crying.

"Nefer, what's happening?"

"Lady Iset is moving from the harem," Merit explained, "into the princess's chamber. Since this is the only room that my lady has ever known, where her mother's image looks down on her at night, you can understand that she is very upset."

Ramesses looked at me again, and his cheeks blazed an angry red. "Who gave permission for this?" he demanded.

"I believe it was the queen, Your Highness."

Ramesses stared at Merit, then turned sharply on his heel and commanded, "Wait here."

I glanced at my nurse. "Is he going to try and change her mind?"

"Of course! She could have asked for any room. Why yours?"

"Because it's closest to Ramesses."

"And who says that her chamber must be near to Pharaoh's? She isn't Chief Wife."

"Not yet," I said fearfully. We waited in the hall, and when Ramesses returned, I saw his face and grasped Merit's hand. "She said no," I whispered.

Ramesses avoided my gaze. "My mother says the move has already been made and that she can't go back on her word." His eyes met mine and he looked deeply unhappy. "I'm sorry, Nefer." I nodded and he continued, "My mother wants me back in the Audience Chamber. But if there's anything you need . . ." His words trailed away. "All of the servants are at your disposal . . ."

I shook my head. "Merit is here."

"My mother says you'll still be in the royal courtyard. I made sure of that."

I smiled thinly. "Thank you." I could see that he didn't want to be the first to leave, so I picked up Merit's basket and said impassively, "We should go. There's a great deal to pack."

Ramesses watched us walk away, but I closed my eyes as I heard him turn and the sound of his footsteps faded.

Inside my chamber was chaos. The perfumes and necklaces that had been in my ebony chests for thirteen years lay strewn in baskets, without any thought of how to keep them from breaking. My Senet board had already been removed, but someone had dropped its gaming pieces, now lying abandoned across the tiled floor.

"What is this?" Merit bellowed, and Iset's harem servants shuddered to a halt, chests still in hand. Even the royal attendants regarded Merit with timid amazement. "Who was responsible for this?" she demanded, and when no one answered, Merit muscled her way through the tangle of baskets and chests. "Somebody is going to clean this up! *No one* will treat Princess Nefertari's belongings with carelessness!"

Servants began picking up the scattered pieces at once, and Merit stood over them with her hands on her hips. I waited in the doorway and noticed that Iset's belongings had been placed on a new cosmetics table. There was a fan of ivory and ostrich feathers, and a dress of netted faience beads in a basket. *Someone has bought all of this for her,* I realized. I wondered if they were wedding gifts from Ramesses, for no one could afford such luxuries in the harem. A gilded bed had been placed against the wall where mine had been, and long silver linens wrapped around its posts. They would be let down at night to cloak Iset from the light of the moon as it fell across the blue tiled walls. *My* walls.

"I know you are small, but I'd rather not walk over you, Nefertari." Iset swept past me with her arms full of sheaths and before I could reply, I saw my mother's wooden *naos* The gold and ebony figure of Mut had been taken from the shrine in order to move it, and my breath caught in my throat when I saw that the statue had been broken in two.

"You broke my mother's statue?" I shrieked, and the commotion in the room came to a second complete halt. I leaned over the goddess my mother had prayed to as a little girl and gathered her in my arms. Her feline head had been separated from her torso, but it might as well have been my body that had been broken.

"I didn't break it," Iset said quickly. "I've never touched it."

"Then who did?" I shouted.

"Maybe one of the servants. Or Woserit," she said quickly. "She was here." Iset looked over her shoulder at the other women, and their faces were full of fear.

"I want to know who did this!" Merit said with soft menace in her voice, and Iset stepped back, afraid. "Woserit would never have touched my lady's shrine! Did you break this image of the goddess?"

Iset gathered herself. "Do you have any idea whom you are speaking to?"

"I have a very good idea who I am speaking to!" Merit replied, rage shaking her small, fierce body. "The granddaughter of a harem wife."

Color flooded Iset's cheeks.

Merit turned away. "Come!" she said sharply to me. In the hall, she took the broken statue from my hands. "Nothing good will come to that scorpion. Don't worry about your shrine, my lady. I will have the court sculptor fix it for you."

But, of course, I couldn't stop worrying. Not just about my mother's shrine, which was dearer to me than anything I owned, but about Woserit's warning, too. Her words echoed in my head like the chants we sang in the Temple of Amun. Already, life was changing for me, and not for the better. I followed Merit's angry footfalls to my new room on the other side of the courtyard. When we arrived, she pushed open the heavy wooden doors and made an oddly satisfied noise in her throat. "Your new chamber," she said.

Inside, the windows swept from ceiling to floor, overlooking the western hills of Thebes. I could see that Tefer had already found his place on the balcony, crouched as proud and confident as a leopard. Everything about the chamber was magnificent, from the tiled balcony to the silver and ivory inlay that shone from the paintings of Hathor on the walls. I turned to Merit in shock. "But this is Woserit's room!"

"She gave it up for you this morning while you were in the edduba," she replied.

So Woserit already knew that Iset had taken my chamber when

she had spoken to me. "But where will she stay when she comes to the palace?"

"She will take a guest room," Merit replied, then regarded me curiously. "She obviously has an interest in you." When I didn't respond, she asked temptingly, "Do you want to see the robing room?"

In most chambers, the robing room is very small, with only enough space for three or four chests and perhaps a table with clay heads for keeping wigs shapely. In my old chamber, the space could barely fit a bronze mirror. But Woserit's robing room was nearly as large as her bedchamber itself, with a limestone shower as well, where water poured down from silver bowls. Merit had arranged my makeup chest near a window that looked out over the gardens. I opened the drawers to see my belongings in their new home. There were my brushes and kohl pots, razors and combs. Even my mother's mirror, in the shape of an ankh with a smooth faience handle, had been carefully laid out.

"If the High Priestess hadn't given me her chamber," I asked, "where would I have gone?"

"To another chamber in the royal courtyard," Merit said. "You will always remain in the royal courtyard, my lady. You are a *princess*."

A princess of another court, I thought bitterly, as a soft body rubbed against my calf.

"You see?" Merit added with forced cheerfulness. "Tefer approves of his new home."

"And you'll still be next door to me in the nurse's quarters?" I looked across the room, and near the foot of the bed I saw the wooden door, that for royalty meant that aid was only a softly spoken word away.

"Of course, my lady."

That evening, I climbed into my bed with Tefer while Merit swept a critical eye over the chamber. Everything was in place. My ala-baster jars in the shape of sleeping cats were arranged on the win-dowsills, and the carnelian belt I would wear the following day had been lain out neatly with my dress. All of my boxes and chests had arrived, but my shrine was missing. And tonight Iset would be sleep-ing beneath the mosaic of Mut that my mother had commissioned.

帀 帀 帀

I AWOKE in Woserit's chamber before even the earliest light had fil-tered through the reed mats.

"Tefer?" I whispered. *"Tefer?"*

But Tefer had disappeared, probably to hunt mice or beg food from the kitchens. I sat up in the same bed I had slept in as a child, then kindled an oil lamp lying by the brazier. A breath upon the em-bers, and then light flickered over unfamiliar walls. Above the door was the image of the mother-goddess Hathor in the form of a blue and yellow cow, a rising sun resting between her horns. Beneath the windows, fish leaped across blue and white tiles, their scales inlaid with mother-of-pearl. And near the balcony Hathor had been de-picted as a woman wearing her sacred *menat,* a beaded necklace with an amulet that could protect the wearer from charms. I thought of the painting of my mother in my old chamber and imagined her confusion at seeing Iset beneath her instead of me. I knew that a painting was nothing more than ochre and ink, not like an image in a mortuary temple to which the *ka* returns every Feast of Wag. Still, my mother's image had watched over me for more than thirteen years, and now, across the courtyard, Iset was in that room preparing for her marriage. I glanced at the corner where my mother's *naos* should have been and anger blurred my vision. Woserit had warned me. She had said that Iset would try to drive me from Thebes.

My feet felt their way uncertainly through the gloom, as my lamp brought color to the robing chamber ahead. I sat at my makeup chest, taking out a pellet of incense and rubbing it under my arms. I tied back my hair and leaned close to the polished bronze. Woserit believed I could challenge Iset, but what about me could ever compare with Iset's beauty? I studied my reflection, turning my face this way and that. There was the smile. My lips curved like an archer's bow, so that I always appeared to be grinning. And there were my eyes. The green of shallow waters touched by the sun.

"My lady?" I heard Merit open my chamber door, and then when she saw that my bed was empty, the heavy pad of her feet into the robing room. "My lady, what are you doing awake?"

I turned from the mirror and felt fierce determination. "I want you to make me as beautiful as Isis today."

Merit stepped back, then a slow smile spread across her face.

"I want you to bring my most expensive sandals," I said hotly, "and dust my eyes with every fleck of gold you can find in the palace."

Merit smiled fully. "Of course, my lady."

"And bring me my mother's favorite collar. The one worth a hundred deben in gold."

I sat before the mirror and inhaled slowly to calm myself. When Merit returned with my mother's jewels, she placed a bowl of figs on my table. "I want you to eat, and I don't mean picking at the food like an egret." She bustled around me, collecting combs and beads for my hair.

"What will happen today?" I asked.

Merit sat on the stool next to me and placed my foot in her lap, rolling cream over my ankle and calf. "First, Pharaoh Ramesses will sail to the Temple of Amun, where the High Priest will anoint that scorpion in marriage. Then there will be a feast."

"And Iset?" I demanded.

"She will be a princess of Egypt and spend her time in the Audience Chamber, helping Pharaoh Ramesses rule. Think of all the petitions he must stamp. Pharaoh's viziers oversee thousands of requests, and the hundreds that they approve must go to Pharaoh for final consent. Pharaoh Seti and Queen Tuya aid him already; he can't do it alone."

"So now Iset will render judgment?" I thought of Iset's hatred for learning. She would rather be at the baths gossiping than translating cuneiform. "Do you think that Ramesses will make her Chief Wife?"

"Let us hope our new Pharaoh has more sense than that." In the cool hours of morning, she stiffened my wig with beeswax and resin, then replaced the beads that had broken in storage. She spent a great deal of time with my kohl, mixing it with palm oil until it was perfectly smooth, then applying it to my eyelids with the thinnest brush I had ever seen. When she turned me around to face the mirror, I inhaled. For the very first time, I looked older than my thirteen years. My face was too small for the wide sweeps of kohl that women like Iset and Henuttawy used, but the fine black lines Merit had extended from the inside of my eyelids to my temples were incredibly flattering. The carnelian beads she'd braided into my wig matched the large carnelian stones of my scarab belt. And the pinch of precious gold dust that she had blown onto the wet kohl highlighted the filigree of my sandals.

I turned to face Merit, and she fastened my mother's jewels around my neck, then let the hair of my wig fall into place.

"You are as beautiful as Isis," she murmured. "But only if you sit like a lady. There will be no running around with Pharaoh Ramesses today. This is a marriage, and princes from Babylon to Punt will bear witness if you are acting like a child."

I nodded firmly. "There will be no running."

Merit scrutinized me. "No matter what Pharaoh wants. He is King of Egypt now and must behave like one."

I imagined Iset in my chamber, and all of the things she would do with Ramesses under the painting of my mother come nightfall. "I promise."

Merit led our path through the crowded halls of the palace. Outside, beyond the linen pavilion, hundreds of courtiers had gathered near the quay where the ships would set sail for the Temple of Amun. Neither Ramesses nor Iset had arrived, and Merit raised a sunshade above our heads to protect us from the rising heat. I couldn't see any of the students from the edduba, but Asha spotted me from across the courtyard and called out, startled, "Nefer!"

"Remember what I told you," Merit said severely.

As Asha approached me, his eyes widened. He took in my wide, carnelian belt and the gold that glittered above my eyes. "You're *beautiful*, Nefer," he said.

"*I* haven't changed," I said heatedly, and Asha stepped back, surprised by my seriousness. "It's everyone else!"

"You mean your chamber." Asha glanced at Merit, who pretended not to be listening. "Yes. And she did it out of spite." Asha lowered his voice. "She may be all sweetness and perfume with Ramesses, but we know the truth. I can tell him—"

"No," I said at once. "He'll think that you're being petty and jealous."

Trumpets echoed from the quayside, and Iset emerged from the palace, answering their call. I knew that once she reached the quay, she would sail alone to the Temple of Amun on the eastern bank. Ramesses would ride in a vessel behind her, and the court would follow them in boats decorated with silver pennants and gold. Once the High Priest anointed Iset a princess, she would return with

Ramesses in his boat, wearing his family ring to signify their union. Then Ramesses would carry her onto the quay and over the threshold of the palace they would come to rule. They would only emerge later that night for the feast. It was his carrying her across the threshold of Malkata that would bind their marriage. Nothing the priests did in the temple could make them married in the eyes of Amun unless he chose to carry her inside, and for a wild moment I imagined that he might refuse. He might realize that Iset was not the rose she pretended to be, but a tangle of thorns, and he would change his mind.

But, of course, this did not happen. Instead, we sailed in a long flotilla of boats down the river, and all along the shore the people began chanting Iset's name. The women raised ivory clappers above their heads, and those who couldn't afford such luxuries used their hands as they shouted for their queen. It was as though a goddess had descended to earth. Children floated lotus blossoms on the water, and little girls who caught sight of her face wept with excited joy. When we reached the temple, Ramesses took Iset as his wife, and they returned to the cheers of a thousand guests. Then he took her up in his arms, and they disappeared together into the palace.

The festivity was so joyous that all formality was dismissed, and Asha seized the chance to join me at the viziers' table. "So Iset is a princess now," he said. He looked down the length of the pavilion to the closed double doors of the palace. "At least you won't have to see her anymore. She'll spend all of her time in the Audience Chamber."

"Yes. With Ramesses," I pointed out.

But Asha shook his head. "No. Ramesses will be with me. There is going to be war with the Hittites."

I put down my cup of wine. "What do you mean?"

"The city of Kadesh has belonged to Egypt since the time of Thutmose. It was the Heretic King who allowed the Hittites to take

Kadesh, and all of the port cities that made Egypt wealthy are en-
riching Hatti now. Pharaoh Seti won't stand for it anymore. He has
reconquered all of the lands that the Heretic lost, and all that remains to be retaken is Kadesh."

"I know this," I said, impatient. "I've studied it all with Paser. But
he never said Egypt was preparing for war *now*."

Asha nodded. "Probably by Phaophi."

"But what if Ramesses is killed? Or if you come back maimed?
Asha, you've seen the soldiers—"

"That won't happen to us. It's our first battle. We'll be well
protected."

"Pharaoh Tutankhamun was well protected, and it didn't stop his
chariot from overturning. He died from that broken leg!"

Asha put his arm around my shoulders. "A king is expected to lead
his men into battle. It's too bad you weren't born a man, Nefer. You
might have come with us. But we'll come back," he promised easily.
"And you'll see. Nothing will change."

I smiled, and hoped it would be so. But in the blur of events, I was
learning how poorly hope alone would serve me.

　　　　　　　　　　　　⊡ ⊡ ⊡

THAT EVENING, Merit brought me a stick of wax. She held the tip
to the flame of the candle, then dripped it slowly onto the papyrus.
I waited until the droplets had hardened before pressing my signet
ring into the wax. Then I handed the letter to Merit.

"Are you sure you want to send this, my lady? Perhaps you need a
few days to think?"

I shook my head. "No, I am certain."

CHAPTER FOUR

◻◻

THE WAYS OF HATHOR

◻◻ ON MY FOURTEENTH Naming Day, I went to the edduba as usual. I slipped off my sandals in front of the door, but inside, Paser was not sitting at his table. For the first time since he had been my tutor, Paser was absent. On the reed mats, the students were taking full advantage, chattering among themselves.

"Nefertari!" Baki exclaimed. "Have you heard?"

I set out my reed pen and bottle of ink deliberately. "What?"

"Paser is no longer going to be our tutor. He is vizier to Pharaoh Ramesses now."

I scrambled from my reed mat. "When did this happen?"

"Yesterday. My father told me this morning." Then he smiled wide enough that I could see his crooked teeth. "And we are to get a new tutor!"

A female shape appeared in the doorway. The students leaped to their feet, and unlike Henuttawy's entrance, they bowed deeply as Woserit approached, dressed in the long blue robes of Hathor. Her earrings and bracelets and belt were all of lapis, and the crown on her head was crested with small horns.

60

"Nefertari," she said. "It's time."

The students all looked at me for an explanation, and when the words stuck in my mouth, Woserit explained. "Your new tutor is coming. But Princess Nefertari's time with you is over. She will be joining me to learn the rites of our temple. She will become a priestess of Hathor."

A collective gasp arose in the room, but Woserit gave me a nod that meant I should smile and take my leave, and as I made my way past the curious faces, it occurred to me that an important part of my life had finished. No tutor would await me ever again. And although I'd always thought I would feel like an animal released from its cage when my student days were finished, I felt more like a bird that had been pushed from its nest and told it must fly.

I followed Woserit down the path along the lake. Though my heart was pounding, she retained her usual calm, that always seemed to hint at some great purpose. "I visited Merit this morning," she said, after some time. "Your most important belongings have been packed, and as soon as they're loaded on Hathor's ship, we'll set sail."

Thebes is a city cleaved in two by water. On the western bank of the River Nile is the palace of Malkata, and on the eastern bank are all of our most sacred temples. Each temple has its own ship, and this is what Woserit used each afternoon when she came to the Audience Chamber, or many evenings when she visited her brother in the Great Hall. Adult life, it seemed, meant movement. For fourteen years I had lived in the same chamber in the palace, and now, within fifteen days, I would be moving twice. Perhaps Woserit understood more than she let on, because her voice softened.

"Moving again and saying farewell will not be as terrible as you think," she promised.

In the courtyard outside my chamber, a small group had gathered to watch the servants collect my belongings. When I noticed Ramesses and Asha, my heart leaped.

"Nefer!" Asha exclaimed, and Woserit raised her brows.

"Nefer*tari*," she corrected as he came over. "In the Temple of Hathor she will be properly known as such," Woserit explained. "Ramesses." She bowed politely to her nephew. "I will leave you to say your farewell."

Woserit disappeared inside my chamber, and both Ramesses and Asha spoke at once.

"What does she mean?"

I shrugged. "I'm leaving."

Ramesses blurted, "Leaving *where*?"

"To the Temple of Hathor," I said.

"What? To become a priestess? To clean tiles and light incense?" Asha asked.

I am sure part of his shock was in knowing that priestesses must train for twelve months. And although they may marry, many never do.

I suppressed the urge to change my mind. "Yes. Or perhaps to be a temple scribe."

Ramesses glanced at Asha, to see if he could believe this. "But *why*?"

"What else am I to do?" I asked solemnly. "I have no place in this palace, Ramesses. You're married now and belong in the Audience Chamber. And soon you'll be going off to war with Asha."

"But it won't last for a year!" Ramesses said. Iset entered the courtyard, and when she saw that Ramesses was with me, she halted sharply in place. "Iset," he called, "come and bid farewell."

"Why? Is the princess leaving us?" she asked.

"For the Temple of Hathor," Ramesses said disbelievingly. "To become a priestess."

Iset put on her most sympathetic look as she approached. "Ramesses will be so very sorry to see you go. He's always telling me how much you're like a little sister to him." She smiled as she said *little*, and I bit my tongue against saying something nasty. "It's simply unfortunate we didn't know sooner. We could have thrown a feast of farewell." She looked up at Ramesses through her long lashes. "After all, it's not as though she'll be returning."

"Of course she'll be returning," Ramesses retorted. "A priestess's training only lasts a year."

"But then she'll be serving Hathor. Across the river."

He blinked quickly, and there was a moment when he might have embraced me, even in front of Iset. I could see that there was more that Asha wanted to say. But then Woseret appeared with Merit at the head of a caravan of basket-laden servants.

"You can visit her anytime," Woseret promised. "Come, Nefertari. The boat is waiting."

I reached around my neck and took off the simple ox-hair's necklace that Merit hated. "What is *that*?" Iset sneered.

"I made it for her," Ramesses said defensively, then met my gaze.

"Yes. When I was seven." I smiled. "I want you to have it to remember me by."

I placed the necklace in his hands, and it took all of my strength not to look behind me at his crestfallen face as I walked to the quay. From the deck of Hathor's ship, I looked back at the life that I had always known. Ramesses and Asha waved from the banks, and a small group of students from the edduba had joined them.

"That was very clever, what you did back there. Giving him the necklace."

I nodded numbly, thinking that it wasn't cleverness, just love, and Merit placed her arm across my shoulder. "It's not forever, my lady."

I pressed my lips together. As I watched the fading shoreline, only one figure remained. She was dressed in red.

"Henuttawy." Woserit saw the direction of my gaze and nodded, "She thinks that you've retreated now, and that it's only a matter of time before Ramesses forgets about you and turns to Iset for his companionship."

I prayed that she were wrong but held my tongue, for now I had placed all those prayers in Woserit's hands.

🝔 🝔 🝔

IT WAS not a long journey to the Temple of Hathor, and as the boat neared the quay, Merit rose from her stool to gaze at the forest of granite pillars soaring above a polished courtyard.

"No wonder her sister is jealous," she whispered out of Woserit's earshot.

Towering obelisks rose against the sky, and beyond the temple, workers in blue kilts tended to Hathor's sycamore groves. The fresh shoots of the goddess's sacred trees shone like green jewels.

"Surprised?" Woserit asked us.

Merit admitted, "I knew this was the largest temple in Thebes, but I didn't realize—"

Woserit smiled. "We have more pilgrims to Hathor in a single month than my sister has in the Temple of Isis in six."

"Because Hathor's temple is larger?" I asked.

"Because the pilgrims know that when they bring offerings of deben or lapis lazuli," Woserit replied, "the offerings will be used to preserve the beauty of the goddess; in her groves, and in the way we keep her temple. But when pilgrims go to the Temple of Isis, their offerings are melted into jewelry that Henuttawy can wear to my

64

brother's feasts. The most beautiful room in my sister's temple isn't the inner sanctum of Isis. It's her own chamber."

Now that we had reached the quay, it was possible to see just how large the Temple of Hathor truly was. The painted columns were cast in the sun's golden light, and gilded images of the cow goddess crowned every limestone pillar. Our ship was greeted by a dozen of Hathor's priestesses, and servants stood on the shore to unload our belongings.

One of the young women in Hathor's blue robes approached us with a pair of sandals, handing them to Merit and explaining, "Leather is forbidden in the Temple of Hathor. Sandals must be made of papyrus."

"Thank you, Aloli," said Woserit. The young priestess bowed, and a tangle of red curls bounced on her head. "Will you please take Lady Merit and Princess Nefertari to their chambers?"

"Of course, Your Holiness." She waited while Merit and I replaced our sandals, and as my leather sandals were taken away, I wondered what other pieces of my old life I would have to lose. "May I show you to your rooms?" Aloli asked.

We followed the priestess through the heavy bronze gates of the temple, and through the chambers for the pilgrims to Hathor. As we passed through the halls, I was careful not to step on her sweeping train. Her hips moved with a mesmerizing sway, and I wondered where she'd learned to walk the way she did. "This way," she instructed, and she led us into the cool recesses of the temple, where silent priestesses moved among the offerants, spreading incense from golden balls.

"The High Priestess has requested that you both be given chambers near to hers," Aloli said. "But do not expect to see much of her here. This temple requires a great deal of care, and when she's not in the palace, she's out in the groves or meeting with pilgrims. This is where the priestesses eat."

She gestured into a wide room that seemed not so different from the Great Hall of Malkata.

"Trumpets will call the priestesses to ritual once in the morning and once at sunset. After Hathor's rites are finished they meet in this hall. I think you will find our food similar to what you are used to in the palace." She looked at me. "Although I would not touch the wine," she whispered. "The priestesses here like it strong, and a girl of your size might never wake up!" She laughed at her own joke, and Merit's lips thinned.

"This is where temple patrons come to worship," Aloli continued. A vast hall spread beneath mosaics of the goddess, and at the foot of a polished statuary worshippers had left bowls of meat and bread. "In Shemu, a woman came who had lost all five of her pregnancies. We found her in the farthest corner." Aloli pointed to a shadowy niche near a statue of Hathor. "With her husband!" She giggled, and Merit cleared her throat.

"But weren't they in trouble?" I gasped.

"Of course. But nine months later she had two healthy sons!"

Merit glared at me in case I should ever conceive such an idea. We turned into a beautifully kept courtyard ringed by sycamore trees. Aloli announced grandly, "This is where our most important guests stay." She gestured to the windows that faced the square. "And this is where you will be." We entered a chamber with blue-glazed tiles that swam with painted fish. Inlaid images of cows filled the western wall, opposite an ebony bed with lion's-paw feet raised upon a platform. Aloli walked across the chamber and threw open a pair of heavy wooden doors. "And for Lady Merit," she announced.

The walls of Merit's adjoining room had been brightly painted, and fresh linen was stacked on a low cedar table. Merit hummed her approval. "This will do well. Now I must go and direct the servants with our belongings."

When she left, I turned to Aloli. "What am I to do here?" I asked.

The red-haired priestess looked surprised. "Didn't the High Priestess tell you? She said that you have been brought here to study."

"To study what?"

"Temple rituals, the harp . . ." Aloli shrugged. "Perhaps she hopes you might become the next High Priestess of Hathor." A trumpet blared on the other side of the temple, and Aloli quickly twisted her ringlets into a knot. "I will see you tonight in the Great Hall." She paused at the door. "It is a pleasure to have you here, Princess. I have heard a great deal about you."

But before I could ask what she had heard, she disappeared into the hall. I crossed the chamber and stood at Merit's window, looking out over the groves. On the western bank of the River Nile, Ramesses would be taking his afternoon meal with Asha and Iset. There would be dancing in the Great Hall come nightfall, and the news would spread that I had chosen to become a priestess of Hathor. I wondered if Henuttawy would swallow her sister's lie.

"Beautiful, isn't it?"

I jumped, startled by Woserit's silent approach. "Yes, very," I acknowledged.

"Tell me, Nefertari. When you look out on these groves, what do you see?"

I hesitated. The sun was directly over the river, and birds flew between the long stalks of papyrus, calling to one another as kilted men worked in the fields. "I see a small clay model," I said. "Like the ones in the tombs, only this one is filled with moving people."

Woserit raised her brows. "That's very creative."

I flushed and looked out over the balcony again, to see if there was something else I had missed.

"What about the groves of sycamores?" she asked. "What do they look like to you?"

"They are beautiful as well," I said cautiously.

"But do you think they always looked so beautiful?"

"Not when they were saplings," I guessed. "Then their limbs wouldn't have touched and they couldn't have formed the tunnel that they are creating now."

Woserit was satisfied with my answer. "That's right. It took many years for them to grow and eventually bend into that form. When they were first planted here, I was your age. I can remember visiting the High Priestess of Hathor and thinking that her garden was extremely ugly compared to the ones we had in Malkata. I didn't see then that she was planning for the future. Do you understand what I'm saying, Nefertari?"

I nodded, because I thought I did.

"You are like a young sycamore right now. The viziers look at you and see a wild and untended garden. But together we are going to shape you for the future, so that when Ramesses looks at you, he doesn't see a little sister, but a woman and a queen."

Woserit's voice grew firm. "However, if you want my help, it will mean following my advice even when you do not understand it. In the past, I have heard that you disobeyed your nurse. There will be no disobedience if I'm instructing you."

"Of course not," I said quickly.

"And there will be times when what I'm saying may seem to con-flict with advice your nurse has given you, but you will simply have to trust it."

I looked up to see what Woserit meant, and she explained.

"I am sure your nurse has told you never to lie. But a queen must learn to be a very good liar about many things. Is that something you are willing to do?" she questioned. "Lie when you must? Smile when you're not happy? Pray when the gods don't seem to be listening? How much is a place at court, and Ramesses's love, worth to you?"

I looked out beyond the sycamore groves to the crests of dunes that vaulted one beyond another. If the wind, which only had the power of breath, could make a hill, then surely Woserit could make a princess into a queen. "Everything."

Woserit smiled. "Come then."

I followed her into Merit's robing room, and she indicated the leather chair in front of the mirror. When I took a seat, she watched me from behind in the polished bronze.

"Do you know what they say about you at court?"

I met her gaze and shook my head.

"That your best feature is your smile. Now it's time you learn how to use it. Pretend that I'm an old friend," she said, "and you've seen me in the market. How would you smile?"

Even though I felt foolish, I grinned widely, and Woserit nodded.

"Good. Now, I'm an emissary that you've just met. How do you greet me?"

I smiled widely again and Woserit frowned. "You're like an easy girl in the harem of Mi-Wer, giving it all away," she criticized. "Start slow. You don't know him yet."

I let my lips curve upward but didn't show my teeth. This time, Woserit nodded. "Good. Now I'm the emissary and I've just complimented you. *My, Queen Nefertari, I never dreamed what a beautiful shade of lapis your eyes were.* How do you respond?"

I smiled so that all my teeth were showing, and Woserit said sharply, "Not so fast! A woman's smile has to be slow, so that a man knows he must work for it. See?" Woserit let her lips curve slightly. "Now compliment me."

I searched for a compliment. "*High Priestess Woserit, you . . . you look lovely today. I'd forgotten what beautiful dark hair you had."* As I spoke, Woserit's smile widened, but it wasn't until I had said my last words that her eyes fixed on mine and she gave me her fullest smile. I felt a sudden hotness in my cheeks.

"You see?" Woserit said. "You want it to feel like a surprise. You want to keep him guessing whether he'll make you smile entirely so that when you do, he will feel like he's been given a gift." She put her arm in mine and led me to the door.

"Watch," she instructed.

We entered the hall outside her chamber and passed through a courtyard where servants were shoveling and toiling at the heavy work of the garden. As soon as they saw us, they scrambled to their feet and bowed. One man, who looked to be the head of the gardeners from the cut of his linen, stepped forward to greet Woserit. "It's an honor to see Her Holiness in the courtyard. We are graced by your presence," he said.

Woserit let her lips curve slightly. "You've done beautiful work," she complimented.

It was true. Myrtle and jasmine grew up around a granite fountain of Hathor, and stone benches had been arranged in clusters beneath the sycamore trees so that the pilgrims to Hathor's temple could sit and contemplate the goddess's splendor.

"It is beautiful," the young gardener agreed. Woserit's smile widened. "But that is only because it is a reflection of you."

Woserit smiled fully. "Very pretty."

She laughed, but the young man didn't laugh. He was taken by her, and there was a light of new fascination in his eyes. "Come," Woserit said to me primly. "I will show you the orchards." When we left the courtyard and passed into the groves, Woserit turned.

"He stared after you until we left the courtyard!" I cried.

"You see what a smile can do? And mine is not even pretty." I made to interrupt her, but she shook her head at my protest. "It's true. It's nothing like yours. You have teeth as white as pearls, and no man who sees your smile will ever forget it."

"I don't think that gardener will ever forget yours," I pointed out.

"That's because I've learned how to use it," Woserit said. "I don't pass it out like an old woman giving free milk to the village cats. It's something that must be controlled, and for you especially. You use it on anyone. You must learn to be more judicious."

She looked down the path and I followed her gaze to a group of men harvesting figs from the sycamore trees. "Do you see one who is handsome?" she asked.

I flushed.

"Don't be shy. There will be plenty of men at court, and some will need to be convinced that they are in your special favor. How will you do that? With a look," she answered. "With a smile. As we walk by, I want you to choose a man," she said. "Make him feel that he has been chosen. And then make him speak to you."

"Without using words?" I exclaimed.

"Using only your smile. So, which one shall it be?" she said slyly.

I looked over at the group of men. Sitting down, sorting the good figs from bad, was a young man with dark hair. "The one who is counting," I said immediately.

I thought a smile alone might not suffice, and the thought came to me to reach for my bracelet. . . . Quickly, I loosened the clasp, and as we passed the group of men I met the expressive eyes of the dark-haired man and smiled slowly. When his eyes widened with the realization that I was acknowledging him specifically, I let the bracelet fall. "My lady!" He jumped up and fetched my bracelet. "You have dropped something!" He held the bracelet up, and I let him have my fullest smile, the way Woserit had with the gardener.

"How clumsy of me!" I took the bracelet from his hand, brushing his palm with my fingertips, and the group of men watched in silence as Woserit and I disappeared through the groves.

At the bank of the River Nile, Woserit nodded approvingly, "Now you are no longer a giggling child, smiling at whoever comes along. You are a woman with power. Learn to control your smile, and you can control what men will think about you. So, the next time you see Ramesses, what will you do?"

I smiled slightly so that only the top of my front teeth could be seen.

"Good. Slow and reserved. You don't give him everything, because you don't know how it will be received. By the time you see him again he may already have decided to make Iset Chief Wife. We also don't want Henuttawy to realize that you haven't retreated. You never want to give away everything at once," she warned. "We are playing a delicate game."

I looked up, still guessing at her true purpose. "What kind of game?"

"The kind you played when you dropped your bracelet," she said with finality.

The sun reflected in Woserit's diadem, and in the golden sun disc at the center of her brow I could see a twisted reflection of myself. "Tomorrow," Woserit went on, "your temple training will begin. If Henuttawy asks one of my women what you are doing here, it must look as though you are truly planning to devote your life to Hathor. I don't expect you to join the priestesses in the Great Hall tonight, but tomorrow morning Aloli will summon you to my chamber and I will explain how we are to proceed."

༺ ༻ ༼

AFTER THE sun sank below the hills that evening, Merit sat on the edge of my bed. "Are you nervous, my lady?"

"No," I said honestly, drawing the covers up to my chest. "We are doing what must be done. Tomorrow, Woserit is going to tell me how I am to spend my year."

"In a manner befitting a princess, I should hope."

"Even if I have to swing a bronze censer from dawn to dusk, if it makes Ramesses miss me, then it will be worth it."

ᗡ ᗡ ᗡ

THE NEXT morning, Aloli knocked on the door to my chamber, and her big eyes grew even wider when she saw me in Hathor's long blue robes. "You are really one of us now!" she exclaimed, and her voice echoed through the silent halls.

"Perhaps we should be quiet," I offered.

"Nonsense! It's practically dawn." She gave me her arm as we walked through the halls. It was so early in the morning that she needed an oil lamp to guide us down the gray passages of the temple. "So, are you nervous?" she asked merrily, and I wondered once more why everyone thought I should be. "I can still remember my first day in temple. I began my career in the Temple of Isis."

"With *Henuttawy?*"

"Yes." Aloli wrinkled her nose. "I don't know why my mother chose that temple. She might have chosen the Temple of Mut, or Sekhmet, or even Hathor. If she were still alive, I'd ask her. But she died when I was ten. I spent five years with the High Priestess. Fetching her water, polishing her sandals, fixing her hair . . ."

"Is that what a priestess is supposed to do?"

"Of course not!"

A door opened at the end of the hall and a voice cried sharply, *"Be quiet!"*

"That's Serapis. The old priestess likes to sleep in late."

"Shouldn't we be silent then?"

"Silent?" Aloli laughed. "Soon she'll be sleeping for eternity. She ought to get up and enjoy the hours she has left." We reached a hall that ended in a pair of double doors, and Aloli said, "Stay here."

Her silhouette dissolved into the chamber's blackness as I waited in the hall beneath a painted image of the Nile in the Sky. When I was younger, Merit had pointed to the band of stars clustered across the void and told me the story of how the cow goddess Hathor had sent her milk across the heavens as a path on which Ra could sail his solar bark. I stared up at the painting, wondering if that was the same path my parents had taken to the heavenly fields of Yaru. Then the creak of a door interrupted my thoughts, and the priestess's hand beckoned to me. "Come. She is willing to see you."

She let me pass into Woserit's private chamber, and as I entered the room I tried to hide my shock. Three chairs had been placed around a lit brazier sunk into the tiled floor, and one of them was taken by Paser. Instead of wearing his hair in a severe scholar's knot, it was now tied back in a lapis band. In the firelight, I could see a cartouche hung at his neck, engraved with Ramesses's full title in gold.

"You may close the door, Aloli." The priestess did as she was told, and Woserit pointed to a seat across from her. "Nefertari," she began when I was seated, "I am sure you are surprised to see your tutor here, especially as he has now become vizier."

I looked at Paser to see how being part of Pharaoh's court had changed him. Wearing a vizier's tunic made him seem somehow different.

"Paser has many new duties in the palace now," Woserit explained, "but he has agreed to continue your education. Every morning, before he reports to the Audience Chamber, he will come to the temple to tutor you in the languages that you have studied with him."

"At sunrise?" I exclaimed.

"And earlier." Paser nodded.

"He knows you will not disappoint him," Woserit said. "You have mastered seven languages in the edduba. This is what will separate you from Iset and make you invaluable."

I frowned. "To Ramesses?"

"A queen's job is more than bearing children," Paser replied. "It is speaking with the people, meeting with viziers, and greeting dignitaries who come into the palace. With a command of Shasu, Hittite, Nubian, who will be best suited for entertaining princes?"

"Of course, Henuttawy will be whispering into Pharaoh Seti's ear," Woserit warned. "And Iset *is* beautiful. Courtiers already adore her, and with Henuttawy at her side they are a perfect pair. Entertaining and pretty . . . But pretty doesn't mean useful."

"And I am to be the useful princess?" I asked, hurt.

"Hopefully, you will be more than that," Woserit replied. "It will take much more to make you Chief Wife when everyone is looking to Iset. This means that every morning, at sunrise, you will meet Vizier Paser in this room."

"*Your* room?"

"Yes, and you will come prepared. I hope never to hear that you have been careless or idle in your work. Paser has told me that there have been times when you did not attend classes in the edduba. That will never happen here. Once you are finished with your lessons, Aloli will meet you outside these doors and instruct you in the morning's ritual. When your duties as a priestess are finished, we will meet in the Great Hall and you will sit with me, where I will instruct you on how to behave when you are dining with the court."

Woserit saw my look and added, "I hope you don't think that you know how already." She waited for my response, and I dutifully shook my head.

"Good. When our meal is finished, you will accompany Aloli to the eastern sanctuary where she will teach you harp."

"But I already *know* how to play harp," I protested.

"Properly? Like my sister or Iset?"

"No, but my talent is in languages—"

"And now it will be in harp, as well."

I looked to Paser, as if he might offer me some reversal, but his face was set.

"When you are finished with harp," Woserit continued, "you may return to your chamber to study. Then I expect that you will join the priestesses in their sunset ritual. When your day is finished, if you would like to join the priestesses at their dinner, you may go to the Great Hall. Otherwise, you may enjoy a quieter meal in your room." She stood to excuse herself. "I know this sounds like a great deal to learn," she said softly, "but there is a purpose for everything. The longer you are away from Ramesses, the more he will miss you, and the more time we will have to transform you from a sapling into a tree that can withstand even the strongest winds."

I nodded as if I believed her, and when she left, Paser said quietly, "And there will be winds. Trust her, Princess." He stood and retrieved a large model from a desk across the room. He placed it on the table between our chairs. "Do you know what this is?" he asked.

I leaned forward to get a better look. An artist had carefully sculpted a long chamber with more than three dozen columns holding up a roof of blue tiles from clay. On one end of the room was a pair of bronze doors that I recognized from the palace. On the other was a raised and polished dais. Its steps were painted with images of bound captives, so that whenever Pharaoh ascended the platform he could crush his enemies beneath his braided sandals. Three thrones had been placed on top of the dais, each of them gilt in gold. Although members of the court had to be at least fourteen to enter, I recognized the room by sight. "It's the Audience Chamber," I said.

Paser smiled. "Very good. But how do you know if you've never been inside?"

"Because I recognize the doors."

"Every morning, Pharaoh enters here." Paser picked up a reed pen from the table and pointed to the front of the chamber. "He passes the viziers." He indicated a long table inside the model that was nearly as wide as the room. "Then the viziers stand and make obeisance to him. Once he has crossed the wide distance between the viziers and the dais, he takes his throne, and petitioners are let into the Audience Chamber. Each petitioner approaches one of the four viziers with his complaint."

"Any vizier?"

"Yes. If the vizier does not have the authority to help him, guards search the petitioner and he is allowed to approach Pharaoh. But it is not Pharaoh alone on the dais. There are three thrones." He indicated the three golden chairs. "Four today."

"For Pharaoh Seti, Queen Tuya, Pharaoh Ramesses, and Iset."

"*Princess* Iset," Paser reminded. "And here, on this dais, is where futures are decided. Will you be a queen like Tuya, disinterested in everything but the happiness of your *iwiw*?" I thought I heard disapproval in his voice, but I couldn't be certain. "Or will you be a queen like your aunt, clever and watchful, prepared in deed if not in name to make yourself coregent?"

I inhaled sharply. "I'll *never* be like my aunt! I'm not a whore."

"And neither was Nefertiti."

I had never heard anyone but Merit speak her name, and in the amber light of dawn Paser's face appeared stern and defiant. "Your aunt never used her body to command the Audience Chamber, whatever you may have heard."

"How do you know that?"

"You may ask your nurse. She knew Nefertiti, and there's no one in Thebes with a greater interest in gossip." Paser might have smiled, but he was serious. "Why do you think the people tolerated your aunt's policies, the removal of their royal city, the banishment of their gods?"

"Because she had the power of a Pharaoh."

Paser shook his head. "Because she knew what the people wanted and gave it to them. Her husband took away their goddesses, so she became their goddess on earth."

"That's *heresy*," I whispered.

"Or wisdom? She knew what her husband was doing was danger- ous. If the people had rebelled, she would have been the first be- neath the knife. She saved her life by impressing the petitioners in the Audience Chamber. She could paint every wall from Thebes to Memphis with her image, but only words can sway opinion. With each petitioner, she influenced the people."

"And that's what you'd have me do?" I asked him.

"If you wish to stay alive. Or you can follow Queen Tuya's example," he said. "You can leave all but the simplest petitions to your husband, assuming Pharaoh Ramesses takes you as a wife. But as the niece of heretics, I do not believe you have that option. If you find yourself on a throne in the Audience Chamber, your time there will be the only means you have to influence the people. The way your aunt did."

"Egypt *curses* the name of my aunt."

"Not when she was alive. She knew how to control the viziers, when to speak, which friendships to cultivate. But are you willing to learn those things?"

I slumped deeper into the chair. "And become like the Heretic Queen?"

"And become a viable player in this game of Senet." He indicated a polished wooden table. The top had been divided into three rows of ten squares, and he opened a wooden drawer to take out a carved faience piece. "Do you know what this is?"

Of course I did. "It's a pawn."

"There are five for each player. In some games there are seven, or even ten. In a way, like the court." He glanced at me. "Some days, it will feel as if you are playing a game with more pawns than you believe you can control. Other days, there will be fewer pawns to play. But at court, every day ends the same: the first player with all of her pawns on her own squares wins. You will have to learn which courtiers to control, which viziers to move closer, which ambassadors to placate. And whichever wife can lure them all to her squares will someday become queen. It's not an easy game, and there are many rules, but if you are willing to learn . . ."

I thought of Ramesses across the river, waking up in Iset's bed and watching her prepare for her morning in the Audience Chamber. What did she know about petitions? How could she help him in any way? I could be closer to Ramesses with every move Paser showed me how to make. "Yes." The word sounded with an intensity that caught me by surprise.

The beginnings of a smile formed on his lips. "Then tomorrow, you will bring a reed pen and papyrus. We will be adding an eighth language to our studies: Akkadian, the language of the Assyrians. For tonight, you may translate this."

He took a scroll from his belt and handed it to me.

Outside the door, Aloli was waiting.

"What's the matter?" she asked cheerfully. "What are you studying?"

I followed the jangle of her anklets down the hall. Priestesses were awake, and soon the morning ritual would begin. "Languages," I said. I was about to add "Shasu," but Aloli held up her hand. "Hush! We're approaching the inner sanctum."

The inner sanctum was as dark and still as a tomb, and the air rang loud with silence. It lay at the heart of the temple, and the window-less walls and heavy columns protected it from the sun. An altar of ebony rose from the center of the chamber; the polished black stone reflected the light of the flickering torches.

"What do we do?" I whispered, but Aloli didn't respond. She walked to the front of the chamber, where she slowly knelt before the altar of Hathor and held out her hands. I followed silently and did the same. Around us, priestesses in flowing blue robes were taking their places, holding out their palms the way Aloli had done, as if waiting for raindrops. I searched the chamber for Woserit, but as the chanting began and sweet billows of incense filled the inner sanctum, I couldn't see anything but the altar in front of me.

> *Mother of Horus. Wife of Ra. Creator of Egypt.*
> *Mother of Horus. Wife of Ra. Creator of Egypt.*

The priestesses repeated this chant, and Aloli looked in my direction to see if I understood. I intoned the words with her. "Mother of Horus. Wife of Ra. Creator of Egypt." Then someone added, "We come to pay you obeisance," and as the women lowered their arms, Woserit emerged from the eastern passageway in a robe of astonishing material. It rippled as she moved, creating the impression of water in the dimly lit chamber. Her hair was swept back by Hathor's crown, and not for the first time I felt awed by her. She held an alabaster jar above the altar, then poured oil onto the polished surface.

"Mother of Horus, wife of Ra, creator of Egypt, I bring to you the oil of life."

The priestesses raised their palms again, and Woserit washed her hands in a bowl of water. Then she disappeared down the smoky hall.

"That's it?" I asked.

Aloli grinned at me. "In the morning, the altar is crowned with oil, and in the evening the High Priestess brings bread and wine."

"But all of that, just for some oil?"

Aloli's smile vanished. "These are the ways of Hathor," she said sternly. "Every morning and evening they must be performed to invoke her pleasure. Would you risk her wrath by not paying her obeisance?"

I shook my head. "No, of course not."

"Hathor's rites may be simple, but nothing is more important to Egypt's survival."

I was surprised by Aloli's sudden seriousness. We walked across much of the temple in silence. When we reached the entrance, I ventured, "So what do we do now?"

The jovial Aloli returned. "Didn't the High Priestess tell you? Now we clean!"

I felt the blood drain from my face. "You mean, with oil and brushes?"

"And linen and lemons." She stopped walking. "Haven't you ever cleaned?"

"My sandals," I said. "When there was mud on them after a hunt."

"But never a floor, or a table, or a mosaic?" She saw my face and realized, "You have never cleaned in your life, have you?"

I shook my head.

"It's not difficult," she promised brightly. "The priestesses do it every day before their afternoon meal." She took off her robe and bundled it under her arm. Beneath, she wore the same blue sheath that I'd been given. "We will clean the hall leading out into the groves. The men come through with mud on their sandals and dirt in their kilts. Every priestess has her own hall, and this one is mine!"

She strode ahead and I followed. I didn't understand why she was so merry until she opened the doors leading onto the groves. As she bent over to clean, the barrel-chested grove workers watched as her sheath moved slowly up her thighs. She made no effort to move herself from their view. I squatted over the tiles at the other end of the hall and arranged my sheath over my knees. I dabbed a piece of linen into a bowl of water, then leaned over and wiped it gently across the floor.

"It will go easier if you are on your knees." Aloli laughed. "Don't worry, no one will be watching you. They're all watching me."

※ ※ ※

WHEN THE piercing sound of trumpets sent the workers heading to their homes beyond the temple, Aloli handed me my robe. An eternity of scrubbing, over at last.

We entered the Great Hall with its towering mosaics of Hathor, and the scent of roasted duck in steaming bowls of pomegranate sauce filled the lively chamber. Row upon row of polished cedar tables were taken up by priestesses who had already taken their seats.

"Where do we sit?"

"Next to the High Priestess."

I could see Woserit's crown above the heads of even the tallest women, and when she saw us, she gave a small nod. I sat on Woserit's right, and Aloli sat to her left. As I reached for my bowl, Woserit said sharply, "I hope you don't snatch your food like that in the palace."

I looked around me, in fear that everyone had heard her rebuke, but the other priestesses were deep in conversation.

"You don't grab for your bowl like a monkey," Woserit said. "You start by rolling up your sleeve." She illustrated, taking her left hand and delicately holding up the sleeve of her right while reaching for the soup. Then she let her sleeve fall into place as she brought the bowl to her mouth. When she had taken a sip, she didn't let her lips linger on the bowl as I might have. She replaced her bowl the same way she had taken it. I imitated what she had done, and she nodded. "Better. Now let me see you take the duck."

The other women had rolled up their sleeves and were taking the meat in both hands and eagerly picking it apart. When I began to do the same, Woserit's look grew dark.

"That is fine for a common priestess, but you are a *princess*." She lifted her sleeve as she had done before, then held the meat between her forefinger and thumb and nibbled on it slowly, using a linen she kept in her left hand to wipe her mouth should the pomegranate paste dribble. "I'm shocked you've never learned this before, sitting at the table beneath the dais for seven years. But then I suppose that you and Ramesses never paid attention to anything besides yourselves."

I hid my shame by lowering my head, then took the leg of the duck in my right hand, just as she had done. She passed me her linen, and when I used it to keep sauce from falling on my robe, her gaze softened. "The next time you come into the Great Hall," she said, "I expect you to bring a table linen with you. Have Merit make it from an old sheath."

I nodded. "And sit straight. And raise your head. None of this is your own personal failing, Nefertari. You are here to learn and that's what you're doing."

ᗏ ᗏ ᗏ

WHEN THE meal was over. I followed Aloli through the halls to the eastern sanctuary. "I think I will like it here," I lied.

Aloli marched ahead, and her long robes swished back and forth.

"The cleaning and the rituals, you'll get used to them," she promised. "And while we're practicing harp," she gloated, "the other priestesses will be out greeting pilgrims."

I stopped walking. "I'm the *only* one practicing harp?"

"The entire temple can't play, can it?" Aloli turned around. "Only a few priestesses have the talent. I'm one of them."

We entered the eastern sanctuary. Tiles of highly polished blue and gold covered the walls, tracing images of the goddess Hathor teaching mortals how to play and sing.

"Impressive, isn't it?" Aloli asked, as she walked to a small platform where two harps had been positioned next to a pair of stools. "Why don't you begin?"

I shook my head firmly at I sat. "No. Please. I'd like to hear you first."

Aloli arranged herself on the wooden stool, then tilted the harp so that it was resting on her shoulder. She sat straight as a reed, the way I had been taught, with her elbows bent out like an ibis about to take flight. Then she positioned her fingers on the strings and an astonishing melody filled the chamber. She closed her eyes and in the echoing strains of her music she was the most beautiful, elegant woman in Egypt. The song resounded in the empty room, first slow, then swift and passionate. Not even Iset or Henuttawy could play the harp with her skill. When her fingers came to rest, I remembered to breathe. "I will never play like that," I said, with awe.

"Remember, you are fourteen and I am seventeen. It will come with practice."

"But I practiced every day at the edduba," I protested.

"In a group, or alone?"

I thought of my music lessons with Asha and Ramesses and flushed at how little we'd ever accomplished. "In a group."

84

"Here, there'll be no one to distract you," she promised. "You may not be playing in Pharaoh's military procession tomorrow, but—"

I stood from my stool so swiftly that it fell. "What do you mean? What procession?"

"Egypt is going to war. There's to be a procession when the army marches through Thebes. News arrived last night." Aloli frowned. "Why, my lady?"

"Paser never told me! I have to bid Ramesses farewell! I have to tell Asha!"

"But you're in the temple now. Priestesses in training don't leave for a year."

"I'm not a priestess in training!"

Aloli stood up her harp. "I thought you were here to take the High Priestess's place?"

"No. I am here to stay away from Ramesses. Woserit thinks I can learn how to behave like a queen, and that Ramesses will take me as Chief Wife."

Aloli's eyes grew as wide as lotus blossoms. "So that is why I am tutoring you," she whispered. "With the flute or the lyre, you're one of a group. With the harp, you are alone onstage, commanding an audience with your skill. And if you can command the Great Hall by yourself with the harp, why not the Audience Chamber with Pharaoh?"

I knew at once that Aloli was right. This was why Woserit had brought us together. "But I am going to that military procession," I said, not to be dissuaded.

Aloli looked uneasy. "I don't think the High Priestess will allow it."

I said nothing more about the procession. We began our lessons, but all I could think about was war, and as soon as our time together was finished, I asked her where I could find the High Priestess. "I can take you to her," Aloli said. "But she will not be happy to be disturbed. This is her time for writing letters."

I followed Aloli through the halls of the temple to a pair of heavy wooden doors. "The Per Medjat," she said.

"She writes in the library?"

"Every afternoon before she sails to the palace." I hesitated in front of the doors, and Aloli slowly backed away. "You can knock," she said tentatively, "but do not expect her to answer." I raised my fist and rapped on the door. When there was silence, I banged again. One of the heavy doors swung open.

"What are you doing here?" Woserit demanded. She had taken off the crown of Hathor, and her hands were stained with sand and ink.

"I have come to make an urgent request," I said. Woserit looked to Aloli and made no sign of inviting either of us in. "I am guessing she has told you about the procession?"

"Yes," I said desperately, "and I have come to ask you whether I may attend."

"Of course not."

"But—"

"Do you remember when I said there will be times you don't understand my advice, but that you would need to take it regardless? And do you remember agreeing to that?"

"Yes," I mumbled.

"Then I expect I won't have to hear about this again."

She shut the door. I turned to face Aloli, and I couldn't keep the tears from my eyes. "If I were his wife, I could be going to war with him."

"War?" Aloli exclaimed. "You're a woman!"

"What does it matter? I could be his translator."

Aloli put her arm around my shoulders. "In a year, my lady, you can see him as often as you choose. It's not as long as you think."

"But he will think I am angry with him," I protested. "He won't be-lieve that I am forbidden from seeing him because I'm a priestess in training. I'm a princess—there's nothing a princess is forbidden."

"Except this. You have given the High Priestess your word."

"But she doesn't understand!" I exclaimed.

"When I was in the Temple of Isis, I thought of running away to my mother to tell her how terrible it was. Or of seeing my uncles and begging one of them to take me in. But I didn't, because if I were caught, I would be banished from the priesthood forever."

"But isn't that what you wanted?"

"Of course not! I only wanted to escape from Henuttawy."

"Then how did you manage?"

"I didn't. The High Priestess of Hathor did. Woserit heard me per-form during a Festival of Opet, and when she came to offer me her compliments, she saw how miserable I was. So she arranged to pur-chase me from Henuttawy."

I sucked in my breath. "She bought you like a slave?"

"Henuttawy wouldn't give me up otherwise."

"And what did she pay?"

"The same price as seven men. She did it because she knew that my life under Henuttawy was unbearable. So you see, Princess? It would have been a foolish thing for me to have run away. The god-dess saw how unhappy I was, and by honoring my vow to Isis, she delivered me from that viper." She reached across and patted my knee. "You must honor your promise to Hathor, and she will see that you are given your desire as well."

"But I haven't made any promise to Hathor."

"Then honor your vow to Woserit. The High Priestess knows what she is doing."

꒰ ꒰ ꒰

THE NEXT morning, I was surprised to see Woserit still in her chamber. She and Paser were crouched, whispering, and when I appeared, they fell silent.

"Princess Nefertari," Woserit said in greeting. I wondered why she wasn't in the inner sanctum. "I know how badly you wanted to attend—"

"No," I said firmly. "I was mistaken."

Woserit hesitated, as if to take the measure of my words. "I had hoped when you came to this temple, Nefertari, that I would be able to instruct you daily. But with my brother's war in Kadesh, I am going to be needed in the Audience Chamber more frequently. There will be times I may not see you for days. A month even."

I looked to Paser, who nodded. "In the mornings, I will still be here, as will all of the priestesses."

"And they will be able to instruct you as I direct. My hope is that whenever I ask of your progress, I will hear that it is satisfactory."

"Of course," I promised, but Woserit did not seem certain.

CHAPTER FIVE

A SWEET SCENT OF FIGS

Thebes, 1 2 8 3 – 1 2 8 2 BC

IN THE TEMPLE of Hathor I fell into a routine. In the dark before sunrise, Merit would wake me, and half asleep I would put on a fresh sheath and light a cone of incense beneath my mother's shrine. When the cone had burned itself into ashes, I would make my way through the shadowy halls of the temple to Woserit's chamber. And just as Woserit had promised, I rarely saw her.

Vizier Paser proved to be different from Tutor Paser. He taught me the proper way to greet a Sumerian, and how to know whether a Hittite soldier had made his first kill. "If he has shorn the hair on his face, then he has demonstrated his heroism by slaughtering an enemy." He wanted me to memorize the customs of foreign people: that Sumerians bury their dead on reed mats and that Assyrians value feathers above any precious stone. We spent entire mornings on politics. "The Hittites are the only power in the world that can rise against Egypt," Paser insisted. "No other country is more important than Hatti." So I learned everything I could about Emperor Muwatallis and his son, Prince Urhi; how both men dressed in colorful robes and used swords made of iron. I drew maps of the lands that Muwatallis had conquered, including Ugarit and Syria.

"And the land of Kadesh," Paser said solemnly, "that once belonged to Egypt. But the Heretic King let the Hittites claim it, and now its wealthy ports—where goods come in from the Northern Sea—all belong to the Hittites. Do you understand what that means?"

"It means that we have to find longer routes for trading ivory, copper, and timber. It means that the Hittites profit from it first. But that is about to change," I added. "Because Pharaoh Seti and Ramesses are going to take it back!"

Paser allowed himself a smile. "Yes."

"Is there any news—"

"None."

I waited for word every night, and on the twenty-seventh day of Choiak, Pharaoh's army returned from Kadesh. Heralds ran ahead of the men with news of their victory and lists of the dead, and Merit awakened me before sunrise to say that Asha and Ramesses had both survived.

From the window of the western sanctuary, I could see the priestesses of Hathor gathering at the quay. Their jeweled belts winked in the sun, and their open-fronted gowns revealed breasts that had been exquisitely hennaed. Aloli joined me at the window. "Aren't you going to be a part of the celebration?" I asked.

"The High Priestess instructed that I stay here with you."

"Why? Does she think I'll run away?"

Aloli grinned slyly. "You wouldn't?"

"No," I said quietly. "I wouldn't." Below us, the priestesses were now crossing the river, and the bright turquoise sails of Hathor's ships began to disappear beyond the sycamore groves. I turned to Aloli. "Do you remember the first time I came to this temple?"

"Of course. With your big green eyes you seemed a frightened cat. I didn't think you were truly a princess."

I was startled. "Why?"

"Because I knew the princess Nefertari was just fourteen, yet you looked like you were eight or nine."

"But do you remember saying that you had heard about me?"

"Certainly." Aloli crossed from the window and took her place at the harp. "I heard that you and Pharaoh Ramesses were fast friends. And when news of his marriage came, the court assumed that it would be you."

"But I was only thirteen! And I'm the niece of the Heretic King."

Aloli shrugged. "Everyone believed Pharaoh Ramesses would overlook that. No one imagined he would take a harem girl up the dais. So when you came to this temple we thought perhaps you didn't want to be married."

"No. I was never asked. As soon as Ramesses was crowned, Henuttawy went to Pharaoh Seti and spoke for Iset." I told Aloli about Woserit's theory, that she believed Henuttawy was helping Iset toward the crown in exchange for something. "But what could it be?"

"Power," Aloli said quickly. "Gold. With both she could build the greatest temple in Thebes, bigger than Hathor's. Pilgrims would go simply to see its magnificence."

"Leaving their riches as offerings," I agreed. I thought of Ramesses and felt my cheeks warm. "There is no one else I can imagine marrying besides Ramesses," I admitted.

"Then it's not enough to study harp," she said. "If you are going to become Chief Wife, you will need to know how to please a man."

Aloli stood, and the silver bangles that jangled when she walked slid down her wrist. "The Temple of Isis was full of Henuttawy's men," she explained. "So long as they were wealthy, she welcomed anyone inside. Hittite, Assyrian . . . I learned more than how to please Isis in that temple. You should learn all the secrets that Henuttawy is teaching to Iset."

I was embarrassed. "Such as?"

"Such as how to satisfy a man beneath his kilt. How to use your mouth to give him pleasure." My eyes must have betrayed my thoughts because Aloli added, "You will be the difference between a Thebes ruled by Henuttawy and a Thebes ruled by Woserit."

Ｌ Ｌ Ｌ

WHETHER FROM horror at that prospect, or love for Ramesses, I became the perfect student. I was never late, my work was never incomplete, and soon I could have sailed to Assyria and survived on my command of Akkadian alone. Paser didn't see how this language came to me so quickly, but the truth was, everywhere I went I practiced; in the baths, around the courtyard—even at my mother's shrine, I prayed to Mut in Akkadian. My harp lessons with Aloli also took on a new intensity, as if the priestess could will her own talent into my hands. With practice I became competent enough that if the queen ever called upon me at court, I would not embarrass myself in front of them. Iset had always prided herself on being talented at music, but now I saw that it was not so difficult with time and patience.

But it wasn't the harp that kept me late each day in the eastern chamber. One day Merit remarked, "You seem to be enjoying your music, my lady." I hid my blush behind the feathers of my fan, and the next day when Merit said approvingly, "You stay longer and longer at every lesson," I finally told her, "That's because Aloli has been speaking with me about more than just the harp."

Merit stopped filling my alabaster jar with perfume and came inside from the balcony. "What does she teach you?" she asked flatly.

I put down my reed pen. "Other things. Such as what I should do on my wedding night."

Merit gave a sharp cry.

"I have to know everything! Iset does," I added quickly.

"You are not some girl from the harem!"

"No. I am the princess from a family that's been erased from history. You know as well as I do what it will mean if I become Chief Wife. My family's name will be rewritten in the scrolls. It will save my family, and it will save us all from Henuttawy. Can you imagine a Thebes where Henuttawy is as powerful as the queen?"

"But for the Priestess Aloli to teach you such things—"

"Why not, if they will keep us safe? If it will keep my mother's name alive?" I glanced at my broken shrine. Although the court sculptor had done his best, I could still see the thin line where the goddess's neck had been broken from her body. "You will always be my *mawat*," I promised. "But I had another mother who gave her life for me. And what have I given her? What has Egypt given her? As Chief Wife I could make sure that she is never forgotten, that *we* are never forgotten," I corrected. "My family ruled Egypt for more than a hundred years and there's not a single mortuary temple to remember them by! But I could build one in the hills for you, and for my parents." A warm wind blew the sweet scent of figs from the sycamore trees, and I inhaled. Merit always said that my mother had loved their smell. "There are so many reasons to become Chief Wife. But what if Ramesses doesn't love me?"

Merit's face softened. "He has always loved you."

"As a sister," I protested. "But what if he can't love me as a wife?"

🔲 🔲 🔲

WHEN THE season of Shemu came, the court prepared for its annual progress north to the palace of Pi-Ramesses, where the suffocating windless heat of Thebes could be relieved by the ocean breezes. It was the first time I wasn't going to sail with the flotilla of brightly painted ships or stand on a deck with Pharaoh's golden standards snapping above me in the warm Payni sun. I stood on the balcony of my chamber one day and imagined the world sailing away from me with only Tefer left for company. And even he wasn't much good, spending all his time chasing mice in the fields. He didn't need me. No one needed me.

"What's wrong with you?" Merit challenged from the door. "Every afternoon you come out here. These groves haven't changed since yesterday."

"I'm missing everything! When Thoth comes and a new year begins, I'll miss the Feast of Wag, too." Wag is the only night when a person's *akhu* can return to the land of the living and enjoy the earthly food that's presented to them.

But Merit shook her head slyly. "I don't believe you will miss the feast. Yesterday, I saw the High Priestess while you were practicing harp. She said that in two months you will have been away from court for an entire year, and that soon . . ." Merit paused for effect. "You may be ready to return."

ᛒ ᛒ ᛒ

ON THE tenth of Thoth, Merit shook me out of bed. "My lady, the High Priestess is waiting!"

I sat up and wiped the sleep from my eyes. "What?"

"You are not to study with the vizier today. The High Priestess wants to see you instead!"

We rushed to the mirror, and I sat patiently while Merit applied my paint. "We will use the malachite," she determined, and opened the jar of expensive green powder. I closed my eyes while she applied it to my lids, and she spent extra time outlining my eyes with kohl. When Merit took my wig from its box, I saw that she had added green faience beads. "How—"

"For the occasion," she said eagerly.

In all the many months since I first entered the Temple of Hathor, Woserit had rarely seen me. Merit hennaed my nails with a brush meant for kohl, and when she gave me my gown I saw that it was new. I stood, and Merit sucked in her breath. "You are a woman," she said, as if she could hardly believe it. She narrowed her small eyes as she studied my face, my gown, my nails. When she came to my sandals, her face smoothed itself out and she said frankly, "You are ready." Her voice choked with tears and she embraced me tightly, "Good luck, my lady."

"Thank you, *mawat.*" I pulled away to look her in the eyes. "Thank you," I said again. "Not just for coming here with me but . . . but for everything."

Merit straightened her shoulders. "Go. Go before she changes her mind!"

Woserit's chamber was not far from mine, but even so, the walk had never felt so long. I glanced up at the painted walls with their images of Hathor and Ra and wondered if this would be one of the last times that I would ever see them. At her door, a servant bowed. "The High Priestess is waiting for you, my lady."

She opened the door and inside, Woserit was sitting at her table, surrounded by flowers for Thoth and the new year. The bright blooms had been arranged in faience vases, and the lilies perfumed the entire chamber. She looked up, and when she saw me, the expression on her face went from one of deep surprise to pleasure.

"Nefertari?" She stood from behind her table and came over to me. "Look at your cheeks," she gushed. "They've filled out! And your eyes . . . they're absolutely stunning." She made me turn around a first time, then a second, and the third time she exclaimed, "Look how you've changed." She reached over and pinched the back of my gown so that she could see the outline of my waist and breasts. "Enough of these shapeless sheaths," she announced. "I want Merit to measure you for new gowns. You have grown into a woman while I was busy! When Iset gets big and fat with Ramesses's child, you will still be light and beautiful," Woserit promised. "And you will never complain. I can promise you, Ramesses will grow tired of her whining."

"He doesn't love her?" I asked quickly.

Woserit raised her brows. "I didn't say that."

"But what does he like about her if she whines?"

"Oh, she can be charming when she wants, and she's exceptionally beautiful. But her charm and beauty will be a lot less appealing once he has you to compare her with eight days from now."

"On the Feast of Wag?" I exclaimed.

Woserit smiled. "Yes. I think we are ready."

CHAPTER SIX

THE FEAST OF WAG

1282 BC

AT THE END of our lesson on the eighteenth of Thoth, Paser put down his reed pen and asked, "Are you prepared for the feast tonight?"

"Yes." I tried to hide my excitement. "My nurse has prepared an offering bowl of food for Pharaoh Seti's temple, and another bowl—"

"I don't mean food," Paser interrupted. And there was irony in his voice when he said, "I'm sure Pharaoh's *akhu* as well as yours will be very happy with the offerings you bring them. What I'm wondering is whether anyone has prepared you for the shock of visiting the court. Especially when you won't be remaining there."

"Yes," I said quietly. "Woserit has warned me I may only speak to Ramesses briefly."

Across the table Paser nodded. "And you will not be staying for the three nights of drinking. Unless you want to see Henuttawy falling over herself," he said under his breath as he stood. I snickered, because I had heard the same stories about Woserit's older sister. "Nefertari," Paser said, growing serious, "soon our lessons are going to become less frequent. And as Pharaoh Ramesses becomes more involved in the Audience Chamber, so will I. Besides, there's not much more that I can teach you. You already have an extraordinary command of each of the eight languages we've studied." He walked me to the door of Woserit's chamber. "But I hope you have taken Woserit's advice to heart. Woserit is a wise woman and if anyone can chart your path to the throne, it is she."

"Not Henuttawy?" I asked curiously.

"Henuttawy knows how to trick and lie. She might teach Iset how to beguile, but eventually, that spell of enchantment will wear off."

"Isn't that what I'm doing? Tricking and beguiling?"

"By keeping away from Pharaoh Ramesses?" Paser asked. "No. You'll simply remind him of the friendship he's been missing."

When I entered my chamber, I was surprised to see both Woserit and Aloli. They were standing with Merit over two pairs of sandals. "The pair with the thick heels and braided gold," Woserit decided. "She'll be walking tonight, but we don't want her looking like a shepherd's daughter trekking through the hills."

Aloli spoke to me first. "Are you ready?"

I nodded, even as I realized that the only hooded robe I owned would never match the sandals that Woserit had just chosen for me. The Feast of Wag always began with a pilgrimage to Pharaoh Seti's mortuary temple in Thebes. Once we paid obeisance to Seti's ancestors, we were allowed to carry food to the mortuary temples of our own *akhu*. There was no mortuary temple for my family. Every year I went to see Horemheb, who had stolen my grandfather's temple in the city of Djamet and made it his, carving my family's faces from the walls, with the exception of a single image of my mother. The progress began once the sun had set, and although the nights of Thoth were warm, in the temples it could be cold and dank. What would I do without a proper robe? I glanced at Merit. "What will I wear?"

"The High Priestess has been kind enough to give you this," Merit said, and she indicated an exquisite white cloak on the bed. The hood was trimmed in fur, and the flowing sleeves were elaborately edged. With the sandals that Woserit had chosen, I would be a vision of white-gold in the dark of the tombs.

"This may be the festival that will change the course of your life," Woserit said. "Merit has altered one of my dresses for you as well." She went to the bed and lifted the cloak, revealing a netted dress of faience beads. "The lapis beads will match your eyes. When I return," she said, moving toward the door, "I expect you to be ready."

She left, and I went over to the bed, astonished by a garment so delicate and revealing.

"It's a rare dress," Aloli said. "I have never seen the High Priestess give it to anyone, even to repair. Hold up your arms."

I took off my sheath and did as I was told. Aloli eased the dress over my head while Merit pulled it down over my thighs. Then I put on the cloak and seated myself in front of the mirror.

"We are not going to use lapis for your eyelids," Merit determined. "It won't stand out in the half light." She opened a jar of gold dust and mixed it with oil. "Even if no one can see your hair beneath that cloak," she promised, "they will still see your eyes."

It took until sunset to henna my nails, and Merit paid careful attention to the design on my feet. In the mirror, a gleam of white and gold shimmered back at me. The soft white of Woserit's cloak framed my face, and the fur trim stood out against my cheeks. When the door to my chamber opened, I heard a slow intake of breath.

"Magnificent."

Woserit came forward and I could see her reflected in the polished brass. A long, white sheath was pressed against her hips with a belt of polished lapis. Her ankle-length cloak was trimmed in thread of the most stunning turquoise, and a golden cow with lapis eyes fastened it at her neck. Her hair had been brushed to the side, so that anyone standing behind her could see the counterweight of the *menat* worn by every priestess of Hathor. The sacred necklace had been made of faience, ending in a golden amulet that kept the wearer from harm. There was no part of Woserit that wasn't remarkable, from her golden anklets to her translucent sheath. I turned in my chair to see her better. "You look beautiful," I whispered, and I was surprised to realize she was just as striking as her sister, Henuttawy.

She motioned for me to stand, then inspected me as I turned. She lifted the edge of my cloak to see what Merit had done with my feet, then hummed her approval. "You'll be careful not to cover the henna in dust," she said. "And do not drag your feet through the sand. Walk carefully tonight." She drew the hood of my cloak over my fore-head, and Aloli arranged my braids, one over each shoulder.

I stared at myself in the mirror and didn't recognize the woman who looked back at me. She was the kind of woman who spent her days in the baths, gossiping with friends, and buying beads from palace vendors.

"Aloli, it's time for you to get ready," Woserit said. "You and Merit have done an exquisite job."

When Aloli and Merit left for their own chambers, Woserit took a seat. She appeared tense. Later, I would come to understand that in many ways the year had been easier for me than it had for her. All I had to do was learn, soaking up the information around me like a pa-pyrus reed, whereas she had to arrange, and plot, and plan. She knew the consequences of failing, whereas I only imagined that I did. But for all her generosity—giving me her room in the palace, keeping me in the Temple of Hathor, arranging Paser as my tutor, and providing me with clothes—she had never asked for anything in return. When I could hear that Merit was snapping and folding sheaths in the ante-chamber, I asked quietly, "What will I owe you for all of this?"

A smile touched Woserit's lips. "I am not like Henuttawy," she said. "There's nothing to repay."

"But all of this work and time you've put into me. Why? For what?"

"You have grown into a mature, clever woman," she said, and she seemed pleased that I had asked. "I expect you to take Iset's place and make certain that Henuttawy never becomes as powerful as she wishes to be. That is what I expect," she said firmly. "A Thebes that doesn't dance to Henuttawy's tune, and nothing else."

I sensed there must be more, but that was all she said. I wondered if someday a larger reckoning would come.

꒦ ꒦ ꒦

WE LEFT as the sun sank beyond the hills, reaching the quay in front of Hathor's temple as the water turned the color of wine in the disappearing light. In a boat filled with Hathor's songstresses, we sailed to the mortuary temple that Pharaoh Seti had built for his *akhu*. Like the palace, the temple had been built on the western bank, since this is where the sun dies every day and the journey to the Afterlife begins. I had gone with the court many times on its annual progress to Seti's temple, but tonight was different. As lights flickered on the approaching shore, I felt a nervousness in my stomach that had never been there before. Merit stood next to me on the prow and raised my hood so that the fur framed my face.

"Delicate," she said as darkness descended. "Soft."

The full moon reflected on the River Nile and I thought of something Woserit had said. *When Iset gets big and bloated with Ramesses's child, you will still be light and pretty.* I asked Merit over the splashing of the oars, "What if Iset is already pregnant?"

"Then there is even more reason to make her queen," she said. "Ramesses is eighteen. This is the year he will choose a Chief Wife."

As the boat slipped into the quay, Woserit spoke in my direction. "I should think the court will already have arrived, but the rites won't begin without us. Or without Henuttawy," she added. "And we can expect her to be late."

Palace servants, who were waiting on the shore, held up torches to escort us through the darkness. And ahead, within the courtyard of the mortuary temple, a hundred lamps lit up its towering pylons, casting their glow across the painted murals. In one scene, Osiris, the prince of the gods, was being murdered by his brother, Set. In the light of the reed torches, I could see Set dismembering Osiris's corpse and scattering the pieces up and down the River Nile. Further along, a painter had depicted Osiris's wife, Isis, who wore the same scarlet robes as Henuttawy. On the wall, she was shown searching far and wide, gathering her husband's body parts and piecing them together to resurrect him. Above the gates of the temple the last scene had been painted. The resurrected Osiris had given Isis a child. He was Horus, the falcon-headed god of the sky, and he was avenging his father by destroying Set. Once Set was banished, he joined the jackal-headed god Anubis in the Underworld. Those who had crossed to the land of the dead had to pass the judgment of Anubis before becoming *akhu*. Gazing up, I wondered how many of my own ancestors had passed this judgment, and whether I would see my mother again on that distant shore.

As we approached the open gates, the chants of the Amun priests grew louder. Woserit turned to me. "Stay close to me, even when I place the offering before my *akhu*. And when my priestesses begin their hymn to Hathor, remain by my side. There will be hundreds of people in the temple tonight. I want you where Ramesses can see you."

Merit shot me a warning look, and I promised to keep by Woserit.

"We are here to remind Ramesses what he's been missing," Woserit continued as we walked. "If you give too much away, it will be as though you've never been gone. And if anyone asks why you aren't dressed in Hathor's robes, tell them you're not sure you want to become a priestess—"

"*Especially* Ramesses," Aloli said. "Let him know you are uncertain of where you belong."

I thought Woserit would be angry at being interrupted, but she nodded. "Yes. He is intelligent enough to make the leap for himself."

I didn't like tricking Ramesses in this way, but wasn't there some truth in it, too? What else would my future hold once my inheritance was gone and I no longer had a place at court? And if he didn't want me, what was the point of marriage? Who else would ever share my desire for languages and hunting? I might as well become a priestess. My stomach clenched as we passed through the temple gates and into the dark sanctuary that Pharaoh Seti had built for himself and his ancestors. On every wall were scenes of his family story. There was Ramesses I, the general who had been chosen as Pharaoh when childless Horemheb realized he would die without issue. And there was Pharaoh Seti with his quiet, unassuming queen, who stayed in the gardens away from court politics. There were images of Ramesses II being born, with his fiery red hair painted into the scenes. My family had sat on the throne of Egypt for generation upon generation. Where was such a monument to them?

"Stop thinking," Merit whispered as we walked. "You'll become upset."

I steadied my lip as we entered the eastern sanctuary. The Amun priests had finished their chants and hundreds of courtiers filled the chamber. They turned to see Woserit's procession, and I had the sudden urge to hide deeper beneath the fur of my cloak. Incense filled the room, as did the dank cold scent of walls that had never been exposed to the sun. I followed Woserit to the head of the chamber where her priestesses began the hymn to Hathor. Woserit herself stepped away from the women, placing the bowl she had brought with her before a statue of Ramesses I. To our right, I could see the gleam of Pharaoh Seti's crown, and next to him, the blue and gold crown of Ramesses in profile. He was taller. And more handsome than I had remembered. The *nemes* crown framed a lean face with long cheekbones and a soldier's strong jaw. We were separated by an image of his grandfather, a towering granite statue cast in golden light. I could see Iset standing next to him, the glittering diadem of a princess on her brow, but there was no sign of Henuttawy. Merit noticed, too, and shook her head. "Late as usual."

"She does it to draw attention," I said. I had begun to understand the games women played. The voices of Hathor's songstresses echoed in the chamber, but their chants were now disturbed by the noise of a large group in the hall. When the new arrivals emerged into the chamber, we could see they were wearing the unmistakable red robes of Isis. But no one was dressed in a color so deep or striking as Henuttawy. Her long crimson cloak was held by a priestess, and her hair was swept up in magnificent curls behind the golden *seshed* circlet of a princess. She cut a path through the crowded chamber, leading her priestesses across the temple to the front. "For the *akhu* of the greatest family in Egypt," Henuttawy said loudly, withdrawing from her robes a gilded bowl. I wondered how many offerings from the Temple of Isis had gone to pay for such a lavish gift. She placed the bowl next to Woserit's, making her sister's look small and inferior. Then she bowed very low to her brother, and her own songstresses began their chant.

"You are late," Seti said, and Henuttawy leaned forward and whispered something in her brother's ear. For a moment he looked angry, then he laughed.

"Beautiful, charming Henuttawy," Woserit whispered in my ear. "Always ready with an excuse. And my brother, ready as always to forgive. That is something that Ramesses has learned from his father. You must watch for that."

The priests of Amun came forward again, and as their chants rose I couldn't take my eyes from Ramesses. But he was looking to the priests, whose deep song resounded in the hollow chamber. Woserit lifted her arm so that her bangles made a noise like small bells, and when Ramesses looked across at us, he froze. Then he peered forward in the darkness, and I let my hood slip back slowly from my face.

"*Nefer?*" he mouthed.

I smiled to let him know it was me. Then I saw that he was wearing the ox-hair necklace on top of his cloak, and my breath caught in my throat.

"You may meet him in the courtyard," Woserit whispered. "But you will only have a few minutes after the chanting is done."

I was never so impatient for my time in Pharaoh Seti's temple to be finished. Every hymn to Amun felt like an eternity. When they had finally finished, I glanced at Woserit and she smiled to indicate that this was the time. In the courtyard outside the mortuary temple, Ramesses and Asha moved through the crowd. "Nefer!" Ramesses shouted, and when he saw me beneath the statue of Amun, I restrained myself from rushing forward and embracing him.

From his side, Asha regarded me with wide, approving eyes. He took in my netted faience dress under which my breasts had been carefully hennaed. "Nefertari, you've become a real princess."

"And you've become a real soldier," I complimented, noting the heavy sword at his side.

Ramesses looked between us, and I'm sure that I saw his shoulders stiffen. "Where have you been?" he exclaimed. "Did Woserit tell you we've been to the temple *six* times?"

I refused to show that I was shocked by the news. Instead, I smiled. "Yes, but priestesses are forbidden from seeing anyone outside the temple during their apprenticeship," I reminded him.

"But we came inside twice," Asha interrupted, "pretending to worship just to look for you!"

I laughed, to hide my surprise. "And you think Woserit didn't know? She wanted to keep me away, in case I should change my mind about the temple!"

Ramesses met my gaze and stepped closer to me. "And now?" he asked quietly. I could smell the mint on his breath, and if I reached out slightly, I could have touched the ox-hair's necklace. "You aren't dressed in the robes of Hathor," he said. He looked down at my beaded dress, and a brilliant flush crept into his cheeks.

I glanced at Asha, who was looking between Ramesses and me with a curious expression. "Because I'm not certain I want to be a priestess," I said. Before they could question me, I continued with the speech that I had rehearsed. "I don't know where my place is at this court, or in the temple."

"Then you should come back!" Asha exclaimed.

Ramesses searched my face, to see if I truly meant what I was saying, and suddenly Iset was at his side. "There you are!" Iset laughed easily. "Henuttawy told me you had gone, but I knew you wouldn't leave without telling me."

"How far could he have gone?" Asha scowled. "It's the Feast of Wag."

Iset ignored him and put her arm around Ramesses's waist. I was surprised by her familiarity, and the confident way she met his gaze.

"Have you seen Nefertari?" Ramesses asked.

Iset looked at me. "Nefertari." She smiled and even managed to sound delighted. "I didn't recognize you in so much paint." She turned back to Ramesses. "There is an emissary who would like to speak with you," she said. "He wants to bring news back to Mitanni about your victory in Kadesh, but he only speaks Hurrian."

"Then perhaps Nefertari can converse with him," Ramesses said, looking at me. "She's probably better at Hurrian than I am. Could you speak with the emissary from Mitanni?"

I gave Ramesses my widest smile. "Why not?"

As the four of us crossed the courtyard, students from the edduba recognized me and called out my name. "You see how much you've been missed?" Asha asked, "I can't imagine why you'd want to be a priestess of Hathor."

"I think she'd make a wonderful priestess," Iset offered. She hooked Ramesses by the elbow and led him on.

Asha leaned over to me and whispered, "Of course she does. Without you here, there's no other woman Ramesses is interested in."

Asha and I trailed behind Ramesses and Iset, our voices lost in the cacophony of feasting. "So is she always with him?"

"Yes. It's unbearable. The only place she won't follow him is the Arena. She even tries to stop Ramesses from racing, or hunting in the marshes."

I inhaled sharply. "And does he listen?"

"With one ear. He promises her that he will always be careful and tries to quiet her whining with gifts."

"Why does he put up with it?" I exclaimed.

"Because half the men at court are in love with her. All of Thebes is singing her praises, and the people are hopelessly charmed."

We both looked at Iset. She was not as tall as Ramesses, but tall enough that everyone in the courtyard noticed when she passed by. Students may have waved and smiled at me, but it was Iset their eyes followed.

"And you?" I asked curiously as we walked together. "Is she charming to you?"

"I see her for what she is. A fool. And she's completely lost in the Audience Chamber."

"But Ramesses loves her, doesn't he?" I asked, and Asha studied me by the light of the torches. "Oh, no." He shook his head. "Not you as well! All of the priestesses fawn over Ramesses. Visiting princesses practically throw themselves at his feet, begging to be his wife!"

"Who said I wanted to be his wife?" I exclaimed.

"I saw the way he was looking at you! And you were looking back," he accused. "Nefer—"

"Nefertari," I corrected, and I could see that Asha was hurt.

"Nefer*tari*," he repeated indignantly. "I have always been like a brother to you. And so has Ramesses. To change that relationship now would be to risk great danger."

"I don't see why," I lied.

"Then think of Iset! Of Henuttawy! The High Priestess instructs Iset in everything she does. You would be making enemies of all of the women who want Ramesses for themselves. Why sleep in a bed of scorpions, when you could marry a nobleman and live in peace? Your mother was forced to become Pharaoh Horemheb's wife, and she hated it every day she drew breath."

"How do you know that?" I demanded angrily.

Asha gave me a look. "You know it as well as I do! So why follow in her path?"

But Asha was cut off when Ramesses recognized the emissary from Mitanni. Although the Hittite empire had crushed their kingdom, the Mitanni people still had their own leaders, and there always smoldered a hope of rebellion. I watched as Ramesses strode ahead. I tried to avoid Asha's interrogating gaze, since I already knew the answer to his question. *Why follow in her path?* Because unlike my mother, I was in love.

"You are Kikkuli of Mitanni?" Ramesses asked.

The fat man paused in his conversation with an emissary from Assyria. "Yes, Your Highness." He bowed his head, and the Assyrian emissary did the same.

"My wife tells me you have some interest in our victory over the Hittites," Ramesses said in Hurrian.

"Yes. Very, very interested," Kikkuli replied.

"Then perhaps the princess Nefertari can explain, since her Hurrian is much better than mine."

It was true. My Hurrian was better, but Ramesses seemed to follow all that was said. I introduced myself and Kikkuli bowed again.

"I am glad to make your acquaintance, Princess. I have been sent to the court of Egypt to learn how to speak your language."

I was surprised. "Aren't there any teachers of Egyptian in Mitanni?"

"Plenty! And all of them speak worse Egyptian than I do!"

Ramesses and I both laughed, while Asha and Iset stood quietly.

"But I believe you wanted to know about Pharaoh's victory in Kadesh," I said. I told him what I had learned while at the temple. When I was finished, Kikkuli looked humbled.

"Thank you, my lady. I had no idea that anyone in the court of Egypt spoke such fluent Hurrian."

"Many royals study your language," I flattered. "And we greatly admire the captive kingdom of Mitanni."

Kikkuli's eyes widened. "I shall be certain to report such warm feelings to my people."

"Yes, please do," Ramesses said. "For Egypt hopes to remain great friends with Mitanni, and we trust that your governor would send word if ever your invaders planned an attack against us."

Kikkuli bobbed his head like an ibis. "If the Hittites should dare to march south through Aleppo, or even Nuzi, you have our word that Egypt will know of it."

Ramesses smiled, but Kikkuli only had eyes for me. "Your princess is exceptional," he complimented.

Ramesses met my gaze. Although he didn't reply, his eyes said more than his words ever could, and I knew that I had made him proud.

"What? What did he say?" Asha asked.

Next to him, Iset had gone still and hard as stone. Her beauty might fascinate men, but it was difficult to charm them when she stood mute as an obelisk.

"He said he would bring back the news of how powerful Egypt's army has become to his people," I translated.

Next to Kikkuli, the emissary from Assyria cleared his throat. "And if the Hittites try to reclaim Kadesh?"

Ramesses shook his head. "I apologize, but your Akkadian is one language I cannot speak."

"He is asking what will happen if the Hittites try to reclaim Kadesh," I relayed, and turned to the emissary. "Then Egypt will march north with the might of twenty thousand men," I promised, "and take it back for a second time."

Ramesses stared at me. "Since when have you spoken Akkadian?"

"Since I've been at the Temple of Hathor."

Ramesses regarded me with deep admiration, and Iset announced, "Look, it's your aunt!"

I caught Woserit's gaze across the courtyard, and I knew what was about to happen. When she smiled at Ramesses, my heart raced. "Enjoying the Feast of Wag?" she asked him. "I'm sure you were surprised to see Nefertari."

"Yes," he said, and his eyes lingered on mine. Standing beside him,

I was aware of how fighting had sculpted him into a man. "Well, Nefertari," Woserit said. "I believe you still have to visit the mortuary
temple in Djamet tonight. Are you ready?"

"Perhaps we can go with you," Ramesses offered.

But Woserit shook her head. "Nefertari should pay her respects
alone."

Ramesses and Asha both looked at me, as if I could offer them
some reversal, but I understood Woserit perfectly. "Ramesses, Asha."
I smiled at each of them. "I very much enjoyed seeing you tonight.
Iset," I acknowledged.

"Will you bid us farewell at the procession?" Ramesses asked
quietly.

"What do you mean?" I looked to Asha. "Pharaoh's army just returned from Kadesh! You're not going to war *again*?"

"The Nubians are rebelling. Ramesses is going to teach them a
lesson."

Ramesses nodded, and his eyes were fixed on mine

"Then we shall see when the time comes whether Nefertari will be
there," Woserit said. "Until then, or perhaps until the next Feast of
Wag, wish Nefertari well on the path she has chosen."

This time, Iset's smile was real. I followed Woserit dutifully be-
yond the courtyard, where Merit was waiting with chariots for hire.
"Take the princess and her nurse to Horemheb's mortuary temple in
Djamet," Woserit said.

The young man helped me into the chariot, and as the horses
pulled away, I looked behind us. The court had left the mortuary
temple, and Ramesses was gone.

"Well, what did he say?" Merit asked.

"I . . . I don't know," I said breathlessly. "But he looked different.
Older."

"But what did he *say*?" she repeated.

"He asked me to speak with the emissary from Mitanni." I looked at Merit as we sped through the night and wondered aloud, "What if he only values me for my talent?"

"Would it matter, my lady, as long as he's interested? Your goal is to become Chief Wife."

"No." I shook my head in realization. "It's not. I want him to love me."

We had reached Djamet, and Horemheb's temple rose from a vast plateau of sand. Its wide black gates were thrown open, for pilgrims who wished to remember the Pharaoh who had eradicated the Heretic King's influence. Only members of Seti's court could visit the temple at any time, but on the first night of Wag the doors of every temple were opened to anyone. Merit brushed the dust from my cloak, then paid the boy who had driven us through the night. Her steps slowed as we approached the heavy gates. On every Feast of Wag, I entered the temple alone, while Merit left to pay obeisance at the small shrine her father had built nearby. "Shall I leave you here?" she asked quietly.

I nodded. "Yes."

"Of course, you will not talk with anyone," she warned. "And raise your hood." She handed me my bowl. "Can you see where you are going?"

"There are reed torches inside. I have good eyes."

I watched as Merit disappeared into the darkness, then I passed through the gates of Horemheb's temple. I tried not to think of how it had once been the exclusive shrine to my *akhu*. It had been built by my grandfather, Pharaoh Ay, but all that was left of him now were the paintings in his tomb, somewhere deep within the Valley of the Kings.

Ahead of me, I heard voices. They might have been descendants of Horemheb's, or commoners who had come to gape at the paintings. In the light of the torches, the old general's eyes watched my progress through the halls. In every image he had been painted tall and fit, wearing the *khepresh* crown that had once belonged to my grandfather. Ay had died an old man, with no heir to take his throne. Only my mother had been left, and General Horemheb took her by force as his wife. Had I been a son, he would have claimed me as his own. But my mother had died in childbirth with only a girl to survive her.

I reached the end of the hall and touched the only painting that remained of my mother. A great deal of care had been taken to portray her. She was tall and thin, with green eyes that shone like emeralds from her long, dark face. She was the opposite of me in every way, but for her eyes. *"Mawat,"* I whispered. Hers was the only painting that Horemheb had kept from Ay's temple. He had ordered the others chiseled away, and with each stroke of the mallet they had erased my family from Egypt's past.

"What a shame that this is all that's left of her now."

I felt my heart drop, for I knew the voice behind me. And before I could stop myself, I asked angrily, "What are you doing here?"

Henuttawy stepped out of the darkness into the light of the torches. She smiled. "Not happy to see me? I shouldn't think you have anything to worry about. You're not acting foolishly enough for me to slap you again. Although I should think that's just a matter of time."

I pushed back my hood, so she wouldn't think I was hiding. Her eyes grew wide in mock surprise. "So the little princess has grown up." She swept her gaze over my body and studied the way I filled out my tunic. "I'm guessing that's Woserit's cloak? You don't have enough sense to dress yourself properly for a drunken revel, let alone the Feast of Wag."

"Why have you come here?"

Henuttawy took a step forward to see if she could frighten me, but I didn't move.

"Like a cat standing its ground. Or maybe you're just too scared to move." She looked up at the painting of my mother. "A pair of green-eyed little kittens, and just as curious."

"I think you've come because you knew you'd find me in my family's temple."

Henuttawy narrowed her eyes, and her beauty looked cold and hard in the torchlight. "It's no wonder Woserit took you in. She's always taken pity on fools. It will come as a great surprise to know that the court doesn't revolve around what Princess Nefertari is doing. But it may interest you to know I've come for Iset." She opened her cloak and took out a small silver jar. "Of course, I'm not supposed to tell anyone, but since you've been such a good little friend to Ramesses, you might as well know." She leaned close and whispered, "His wife is carrying the heir to the throne."

I tried to hide my shock while Henuttawy placed Iset's silver jar on the shrine below my mother and Horemheb's image.

"Even Ramesses hasn't been told," she said with delight, "but when he finds out, there is no one at court who will doubt that he will make her queen. In light of such good fortune, it is only natural that Iset would want to thank her *akhu*. As a queen, she'll want everyone to remember that her grandmother was Horemheb's harem wife. So, you see, this *was* your family's temple." Henuttawy looked up and placed her hand on my mother's cheek. "But when Iset is crowned, I wouldn't be surprised if she changes a few of the paintings to remind the gods of her grandmother's importance at court."

She turned, and as she disappeared through the doors of the temple, I looked up to the painting of my mother and gasped. "Henuttawy!" I screamed, and two children who had come to gawk at the paintings inside the temple ran away in fear. I put my hand on my mother's cheek, where Henuttawy had scraped her fingernail along the side of her face. My mother's beauty was marred. I felt the kind of blinding hatred that whole kingdoms must have for invading armies. As my voice echoed through the corridors of the temple, Merit hurried in with a reed torch before her.

"My lady, what is it?" she cried.

I pointed to my mother's cheek. "Henuttawy," I said between clenched teeth. "She's ruined it!"

"We will tell Pharaoh Seti!" she vowed.

"And who will he believe? You saw her tonight. She wears him like a cloak!"

The tears coursed down my cheeks, and Merit placed her arm around my shoulder. "Don't worry, my lady. We will hire a painter to fix it."

"But this is all that I have of her," I sobbed. "And even if a painter comes, what does it matter when her entire image is going to be erased?"

"Says who?" Merit cried.

"That's why Henuttawy was here. She came to tell me that Iset is pregnant with Ramesses's child. And if Iset is made queen, she'll take this temple for her *akhu*."

Merit narrowed her eyes. "She's seen tonight that you are competition and wants to frighten you away. By telling you this, she imagines you'll have no incentive to return to the palace."

"Then she is wrong!" I swore. And suddenly, I could see the future clearly. I was going to be relegated to a temple in the Fayyum, just as Woserit had predicted. I would never be allowed at court, and if I were, Henuttawy and Iset would be there to make life miserable for me. Ramesses would make Iset Chief Wife, and when he shared a joke with her, Iset's laugh would ring hollow as a reed. But no matter. She would be his queen and mother to the crown prince, and he would tolerate her ignorance for her great beauty. If ever he thought of me, it would be only to wonder where I had gone and why I had chosen never to come back. And my closest friend would be lost to me forever. I looked at Merit beneath the moonlight and repeated, "Then Henuttawy is very, very wrong."

I had every incentive to return.

CHAPTER SEVEN

PRAY TO SEKHMET

IN THE TEMPLE of Hathor, Aloli pressed me for details on what happened that night. For several days, I avoided her questions, until finally I blurted, "She's already pregnant!"

Aloli stood up her harp, and frowned. "*Who's* pregnant?"

"Iset." I blinked away tears. "With Ramesses's first child."

Aloli's look was compassionate. "It might be a girl," she said helpfully. "Or she might not even carry it to term. What's most important is what he said. Had he missed you?"

I thought of the way Ramesses's cheeks had reddened when he looked at my beaded dress, and I nodded. "Yes. Woserit thinks that by the time he returns from battle, he'll have made his decision about who will be Chief Wife. If the army is victorious, she wants me to attend his procession."

Aloli clapped her hands. "That's excellent news!" She searched my face. "So why aren't you happy? You were his closest friend when you were children. And now you are a woman. A *beautiful* woman. What more could he want from a queen?"

"A child."

"So who's to say you won't give him one?"

"Aloli," I said miserably, "my mother died in childbirth with me."

She sat back and her jewels caught the light of the oil lamps. "And you think the gods won't watch over a princess of Egypt?"

"My mother was a queen, and they didn't watch over her! Besides, what if I don't want a child?"

Aloli sucked in her breath. "Every woman wants one."

"Even you?"

She waved her hand, as if swatting at one of her loose curls. "Who cares about me? I'll never become queen."

"But would you risk childbirth?" I persisted.

"I suppose that if I ever find a man who can afford to keep me in necklaces and jewels," she said lightly, "then yes. I will want to have children with him." She saw my look and swore earnestly, "I'm not lying! When I dream at night, I never see just a man. It's always a family." She frowned. "Why? What do you dream about?"

I flushed.

"You dream about Pharaoh!" she exclaimed.

"But there are never any children! It's always just the two of us."

"Alone? In bed together?"

I knew my cheeks were red, but I nodded.

"And are you practicing what we've been talking about?" she asked swiftly.

"*Aloli!*"

"This is important!" she cried.

"Yes. Since Ramesses left with the army, I can't stop thinking about him. In the baths, at the shrine, even here in the eastern sanctuary."

"Then if you are dreaming of him every night," she said eagerly, "he must be dreaming of you!"

I stared at her. "How can you possibly know that?" I demanded.

"Because you've caught his eye." She smiled widely. "Trust me, Princess. And when he returns, he'll be looking to make those dreams come to life."

I wondered if Ramesses's dreams were like mine, and whether he could smell the scent of my hair the way I could smell the scent of his skin when I closed my eyes. Did he imagine us lying alone together, with only the warm summer's air between us? Or tumbling on his bed between the soft linen sheets perfumed with lavender? I thought of everything Aloli had taught me, about where to kiss tenderly and places where my kisses could bring him to tears, and soon my dreams became more vivid. In the night, I lay in his imaginary arms, and in the day I worried about what was happening in the south, and whether he would ever come back to Thebes.

ONE MORNING in the beginning of Aythyr, Paser asked, "Have you been practicing your Akkadian at all?"

"How can I practice," I asked him, "when Ramesses might be killed in this Nubian rebellion?"

Paser took a long look at me from across Woserit's table. "If you are worried about Ramesses in Nubia," he said, "then you will be spending the rest of your life without sleep. To be a Pharaoh is to fight against the enemies who would like to make your kingdom theirs. And when a Pharaoh isn't fighting invaders, he is settling rebellions. Even the Heretic King held on to the territory of Nubia, with its gold mines and electrum. I wouldn't expect Pharaoh Ramesses to return until the uprising is crushed completely. There is nothing for you to do—"

"But there is," I interrupted. "I can go with him."

Paser looked at me as if an ibis had suddenly perched on my head. "And what do you think you would do?" he demanded. "Pharaoh

Ramesses has trained for war since he was a child. There would be bloodshed, and death, and men crying in the night—"

"Women go to tend the sick," I argued.

"Have you ever seen a man's arm taken off by an enemy's blade?"

I forced myself not to blanch. "No."

"How about the sight of a soldier's intestines gouged by an arrow?"

"No. But I have seen the chariot races in the Arena, where soldiers have been crushed by wheels and by horses."

"Battle is not a game, and it is certainly not a sport!" Paser sighed with a great deal of exasperation. "What do you think would happen to you if Pharaoh was killed in battle? You would be taken by the enemy and abused," he answered himself. "And the rest of Egypt would be thrown into chaos. Who would become coregent? Who would succeed Pharaoh Seti on the throne? There would be civil war, and every wise person with gold would flee."

"But you said there was no danger in Nubia. You said he would return—"

"Perhaps not in Nubia, but what about Hatti, or Assyria, or Kadesh? War is no place for a princess. If you want to help Pharaoh, then pray to Sekhmet that he will be safe, and that the goddess of war will bring him home. Now study your Akkadian."

But I couldn't concentrate. I couldn't sleep. I couldn't even eat. Merit ordered tempting bowls from the kitchens, roasted goose in garlic and honeyed nut cakes, but my appetite was gone. "You cannot continue like this!" she exclaimed. "You will shrink away to nothing. Already, look at you." She held up my arm. "You will disappear!"

Finally, when the army had been gone for almost three months, Woserit came in to my chamber and said, "Merit tells me you are not eating. Do you want to look like a mangy cat next to Iset when Ramesses returns from Nubia?"

I stared at her in horror from the edge of my bed. "Of course not!"

"Then I will send to the cooks for several bowls," she said sternly. "And you will eat from all of them." She turned to leave, then hesitated at the door. "Messengers arrived this morning. Pharaoh's army has crushed the rebellion."

CHAPTER EIGHT

FIRST VICTORY

WHEN A PHARAOH comes home victorious from battle it means the gods are not only watching us, but have extended their hands to our kingdom in aid. Throughout the city of Thebes, crowds celebrated in the streets, eating the honeyed cakes being sold by vendors and washing them down with pomegranate wine. The men wore long kilts to protect them from the cold, and I was shielded against the wind by the soft fur of Woserit's cloak. I stood with the court on the Avenue of Sphinxes by the Amun temple, and Woserit whispered nervously, "Remember what I taught you."

"That Ramesses must come to me first," I repeated.

"You must not run to him like a fish-starved cat. But if he wants a private audience with you, then you may give him one."

I looked up in surprise, since Woserit had never said this before.

"Men are like *iwiw*," she explained, making me think of Queen Tuya's pampered dog. "Give them a good meal and they'll come around wanting it again. But you will make sure he understands that meals don't come free," she said sternly, and I wondered why she sounded more nervous than I was. "Make him understand that you will return to the temple if he doesn't decide." Woserit's gaze flicked across my golden diadem and the lined cloak that was opened to reveal my diaphanous sheath. "I'd be very surprised . . ."

But her words were cut off by the sound of trumpets and the cheers of the crowd heralding the approaching army.

Above us, on the temple's steps, Pharaoh Seti and Queen Tuya waited proudly for their son's return, surrounded by the most important men at court. But of everyone who stood above us, dressed in gold bangles and heavy wigs, Iset appeared the most triumphant. Her five-month belly curved beautifully beneath her cloak, and across her chest a servant had powdered the skin with crushed mother-of-pearl.

By stepping forward and craning my neck with the crowd, I could see the war chariots with their polished wheels and gilded sides. The scent of horses intermingled with incense and roses. As the army approached, the cheers of the crowds reached a feverish pitch, and I felt a pair of hands push me forward. I looked back and saw Aloli's brazen smile from among the priestesses of Hathor.

"You want him to notice, don't you?" she demanded.

Merit tugged at my shoulder. "She also wants to avoid being crushed by the chariots."

At the end of the Avenue I recognized Ramesses's *khepresh* crown of war. He was sharing a chariot with Asha, and both of them absorbed the adoration of the people. As Asha reined in a pair of sleek black horses, Ramesses searched the crowd, and when he found me, I felt a strange heat under my cloak despite the chill in the wind. Then Pharaoh Seti spread his arms in a gesture of welcome, and Ramesses tore his gaze away from my face. He dismounted at the steps of the temple to bow before his parents, then he slowly withdrew his sword from its sheath. Around us, the cheering grew even more frenzied as Ramesses prepared to give his sword of victory to Iset. To be presented with this is the greatest honor any person can receive. I arranged a smile on my face; then I noticed that Asha was staring in our direction.

"Who is *that?*" Aloli whispered.

"*Asha?* He's the commander of Ramesses's charioteers."

"So why is he staring at us?"

"Probably because he's never seen anyone like you before." Aloli was the only priestess of Hathor whose hair outshone Ramesses's. She wore a heavy turquoise cloak that brought out the vivid blue of her eyes, and the sheath beneath it was spun from a linen so fine it was nearly transparent. When Iset accepted the sword and the ceremony was finished, Aloli stepped forward to make sure that Asha didn't miss her.

"Don't bother," I said as the army made its way to the palace. "Pharaoh Seti calls him Asha the Cautious."

"Then perhaps what he needs is a woman with spirit."

I laughed, but Aloli's voice was earnest. "This will be my first celebration in the palace, and I don't plan to sleep at all," she admitted.

Because it was Choiak, it was growing too cool to feast in the courtyard of Malkata. The victory celebration would be held in the warmth of the Great Hall, where cinnamon would burn all night on the braziers and the doors would be shut against the wind. That afternoon, when I entered the chamber, it wasn't the number of soldiers that surprised me, or that Ramesses's horses had been brought into the hall and decorated with flowers. It was the long, polished table on the dais, with four thrones in the middle and two dozen chairs around them.

Woserit saw the direction of my gaze, and nodded. "You haven't been inside the Great Hall since Ramesses changed court tradition. The most important members of the court no longer eat below the dais."

"They eat on top? In front of everyone? Why?"

"You can't guess?" she asked. "Iset's conversation isn't as interesting as he had hoped. What could he possibly have to talk about with her and his parents, night after night?"

Now he had his viziers and emissaries from foreign kingdoms on the dais. So while the rest of the court ate below, Pharaoh's closest advisers and friends would be eating on the highest step. Ramesses had not yet taken his throne. I imagined that he was probably in his chamber, changing from his armor to a long kilt and thick cloak. He would probably put on his blue and gold *nemes* crown, since the *khepresh* was tall and burdensome. And then what would he do? My heart raced. Would he speak with me at the table? Or would he have eyes only for his pregnant wife?

"I've never seen anything like this," Aloli murmured. I had forgotten that it was her first time in the Great Hall. Harpists played in all corners of the room, and the rich scents of roasted beef and wine filled the warm chamber. Every woman had come attired in her best jewels, and at night, their thick collars of gold would reflect in the light of the oil lamps. In the polished glaze of the tiles I could already see a thousand sandaled feet reflected, walking and dancing and secretly touching under the tables.

As we moved through the crowded hall toward the dais, someone approached from behind a column and touched my shoulder. I turned, and there was Ramesses, dressed in a long linen kilt, trimmed with gold thread and painted with images of charioteers at war. His belt was wide, and beneath the gold pectoral on his chest was a fresh scar where he'd been hurt in battle. I opened my mouth to exclaim about the wound, but Ramesses put a finger to his lips. I glanced at Woserit, who took Aloli's arm and escorted her toward the dais. Ramesses never stopped looking at me.

"It's true," he whispered.

Suddenly, I was aware of how close we were standing, so close I could touch the square of his jaw or the chiseled planes of his face. "What's true?"

"You are as beautiful as I remembered. Nefer," he said, and his breath came quickly. "Perhaps you want to simply remain my friend, but when I was gone, all I could think about was you. When I was supposed to be thinking about the rebellion, or how my men would find fresh water in the desert, all I could think of was how you wanted to be hidden away in the Temple of Hathor. Nefer," he said passionately, "you *can't* be a priestess."

I wanted to close my eyes and step into the shelter of his embrace, but beyond the column the entire court was gathering. "But if I'm not to be a priestess," I asked him, "where will my place be in Thebes?" I held my breath, waiting for the right answer to come, willing it into his heart. Then he took me in his arms and brushed his lips against mine.

"With me," he said firmly. "As my queen."

🜍 🜍 🜍

LEAVING BEHIND the entire court, now feasting in the Great Hall, we headed directly to his chamber, and Ramesses immediately barred the door. His room was neatly kept, and the blue and green tiles of the floor had been polished for his arrival. Cuneiform tablets were stacked on a low table, and a Senet board that could not have been used in many months was ready to be played. He took my hand and led me to the bed, stopping only to whisper, "And you are sure you want me the way I want you?"

I didn't respond. I simply brushed my lips against his, then kissed him the way I had imagined kissing him all of those nights when he had been gone in Nubia. We fell together on his pillows, and the victory feast might as well have been in another kingdom.

"Nefer." Ramesses pressed his hands against the bed so that his muscular arms were on either side of my face. I reached up and stroked him the way Aloli had told me I should. He closed his eyes, allowing me to trace my finger along his shaft.

"Let me taste you," I whispered.

He rolled so that his back was against the pillows, and I began with the inside of his thighs, licking my way up to his chest and the tender flesh around his new scar. He cupped my breasts in his hands, feeling the nipples harden beneath my sheath, and he groaned as I licked my way back down to the hardness between his legs.

"Undress for me," he begged.

I knelt above him, slowly unfastening the cloak, then my sheath, and finally taking off my wig so that my nakedness was covered only by my hair.

"You are even more beautiful than I thought." Ramesses sighed. I'm sure that I flushed at being called so. Henuttawy was beautiful. Iset was beautiful. But as I straddled him in the position that Aloli promised would increase fertility, I wondered for the first time if it might be true. His breath was ragged, and as I balanced above him, he thrust his hips forward in his eagerness to be inside of me.

I had dreamed of what it would be like with Ramesses a hundred different times. Yet when the moment came, everything that Aloli had taught me flew out of my head and I knew nothing but the feel of his body against mine, the taste of his skin, and the burning sensation that began as pain and soon became pleasure. When it was done, and Ramesses had spent himself inside of me, I looked down at the linens. I was no longer a virgin.

In the amber light of a setting sun, Ramesses caressed my cheek. Our reverie was only broken when a heavy fist pounded on the door outside of his chamber. He looked at me, and then both of us were rushing to find our clothes.

"Your Majesty," someone called from without. "The feast has begun and Pharaoh wishes to know where you are!"

"How long has he been knocking?" I exclaimed.

"Probably for a while!" Ramesses laughed, then took me in his arms. "You must move back into your chamber," he said. "No more of the temple."

"I shall have to ask Woserit," I said coyly.

"Forget Woserit! If I make you my wife, she can't take you back. I *need* you here." He cupped my breast in his palm. "I *want* you here."

"And they want you in the Great Hall," I said teasingly.

꼬 꼬 꼬

EVERY NIGHT since he had been married, Ramesses had entered the Great Hall with Iset. But that night, on the celebration of his first victory as leader of Pharaoh's army, he would enter with me and everyone would know where he had been. From the table on the dais, Henuttawy would see us, and Iset would turn to her ladies from the harem and unleash a storm.

Be brave, I told myself. *Iset is the granddaughter of a harem wife but I am the daughter of a queen.* We left the royal courtyard as the chill of evening had settled over the palace. I sheltered beneath Ramesses's strong arm, and as we passed through the halls the whispering began. I heard my name behind me and I shivered.

"You'll grow used to it," Ramesses promised.

"The whispering or the cold?"

He laughed, but as we approached the Great Hall and the herald who would announce our presence, my stomach clenched. I could already hear the murmur of surprise from within.

"Pharaoh Ramesses II," the herald declared, "Lord of the Two Lands and son of Pharaoh Seti."

Ramesses stepped forward and waited for me.

"Princesses Nefertari, daughter of Queen Mutnodjmet and General Nakhtmin."

Ramesses took my arm, and as we moved through the hall a horrified murmur passed through the court, that on this night—of *all* nights—Ramesses should appear with me instead of his wife, who would bear his child. I caught my name several times before we reached the royal thrones, and at the table on the dais, a servant hastily added a chair between Pharaoh Seti and Ramesses. Iset's eyes narrowed into tiny slits, and next to her, Queen Tuya's face became hard as stone. Her *iwiw*, Adjo, sniffed at the air, and though there was no one else in Thebes he seemed to dislike he raised his lips in a silent growl as I passed.

I took my seat in the uncomfortable silence, and it was Queen Tuya who finally spoke. "How nice of you to escort the princess Nefertari into the Great Hall. I would have thought you might have chosen to escort your wife."

Woserit caught my gaze across the table, and I knew that she was willing her strength into me. I kept a smile on my face and replied, "I'm afraid it is my fault, Your Highness."

"What does it matter?" Seti demanded. "My son is returned from war, and the Nubians are crushed!" He raised his cup, and the rest of the table did the same. "So Nefertari," Pharaoh Seti exclaimed with mock surprise. "Not so little anymore."

I lowered my head bashfully. "No, Your Highness."

"Well, we have missed your smile in Malkata. My son, especially, I believe." He glanced at Iset, who was sulking next to the queen. The pair of them looked like Tuya's long-faced *iwiw*.

"It's true," Ramesses replied, meeting my gaze. I knew there was more he wanted to say.

"So tell me, Nefertari." Henuttawy lowered her cup. "What was it that you and my nephew discussed? He must have told some very exciting tales to have taken all afternoon. Why don't you share one with the table?"

I'm sure my face turned as red as the cinnamon burning in the braziers, and Ramesses said firmly, "We spent our time discussing how Nefertari will be returning to the palace."

Henuttawy exchanged a look with the High Priest, Rahotep. *"Really?* Was her time at my sister's temple so unbearable?"

"Of course not." Ramesses's voice became stern. "But she is of greater use here than in the Temple of Hathor."

I looked across the table at Woserit. Was it true? Did he want me simply because he thought I was useful to him? But Woserit avoided my gaze.

"So you have decided not to become a priestess?" Pharaoh Seti confirmed.

I nodded. "My wish is to return to the palace of Malkata as soon as possible."

Pharaoh Seti sat back. "Then perhaps you will be here for my announcement in the Audience Chamber tomorrow. In a few days, my court will be leaving for Avaris."

I glanced at the queen, whose face was still drawn. *"Permanently?"*

Pharaoh Seti nodded and began to cough. "I shall make Avaris the capital of Lower Egypt," he said, "and be closer to our northern border. I want to keep an eye on the kingdom of Hatti."

In that moment I realized how difficult it must have been for him to watch his son lead the army into Nubia. *He still wants to protect Egypt and watch over her enemies, even if he can't join his son on the battlefield.* When he continued to wheeze, Ramesses scowled.

"It will also be better for his health to be away from the heat and disease of a large city like Thebes. That is the most important reason."

But Pharaoh Seti waved Ramesses's concern away. "I will be taking a few of the viziers with me. And half of the army. We want to sail before the weather turns." His kind eyes rested on me. "I hope you will be able to bid us farewell when we leave."

Ramesses placed his open palm on my knee, and I smiled. "Of course, Your Highness."

ON THE boat ride back to the temple, I told Woserit what Ramesses had said before we left his chamber. "We will pack tonight to be ready for the Audience Chamber in the morning," she said, sounding pleased. "Shall I assume that you—"

"Of course they did!" Aloli cried over the splashing of the oars. "Look at her face. You did, didn't you?"

I nodded, and Merit stifled a gasp. "This *afternoon*, my lady?"

"There is no point in leaving love up to the gods," Woserit said. "He wants her now, and we had to put her in front of him so that he knows what he'll be fighting for."

I tried to make out Woserit's expression in the dark, but there was only a single oil lamp in our boat. *"Fight?"*

"It will certainly be a fight. And not just between my brother and Queen Tuya. While we were on the dais, Aloli was sitting among the court. She heard their whispers."

"About me? What did they say?"

Aloli nodded. "Things I shouldn't repeat, my lady."

"And you saw Henuttawy's reaction tonight," Woserit went on. "The High Priest's response will be even worse if Ramesses asks to marry you. Especially if the gossip is true and Rahotep has been visiting my sister's chamber. But my brother loves Ramesses and rarely denies him. I doubt he will now."

"But Henuttawy can be persuasive," I said.

"Not as persuasive as a man in love."

"But what if he's not in love with me? You heard what Ramesses said at the feast — that I'm more useful in the palace than in the temple."

Woserit gave me a long look from beneath her cloak. "He will say what he must to convince his father. Pharaoh Seti may see you as a daughter, but thinking that you are a good choice for a wife is something different."

I turned my face to the river, so that no one would see my hurt.

Aloli added gently, "You'll know if he loves you by how long he's willing to fight."

"And if he gives up the fight, he'll have decided I'm not worth it," I said as the boat approached the quay.

"So make sure you are," Woserit remarked.

We passed through the gates of Hathor's temple, and Woserit sent an army of servants to help pack my belongings. In my chamber, Merit ordered hot water for my bath.

"At this hour?" one of the servants questioned.

"Of course, at this hour. Do you think I want it for the morning?" Merit chided.

When the hot water came, I lay back in the tub and tried to remember everything that had happened in Ramesses's chamber. I wanted to go over it again and again so there was no detail I would ever forget. As Merit scrubbed at my back, I told her what had happened from beginning to end, and when I was finished, she let out a huge sigh and wept, "Oh, my lady, you are a woman now! And soon . . ." She sniffed. "Soon, you will belong to Ramesses."

"Oh, *mawat*, don't cry. I will never leave you. Not for a hundred Pharaohs."

Merit blinked and raised her chin. "I'm crying tears of joy, not sorrow," she promised. "It is what I always imagined. Queen Nefertari. Mother to the future King of Egypt."

I lay in the warm water and sighed. "And we wouldn't be afraid of anyone," I said. "Not the High Priest or Henuttawy. Even Iset couldn't touch us if I were queen." I stood from the water and Merit handed me a heavy linen. I wrapped myself in its length and shivered. "But what if I can't have children?" I worried.

"Who would say such a thing?" Merit hissed. "Why wouldn't you be able to have children?" she demanded.

"I am small."

"Many women are small."

"Not as small as I am, and my mother died giving birth to me," I whispered.

"You will have plenty of children," Merit blustered. "As many as you wish."

I put on a sheath. Outside the robing room I could hear the servants moving baskets and placing my belongings into the many chests I had returned with from Malkata. I passed through the bustle and stood on the balcony overlooking the groves. The sycamores were bent like old women in the moonlight, thin and twisted, and I wondered when I would see them again. I shivered in my linen, and when Merit saw me she gave a sharp cry.

"My lady! What are you doing outside?"

"This will be the last night I look out over this," I said.

She marched onto the balcony and took my arm. "And it will be your last night in Egypt if you catch sick and die. Get yourself into bed. You must sleep for tomorrow!"

But I looked behind me to catch a last glimpse of Hathor's groves. *These will be my last moments of peace,* I thought. *From now on, my love for Ramesses will bring nothing but chaos.*

"My lady is sleeping now," Merit announced to the servants in the chamber. "We will finish in the morning." When the servants disappeared, she shut the heavy doors and came to my bedside. "You are a woman," she marveled again, looking down at me.

Tefer curled against my pillow, and I laughed. "I have been a woman for two years."

"But a woman is not really a woman until . . . Perhaps in a few months we will be preparing the birthing chamber for you," she said proudly.

When Merit left, I lay in my bed and looked up at the painted ceiling. I had probably seen that painting a hundred times, but do you think that I can recall it now? This is how memories are; what seems so clear and unforgettable at one moment vanishes like steam the next. I didn't want this to happen to the afternoon that Ramesses and I had shared together, so I imagined it again and again in my mind, committing to memory the look in his eyes, the smell of his skin, the feel of his strong legs between mine. I felt a deep longing to be with him, and I wondered whether he was thinking of me in the palace, too.

I slept fitfully that night, worried that in the morning I would awake and find it all to have been a dream. But when the milky sun filtered through the reed mats, I opened my eyes and saw that the servants were already packing. Merit smiled at me over a handful of linens.

"I wondered if you were planning to get up at all, my lady."

I scrambled from my bed. "Are we leaving?"

"As soon as you've dressed and braided your hair. Then I expect that Woserit will want to speak with you."

I had become skilled at dressing quickly in the cold, and by the time Merit had finished with my hair, Woserit came in to survey the chamber. The servants had removed my bottles and heavy chests. Even my sheaths, and robes, and beaded gowns had been folded into baskets and whisked away. The chamber looked large and empty, and the glazed tile walls and high ceilings echoed with our voices.

"They have done well," Woserit said approvingly. "Are you prepared to leave?"

I felt a rising panic in my chest. The temple was not my home, but it was where I had become a woman and learned to be a princess. "I would like to say farewell to Aloli first," I said. "And some of the other priestesses."

"There will be time for that." Woserit took a seat and motioned for me to do the same. I sat, and Woserit made a face. "I shall hope you don't take your throne that way! Like some weary petitioner who's stood outside the court all day and is willing to throw herself on the first available surface for relief."

I tried again, standing and then slowly seating myself. I pressed my knees together and straightened my back. I folded my hands over my lap and looked at her.

"Much better. The way you take your chair this morning will say as much about you as the words that come out of your mouth." She motioned with her hand. "Let's get Tefer into a basket and make your farewells. This will be a busy day. If Ramesses does plan to make you his wife, he will have to fight for you in the Audience Chamber. Do you recall what Paser told you about being inside?"

"That it's like the Great Hall, but instead there's only one table with petitioners."

"And on the dais, there will be four thrones."

"For Ramesses, Pharaoh Seti, Queen Tuya, and Iset."

"And if Ramesses makes you his queen, you will take Iset's place. She will not be welcome in the Great Hall after that."

I pressed my lips together and acknowledged the gravity of displacing Iset.

"Of course, Ramesses must never know that you want to be Chief Wife. Let him come to that decision on his own. But even if he makes you queen, he will divide his time between you and Iset." Woserit saw my expression and added, "If you love Ramesses, you will not make it difficult for him. Heirs for the throne of Egypt are more important than any wife's petty jealousy."

I felt stung, but nodded in agreement. "I will be pleasant at all times," I promised her.

"And cheerful," she added, "and welcoming."

Eventually, we made our way out of the temple and reached the quay, where all of my belongings were being carried in cedar chests onto Hathor's ship. While Merit supervised the move, I bade my farewells to the priestesses of Hathor. Aloli was particularly sad to see me go.

"Who will I share my secrets with now?" she complained.

"You'll find some innocent priestess to lead astray," I teased. "But truly," I said, and my words were in earnest, "thank you. For every-thing." I gave her a farewell embrace, and Merit brought a mewling Tefer onto the boat as the last of our belongings. I stood on the stern of Hathor's ship, surrounded by baskets and heavy chests, and waved to the priestesses on the shore.

CHAPTER NINE

✦

SIMPLY A MARRIAGE

WHEN WE ARRIVED in Malkata, the quay was filled with the towering prows of Pharaoh Seti's ships. Their blue and gold pennants snapped in the wind, while below them an army of servants was packing the royal belongings for a journey north. There was the royal statuary wrapped carefully in linen, and chests so large that four men shouldered poles simply to carry them. Chamberlains, scribes, fan bearers, sandal bearers, even emissaries were rushing to pack for Avaris, where Seti would rule Lower Egypt while Ramesses governed the upper kingdom from Thebes.

"I thought Pharaoh was going to announce his move today?" I asked.

"Officially, yes," Woserit replied.

"But the court already knows?"

"Certainly. But the rest of Egypt must be told. My brother will make his announcement in the Audience Chamber, and his scribes will post the news at the door of every temple."

Woserit instructed the boatsmen to carry my chests into the royal courtyard, and Merit passed the basket with Tefer to a young girl who promised to take him to the chamber that Woserit had given me. As we walked through the towering gates of Malkata, Merit whispered, "Stop fidgeting." I was twisting the linen edges of my belt. "There's nothing you can do now," she added. "It's in the hands of the gods."

In the palace, there was a tense energy, as if the court knew what Ramesses was about to request, and how the viziers and High Priestess of Isis would respond. Courtiers darted furtive glances at me, and a young serving girl lowered her heavy linen basket to watch us pass. In the golden hall before the Audience Chamber, Woserit said firmly, "Stay here with Merit until the herald calls for you."

We seated ourselves on an ebony bench whose legs had been carved into the heads of swans. "Are there petitioners inside?"

"No. They have been dismissed. Today is for my brother's private business."

"And Iset?" I asked quickly.

Woserit sniffed. "Without the petitioners, there's no reason for her to be here. She's probably hennaing her toenails in the baths." She pulled open one of the heavy bronze doors, and as she entered, she left it wide open behind her. I glanced at Merit.

"This is why we arrived late," she whispered.

So that Woserit could be the last in the chamber and leave the door open for us to listen. I looked up at the guards, but both of their faces were expressionless, and I wondered if they had been paid to cooperate. I leaned forward on the bench and looked in. The Audience Chamber was as wide and impressive as both Paser and Woserit had described it. A forest of columns held up the painted ceiling, and from the high windows you could see the crests of the western hills. Ramesses was seated between his parents. Below him, at a table for viziers and dignitaries, I recognized Henuttawy by the red of her cloak. Her back was to us, and only those who were sitting on the dais could look down the long aisle of the Audience Chamber and see that the door had been left open. But today no one would be interested in what was happening outside.

At first, there were too many voices from within to make out anything clearly. Then I heard Pharaoh's golden crook strike the dais, and suddenly there was silence. The announcement was made that he and Queen Tuya would leave for Avaris in two days on the thirteenth of Choiak.

We listened as Pharaoh Seti told his court sculptor what sort of image should be carved on the Wall of Proclamation outside of Karnak to let visitors know his court had moved to Avaris. He wanted a painting of a fleet of ships, with him and the queen standing on a prow in their golden crowns. In the next scene, he imagined himself standing on the quay in Avaris. There was a moment of silence as the sculptor took notes, then I heard Paser's voice addressing Pharaoh Seti, "There is something His Highness Ramesses would like to request."

Courtiers shifted uncomfortably, and their gold bangles clinked loudly in the uneasy silence. The court knew what Ramesses was going to ask, and Henuttawy had made certain to be in the Audience Chamber for the announcement. Next to her I could see the leopard cloak of the High Priest. Although I couldn't see his face, I could imagine Rahotep's carnelian eye moving as he followed the proceedings, and how his lips were stretched into his grotesque hyena's grin.

Ramesses stood from his throne. "Father," he said formally, "in two days you will make the journey from the palace of Malkata to your father's palace of Pi-Ramesses. But before you leave, I would like your permission to marry the princess Nefertari."

Whispered murmurs rippled through the court, and I imagined Henuttawy's beautiful face frozen like a funerary mask. I supposed that Ramesses glanced at her when he said, "I have made Iset a princess and wife to me. Although I love her, I love Nefertari as well." He argued, "Princess Nefertari is well studied. She can speak eight languages and will be a valuable asset in this chamber. She is—"

"The niece of a Heretic King?" Henuttawy offered.

Ramesses replied with heat, "That was many years ago."

"Not so many that the people don't remember." The Vizier Nebamun stepped forward and blocked my view of Henuttawy. "Your Highnesses, love alone does not make a good wife."

"Which is why we are fortunate that Nefertari is also wise enough to serve in this chamber," Ramesses said.

Courtiers began talking over one another, and Pharaoh Seti raised his crook and struck it twice on the base of the dais. "Nebamun and Henuttawy, we have heard what you both have to say. Vizier Anemro?"

Vizier Anemro stood from a table at the base of the dais, and I could hear him address Pharaoh Seti politely before saying, "I agree with the High Priestess of Isis. Looking to the future, to make the princess Nefertari Chief Wife would be dangerous to His Highness's reign."

Beneath the dais, Rahotep remained silent. Ramesses asked sternly, "Vizier Paser?"

Paser stood, and his was the first voice raised in my defense. "I do not see any harm or danger in making Princess Nefertari queen."

"Nor I," Woserit said firmly.

The High Priest of Amun finally spoke. "Even though her family murdered my father and abolished Egypt's gods?" he spat. "Has that already been forgotten? The blood of heretics runs through her veins!"

Pharaoh Seti struck his crook on the dais and declared, "Princess

Nefertari is a daughter to me. I do not care what blood runs in her veins."

"But the people will," Henuttawy snapped. She understood that Seti was going to allow Ramesses to wed and added quickly, "At least wait until after the marriage to choose a Chief Wife." I could see her face now. She turned to Ramesses. "Wait to see how the people will react. For the sake of peace throughout your long reign, wait until the ceremony is finished."

"I fear a rebellion," Rahotep warned.

"Wait," Henuttawy suggested. "Then, if you still want to make her queen over Iset—"

"I wouldn't call it *over* Iset," Ramesses said quickly.

"*Instead* of Iset," Henuttawy corrected, coarsely. "Then there will be two feasts to celebrate."

Pharaoh Seti sighed. "The decision of Chief Wife will wait. But what does Nefertari have to say about this? I hope you haven't pressured her into marriage."

"Bring her in," Ramesses answered. "She can tell you herself."

I looked at Merit, who rushed to straighten my wig. When the herald discovered the open door, he glanced at the guards, then at us. We both stood quickly.

"You are wanted in the Audience Chamber," he said.

We followed him through the great doors of carved bronze, and I was shocked by how large the room really was once I was inside of it. Not even Paser's careful model had captured the true grandeur of the hall. *This is where my mother sat with Nefertiti when she was my age*, I realized, *and where she ruled alongside Pharaoh Horemheb*. I studied the long expanse of polished tiles and the vaulted roof of gold. The limestone columns depicted scenes of previous kings in their triumphs. Ebony chairs with ivory inlay were clustered around Senet boards throughout the chamber. I imagined that courtiers usually filled those seats, laughing together and ready to entertain Pharaoh whenever he grew bored.

Henuttawy and Woserit watched our entrance, and as we reached the thrones, the heated whispers between the viziers increased. Courtiers gathered like thick clusters of grapes around the dais while we held out our arms in obeisance and bowed. When I arose, Ramesses met my gaze.

"Princess Nefertari." Pharaoh Seti smiled. "You have returned to Malkata to be married to Ramesses. But tell me." He leaned forward. "Is this what you wish?"

I closed my eyes briefly and nodded. "More than anything," I whispered.

"And you are certain of this? My son can be very persuasive. If you're afraid to hurt his feelings, he'll recover."

"There is nothing for him to recover from except my excessive love," I said.

"Very pretty." Henuttawy clapped. "If the Passion Plays of Osiris are missing an actress we will know who to send them."

"It's not an act," I said simply, and something in my voice prompted Pharaoh Seti to sit back. He regarded me for a moment, and I hoped he could see the earnestness in my stare.

"Let them be wed," Seti pronounced with a wave, and I exhaled.

Ramesses stepped down from the dais and took my hand firmly. It was real. We were going to be married.

"Think of what the people will say," Henuttawy shrieked. "Brother, think of what you are doing!"

"There will not be a coronation. Yet," he conceded. "Simply a marriage."

From behind the table, Woserit asked lightly, "What is it that you have against this princess, Henuttawy?"

Henuttawy replied with terrifying sweetness. "I suppose it's that she's so ambitious and clever," she said. "Clever Nefertari, who began life as a worm and emerged as a butterfly."

"Enough!" Pharaoh Seti warned. He looked to the High Priest. "I wish to see them joined in marriage before my court leaves for Avaris. Arrange a royal wedding."

The hyena stepped forward, and his bald head reflected the late afternoon light. "Within two days?" he questioned. "Perhaps it would be better if His Highness waited until the auspicious month of Pharmuthi."

When Iset will give birth, I thought.

"We will marry tomorrow," Ramesses swore. "If it's not possible to ready the Temple of Amun, I'm sure that Hathor or Isis can be readied."

Rahotep's face lost some of its color. "Amun's temple can be ready, Your Highness."

Henuttawy and the other viziers made to speak, but Pharaoh Seti stood and pounded his crook on the dais. "The proclamation will read as such: Tomorrow, there shall be a wedding between Pharaoh Ramesses and Princess Nefertari."

For the first time, Queen Tuya spoke. "I don't understand why it has to be so soon."

"Because if not tomorrow, then when?" Seti asked. "How do you know when the gods will bring us back to Thebes? Or do you propose to miss our son's Marriage Feast?"

Tuya's hand tightened around her *iwiw*'s leash. "I am sure he will have many Feasts of Marriage we will miss."

"Perhaps. But none to a princess of Egypt."

Queen Tuya settled unhappily back into her throne, and when her hand rested lightly on Adjo's head, the *iwiw* wagged his tail contentedly.

"So will she greet the people?" Henuttawy demanded. "If she's going to be queen, she should walk through Thebes and meet her subjects."

Woserit glanced at her brother. "Nefertari doesn't need to go among them yet."

"Why not?" Pharaoh Seti frowned. "Let them become accustomed to seeing her with Ramesses."

I was too full of my own joy to see then what Henuttawy had done.

Court business being concluded, we left the chamber and Ramesses took me in his arms. "By tomorrow, you will be at my side in the Audience Chamber, and there's no one who will dare to say a word against you."

And of course, because I was naïve and hopeful, I allowed myself to believe him—even though I knew what the courtiers thought. They believed I had my aunt's blood and that I'd be the new Heretic Queen. Merit came to my side and her face was as bright as an oil lamp.

"Congratulations, Your Highness. It is a union sure to be blessed by Amun."

"Thank you, Nurse. I was hoping Nefertari would join me in the Arena. Do you think that will be possible?"

"With a dozen things to do and arrange before tomorrow?" Merit cried.

Ramesses laughed, and I knew he hadn't really expected her to say yes.

"There is the matter of a dress to arrange," she said, "and a wig and malachite paint . . ."

"I believe she's saying no," I told Ramesses, and he put his arms around my waist.

"Then may I come to you tonight?" he asked quietly.

Courtiers were watching us and I forced myself not to look back at them. *They will always be watching us,* I reminded myself. *I will never enjoy a private kiss. There will always be eyes upon me, and I must simply get used to it.* That was the price for loving a Pharaoh. "Of course you can come to me."

A hundred pairs of eyes followed my walk through the halls with Woserit and Merit, and one of them was Henuttawy's. I smiled widely. If I had been a commoner about to marry some farmer's son, the women of my house would never have allowed my husband to climb into my bed before he had carried me over the threshold of his home. But Ramesses was Pharaoh. He could do as he pleased. By coming to my room before our wedding, he was telling the court that a single night couldn't be wasted in trying to create an heir with me.

CHAPTER TEN

┴┴

A PHARAOH'S
MARRIAGE BEGINS
ON THE WATER

┴┴ ┴┴ IN THE GREAT Hall that evening, the whole court appeared to see the worm that had turned into a butterfly. Everyone was eager to see the niece of the Heretic Queen, whom Ramesses was going to take to wife.

At the long, polished table on the dais, a servant led me to my seat between Ramesses and Woserit, while Iset had been placed at the side of Queen Tuya. I felt sorry for Iset, who didn't have the sense to laugh and pretend to be joyful. Though she should have felt triumphant in knowing that she was carrying Ramesses's first child, her face was as sour as a tamarind. I wondered if it was because he had not turned out to be the husband she'd imagined. I knew she enjoyed the exquisite jewels and fur-lined cloaks, but what did she and Ramesses have in common? But if Iset appeared dark and glowering, then across from her, Henuttawy was at her best. The viziers were laughing at her jokes, and when she saw me, she announced brightly to the table, "The butterfly emerges."

But Ramesses heard the edge in her voice. "She *is* like a butterfly," he said. "Hidden away for a year, and emerging more beautiful and talented than ever."

"When she told me she was not going to become a priestess of Hathor, I was worried she would not find a place in Thebes." Woserit turned to her sister. "But it seems that she has found a place on the highest step of all."

Henuttawy's smile vanished, and Rahotep's face looked immensely pained.

"Come," Woserit said cheerfully, "let us raise our cups." She lifted her wine and the rest of the table did the same. "To the princess Nefertari," she said.

"To the princess," Vizier Anemro repeated, though I wondered which princess he meant.

"And let us all hope that the curse of the Heretic King does not run in her veins."

Henuttawy had gone too far. Pharaoh Seti clenched his cup in his hand. "Nefertari is no more of a heretic than *you* are. I trust that she will make good decisions in the Audience Chamber. She may not be popular yet, but she's certainly no fool."

Everyone at the table knew who he meant, but no one dared to look in Iset's direction.

Queen Tuya shook her head, and Ramesses added indignantly, "She's also my *wife*." But Pharaoh Seti remained silent, and soon steaming bowls of roasted duck were brought from the kitchens.

Ramesses turned to me. "I'm sorry," he said softly.

I smiled the way Woserit had taught me to smile in the face of disappointment. "I believe the court is waiting for your blessing."

Ramesses looked to his father, who nodded, then stood from his throne while the room fell silent. "We dedicate this feast to Pharaoh Seti the Great, beloved of Amun and Reconquerer of a dozen lands."

A loud cheer went up in the hall and Ramesses proclaimed, "May the gods watch over your journey to Avaris, and may they watch over the joyous union tomorrow that shall precede it."

The court's cheers reverberated beneath the columns, because it would have been foolish to do otherwise. But I wondered how many of them were like the High Priest of Amun, who had fathers and grandfathers murdered by Akhenaten and Nefertiti.

As the cheers still echoed, Seti leaned over and whispered to me, "I am allowing you to put yourself in danger at this court. But there is no one else in the kingdom of Egypt I would rather see on the throne with my son than you. . . Did you know that if Pili was alive, this would have been the year of her marriage as well? You would have been like two sisters in your bridal boats." He patted my hand, and I saw in that moment why his care for me had always been so tender.

I took my free hand and placed it over Pharaoh's. "Thank you," I told him. "I will try never to disappoint you."

He smiled, but not at me. His look was far away, and only later would I understand how a son's marriage can be both happy and sad. Of course, a father is hopeful for all of the events in the future, but he is also reminded of the family members who are not there to celebrate with him. And when a son begins producing heirs, spinning Khnum's potter wheel of creation faster and faster, he must begin to imagine his own potter's wheel slowing down. But I was too young to understand this then.

🜔 🜔 🜔

IN THE tiled hall outside my chamber, Asha was waiting. His arms were folded over his chest, and in the light of the torches, I searched his face to see if he was angry. As soon as he saw us, he straightened, and Woserit was discreet enough to join Merit inside my room.

"Asha," I said cautiously. "I'm sorry I missed you in the Great Hall tonight."

"You were surrounded by courtiers. I'll have to grow used to that now." I felt as though a heavy stone had been lifted from my chest, and when he stepped forward to embrace me, I did the same. "I'm very happy for you," he said.

"But you told me—"

He nodded. "That was before I knew how much Ramesses needed you."

I flinched at the word. Did he need me, or love me?

"But I still think you've chosen a dangerous road. Tomorrow, Pharaoh wants you to meet the people. He wants Ramesses to see their reaction before he makes a choice about Chief Wife. There are many other women in the harem."

"If you have come here to insult me—"

Asha grabbed my arm. "Nefertari, I'm only trying to tell you the truth. Pharaoh Seti and Ramesses live their lives sheltered inside this palace. *I* see the people on the streets. I hear what they say, and you need to be careful tomorrow."

I saw the concern in his eyes and nodded. "We will take guards," I assured him.

"Make sure there are enough. At least two dozen, no matter what Ramesses says."

"Do you think they'll be that angry?" I whispered.

"I don't know. There are many people who still remember . . ." But he didn't finish. "This will be the fourth year that the Nile has been low, and there's talk that in the poorer sections of Thebes people are already starving. If the river doesn't flood its banks by the end of this month, famine will spread, and the people will want someone to blame."

I felt the color drain from my face. "Not me?"

"Just be prepared."

"I will," I promised. We parted and I entered my chamber. In the light of the brazier, Woserit's face appeared sharp and beautiful.

"How is Asha?"

"Concerned about what might happen tomorrow," I told her.

"Then he's a good friend to have. I will not always be in the palace to help you, Nefertari, so you must learn to recognize who can be trusted and who cannot. Once you marry Ramesses, there is no one in Malkata who will tell you the truth."

"Merit," I protested.

"Yes, Merit. She will be able to hear the whispers in the halls of the palace, but who will tell you about the conspiracies closer to your throne? Those conspiracies inside the Audience Chamber?"

I thought of Seti's words about the dangerous road I had chosen. "On the evenings that Ramesses is with Iset," she suggested, "meet Paser in his chamber. You may trust him to tell you what is truly happening in Thebes. And whenever I can, I will be there as well." The flames of the brazier illuminated the paintings in her old room, and as I stood there in her rich cloak, I wondered again why Woserit was doing so much for me. She reached into her linen belt and produced a small statue of Hathor. "For tonight. Place it under your pillow and she will bring you fertility."

"Thank you," I whispered. I brushed the goddess's face with my thumb. She had been carved from ebony and wore the tall modius headdress that Woserit did, with its small horns and sun disc.

"All will be well tomorrow," she promised. "Be strong of heart." Woserit embraced me, and as the door clicked shut behind her, Merit burst from her chamber next to mine.

"Have you decided which oil you want for your hair?"

I shook my head.

"Then what cream shall we use?"

"I don't know."

"Well, hurry, my lady! Pharaoh is coming!"

Inside the robing room, I slipped from my sheath, and Merit filled the basin with hot water. "What's the matter, my lady? Tomorrow you marry and it will be done!" She tested the surface with her hand, and beckoned me in.

"Asha just told me I should be prepared for anything," I confided. Rainbows swirled over the surface of the water as light from the lamps filtered onto my bath. As I stepped into the tub, I could smell the lotus oil that Merit had added to keep my skin smooth.

"And what is anything?" Merit scrubbed at my hair.

"This is the fourth year the Nile has been low . . . what if they blame me?"

"Why would you say such a thing? You are a princess of Egypt, not some all-powerful goddess. I'm sure the people know the difference."

When my bath was finished, Merit dried my legs and handed me a fresh sheath. I sat before the mirror, studying my reflection while she combed my hair. I opened the lowest drawer of my chest and took out the cream Merit had gone to the farthest market in Thebes to purchase. I rubbed it over my arms, then down my legs.

There was a knock at the door. Merit's chin wobbled furiously. *"Hurry!"*

I rushed to prop myself up against the pillows, allowing my hair to spill onto the white linen, and when Merit opened the door I held my breath just in case it was a dream.

But she bowed very low. "Your Highness."

"Nurse Merit," Ramesses said in greeting.

"The princess Nefertari is waiting for you." She gestured toward me on the bed, and when she reached the door to her chamber, said loudly. "Good night, my lady."

When the door swung shut, Ramesses looked at me, and both of us laughed. "She'll be waiting on the other side of the door all night," I whispered.

"As a good nurse should," he teased. "In case you should scream and want to run away." He approached the bed, and I slipped the *nemes* crown from his brow, running my fingers through his hair. "As you did once before," Ramesses said quietly.

The pain in his eyes wrenched at my heart. "But now I am here," I promised, and let the sheath I was wearing fall from one of my shoulders. "Here with you for eternity."

"And this time I won't let you run away."

WHEN RAMESSES and I emerged from his chamber the next morning, we walked together to the lakeside, and the cheers from the courtiers who were waiting for our arrival must have reached the ears of the gods themselves. Ramesses took my hand in his, and the viziers of Seti's court surrounded us, talking and smiling as though they had supported my marriage all along. Although Iset had claimed an indisposition and remained inside Malkata, the rest of the court was in attendance. Even Queen Tuya spared a smile for me. Her *iwiw* bared his fangs, and a low growl rumbled in his skinny throat.

"Hello, Adjo," I said cheerfully.

I smiled at the thought that I might never have to see him again. Tonight, there would be a feast of both celebration and farewell, and tomorrow Pharaoh Seti would sail with his half of the royal court to the palace in Avaris. Ramesses had been fully trained in the Audience Chamber; now he would rule Upper Egypt on his own. His father, in his advancing age, would reign in the capital of Lower Egypt, where less would be required of him. This move had been planned for many years, yet even though Ramesses had always known it was coming, I saw his lips turn down in sorrow when he gazed across the lake. The eastern horizon was obscured by his father's towering ships. They floated like pregnant herons on the water, their decks filled with some of the most valuable treasures in Thebes: ebony statues and granite tables, rare sedan chairs with wide lion's-paw feet. While some kings were content to remain in the same city as their coregents, governing from the very same Audience Chamber, Pharaoh Seti now wanted a simpler life. Once he reached Avaris, there would not be so many petitioners, and in his summer palace closer to the sea, there would never be the kind of heat that sucked the life from the air as it did nearly every month in Thebes.

The court had assembled itself on the quay, while a small golden vessel was rowed to the shore. It would fit only three people: myself, Merit, and a ferryman. Once Pharaoh Seti gave his permission, we would be rowed the short distance to the Temple of Karnak. Behind us, Ramesses would sail in his own golden bark, accompanied by his parents and rowed by a single soldier from Pharaoh's army: Asha. Behind them the court would follow in a flotilla of brightly painted boats. When I asked Merit once why a Pharaoh's marriage begins on the water instead of the land, she told me that it was because Egypt had been born from the Watery Waste of Nun, and if such a fertile land could be birthed from the water, a fertile marriage would as well.

I stood on the quayside, separated from Ramesses by hundreds of courtiers in their whitest linens and finest gold, waiting for Pharaoh Seti to give his blessing. When the piercing sounds of several trumpets blared, Pharaoh Seti said something I couldn't hear. But he must have given his blessing to set sail, for Merit took my arm and led me to the boat, helping me inside and arranging my cloak so that it fanned out around my legs like a lotus blossom. She seated herself next to me, as straight and serious as Paser. When I opened my mouth to speak, she shook her head firmly. I was meant to be a silent bride, approaching my fate timorously, even though inside my heart was soaring. I knew that I shouldn't turn around. I didn't want to appear like a goose craning its neck to see what was happening in every direction, so I looked ahead as our boat left the lake in front of the palace, and entered the main current of the River Nile itself. Thousands of people stood on the banks, crushed together to see the spectacle of the court sailing beneath Pharaoh's golden pennants. They had chanted eagerly for Iset when she had been married, yet now there was silence.

I glanced at Merit, and she returned my uneasy gaze. It was as if someone had taken a heavy sheet of linen and draped it across the people on the shore. Only the muffled sound of children crying reached us on the river, and Merit turned her sharp eyes on the ferryman.

"What is the talk in Thebes?" she demanded.

"In Thebes?" he repeated.

"Yes! What are they saying about her? She already knows she's the Heretic's niece. There's nothing you can say that will shock her. Just tell us the truth so we can be prepared."

The man looked at me, and his face was sorrowful. "Since Pharaoh Ramesses announced his intention to marry the princess yesterday, my lady, there is talk that she may be the reason for the famine all of these years." The ferryman's voice shook. "They think she has brought bad luck to the city. Her *akhu* angered the gods so deeply that once Pharaoh makes her his wife, they will turn away from Egypt completely. I'm sorry, Princess."

I held on to the sides of the boat so that my sudden dizziness would not overwhelm me, and I looked ahead at the unwelcoming faces of the people on the riverbank. Their silence was terrifying. What were they waiting for? That Ramesses might change his mind?

When we reached the quay in front of the temple, a young priest reached down to help me up. A crowd of priestesses circled around us, chanting and shaking their long bronze sistrums. They led us through the gates of Karnak, and we followed their loud jangling to the inner sanctum, where I ascended the dais and waited for Ramesses. When he arrived, his eyes met mine. Then all I could see was the High Priest in front of me. He took a vessel of oil from the altar, and as he raised it above my head he intoned, "In the name of Amun, Princess Nefertari, daughter of Queen Mutnodjmet and General Nakhtmin, is bound together with Pharaoh Ramesses."

I stole a glance at the throngs of courtiers who filled the inner sanctum. The High Priest approached Ramesses. "In the name of Amun, Pharaoh Ramesses, son of Pharaoh Seti and Queen Tuya, is bound together with Princess Nefertari."

Ramesses held his breath as the oil poured over his *nemes* crown. There was one symbolic gesture left to make. Rahotep produced a golden ring from his robes. Ramesses slipped the band on to my fourth finger, since a vein travels from this finger to the heart. Now, I wore two rings. One bore the insignia of my family, the other bore Ramesses's name in hieroglyphics. Ramesses's ring was gold with an ebony stone, and by placing it on my finger, he had "captured" my heart. Like a *shen*, a design with no beginning and no end, we were joined for eternity. The High Priest announced, "United and blessed before Amun."

Ramesses held my hand above the cheering courtiers of the inner sanctum, who would have forced themselves to look happy even if he'd been marrying his mother's *iwiw*. "Are you ready?" he asked. We would walk from the temple through the city, then sail from the quay in front of the marketplace. Only newly crowned royalty made such a walk. When I nodded, he took my hand firmly in his and pressed forward.

The noise of the procession grew deafening. The priestesses of Isis were playing their tambourines and Hathor's women were singing as we passed through the magnificent halls of Karnak into the city. Thousands of people filled the streets, but I saw with a rising sense of alarm that only a handful of them waved palm branches or cheered. We passed through the marketplace, and the noise of our procession made an awkward contrast to the continuing silence of the people. Ramesses raised his hand in mine and shouted jubilantly, "Princess Nefertari!"

Behind us, the court echoed his cry, but in the streets the old women watched me with their arms across their breasts. At the end of the market an old woman shouted, "Another Heretic Queen!" and then the people of the marketplace began to chant.

"HER-E-TIC. HER-E-TIC."

"Stop them!" Ramesses shouted angrily. His guards formed a tighter circle around us, but the people's chanting was quickly building to a feverish pitch. Even children, who didn't know what they were shouting, squinted into my face and yelled, "Another Heretic Queen!"

The songs of the priestesses grew louder to drown out the people's chants, but soon it became impossible. Ramesses might have ordered violence on the surging mob. But there were old women and children, so instead he called, "Get back to the boats!"

ᴛ ᴛ ᴛ

ONCE WE had cast off from the quay, Ramesses took me in his arms, soothing me while I shook. The faces of the women were terrible to see. Many of the young girls were weeping into their hands. Henuttawy asked, "Have you *ever* seen anything like that?"

Queen Tuya used a linen to dab her eyes, and a sob escaped from her lips.

I looked up into Ramesses's face, and I was the one who spoke the embarrassing truth first. "You won't be able to make me queen."

"They'll change their minds," he vowed. "Once they know you . . ." But he looked at his father, and entire conversations were conveyed in that glance.

"Let us proceed to the feast," Woserit announced. "This is still a celebration." But her good cheer rang hollow, and the courtiers who sailed with us did so in silence.

In the Great Hall, the cheerful laughter of the servants and the comforting crackle of the fires contrasted with the mood of the court. The rich smell of wine and roasted duck filled the chamber, and musicians began to play as we appeared. Pharaoh Seti ascended the dais as if nothing had happened, and I took my place next to Ramesses at the table. Because the court knew its purpose, there was suddenly merrymaking and dance. Even the young girls had dried their eyes and repainted their cheeks, now that the scare was over.

Pharaoh Seti took my hand. "There is nothing you could have done differently," he said. "They don't know that you are as much my daughter as Ramesses is my son."

I lowered my head in shame. It was Seti's final day of rule in the palace, and instead of leaving Thebes in triumph, he would depart wondering if the next time he returned it might be to rebellion. Then I noticed that while others were taking their seats, our table on the dais remained empty. "Where are Woserit and Henuttawy?" I asked.

Ramesses followed my gaze. "And where are the viziers?" He stood from his throne and appealed to his father. "They are meeting without us!"

Pharaoh Seti shook his head. "Tomorrow, this will become your city," he challenged. "What will you do?"

Ramesses pulled me with him, and we rushed down the dais, crossing the Great Hall as courtiers scrambled to move out of our way. Ramesses flung open the doors to the Audience Chamber. Inside, the conversation immediately stopped. At the base of the dais, Asha was standing with his father. The viziers and generals of Egypt were present, and so were Woserit and Henuttawy. Woserit passed me a warning look.

"What is this?" Ramesses demanded.

"Your Highness," Rahotep began, "I think you know why we are meeting here."

"Behind my back?" Ramesses challenged, and glared at Asha.

"The people," Henuttawy spoke sharply, "are against Nefertari, as I warned you—"

"And who rules this kingdom?" Ramesses asked angrily. "The people, or me?"

"Did the people rise against Iset when you married her?" Henuttawy spoke swiftly. "Did they shout *Heretic Queen* in the streets?"

"Iset wasn't taken through the city," Woserit rejoined. "In fact, I believe that idea was yours."

Henuttawy turned on her sister, and it was like watching a lioness attack one of its own pride. "Are you saying I planned this?"

"I don't know," Woserit said calmly. "How many temple offerings would you need to sell in order to buy the people?"

Paser stepped forward. "Give the people time. They haven't seen the princess in the Audience Chamber. She is wise and just."

Henuttawy smiled sweetly, and I knew that something vicious was coming. "Vizier Paser is willing to say and do whatever pleases my sister," she said bitterly. "Listen to reason!"

I put my hand on Ramesses's arm. "It's true." Everyone turned in shock, and Woserit watched me with a strange expression. But I thought of the hatred I had seen in the streets. Even if Henuttawy had paid the women to chant, they had been angry enough to risk their lives by raising their voices against a Pharaoh. "Remember what happened under Akhenaten," I said.

"Wait to choose a queen," Rahotep suggested. "There is no harm in waiting."

"For how long?" Ramesses demanded.

Asha's father, General Anhuri, had been listening, and now he stepped forward. "If Pharaoh doesn't choose a Chief Wife, how will the thrones be arranged on the dais? Who will the petitioners see?"

"There can be two thrones flanking Pharaoh," Rahotep said. The other viziers immediately raised their voices in displeasure.

"*Two* thrones on each side of Pharaoh?" Woserit exclaimed. "And they will both wear the diadem of a princess? Neither will be queen?"

"The people were outraged to see me at Ramesses's side," I said, feeling pained. I couldn't meet Woserit's gaze.

"Give your decision time," Henuttawy suggested, taking the advantage. "Place three thrones on the dais. In the Audience Chamber, let the petitioners be divided between the two princesses."

"Then who will be Pharaoh's heirs?" Woserit asked. "The children of Iset or Nefertari?"

"Nefertari, of course." Ramesses's voice was adamant.

"*If* the people accept her," Henuttawy said.

Ramesses looked to me. I made no motion to protest, and he said quietly, "We will wait. But this court knows who will make the better queen for Egypt."

卍 卍 卍

"YOU DID what was right," Merit said quietly.

I watched while the servants filled my bath with hot water. When the women left, I crouched in the tub, putting my arms around my knees. "You should have seen their faces," I whispered.

"I did, my lady. It was not so terrible as you think."

"But from the front of the procession," I told her, and my eyes welled with tears. "Their faces were so full of hate."

There was a brief knock on the door. It was the quiet tap of a servant, and I answered carelessly, "Come in." Neither of us turned. "You know as well as I do that the only reason I am in Paser's favor is because of Woserit."

"I don't think you give yourself enough credit."

Merit and I both spun, and Woserit emerged from the darkness of the doorway. "Even if Paser wasn't in love with me, I don't believe he'd want to see a fool like Iset in the Audience Chamber." Woserit laughed at the shock apparent on Merit's face. "It was never a secret."

I stood from my bath, wrapping myself in a long linen robe before joining Woserit at the brazier.

"Nefertari asked why I was willing to help her become Chief Wife." Woserit seated herself on the largest chair. "I told her that I was doing it for myself as much as for her. Not only do I fear a city where Henuttawy is as wealthy as she wishes to be, I am also afraid of what my sister might do out of jealousy."

"But what can she have to be jealous of?" Merit asked.

"That I was the first to be asked for in marriage."

I took a seat and named the man to whom she was referring. "Vizier Paser?"

Woserit nodded. "Paser asked my father if we could marry. We were seventeen and had studied together in the edduba. He was being groomed for the job of vizier. But when Henuttawy heard he wanted to marry me, she flew into a rage. There were a hundred men at her door, but she couldn't stand the thought that there was one at mine. She went to our father and begged him not to shame her by letting me marry before she did. He asked Henuttawy if there was someone she wanted to marry. She said there was. Paser."

"She could have asked for anyone!" I cried. "Even the prince of a foreign nation."

"Egypt never gives away her princesses," Merit corrected me.

"Then another vizier's son," I said. "Or a wealthy merchant. Or a prince willing to live in Egypt."

"It's true. My sister's beauty was as tempting then as it is now. When Henuttawy said she wanted Paser, my father summoned him to the Audience Chamber to see which sister he would choose."

"And Paser chose you."

"Yes. And when he told Pharaoh this, Henuttawy vowed that she would never take a husband."

"So that you could never marry."

Merit clucked her tongue. "How cruel."

"If Iset becomes Chief Wife with Henuttawy whispering in her ear, then there is little hope for Paser and me. But now you are here, and the risk is worth taking . . ."

I flinched at the callousness of her statement. I was a Senet piece that she had polished and moved across the board for her own benefit.

Woserit saw the betrayal on my face. "If I did not like you, I would never suggest you to Ramesses as Chief Wife, whatever the reward for myself. There are things more important than whether or not I marry. Stability in the kingdom and a wise queen for the throne. You are getting what you want, and perhaps someday I will get what I want. And if we can help each other to that end—"

"But your father is gone," I protested. "Can't you marry now?"

"And leave the Temple of Hathor?" Woserit asked. "For what? If Iset becomes queen and I marry Paser, what will happen to him once my brother is gone?"

"Henuttawy and Iset will drive him from court, and he'll lose everything."

Woserit nodded.

"But why didn't you tell me any of this?"

"Because there are enough burdens resting on your shoulders," she said. "You don't need the weight of my destiny on you as well. Your first responsibility is to Ramesses, and then the people."

I glanced at Merit, who knew what I was going to ask. "Do you think those people will rebel because of me?"

Woserit was honest. "Anything might happen," she replied. "Especially when the Nile runs low. What does Ramesses say?"

"He is horrified," I whispered.

"Good. And you will never mention becoming Chief Wife. He has made his decision to wait. Let Iset complain and drive him away. You will be silent and long-suffering and he will love you even more."

"And his decision?" Merit asked.

"It all depends on how soon Nefertari can change the people's minds—by being wise and judicious in the Audience Chamber. Tomorrow, Pharaoh Seti will be gone, and there will only be Pharaoh Ramesses to rule in Thebes. She must build her reputation as the clever princess."

"I am a danger to Ramesses's crown," I said. "Did I do what was right in the Audience Chamber today?"

Woserit hesitated. "You stopped him when his rashness might have made you queen tonight. You placed the kingdom of Egypt and Ramesses's welfare before your own." She smiled sadly. "You love him."

I nodded. I did, and in the end, I knew such love might prove costly.

🜚 🜚 🜚

LATER THAT night, when Ramesses came into my chamber, Merit disappeared into her own room. There was nothing that Ramesses needed to say. He embraced me, stroking my hair. "I'm sorry," he whispered again and again. "I'm sorry for what happened."

"It's fine," I told him, but we both knew it wasn't. On a day that Egypt should have been celebrating, the people couldn't have been angrier. They had risen up against Pharaoh's guards, something that had not happened since the reign of Akhenaten.

"Tomorrow," Ramesses promised, "things will be different. You don't belong in the streets of Thebes. You belong with me, in the Audience Chamber." He guided me to the edge of my bed and drew a cloth-wrapped object from inside his cloak. "For you," he said softly.

The linen wrapping had been painted with images of Seshat, the goddess of learning. When I unveiled the gift within, I thought my heart would stop in my chest. I held the heavy scroll up to the oil lamps, slowly unrolling the papyrus, as light illuminated the painted text. "Ramesses, where did you find this?" I asked. It was a history of every major kingdom in the world, from Hatti to Cyprus, written first in hieroglyphics and then in the language of each country. Not even Paser owned such a book.

"The scribes have been compiling it for you for more than a year."

"A *year?* But I was in the Temple of Hathor—"

I stopped, realizing what he meant. Every misery of the afternoon disappeared. It didn't matter that the people hated me. We fell onto the bed and thought only of each other that night.

CHAPTER ELEVEN

THE AUDIENCE
CHAMBER

WHAT SHOULD HAVE been Pharaoh's triumphant departure from Thebes became instead a quiet lakeside farewell. I wondered if the court members were as angry with Seti as they were with me. He had allowed my marriage to Ramesses to proceed, and he knew that if there was plague, or further drought in Thebes, the blame would likely fall on me. Tuya held back tears while she embraced her only son, and Ramesses's face was solemn. No one knew what might happen once Seti's ships left, and over the crying of the gulls I heard him remind Ramesses, "Half of my army stays with you. If there is any talk of rebellion—"

"There *won't* be rebellion."

But Seti wasn't placated. "Have your men watch over the city. Four viziers are staying behind. Send one of them to walk the streets and listen to what the people are saying. This is your capital now." Behind him, the white palace of Malkata gleamed like a pearl against the darkening sky. "Its glory will reflect your reign. You should begin rebuilding the Temple of Luxor, and let the people see that there is nothing more important to you than honoring the gods."

Seti beckoned to me with a jeweled finger. "Little Nefertari." I embraced him as tightly as I could. "I want you to be careful on the eastern bank," he cautioned. "Be patient with the people."

"I will," I promised.

Then Seti took my arm and led me aside. I felt certain that he was going to say something about what had happened in the streets the day before. But instead, he said in a conspiratorial whisper, "I also want you to take care of my son. Ramesses is rash, and he needs a head with reason—"

I flushed. "I think you should be talking to Asha . . ."

"Asha will keep my son from trouble on the battlefield. It's trouble at court I'm worried about. Not everyone lives their life according to the rules of Ma'at, and I suspect that behind those pretty green eyes you have a good understanding of this."

Seti stepped back, and as I reached forward to embrace Tuya farewell, Adjo strained at his leash and snapped angrily at the air.

"That's enough!" Tuya reprimanded. She gave me a long look from beneath her wide Nubian wig. "He never barks at anyone else."

The trumpets blared, and the clanging of sistrums filled the air. Seti and Tuya went on board and soon waved from the prow of their ship. As Ramesses and I waved back, Iset appeared beside us and asked, "What does it feel like to be the Pharaoh of all of Thebes?"

Ramesses looked at her as if to ask how she could wonder such a thing. "Lonely," he replied.

An hour remained until the Audience Chamber, so as the court returned to the palace, Ramesses took my hand and it became clear to everyone where he intended to be. After all, we had only been married for a day.

By the time Merit knocked on our door and told us that the petitioners had arrived, Ramesses was not feeling so lonely. I took his arm, and we walked together into the Audience Chamber where the herald grandly announced our presence. Inside, the entire court had gathered. Courtiers rolled knucklebones next to the warmth of the braziers, and musicians huddled around the dais, performing on their double flutes and lyres. Women laughed at the back of the room, and a few old noblemen in warm furs were playing Senet. It looked more like a feast in the Great Hall than a place for the affairs of state. I was shocked. "Is it always so merry?"

Ramesses laughed at my surprise. "Until the business begins."

"And then where do all of these people go?"

"Oh, most of them will remain. But the musicians will leave, and the courtiers will keep quiet."

In the middle of the Audience Chamber, the viziers were already seated at their tables. They stood as we passed, and I nodded briefly to Paser. "Your Majesty," they murmured. "Princess Nefertari." I caught the bloodied eye of Rahotep and thought, *He will send me all of the difficult petitioners. He will try to embarrass me.*

On the dais, Iset was already seated at her throne. She was dressed in a wide collar I had never seen on her before, and she had left the front of her heavy cloak open to remind the court of her swelling belly. *Five months, with only four to go,* I thought. *If she births a son, and a Chief Wife has not been announced, her child will be the heir to Egypt's throne until Ramesses declares otherwise.* I knew that everyone was watching me, and I was careful as I ascended the steps. The thrones had been set close enough together so that if Ramesses wanted, he could stretch his arms from the center of the dais and touch both of his wives. In the history of Egypt, there had never been two thrones for dueling princesses.

"Are you ready?" Ramesses asked both of us, and I nodded. He struck his crook on the dais and declared, "Bring forth the petitioners!"

Courtiers sprang into action. The wide doors leading to the courtyard of Malkata were thrown open, and the first petitioners were led inside. Three men approached the viziers' table, and all of them bore scrolls that they handed to the viziers. I watched while Paser, Rahotep, and Anemro read the petitions, then took out their reed pens and signed a name on the bottom of each scroll. Then all three men approached the dais, and the oldest one held his petition out to me with a bow.

"For the princess Nefertari," he said. My family's seal had been drawn on the scroll, but it wasn't in Paser's hand. The old man watched me with plain distrust. "I asked to see the princess Iset, but the High Priest sent me to you. I specifically requested—"

"Whatever you specifically requested," I snapped, "I will be the one who reads your petition." Woserit had warned that if I allowed a single petitioner to treat me as though I was less important than Iset, he would leave the palace and tell of my timidity to the others still waiting in line. I looked at the open scroll. The man had come to request entry into the Temple of Amun at Karnak. Commoners were not allowed inside, yet he was requesting a special dispensation to see the High Priest. "What is this for?" I asked him quietly.

"My daughter is sick, and the offerings I've placed at our shrines have not been enough." The old man narrowed his eyes. He watched me pick up the reed pen from the small table at my side, then write across the bottom of his scroll. "You may enter the temple," I said.

The old man stepped back as if to see me better. "I was alive during the time of Amarna," he said. "I saw the Heretic break the statues of Amun and murder the god's priests."

I tightened my fist around his petition. "And what does that have to do with me?"

The man squinted up into my face. "You look like your aunt."

I suppressed the strong desire to ask him how. Was it my nose, my lips, my high cheekbones, my build? But I knew what he was trying to imply, and instead, I shoved the scroll at him and said darkly, "Go. Go before I change my mind!"

Ramesses glanced at me instead of paying attention to his own petitioner, and his look was one of pity, not admiration. I felt the fire in my stomach spread.

"Next!" *Whatever happens, keep smiling,* Woserit had warned. A farmer came forward and I smiled beautifully. "Your petition?" He held out his scroll. I read it, then looked down at the man. His kilt had been neatly pressed for the occasion, and he was wearing leather sandals instead of papyrus. "You come from Thebes and wish to claim access to your neighbor's well? And why should your neighbor grant you this access?"

"Because I have given his cows grazing in my fields! I have no water on my land and I want something in return."

"So if he will not give you water, stop giving his cows feed."

"My son would let the beasts starve! And he would do it to spite me!"

I sat back on my throne. "Your neighbor is your son?"

"I gave him a piece of my land when he married, and now he won't give me access to my well because of his wife!"

"What's wrong with his wife?"

"She is against me!" he cried. "When I told my son I didn't want a harlot like her for a daughter, he married her anyway. And now the girl wants to ruin me," he raged.

The viziers stopped to watch us, but I resisted the temptation to see which had sent the farmer to me. "And what has your daughter-in-law done to make you think that she is unfaithful?"

"She has slept with half of Thebes. She knows it as well as Ma'at! My son's heirs might be any man's children, and now she won't even give me access to my land!"

"Did you deed your son the land?" I asked him.

"I gave him my word."

"But not the deed?" The man clearly didn't understand. "It is not enough to give your word," I explained. "It must be set down in writing."

The farmer smiled widely. "I have not given anything in writing."

"Then it is your well to use," I said firmly, "and she will have to live with it until you've signed away your deed or your son finds his own land."

The old man's face was a picture of shock. I took up my reed pen and wrote the verdict on the bottom of his papyrus. When I handed him the scroll, he watched me with a guarded look. "You . . . you are not like they say."

Every day will be like this, I thought. *Every morning for the rest of my life I will be treated as the Heretic's niece. If I don't change their opinion of me, I will never escape it.* My back stiffened as a third petitioner made his way to me. He held out a scroll and I read the contents quickly.

"Give me the whole story," I said, but the young man shook his head.

"I ask to see Pharaoh, who speak my language, but Vizier Paser send me you," he stumbled in a heavy accent.

"And is there something wrong with me?" I demanded in Hurrian.

The foreigner stepped back. "You speak Hurrian," he whispered.

"Well, what have you come for?" I demanded.

For every petitioner who watched me with mistrust, there was another from Babylon, Assyria, or Nubia whose language I could speak. Before the day was finished I could see the interested glances that courtiers made in my direction. I sat straighter on my throne. Even without the signature at the bottom of each scroll, I could guess where each petition had come from. Foreigners from kingdoms whose languages I could speak were sent by Paser. The angriest and most contentious men were from Rahotep.

When a trumpet sounded in the distance, there was a sudden shifting in the room. A table was brought and placed at the base of the dais, and servants began positioning chairs with large arms and padded cushions.

I turned to Ramesses. "What are they preparing for?"

"Obviously, we're done with petitions," Iset replied.

Ramesses ignored her and said quietly, "At noon we finish and move on to private business."

The remaining petitioners were led away, and from a small door on the side of the room a group of women entered the chamber. Although Henuttawy and Woserit were among them, they never looked at each other. *Like a pair of horses wearing blinders,* I thought. As they seated themselves around the table, Ramesses struck his crook against the dais.

"We are ready to begin the business of the court," he declared. "Bring in the architect Penre."

The doors of the Audience Chamber were thrown open and Penre appeared. He was a strapping man, with a lean jaw and a straight nose that would have been too large on any other man's face. His long kilt was banded with yellow, and his golden pectoral had been a gift from Pharaoh Seti. He looked more like a warrior than an architect to me. "Your Majesties." He bowed efficiently, then wasted no time unfurling his scroll. "You have requested an undertaking that no other architect has ever accomplished. A courtyard in the Temple of Luxor, with obelisks so tall that the gods themselves can touch them. So I have drawn for Your Highness one vision of what might be built." He offered up a scroll and produced another two from the bag that hung at his side. These, he gave to myself and Iset.

I unfurled the papyrus and saw that the changes to Luxor that

Penre had drawn were magnificent. Dark limestone pillars rose from pink sands, decorated with reliefs and hieroglyphics.

"What is this?" Iset demanded haughtily. She looked at Ramesses. "I thought your first act would be to build on to the palace."

Ramesses shook his head, and the *nemes* head cloth brushed against his wide shoulders. "You heard my father request that we rebuild the Temple of Luxor."

"But we're living in the palace, not the temple," Iset whined. "And what about a birthing pavilion for our heir?"

Ramesses sighed. "There is a pavilion already built. The people must see that Pharaoh's first project is for Amun, not us."

"We all know what happened when another Pharaoh built only for himself," Rahotep reminded.

Iset glanced at the bottom of the dais to where Henuttawy was sitting. "Then perhaps we should rebuild the Temple of Isis?"

Ramesses didn't understand her persistence. "The Temple of Isis was rebuilt by my grandfather!"

"That was many years ago. And since then Hathor's temple has been made new. Don't we want the people to know that Pharaoh values Isis as much as Hathor?"

Rahotep nodded, and I sensed an unspoken message in the glance he flashed at Iset.

But her persistence seemed only to baffle Ramesses.

"There is only so much time and gold," he said shortly. "I would rebuild every temple from here to Memphis if I could, but Amun must come first."

Iset saw that she had lost. "The Temple of Luxor then," she said. "And think . . ." She touched Ramesses's arm with her hand, and the brush of her fingertips seemed sensual. "If the temple can be completed by Thoth, your father will be able to see it when he arrives for the next Feast of Wag."

This was what Ramesses wanted to hear. He straightened. "Are there changes you think should be made?"

He was asking us both. Iset said swiftly, "I wouldn't change anything."

"I would."

The court turned to me, expectantly. Penre's design was skillful. In his vision, two towering granite obelisks guarded the gates, piercing the sky in magnificent testaments to Ramesses's reign. But there was nowhere to remind the people of Ramesses's deeds. In a hundred years, how would the people know what he had done if there was nowhere to record it? Time might rot the gates of the palace, but Amun's stone temples would be forever.

"I think there should be a pylon," I said. "Outside the Temple at Karnak is the Wall of Proclamation." On this wall, images are carved and erased with every new triumph. "So why not outside of Luxor as well?"

Ramesses looked to Penre. "Could you erect a pylon?"

"Certainly, Your Majesty. And you may use it as a Wall of Proclamation as well."

Ramesses glanced approvingly at me, but Iset was not to be outdone. "Then what about a hall?" she suggested. "A columned hall in front of the temple?"

"What purpose would that serve?" I asked.

"It doesn't need a purpose! There should be a hall, shouldn't there, Ramesses?"

Ramesses looked between us, then down at Penre. "Can a hall be constructed?" he asked wearily.

"Of course. Whatever Your Highness would like."

☖ ☖ ☖

THAT EVENING, only a day after our own wedding, Ramesses began his ten nights with Iset. And even though I understood that every king in the history of Egypt had divided his nights equally between his most important wives, I sat in front of my bronze mirror and wondered if he had left me because he loved her more.

"Nonsense," Merit said with absolute conviction. "You told me yourself what she did in the Audience Chamber. Nothing but whine."

"But not in bed," I said, and I imagined her naked in front of Ramesses, rubbing lotus oil over her breasts. "I'll bet Henuttawy taught her every trick she knows. She's beautiful, Merit. Everyone sees it."

The pouch beneath my nurse's neck grew rigid. "And how long is beauty entertaining for? An hour? Two hours? Stop complaining, or you'll be just as bad as she is."

"But if I can't whine to you, then who can I whine to?"

Merit looked across the chamber to my mother's wooden *naos*, with its tall statue of the feline goddess Mut. "Go tell her. Maybe she'll want to listen."

I folded my arms across my chest. Even though I felt like sitting in my robing room and complaining to Merit, I *had* promised Woserit that each evening Ramesses spent away from me, I would meet with Paser. So I made my way through the dimly lit halls around the royal courtyard, and when Paser's body servant opened his door, I saw my former tutor sitting with Woserit at his brazier. At once, they moved apart, but the scene had been so intimate that I stepped back. Paser's long hair was loosened from its braid, and in the firelight it gleamed like a raven's wings. *He is beautiful*, I realized. I immediately thought the same of Woserit, whose face seemed suddenly younger. She was only twenty-five, but the weight of life at court had etched thin lines between her brows.

"Princess Nefertari," Paser said, and stood to greet me. His chamber was large, painted with murals and decorated with expensive hangings from Mitanni. Above the bed were carvings from Assyria, sphinxes whose tightly curled beards gave away their origin. And at the entrance to his robing room, the carved wooden faces of Babylonian gods stared back. *Has he been to all of these lands?* I wondered.

It was cold, and Woserit was wearing her heaviest cloak. "You did well today," she said while I took an empty seat. "Especially with your entrance. There was no one in that chamber who couldn't tell that you were a princess, born and bred."

"And you judged wisely," Paser added.

"Then I must thank you for sending me all of your simplest petitions."

Paser raised his brows. "Those foreign petitioners wouldn't have been simple for Iset. Once the court begins to recognize your talent for languages, perhaps we'll start sending those cases to her instead." He smiled at Woserit. "If Rahotep thinks he's the only one who can play this game, then he'll discover very quickly that he's wrong."

"What were your impressions of the Audience Chamber?" Woserit asked.

I looked between them, wondering what she wanted me to say. "It was filled with interesting people," I said carefully.

"Did you find it tiresome?" Paser asked.

"With so many petitioners to talk to?" I exclaimed. "No."

Paser glanced at Woserit. "She's not another Iset," he said thankfully, then turned to me. "When the people see how valuable you are, the tide of love for Iset may change."

"Especially if you are pregnant," Woserit added.

We both looked down at my tunic, with its amber studded belt emphasizing the smallness of my waist. They both knew the story of my mother. It was a legend now at court, how she had been poisoned by the Heretic King and lost her first child. She had been tall, with wide hips for childbearing, but it was years before Tawaret blessed her womb again with my brother. Yet she'd wanted more children, and I could only imagine how she must have felt when her third had come into the world robbed of its breath. And then, while she had been pregnant with me, there was the fire in the royal courtyard. I shuddered to think of her gentle heart having to bear the news that everyone she had ever loved—her mother and father, her son and husband, both of Nefertiti's remaining daughters—was gone. Was it any wonder that after my birth, she had no more energy left for living?

"We are not always our mother's daughters." Woserit read my mind. "Your aunt gave Pharaoh six healthy girls."

"Then I should hope to be more like the Heretic Queen?" I whispered.

"In this regard, yes."

I was silent for a moment, then asked, "And if I never become pregnant?"

"Why would you say such a thing?" Woserit shot Paser a look, and he said warningly, "Nefertari, a Chief Wife's duty is to give Pharaoh a son."

"My aunt never gave her husband a son!"

"But she gave him children," Woserit said sternly. "Six princesses to marry any prince. Ramesses married you for the children you will bring him."

"He married me for love!"

"And sons," Paser said. "Do not mistake him."

I stood from my chair. "And he would rather have a son than a wife?" I demanded.

There was silence in the chamber, and the crackle of the fire in the brazier seemed unnaturally loud. Paser gave a heavy sigh, and

Woserit reached out to touch my hand. "No man ever thinks of childbirth as a choice between his children and his wife. Every husband hopes for both."

Woserit stood from her stool and wrapped me in her arms. "You are not fated to die in childbirth, Nefertari."

"How do you know?" I pulled back to look at her face.

"Instinct." She shrugged. "You are meant to have a very long reign. *If* you give Ramesses a prince. And *if* he makes you Chief Wife."

"And he would never make me Chief Wife without a son."

Woserit shook her head. "He cannot."

When I returned to my chamber, I went to the balcony and watched the moon drift behind thin wisps of cloud. Even though the wind was cool, there was still no dusty scent of rain in the air. No relief from the drought and the rising hunger. Already, there were reports of men stealing the food offerings from mortuary temples to feed their families. And when a group of these thieves had been brought before their elders, the old men had pardoned them with the belief that it is better to feed the living than the dead. But how long would it be before the gods grew angry, or even the wealthy began to starve and the people rebelled? Then, what would it matter if I was pregnant? Had I seven sons, the people would still blame me.

"You have had a very long day, my lady. You must eat something," Merit chided. Her squat body was framed by the doorway, and she held up the cooked perch for me to see. I left the balcony and she handed me the bowl, slamming the wooden doors shut behind us. "Standing out in the dark and the wind," she grumbled. "Don't you have any sense?"

"It's beautiful," I objected. "It's how Amun must have felt when he emerged from the dark waters at the beginning of time, when everything was possible."

"Was it possible for him to get sick as well? Because that's what you're about to do, my lady. Sit next to that fire."

I did as I was told, and Merit took a blanket from the wooden chest and draped it over my shoulders. "Did you know there's already talk about you in the palace?"

I lowered the bowl. "What kind of talk?"

"First, you must eat!" She crossed her arms over her chest, and when I'd taken a bite of perch to satisfy her, she smiled. "The kind you want," she revealed. "It was about the Audience Chamber. You must have done very well today. There was surprise in the palace that someone so young could command so many languages and deal so justly. I heard it in the baths, and in the kitchens as well."

I put down the bowl of fish. "But those are just servants."

Merit passed me a long look. "And what kind of gossip do you think the people trust? Gossip from the mouths of cooks, or courtiers?"

"Do you think it's possible to change the people's hearts?"

"It might be easier," she said quietly, "if the River Nile would overflow its banks."

I went to my mother's shrine and looked into the face of the feline goddess. In the firelight, it was impossible to see that she'd once been broken.

"Mut watches over you," Merit whispered. "But there is nothing she can do if your body is not strong!" She thrust the half-eaten perch at me again. "Eat!"

I looked over her shoulder and gasped with surprise. "What are you doing here?"

Ramesses stood in the door. Merit inhaled so sharply at the sight of him that her pelican's pouch disappeared. "Your Highness!" She rushed across the room to get him a proper chair. I looked at Ramesses in his short kilt and bedroom sandals and repeated my question. "What are you doing here?"

"I thought I would come here tonight." He added sheepishly, "If you don't mind? Iset is going to sleep, and I want to be with you."

I could see that Merit was shocked, but she excused herself at once. I sat across from Ramesses at the brazier.

"Your first Audience Chamber, and all of Thebes is talking about you. You have a great talent, Nefer. And I was thinking that perhaps . . . although, of course, you don't have to . . . but I was hoping that you would look over the reports from Egypt's spies."

I hid my disappointment. *Was this why he had come to me?* "You don't trust the viziers' translations?" I asked quietly.

Ramesses shifted uncomfortably in his chair. "Bribery is a strong temptation. How do I know what the viziers are giving me is accurate? Or that there isn't more to these reports they are missing or concealing? My court is full of spies."

"Among your *viziers?* They'd be jeopardizing their *ka* to lie to a Pharaoh," I said sternly.

"You can't see your *ka*. But you *can* see a chest full of Babylonian gold. I could work all day and still not finish reading what is sent to me. I must trust my viziers and their scribes. But the most important messages, from Hatti and Kadesh—I'd like you to read them."

This was an opportunity—a chance to make myself more valuable than Iset. "Of course." I smiled. "If you'd like, you can bring them every night."

CHAPTER TWELVE

A HUNGRY PEOPLE

THE ENTIRE COURT knew that it was Iset's time with Pharaoh, so when Ramesses arrived in the Audience Chamber with me on his arm, there was a stiffening of backs among the viziers. Iset wore a look of deep disgust, but it wasn't her sneer that caught my attention. It was the fact that there wasn't a single petitioner in the chamber.

"Where is everyone?" Ramesses questioned. As we reached the viziers' table, Paser rose.

"I have dismissed the petitioners for the day, Your Highness. There is something more important."

Ramesses looked to Vizier Anemro, who rose as well and began to wring his hands. "As you know, Your Highness, the Nile hasn't overflowed its banks in four years. The granaries in Aswan are already empty. And this morning . . ." He glanced uncertainly at Paser. "This morning, the scribes have told us that our Theban stores may only last until Pachons. Six months at the most."

"So little?" Ramesses exclaimed. "That isn't possible. My father said there was enough for another dry season!"

Paser shook his head. "That was before Your Highness's victory feast, and your marriage, and the extra rations of grain that the Theban people received for every celebration."

I saw the blood drain from Ramesses's face. "The scribes gave out extra rations of grain *every* time?"

Anemro swallowed. "It is the custom, Your Highness."

"And no one thought to stop this custom when the Nile has run low for four years?" he shouted. "Our season of overflow is nearly over. If the river doesn't overflow by next month, crops will fail. Come summer there will be famine within this city. And no one can predict how long it might continue. Or what its consequences might be!"

The river's load of black earth gave Egypt not just its name, but its very life as well. I squeezed Ramesses's hand in mine and asked calmly, "So what can be done?"

Paser spread his palms. "I would like to suggest we use this time to address the situation."

"Arrange several tables beneath the dais," Ramesses instructed. "I want everyone in this chamber to offer their suggestions. Nefertari, Iset, you too."

When the servants arranged the viziers' tables beneath the dais, Rahotep spoke first. "I suggest that Your Highness visit each of the granaries, to be certain this is true."

Ramesses turned to Anemro. "Have you verified that the granaries are nearly empty?"

Vizier Anemro nodded swiftly. "Yes, Your Highness. The scribes have not lied. Outside of Thebes, in the city of Nekheb, some of the granaries have lain empty since Thoth, and families are already experiencing famine. Soon, people will be taking to the streets. Murder and theft will increase," he warned fearfully.

"We need a solution before Inundation is over and Harvest arrives," Paser said.

"And what do you suggest we do?" Rahotep demanded.

There was silence in the chamber while everyone waited, then Paser said thoughtfully, "The people of Nekheb must be given food. Begin emptying the temple granaries," he said. "And when those are finished, look to the army's."

"The temple's granaries?" Rahotep exclaimed. "And starve the priests?"

Even Vizier Anemro was shocked. Behind him, courtiers began speaking nervously among themselves.

"In every city the temples have nearly six months of surplus grain," Paser replied. "And here in Thebes, the army has at least three months."

"That is a fool's idea," Rahotep pronounced. "What happens when the army has nothing to feed itself with?" he demanded. "What will be more dangerous?" he asked. "A hungry rabble, or a hungry army?"

Ramesses looked to Paser. "We need to be sure that when the granaries are emptied this summer, new grain is coming in. This court will need to discover a fail-safe way to be sure that the Nile overflows with enough time to plant and harvest. Or if it doesn't overflow," Ramesses said slowly, "that enough water can be taken from the river to irrigate the land."

"So what will Your Highness have the people do?" Rahotep asked. "Carry water from the river back to their fields?"

"Even if a hundred people worked on every farm," Anemro objected, "it would be impossible!"

"What if we built more canals going from the river to farmers' lands?" Ramesses asked.

"There are already *hundreds* of them," Rahotep dismissed. "But when the Nile doesn't flood its banks, they don't flow. No number of men with water jars will change that."

"There *has* to be a way!" Ramesses said. There was a defeated silence in the Audience Chamber, and he looked to me. "Speak. What would you do?"

"Until a method is discovered of bringing water up from the river into the canals, I would do as Paser suggests."

"And if none is ever discovered?" Rahotep raged. I wondered how Henuttawy could bear to look into his deformed eye at night. "How many Pharaohs have endured such years of drought?"

"And how many have brought the greatest minds in Egypt together in order to search for an answer?" Ramesses gripped his father's crook in his hand.

"I am sure the farmers have searched for an answer," Anemro replied feebly. "And with all respect, Your Highness, how do we know that one will be found in two months? Because that's all that's left before it's too late to plant."

Ramesses looked to Paser. "A solution *must* be found by Mechyr. Summon General Anhuri and Asha. We will release grain from the temples of Nekheb today."

"Your Highness!" Rahotep rose in desperation. "Is this wise? If you are doing this because you are afraid that the people will blame the princess Nefertari—"

There was a gasp across the Audience Chamber. Ramesses shouted, "I am not afraid of anything!" The viziers beneath the dais grew still. "We have no other choice but to feed the people. Would you have them starve when there's perfectly good grain?"

"Why don't we ask the princess Iset?" Rahotep suggested. "You have asked for the princess Nefertari's opinion; what does the princess Iset have to say?"

Iset shifted uncomfortably on her throne. Ramesses asked her, "Is there anything you would like to add?"

She glanced at Rahotep. "In three thousand years," she repeated his argument, "no way has ever been found to bring water up from a low river."

"That is certainly true." Ramesses nodded. "But now my viziers and I have two months to find one."

"And if we don't?" Anemro asked.

"Then we will all starve!" Ramesses said angrily. "Not just the people, but the priests and generals with them!" At this, the doors of the Audience Chamber swung open, and Asha approached the dais with his father.

Ramesses stood from his throne to address General Anhuri. "We are opening the temple granaries in Nekheb," he announced. "You and Asha will inform the other generals of this, and notices will be posted on every temple door so the people know what to expect." He turned, then looked between me and Iset. "The largest granary in Nekheb belongs to the Temple of Amun and will require the greatest supervision. Would either of you like to oversee its grain distribution?" His eyes lingered on mine, and I realized what he was doing.

"Yes," I said at once.

"Out there in the dirt?" Iset recoiled. "With all of those people?"

"You are right. Stay here where it is calm," Ramesses said. "I would not want you to risk the child. Asha, take Princess Nefertari to the Temple of Amun. Paser, summon my father's architect, Penre, and every other architect in Thebes. We will not see petitioners until we find a way of flooding the canals."

ᘔ ᘔ ᘔ

IN THE city of Nekheb, I stood between Asha and his father while a swelling crowd filled the temple courtyard, shouting for food.

Behind us, three dozen soldiers with spears and shields at the ready guarded unopened bags of grain.

"Don't bring the heretic to the Temple of Amun!" one of the women shrieked. Another cried, "She'll anger the gods and bring us more hunger!"

Asha glanced at me, but I understood what needed to be done, and I observed the crowd's growing rage without flinching.

"You are brave," Asha whispered.

"I have no other choice. And until Ramesses finds a solution, I will stand here every day."

But the crowds looked at me with loathing. I was the reason for their suffering, the reason their crops had failed in the dry earth and the waters of the River Nile had not flooded their fields.

General Anhuri held up a proclamation. "Under the orders of Pharaoh Ramesses and Princess Nefertari, the granaries of Amun are to be opened to you. Every morning, when the sun begins to rise, a cup of grain will be given to every family that lives between here and the Temple of Isis. Children may not receive cups themselves unless they are orphans. Anyone found to have joined the line twice will forfeit their grain for seven days." There was a rush of questions and exclamations, and over the rising din General Anhuri shouted, "Silence! You will form a line!"

I stood with the soldiers who were passing out grain and, like a common scribe, tallied the number of cups being given. But as the morning wore on, the faces in line grew less and less hostile. By the afternoon, a woman muttered, "Amun bless you, Princess."

Asha smiled at me.

"She is only one woman," I reminded him.

"How else does it start? And that's what Ramesses wants, isn't it? To change their opinion?" Asha seated himself on a bag of grain. "I wonder how he and Penre are doing."

I had been thinking the same thing since I had left the palace, but in the Great Hall that evening, Ramesses was not at the table on the dais, and the architect was missing as well.

"So I hear you are counting grain now," Henuttawy said, as she and Woserit took their places. "From princess to peasant. I must admit, you are capable of the most astonishing transformations, Nefertari."

"I should think that your nephew knows exactly what he's doing," Rahotep remarked, "sending her to the temple to pass out grain. Associating her with food and plenty. I'm sure that's obvious to everyone here."

"Really?" Woserit asked. "It seems to me Nefertari has agreed to help in order to be kind."

Henuttawy looked across the table at Iset. "Then perhaps Iset should be displaying her kindness."

"I'm not mingling with those dirty crowds at Nekheb!"

Vizier Anemro frowned. "There are plenty of soldiers present to protect you."

"I don't care if there's an entire battalion," Iset snapped. "Let Nefertari go, and when the people riot, they can tear *her* to pieces."

Vizier Anemro stiffened at the rebuke, and Henuttawy lost her smile. "The people like to see kindness in their leaders," she warned.

"And I am almost six months pregnant!" Iset shot back, heatedly. "What if some hungry peasant attacks me and hurts the child?"

There was a dark gleam in Henuttawy's eyes. "Ramesses would never forgive himself."

Iset grew enraged. "You would happily see me dead as long as I convinced Ramesses to rebuild your temple first! It's not enough that I have to sit in the Audience Chamber day after day so that Ramesses will pick me instead of that dwarf. It's not enough that I lost Ashai. Now you would have me lose my life as well!"

I glanced at Woserit; Ashai wasn't an Egyptian name. Perhaps it was Habiru?

"Be *quiet*," Henuttawy hissed. She lunged forward, and for a moment I thought she might strike Iset. Then she remembered her place. Next to her, Vizier Anemro's eyes had grown wide. "I think you should remember where you are," Henuttawy suggested.

Iset realized what she had done, and I could see her mind race to catch up with her tongue. "Princess Nefertari wouldn't dare to speak a word against me," she blurted. "If she did, I would make sure that Ramesses knew she was trying to ruin my good name just to pave her own way to the dais."

"Vizier Anemro here isn't deaf," I said sharply.

"No, just impotent." Iset smiled. "He knows he's the least important vizier. If he were to utter the name *Ashai*, he would disappear from court the moment I give Egypt a son."

"You have great confidence it will be a son. What if it's a girl?" Woserit asked.

"Then I will have a son next! What does it matter? Ramesses will never choose Nefertari for Chief Wife. If he was going to, he would already have done it!"

"Then why is he sending her to pass out grain?" Woserit asked archly.

"He asked me as well, but I wasn't enough of a fool to say *yes!*" Iset turned her wrath on me. "Do you think the viziers don't know the *real* reason that Ramesses goes running off to your chamber? He wants someone who will inspect their work, and busy little Nefertari with her skill at languages is willing to spy over their shoulders."

"You are supposed to be supporting Ramesses as well," I hissed.

"I do," Iset said, placing her hand over her belly.

"And if *you* truly loved Ramesses, you would never ask him to make you his queen," Henuttawy added. "You are placing his crown in jeopardy."

Woserit put her arm through mine. It was unlikely that Ramesses would come that night, and we both stood up. "Vizier Anemro, Paser, I wish you a pleasant evening," she said, and we descended the stairs. At the bottom of the dais, she whispered, "So he returned to your chamber after lying with Iset. Was it truly to translate messages for him?"

"Yes," I told her as we crossed the hall. "From the kingdoms of Hatti and Assyria."

"And he also has you overseeing the grain." Woserit gave me a look as we reached the doors. "If all Ramesses wanted were your skills at translation he could hire you as a scribe," she said wryly. "There is only one reason he's sending a princess to do a soldier's work at Nakheb."

It was as though someone had tugged on the ends of a string and loosened the knot in my stomach. "So who is Ashai?"

We passed through the doors, and before Woserit could reply, Ramesses saw us emerge from the Great Hall. "Nefertari!" he called. "Where are you going?"

"She wanted to find you," Woserit answered, "to tell you about the temple."

Ramesses searched my face. "It wasn't chaos, I hope?"

"No. Asha and his father would never have allowed that."

"But the people?" he asked worriedly.

"They were happy to receive the grain. In fact, some of them even thanked me."

Ramesses exhaled, and I could see the immense relief in his eyes. "Good." He placed his hands on my shoulders. "*Good*," he repeated, and in the light of the oil lamps, the flaps of his *nemes* crown framed his face like a lion's golden mane.

"It was a wise idea to send Nefertari to Nekheb," Woserit complimented him. "But tell us what happened in the Audience Chamber
while she was gone."

Ramesses glanced warily at the door to the Great Hall, then took
my arm and led us away from the prying ears of the palace guards. In
the shadow of an alcove, Woserit and I both leaned forward.

"My father's architect, Penre, thinks he may be able to find a
solution."

Woserit frowned. "In one day?" she asked in disbelief. "After farmers have suffered for so many years—"

"But they haven't suffered. Not in Assyria. Or Babylon. Or
Amarna."

This time, it was Woserit who glanced back at the guards. "What
do you mean they didn't suffer in Amarna?"

Amarna was the city that my aunt, Queen Nefertiti, had built with
her husband. From the time of her murder it had been abandoned.
When General Horemheb made himself Pharaoh, he used the building blocks of her city as rubble for his projects all across Thebes. I
had heard people say there was nothing now left of what my aunt
and the Heretic King Akhenaten had built.

Ramesses lowered his voice. "I mean that at least one farmer in
Amarna knew how to take water from the River Nile, even when it
didn't overflow into their canals. Think of it," he said quickly. "The
Heretic King invited emissaries from every kingdom to Amarna.
The Hittites may have brought the plague, but perhaps the Assyrians brought knowledge. Paser checked the records, and in the year
of the Heretic's greatest celebration there was drought. The next
year, under Pharaoh Nefertiti, the silos belonging to the High Priest
of Meryra were bursting with grain. Perhaps the Assyrians saw the
dried-out fields and knew they could help."

"Even if they helped," Woserit said shrewdly, "there's nothing left of Amarna. The city is buried beneath the sands, and what hasn't been buried has been looted or destroyed."

"Not the tombs." Ramesses smiled widely. "When Penre was a boy, he helped his father with the tomb of Meryra in the northern cliffs of Amarna. He swears he can remember his father painting an image of a basket attached to a pole, lifting water out of the Nile. It was unlike anything he'd seen before, and his father told him that this was the device that had made Meryra the wealthiest priest in Egypt."

"Ramesses," Woserit said in a tone I had heard Merit use with me many times. "There are only two months left before it's too late to plant. To place all of your hopes in a painting this architect may or may not remember correctly—"

"Of course we will keep searching for a solution. But this is better than what we had, which was nothing!"

"And what does he plan to do?" I asked. "Return to Meryra's tomb in Amarna?"

"Yes," Ramesses said. "I have given my permission."

I covered my mouth, and Woserit stepped back.

"The tomb was never finished!" Ramesses exclaimed. "We're not disturbing his rest or offending his *akhu*. The tomb was abandoned when the Heretic Queen returned to Thebes. And if Penre can find this image—"

"If," Woserit whispered, and Ramesses turned up his palms.

"You're right. It's not certain. But there is a chance, and it's the best we have. Amarna is closer than any city in Assyria."

"And what about traders? Or Assyrian emissaries?"

"How long before they would arrive in Thebes? Two months? Three? We don't have that kind of time." Ramesses turned to me.

"No one shall know but us. If Penre returns with an image, we'll say it's something that he created. We won't reveal that it's from Amarna."

The heavy double doors of the Great Hall swung open, and Henuttawy appeared.

"He can't go alone," I said quickly. "What if something happens in those hills? You need someone else you can trust."

Ramesses nodded. "You're right. I'll send Asha with him."

꒦ ꒦ ꒦

NIGHT AFTER night Ramesses came into my chamber, regardless of whether it was his time with Iset, but instead of translating foreign petitions with me, he sat at the brazier and studied strange sketches made on papyrus. Knowing that he still wanted to come to me, even when there was nothing I could translate for him, filled my heart with such intense love I thought it would burst. *Iset is wrong*, I thought fervently. *He's not waiting for her to have a son. He's waiting for the people to accept me as his wife before declaring a queen.*

But even though I was happy, I grew afraid for Ramesses's health. In the middle of the night he would crawl from my bed, searching through sketches his architects had submitted, hoping to find something that looked promising. He'd hunch over the low flames of the brazier and wouldn't move until the sun rose in the sky and his eyes looked as red as the High Priest of Amun's.

When Penre had been gone for a month, I wrapped my arms around Ramesses's shoulders and whispered, "Let yourself rest. Without sleep, how can your thoughts be clear?"

"There's only a month before it will be too late to plant. Why didn't my father search for a solution? Or his father? Or Pharaoh Horemheb?"

I ran a soothing hand through Ramesses's hair. "Because the Nile never ran so low."

"But my father knew!"

"How could he have predicted that the Nile wouldn't overflow for *four* years? He was busy planning war in Nubia and Kadesh."

Ramesses shook his head in frustration. "If there was more time we could have sent emissaries to Assyria. We could have asked the farmers—"

I took his hand. "Come to bed. Stop for tonight."

Ramesses let himself be led away, but in bed, I knew he wasn't sleeping. He tossed beneath the linens, and I closed my eyes, willing him to be still. Then I heard three soft knocks outside our chamber. Ramesses looked across at me, and in the warm glow of the brazier, I saw his eyes widen. He rushed to the door, and Penre, the architect who had traveled to Amarna to find and unseal the tomb of Meryra, was standing with sheaves of papyrus in his hand. Behind him, Asha was dressed in a traveling cloak, his long braid arranged in a neat loop at the back of his neck. I scrambled from the bed and put on a robe to cover the thin linen sheath I was wearing.

"Asha! Penre!" Ramesses cried.

Asha stepped inside to embrace Ramesses like a brother. Penre bowed deeply at the waist. I took Asha's arm and led him to the brazier. "It's good to have you home," I said truthfully. "Ramesses hasn't slept for weeks."

Asha laughed. "Neither have we," and I noticed the dark circles under his eyes.

"Your Highness, our ship arrived in Gebtu this evening. We took a chariot the rest of the way, knowing that what we found couldn't wait."

"Everything. Tell me everything!" Ramesses exclaimed. Without his *nemes* crown, his hair fell over his shoulders like brilliant sheets of copper. He guided Penre and Asha to carved wooden chairs, then leaned forward to hear what his father's architect would say.

"It was just as I remembered," Penre revealed. "The very spot."

Ramesses glanced at Asha. "And only you went with him?"

"Of course," Asha replied. "No one else knows."

I looked into Penre's hard gray eyes and knew he would be as trustworthy as Asha. Whether the design he brought back failed or succeeded, no one would ever learn that it came from the Heretic's city and had once been used by a High Priest of Aten. I wondered what my aunt's capital looked like now. Though her name had been chiseled from the walls of Amarna when Horemheb became Pharaoh, perhaps images of her had remained beneath the earth.

"The tomb was in the northern hills," Penre began. "We placed an offering of incense at the door, and inside, this is what we found." He held out an image drawn on a papyrus. The drawing looked like the wooden toy that children play on, with a post in the middle and seats at each end. But instead of seats, the long end had a clay bucket, and the other a heavy stone.

"It's so simple . . . with a fulcrum in the middle." Ramesses passed the drawing to me, then looked at Penre in shock. "Do you think it can work?"

"Yes. With a large reed basket sealed with bitumen, it could do the work of hundreds of men. In fact . . . with a heavy enough stone, it might be able to lift five thousand *des* a day."

Ramesses inhaled sharply. "Are you certain?"

"I've been making the calculations." He shuffled the other sheaves of papyrus and gave one to Ramesses. I didn't understand what was written, but both Ramesses and Asha were nodding in agreement.

"It's unlike anything else in Egypt," Asha promised. "In the tomb . . .

dozens of images of the Heretic King." His eyes found mine, but it was Ramesses who spoke.

"And did you find—"

Asha nodded briefly. "Yes."

Ramesses stood from his chair and addressed Penre. "We will tell the court of your invention tomorrow. You will have your pick of the men for construction. If the first one built works, I will ask you to build them all along the banks of Thebes. You have done a great service to me," Ramesses complimented. "I would not have trusted anyone else."

Penre inclined his head to show that he was humbled. As Ramesses led him to the door, Asha held out a folded sheet of papyrus. "For you," he said quietly.

I glanced at Ramesses, then carefully unfolded the page. Instead of a drawing, there was a small fragment of plaster painted with an image of a woman in a chariot. Her skin was dark, and even if the artist hadn't taken the time to color her eyes, I would have known her name. I pressed my lips together to keep them from trembling.

"Ramesses wanted you to have it," Asha said tenderly. "You are the only star in his sky."

I blinked rapidly. "How did he know—"

"He didn't. But he knew there were dozens of paintings of Amarna's court. I would have brought back an image of your aunt, too, but . . ."

I nodded so he wouldn't have to say the words himself. "They were destroyed."

"But Horemheb left the images of your mother and father."

I pressed the small painting into my palm. I felt somehow that by holding it I could reach the *ka* of my parents. Of the many gifts Ramesses had given me, this was by far the most precious.

I waited until Asha and Penre were both gone before placing the painting inside my mother's *naos*. And when Ramesses asked what I was thinking, I didn't tell him with words.

꙳ ꙳ ꙳

THE NEXT day, Meryra's design was announced in the Audience Chamber. At first, there was silence. Then the court erupted into exclamations of astonishment and joy. But the village elders, who had been invited from surrounding farms for the occasion, looked at one another in confusion.

"If this device succeeds," Penre promised, "there will be harvest this year and every year thereafter!"

I leaned over to Ramesses. "Why aren't the farmers rejoicing?" I whispered.

"They are wary. They'll want to see it working first."

"Well, they should be appreciative," I said. "No Pharaoh in the history of Egypt will have changed the lives of so many people."

But in Paser's chamber later, even Woserit was cautious.

"Why doesn't everyone see what Penre has achieved?" I cried.

"Because it has to work first," Woserit said flatly. Although a large fire warmed the brazier, she was dressed in a heavy blue sheath. "There is still the matter of Iset," she said quietly. "In two months she will be the mother to Ramesses's eldest child."

I felt my throat tighten at my own failure.

"Have you taken mandrakes?" Woserit pressed.

"Of course!" I flushed. "Merit gathers them for me."

"And have you made the right offerings?"

I nodded, ashamed, because it meant that the gods were not listening. What if Tawaret, the goddess of childbirth, could not distinguish my plea among the thousands she received? Why should she? I was one of two wives, and the niece of a heretic who had abandoned the gods.

Woserit sighed. "At least the news is not all bad."

"Your performance in the Audience Chamber is still inspiring a great deal of talk in Thebes," Paser said. "I no longer have to direct foreign emissaries to see you. They ask for you now."

"It is a great honor," Woserit clarified. "No emissary ever seeks out Iset."

"They will if she becomes Chief Wife," I said, seeing into the future. "The people rarely smile at me. I could have passed out grain from now until Thoth, and it wouldn't have mattered."

Paser said firmly, "You cannot help who your family was."

"Then why am I cursed to live in their shadow?" I asked.

"Because they were giants," Woserit said, "and their shadows loom large. But you are creating another path for yourself. You are becoming a partner and adviser to Ramesses. And if you can give Egypt an heir, there will be less reason for the people to want Iset."

CHAPTER THIRTEEN

WEIGH EACH
HEART ALONE

"MY LADY!" Merit cried. "My lady, it's happening!"

I glanced at Woserit, and when Paser opened his chamber door, Merit's face was flushed. "Vizier. My lady," she acknowledged briefly, then stepped inside. "The princess Iset is having her child!"

I stood quickly, but Woserit held out her hand. "Go—dress carefully. You want him to see that while Iset is sweating like a heifer, you are young and fresh."

My heart beat faster. There was always the possibility that Iset wouldn't survive the birth. But I knew I shouldn't let Tawaret hear such thoughts. The goddess would punish unkindness and spite.

"None of us can predict when Anubis will come. Not even for Iset. But if she lives," Woserit added firmly, "don't expect Ramesses to see you at night the way he has these past months. He will follow tradition and spend ten days with her."

"With a crying infant?"

"Of course not," Merit said. "The baby will sleep with its nurse."

I returned to my chamber to put on my best sheath and most elaborate wig. But as Merit began to paint my eyes, bells rang in the courtyards of Malkata.

"Three times if it's a son," Merit whispered.

We held our breath and waited. The bells pealed three times, then there was a pause while the priestesses waited, and rang their bells three times again. I jumped from my stool and ran.

"Your cloak!" Merit cried after me. "It's cold!"

But I couldn't feel the early morning mist. How would fatherhood change Ramesses? Would he come to me less and stay in Iset's chamber more? I rushed through the polished halls toward the very birthing pavilion that had been built by my grandfather. But I stopped when I saw the crowd of courtiers huddled outside the heavy wooden doors. No one was to be allowed within.

Henuttawy saw me and smiled. "Princess Nefertari." She took in the careful beading of my sheath with a quick, calculating glance. "My sister polished you into a little queen and thought to place you next to the king as Chief Wife. But that is not going to happen now."

I met her gaze. "How would you know? No one *truly* believes that you're the mouth of Isis."

She tensed, then saw Woserit coming toward us and whispered triumphantly, "I know because Iset has just given Ramesses a son. A healthy prince of Egypt. Ramesses would be a fool not to make her queen now."

"Ah, Henuttawy!" Woserit said. "You must be happy to hear that Iset has given Ramesses a boy. After all, this child might have been the son of Ashai if not for you."

Henuttawy's red lips formed a dark, thin line, and I realized why Woserit had not mentioned the name of Ashai since Iset had first spoken it in anger. She had been waiting, gathering information. Now she turned to me, and her eyes were very bright.

"You see, Nefertari, before she married Ramesses, Iset was in love with a young Habiru named Ashai. Unfortunately, he was only an artist, and when Iset's grandmother discovered them together in her chamber, she threatened to disinherit her. But Iset didn't care. She was in love, and when my sweet sister heard of this, she saw an opportunity: a beautiful harem daughter the same age as Ramesses who had entered into a secret romance. So easy to manipulate! Knowing my sister, she probably sent someone else to scare off Ashai."

Henuttawy swore angrily, "Still shaming Hathor with your lies!"

"Maybe it was a servant, or perhaps someone more powerful, like the High Priest of Amun. Imagine," Woserit continued in her most conspiratorial voice. "You're a young Habiru artist and the High Priest arrives in his leopard robes and tells you that the woman you love is destined for the prince. Any man would have enough sense to leave her alone. So Ashai left Iset for a Habiru girl, and the path was clear to push Iset toward the dais. All my sister would ask for in exchange would be patronage for her temple. Of course, Iset still believes that Ashai simply lost interest in her. Imagine how she would feel if she knew what my sister had done!"

I didn't know where Woserit had come by her information, but she had placed it like an offering at my feet.

"Nefertari would be a fool to open her mouth. If she ever speaks such nonsense to Ramesses," Henuttawy threatened, "I would turn every priest in Thebes against her."

Woserit shrugged. "They're already against her. You don't think we know that if you had the opportunity to ruin Nefertari, you would have already done so?"

The door to the birthing pavilion swung open. A delighted Ramesses emerged, and I felt a sharp stab of disappointment knowing that Iset had been the one to make him so happy. He saw me, and Woserit whispered, "Put a *smile* on your face."

"Nefertari!" Ramesses shouted from across the courtyard, and I wondered selfishly if Iset could hear him calling my name from inside the pavilion. He was striding toward us, brushing past the courtiers' bows. "Did you hear?" he asked joyously.

"Yes." I smiled, though I'm sure it looked more like the grimace of Bes. "A son."

"And Iset is healthy! She's already asked for a harp to be moved into the pavilion. Have you ever heard of such a swift recovery?"

"No." I swallowed my pain and added, "The gods must be watching over Malkata."

This was what Ramesses wanted to hear. A breath of wind brushed the blue and gold flaps of his *nemes* crown behind his shoulders, and even in the gray of morning he appeared radiant. I had never seen him so proud, and again wished I had been the one to cause it.

"A feast must be prepared," he said. "Tell the viziers that all of Thebes should celebrate. Every worker will have the day off."

ꗞ ꗞ ꗞ

THE REED mats were lowered in Paser's chamber, while outside the priestesses continued to toll their bells.

"What have they named him?" Woserit asked grimly.

"Akori," Paser replied. "But just because it's a son doesn't mean he'll be made heir to the throne. He's simply a prince."

"The eldest prince," I reminded, "and if Ramesses doesn't choose—"

"And he's never mentioned making you Chief Wife?"

I shook my head sadly at Paser's question. "No."

"Not even at night when he goes to your chamber?" Woserit pressed.

"Never."

"So what is he waiting for?" she demanded.

"Maybe he's waiting to see if Nefertari can give him an heir."

We all looked down at my belly, and although my nipples had re-cently darkened and Merit thought that it might be a sign of a child, I looked the same as I had the month before. Then a heavy knock resounded through Paser's chamber, and my heart pounded in my chest.

"My nurse," I whispered. "She promised she'd come with any news." I rushed from my stool, and outside, Merit was wringing her hands.

"Something's happening in the birthing pavilion."

Woserit rose quickly. "How do you know?"

"Three physicians entered and haven't come out. Do you want me to go and deliver the princess fresh linens?"

"You mean spy?" I exclaimed.

"Of course, my lady! We don't know what's going on in there. What if she tempts him to make her Chief Wife?"

Then we'll want to be the first to know, I thought, but stopped myself. "But if it's not in Ramesses's heart to make me queen—"

"Forget such foolishness!" Woserit said. "We all *know* it's in his heart. But Iset will try to tempt his reason. The entire court will be there telling him that he is eighteen and that a Chief Wife must be chosen. Go," she said eagerly. "Go and find out what's happening." Woserit turned to me. "You should be in your own chamber. In case Ramesses comes looking for you. If there is something wrong with Iset, you want it to be your shoulder that he weeps on."

I sat in my chamber and waited for news from the birthing pavil-ion. When the afternoon passed and there was still no word from anyone, I motioned to a passing servant in the hall. Tefer arched his body against my leg, curious to know what was happening as well.

"Do you know what's happening in the birthing pavilion?"

The young girl lowered her reed basket to make the proper obeisance to me, but I waved it away. "Just tell me what you know."

"The princess Iset has just had a son!"

"I know that! But why have the bells stopped ringing?"

She looked at me with wide, uncomprehending eyes. "Perhaps because the priestesses grew tired?"

I sighed in frustration, then made my way out toward the Great Hall, where the court was already celebrating. In a corner with the High Priest of Amun, Henuttawy was laughing. The clink of her bangles, the way she placed her delicate hand on his knee—it was like seeing a swan trying to mate with a hyena. But there was no sign of Woserit or Paser, and Merit was not there either. Platters of duck in roasted onion had been served, and barrels of the kitchen's best wine had been opened. But the servants were watching one another nervously. I approached the cook, who saw me coming and desperately tried to make himself busy. But I caught his eye before he could take a handful of empty bowls from the table.

"What's the matter?" I asked him. "Why isn't anyone preparing for tonight?"

Nervous sweat appeared at the top of his heavy brow. "There are great preparations happening, my lady. There is meat and wine—"

"You don't have to pretend with me," I told him. "What have you heard?"

The cook cleared his throat and placed the bowls back on the table. He exchanged a glance with his two assistants, who quickly disappeared. Lowering his voice, for fear the gossip might reach Henuttawy's ears, he continued. "The prince, my lady. There is talk among the servants that the Birth Feast might not take place tonight."

I stepped forward. *"Why?"*

"Because the young prince is not as well as they thought. There is news he might—" He wouldn't go on, for fear of calling Anubis to a place where new life had just entered.

"Thank you," I told him and went back to my chamber to wait. I kneeled on my reed mat, then lit a cone of incense beneath Mut's feet. I imagined the pain of having my own child taken from me and pleaded for the *ka* of the little boy who might never feel his father's embrace. "He's too young," I beseeched Tawaret. "And Ramesses has just become a father. I know you have never heard Akori's name, but he is my husband's child and hasn't lived long enough to offend anyone in this life."

The door to my chamber opened, and Merit came in, followed by Woserit.

"I heard," I said solemnly, and stood. "A cook in the Great Hall told me."

Woserit sniffed the air and regarded me with a strange expression. "And you were praying for the princess's son?" Woserit shook her head. "Then you can save your incense," she said plainly. "The prince has already died."

"And the woman you were praying for just now," Merit added, "has accused you of stealing her child's *ka* and killing him!"

"*What?* Who did she say this to?" I cried. "When?"

"To everyone in the birthing pavilion," Woserit replied.

I thought I might faint. Merit rushed to bring me a stool, while Woserit said something about everyone in Thebes hearing Iset's accusation by nightfall.

"And Ramesses?" I breathed deeply. "What did Ramesses say?"

"I'm sure he didn't believe her," Merit vowed. "Who *would* believe her?"

"Other grieving mothers! Egyptians who already think the

Heretic's niece has powers of persuasion and magic like her aunt." I looked at Woserit. "I never even saw the prince! She can't believe I stole her child's *ka*."

"She's the superstitious granddaughter of a peasant who was plucked from the river by Horemheb. Of course she believes it."

"How will I convince the people that I haven't done this?" I whispered.

"You won't." Woserit shook her head. "The people will believe what they want to believe. But it won't matter what they say if you have a prince in your womb. Keep by Ramesses's side."

I wept into my hand. "Oh, Ramesses—he's lost his first child!"

"Which will pave the way for one of your own," Woserit said roundly.

I stared at her in horror.

🜚 🜚 🜚

I KNEW that Ramesses wouldn't come to me that night. It would have been wrong to creep away and visit my chamber with Iset still lying in the birthing pavilion, childless. When news spread across Malkata that the prince had died, festivities were quickly abandoned to pay tribute at the Temple of Amun. This time, I didn't light a cone of incense. Instead, I stood on my balcony, inhaling the bitter air and letting the wind snap at my cloak. Not even Merit dared to call me inside. *Why?* I thought. *What have I done to anger you, Amun? It was my akhu who turned from you! Not me!* The wind grew more violent, and all at once, like stars appearing in the night's sky, a stream of lights began twinkling on the road to the palace gates. At first, they were pinpricks in the distance, but as they grew closer I could recognize an unmistakable chant and understood what the blazing river signified.

"Merit!" I shouted.

She rushed onto the balcony, and I pointed fearfully into the darkness.

Thousands of torchlights wavered in front of the palace gates, and the chanting of "Heretic" grew so loud that it drowned out the wind. A pair of soldiers burst into my chamber, and Ramesses was behind them. His face was as pale as the summer's moon. One of the guards stepped forward.

"My lady, we must take you to a place of safety at once. There are crowds of people chanting at the gates." The soldier stole an uneasy glance at Ramesses. "Some believe that Princess Nefertari has had something to do—"

"With the prince's death?" I asked with dread.

Ramesses regarded me with uncertainty. "I'm sure you didn't, Nefer. You never saw the prince."

"Even if I had seen him," I cried, "do you really believe—"

"But he was such a healthy child!" There were tears in Ramesses's eyes.

Slowly, I backed away from him. "You don't really think I could . . ."

"N-no." Ramesses stumbled over his words. "No. Of course not!"

"Then why are you here?"

"Because there are thousands of people at the gates, and there are only a hundred guards on duty tonight. I have sent Asha to call up the army."

I turned to his two soldiers; gray-heads, who had probably seen battle from Assyria to Kadesh, yet there was fear in their eyes. The people of Thebes had been angry enough to cross the river in their boats by night.

"If they break through the gates," the tallest soldier explained, "we cannot assure your safety, Highness. We can take you to the treasury. There is no stronger building in the palace."

I looked out over the balcony. The chant of "Heretic" was as loud as before. I could hear the bronze gates being drummed by angry fists, and the palace guards warning the people to stand back. "No," I said firmly. "I will confront them. There is no way to stop them from believing the unbelievable except to face them myself."

"They will kill you, Highness!" one of the soldiers exclaimed.

But Ramesses looked at me with rash admiration. "I will come with you."

Merit pleaded, "My lady, no! Don't do this!" But we rushed through the halls while Merit simpered behind us. I turned and told her to wait in my chamber. Her eyes were wide with fear, and I knew that what we were doing was unwise. It was the kind of foolish thing that Pharaoh Seti had warned me against.

We hurried along the corridors, while on either side courtiers were locking themselves in their chambers for fear of what was to come. Unless the army was roused quickly, thousands of commoners could break the gates and loot the palace. When we reached the courtyard, the two soldiers who accompanied us stood back in fear, their eyes focused warily on the gates, which shook with the pounding fists of the mob. At the top of the ramparts, archers watched the angry crowd with their bows at the ready. Ramesses held on to my hand as tightly as he could without crushing it, and the sound of my heartbeat was even louder in my ears than the chanting or the wind. We approached the steps leading up the palace walls, and Ramesses's voice cut through the chaos.

"Stand back!" he shouted to his own men, who crowded the stairs leading to the ramparts. "Stand back!" As the guards recognized his *nemes* crown, they moved away.

The men watched us with incredulous eyes as we climbed. For a moment, when we reached the top of the palace walls, I thought the mountains were on fire. Instead, a sea of thousands of torches burned below us in the crisp Pharmuthi night. When the people nearest the gates recognized the crown of a Pharaoh above them, the chanting suddenly grew hesitant and seemed muted by his presence.

I marveled at Ramesses's bravery as he raised his arms and addressed the angry mob. "You have come here chanting for a heretic's blood," he cried above the storm. "But I have come here to tell you that no heretic exists!"

There were angry exclamations in the crowd, and voices rose in protest.

"I am the father of the prince who has died. No one wishes to have an heir more than me. Therefore, if I come to you saying that there was no magic involved in his death, should you not believe me?"

An unsettled murmur passed through the mob, and Ramesses continued. "This is the woman you are calling *heretic*. The princess Nefertari! Does she look to you like a woman who practices magic? Does she look like a heretic?"

"She looks like Nefertiti!" an old man shouted, and the people behind him raised their torches in approbation. There was a sudden push against the gates. Ramesses took my hand and stood firmly in his place. The chant of "Heretic" was taken up again, and Ramesses's voice grew fiercer so he could be heard above the cry.

"And who here thinks their Pharaoh would take a heretic for his wife?" he challenged. "Who here believes that the son of the Reconquerer would risk the wrath of the gods?"

This was clever, for no one would accuse Pharaoh himself of purposefully angering Amun. The angry chant died away again, and Ramesses turned to me.

"It's true!" I shouted. "I am the niece of a heretic. But if you are not responsible for your grandfather's crimes, why should I be? Who in this crowd has chosen their *akhu*? If that were possible, wouldn't we all be born into Pharaoh's family?"

There was a surprised murmur in the crowd, and Ramesses's grip on my hand relaxed.

"Weigh each heart on its own," I shouted, "for how many of us would pass into the Afterlife if Osiris weighed our hearts with those of our *akhu*?"

Ramesses looked at me in shock. There was silence beyond the gates. It seemed as if nobody moved, as if no one was breathing. "Return to your homes!" he cried. "Let the palace of Malkata mourn in peace." He stood motionless, watching as the human sea beneath his feet began to ebb.

Slowly, the crowd began to disperse. Some of the women still shouted "Heretic," and a few made vows to return, but the immediate danger was over. After some minutes of silence, Ramesses turned to take my hand. Inside the palace, he leaned against the wall and closed his eyes. "I'm sorry I ever doubted you," he whispered.

"Thank you," I told him. Yet secretly I knew better. *One day, she will convince him that I really am a heretic, and nothing I do will ever be able to change his mind.*

CHAPTER FOURTEEN

ANOTHER LIFE
IN RETURN

ALTHOUGH FOR TWO nights Ramesses did not visit, new light still found its way into the darkness of my chamber. By the second of Pachons my body gave me confirmation of what Merit had suspected for a month. I whispered it to Woserit and Paser, and when Merit heard, she sent up such a whoop of joy that Tefer scampered fearfully from the bed.

"A *child?*" she exclaimed. "You must tell Pharaoh Ramesses! When he hears—"

"He will think of Prince Akori and wonder if Iset was right."

Merit stepped away from me. "You must *never* repeat that."

"Iset accused me of stealing her child's *ka*, and now I'm pregnant with my own."

"Pharaoh could *never* think such a thing! The princess is a superstitious fool. You must tell him."

"*If* he comes."

"He will, my lady. Give him time."

But several days passed, and on the fifth night, when it was clear he wasn't coming, I wept into my pillow, emptying all of my sorrows into the linen as Merit stroked my hair. It wasn't just loneliness. It was the sadness that hung over the palace like a shroud. I saw Ramesses every morning in the Audience Chamber, but he never laughed, and even when the viziers brought news that the farmers were finding success with his invention, his face was still grim. In the Great Hall, courtiers watched me with suspicion, and even Woserit had very little to say. I begged her to let me tell Ramesses that I was pregnant, but she made me swear not to reveal anything to him until he visited me on his own.

So I waited, and on the seventh of Pachons, Ramesses arrived as the sun rose. He came to the very edge of my bed, and when I sat up to embrace him, tears stained his cheeks. It was as if all of his joy and rash optimism in life had been drained away.

"The priests tell me it was the will of the gods," he whispered, "but how could it be their will that a child of Pharaoh, his first son, should be stolen by Anubis?"

He held his *nemes* crown in his lap, and I caressed his hair. "I can't pretend to understand," I told him. "But perhaps when the gods saw your terrible loss, they gave you another life in return." I took his hand and placed it on my stomach, and his breath caught in his throat. "A *child?*"

I smiled cautiously. "Yes."

Ramesses stood and crushed my hands in his. "Amun has not abandoned us!" he cried. "A child, Nefer!" and he kept repeating it. "Another child!" He pulled me up with him, then searched my face. "You know that night on the balcony—"

"It doesn't matter," I said quickly.

"But I never really believed—"

I placed my finger on his lips. "I know you didn't," I lied. "Those are peasants' superstitions."

"Yes. She comes from superstitious people. And without Akori she's become irrational. And inconsolable," he admitted. "I promised to begin a mortuary temple in Thebes for the prince—for all of us—but it isn't enough. Even the flowers at the gates mean nothing to her."

"What . . . what flowers?"

Ramesses glanced away. But when I pushed back the long linen curtains of the balcony and saw the tribute that women had left for Iset, I brought my hand to my mouth. The heavy bronze bars were twined with flowers, and lilies, the symbol of rebirth, stretched as far as the eye could see beyond the gates. "They love her so much," I whispered, hoping Ramesses wouldn't see how much it hurt me.

"And they will love you," Ramesses swore. "You are to be mother to Pharaoh's eldest child now." Ramesses strode to the door that led to Merit's chamber, calling her out and instructing her to let the palace know that a second child was on its way.

There were to be no petitioners in the Audience Chamber that day. The viziers watched from a large table in front of the dais as Ramesses and I entered together, and only Paser looked happy to see me. Everyone now knew that I was with child. I saw Iset on her throne, and I thought, *Henuttawy has instructed her to be here today.* Her face appeared sunken and hollow; as we ascended the steps her eyes never moved from an invisible spot on the floor.

"Iset." Ramesses gently took her hands. "Why are you here? Did you get enough rest?"

"How can I rest," she asked tonelessly, "when someone has stolen the lifeblood of our prince? The midwives say that he was healthy and screaming when he came."

Ramesses glanced at me. "There was every protection in the birthing pavilion. Tawaret and Bes—"

"And do Tawaret or Bes prevent the evil eye?" she cried, so that even the old men in the back of the Audience Chamber looked up from their Senet games. "Can they stop a charm from stealing a prince's *ka*? There is only one woman who would want to take our child!"

Rahotep rushed forward from the viziers' table. "The princess Iset is not well," the High Priest said quickly. "Let me take her to her chamber."

"I'm perfectly fine!" Iset shrieked. "I'm *fine!*" But the front of her gown where Akori should have been nursing was wet, and her eyes darted wildly across the chamber.

Ramesses placed a steady hand on her arm. "Iset, go and rest. Penre is coming with designs for a temple. As soon as we are finished, I will come to you." But her chest rose and fell with her heavy breaths, and she didn't move. "Even though it's your time with Nefertari?" she challenged.

I heard the hesitation in Ramesses's voice before he answered, "Yes."

Iset shifted her gaze to mine, and I saw fear in her eyes. *She truly believes I stole her child's* ka. *She thinks I'm a murderess.* She composed herself, moving gracefully across the chamber, and as she reached the doors I heard a courtier murmur, "It's only her first child. There are sure to be others."

When the doors swung shut, the viziers watched me, and courtiers whispered.

I tried to keep my voice from trembling. "Shall we summon Penre?"

We waited in silence while he was sent for, a silence unbroken until the herald announced grandly, "The architect Penre, son of Irsu and Keeper of the King's Great Works."

A triumphant Penre entered the chamber, beaming conspicuously. In a single month, his design, based on the painting in Meryra's tomb, had spread up and down the Nile. By the end of Shemu, there would be the first real harvest in four years, and offerings of grain could be placed in the completed Temple of Luxor. Now, Penre would undertake the construction of the greatest mortuary temple in Egypt. Two scribes followed in his wake, carrying a heavy clay model on a large board between them. A linen cloth obscured the details of the model. Penre stretched his arms out in obeisance.

"Your Majesty," he announced. "The Ramesseum." He swept the linen cover away, and a row of viziers murmured their appreciation. "It will be the largest mortuary temple in Thebes," Penre explained, "built next to the Temple of Seti the Reconquerer." He pointed out the intricate details. "Two rows of pylons, towering as large and thick as the pylons at Luxor, will lead one after the other into a courtyard." Chairs scraped on tiles as the court pressed forward to get a better look. "Beyond the second courtyard, a covered hall with forty-eight columns will enclose the inner sanctuary." Another murmur of awe from the viziers' table. "And inside . . ." Penre removed the ceiling, showing the court the blue sky with scattered gold stars that he had painted. "Inside, three rooms that will stand for a million years as a shrine to Ramesses the Great and his reign."

There was a moment of shock in the Audience Chamber. No one dared to give Pharaoh a title; he always chose it for himself. The court looked to Ramesses, to see his reaction.

"Ramesses the Great," he repeated, "and his million-year Ramesseum."

Penre squared his shoulders with confidence. "And to the north of the hall with its forty-eight columns, a temple for the most beautiful princesses in Egypt."

I saw statues of myself and Iset, both equal in height and width. I should have been flattered, but I was worried. The mortuary temple was an undertaking that would require years, and a great deal of the treasury's gold. Before Ramesses went to Iset's chamber that night, he came to mine and I asked him, "Where will the deben come from to build all of this?"

"My father accepts tribute from more than a dozen nations. I've seen the accounts from the treasury. There's enough to build three Ramesseums," he said. "It is what our descendants will remember of us." He looked at my stomach and drew me close to him. "Our little kings," he added lovingly.

CHAPTER FIFTEEN

AHMOSES OF CHALDEA

FOR TWO MONTHS, the gates of Malkata Palace were strewn with flowers, so that whenever we rode out to see the progress of the Ramesseum, the guards had to clear a path for the horses. Iset would descend from her chariot, and no one would speak as she chose the prettiest flower for her hair, reminding everyone that she had borne and lost the first prince of Egypt.

In Paser's chamber, Woserit paced the tiles and demanded, "When will this be over? Every day flowers are burying the gates and women are weeping in the Temple of Hathor. She lost an infant, not twin eighteen-year-old princes!"

"And now there's news that she's with child again," I revealed. "Merit heard it in the baths."

Woserit turned to Paser, "Before Iset has another child," she said irritably, "we must make the people understand that Nefertari is Ramesses's choice for queen. What's wrong with them? She speaks eight languages and has impressed every emissary from Assyria to Rhodes."

"They still remember the Heretic King," Paser replied. "They hear their grandparents speak of the days when the gods were banished and Amun turned his back on Egypt by bringing us plague. But I have intercepted messages from Nubia that speak of a second rebellion. And if Pharaoh Ramesses leaves with his army, Nefertari will be left to rule in his stead."

"It will be your opportunity to show the people how you would govern," Woserit said eagerly.

"*No!*"

Paser and Woserit both stared at me.

"Ramesses promised to take me on his next campaign. Who will be of more help to him?" I demanded. "A Nubian translator or *me?*"

"You are carrying Ramesses's child," Woserit said. "Are you willing to risk his likely heir? There would be no litters. You would travel through the desert entirely by chariot, and water would be scarce. This rebellion may be your only chance to prove at court that you will not be another Heretic Queen."

I looked down at the small swell of my stomach. If Ramesses left me in Thebes, would I be able to change the people's hearts, or would they call my child a heretic as well?

Paser sat forward in his carved wooden chair. "Do not suggest that you go with him. There's nothing more important than the health of this child."

"And Iset?" I asked quietly. "If Ramesses doesn't declare a Chief Wife, would we both rule jointly in the Audience Chamber?"

Woserit raised her sharp brows. "Yes. Which would be very interesting."

𝌆 𝌆 𝌆

THAT NIGHT, Ramesses crept away from Iset, bringing me the scrolls that Paser had seized from a captured Nubian merchant. We sat together on the balcony, and I translated letter after careless letter detailing a rebellion that was planned for the first of Mesore, when the heat was so brutal that Egypt's soldiers were unlikely to travel very far south.

"They have more than a thousand men," I confirmed, "who are willing to overtake the palace and kill the Egyptian viceroy."

"So Paser was correct." Ramesses stood from his chair and looked out over the balcony. An early summer's breeze bore the scent of lavender, and the chirp of insects from the dark gardens below. If Ramesses left, there was no telling when he might return, or what might happen in his absence.

"I must write to my father and speak with my generals," he announced. "In a month, I will lead Egypt's charioteers into Napata and remind Nubia to whom she owes her allegiance." When he saw the look on my face, his voice faltered. "You could come." He hesitated, and we both looked down at my three-month belly.

"No. It would be too dangerous," I said, rising to join him. But we both knew what I wanted. Ramesses took my hand and we stared into the night, listening to the wind as it eased through the boughs of the sycamore trees.

"I will return to you safely," he promised. "And if I ever leave again, you will come. Even if it's to the farthest reaches of Assyria."

I laughed miserably. "And how would I survive?"

"I would have the army carry you by litter. They would bear you across the desert like Amun's shrine." When my laughter was genuine, he smiled. "While I'm gone, I want you to oversee the building. Luxor is finished, but there is Nubian gold and shiploads of ebony bound for the Ramesseum. There's no one else I trust."

"What about Iset?"

"She can't oversee the Ramesseum," he dismissed. "Perhaps the Feast of Wag. But in the Audience Chamber, if there's something she doesn't understand, Nefer, you will help her, won't you? I don't want foreign emissaries to think she's a fool."

Too late, I thought sharply, holding my smile. "Of course I will."

🛗 🛗 🛗

IN THE hours before dawn, a flotilla of ships crowded the bay, while Asha ushered the charioteers aboard. A month had passed since Ramesses had learned of the plot for rebellion in Nubia, and now two thousand men, with their weapons and horses, shouted farewells from the vessels to their wives and children. On the quay, Ramesses cupped my chin in his palm

"Sometimes, I forget how small you are," he said tenderly. "Promise that you'll let Merit take care of you. Listen to what she tells you while I'm gone, even if you don't like it. There are two of you now to watch over."

I looked down at my small stomach and wondered if Tawaret would abandon me in childbirth the way she had abandoned my mother. Perhaps if I lit incense every day and reminded her that I was the Heretic's *niece,* not the Heretic's daughter, she would forgive the crimes of my *akhu.* Or would my prayers only attract their attention, and bring Anubis back to stalk the palace once more? "I will listen," I assured him.

The sound of trumpets pierced the morning air, and the priestesses of Hathor joined with Isis in shaking their sistrums and singing a hymn to Sekhmet, the lion-goddess of war.

Ramesses made his way to Iset and kissed her briefly, then he came back to me. "I will return before the month is over," he swore.

We watched the fleet as it worked its way through the channel, and then slowly upstream. When the last pennant had disappeared, Woserit took my arm and led me through the doors of the palace. In the Audience Chamber, the court took its place while musicians played "The Song of Sekhmet." I had thought I was prepared for Ramesses to leave, but at the sight of his empty throne on the dais, I drew an uneven breath.

"This is an opportunity," Woserit said bracingly as we crossed the chamber.

"What if the people return?" I worried. "What if they shout *Heretic* at the gates?"

"Then four hundred guards will be here to protect you. The greater threat is in the Temple of Isis. Think of what my sister could do if her temple became the largest in Thebes! Pilgrims from all across Egypt would leave their gold at her shrines. If Henuttawy and Rahotep were to use their resources collectively, they would be wealthy enough to tell Ramesses which wars should be waged and which monuments should be built. Why do you think the Heretic abolished the priestship of Amun? He was willing to risk the wrath of the gods to destroy such rivals to his power."

"Why doesn't Ramesses see what Henuttawy is after?"

"Why should he? My sister is his beloved aunt. The one who taught him how to balance the *khepresh* crown on his head and to write his name in hieroglyphics as a child. Would he believe me if I told him what she really wants?"

With that, she left the Audience Chamber, her long blue robes swishing across the tiled floor. The turquoise jewels of the goddess Hathor encircled her arms, and I wished I looked so tall and splendid. Like Henuttawy and Iset, she commanded the chamber, but as the heavy doors swung shut in her wake, I noticed that the room was nearly empty. "Where is everyone?" I exclaimed.

Rahotep turned in his chair. "Who is *everyone?*"

My neck grew hot beneath my wig. "Where is Iset? Where is the rest of the court?"

"Preparing for the Feast of Wag," he said dismissively.

"Doesn't she plan to hear the petitioners?" I demanded.

Rahotep raised his brow. "I suppose she will come when she is ready."

The musicians kept playing. They would play until the herald announced the petitioners. I sat on my throne and felt the heat creep from my neck into my cheeks. The entire court was attending Iset; the only courtiers who had remained with me were the old men playing Senet in the back of the chamber. Gone was the pretty laughter of noblemen's daughters. Even the girls from the edduba, who had never liked Iset, were missing. *They all believe she is the future of Egypt.*

I struck Ramesses's golden crook on the dais. "Bring forth the petitioners," I announced.

Three men approached the viziers' table, but only two held out written petitions. The third gripped a wooden staff in his hands. His long beard was the milky color of moringa blossoms. I tried to guess what his language might be, as only foreigners wear hair on their faces.

"Where is your petition?" Paser demanded.

The bearded man shook his head. "It is for the princess Nefertari alone."

"And while the princess may eventually read your petition, it will go through me first." Paser held out his hand, but the old man was firm.

"It is for the princess Nefertari alone," he repeated.

Paser exhaled impatiently. "Send this man away!"

But when several guards stepped forward, the old man shouted, "Wait! *Wait!* My name is Ahmoses."

"That means nothing to me," Paser remarked sharply.

"Ahmoses of the kingdom of *Chaldea.*"

Paser held up his hand, and the guards backed away. "There is no such kingdom," he challenged. "It was conquered by the Babylonian King Hammurabi, and then the Hittites."

The bearded man nodded. "When the Hittites came, my people fled to Canaan. And when Egypt conquered Canaan, my mother was taken as a prisoner to Thebes."

Even across the chamber, I could hear Paser's breath catch. "Then you are a Habiru?"

Rahotep trained his red eye on the old man, and the courtiers at their Senet tables stopped what they were doing. The Habiru were heretics, dangerous men who dwelled in desert tents, not cities. But Ahmoses of Chaldea nodded. "Yes. I am a Habiru," he replied, "and my petition is for the princess Nefertari."

He needs help with some runaway daughter, I thought, *and he is too embarrassed to tell the truth.* "Bring him to me," I called across the chamber.

"My lady, this man is a *Habiru*," Paser warned.

"And if he has a petition, I will see him," I announced. I knew the fact that I was willing to listen to a heretic's plea would scandalize the few members of court who were present. But *I* was the one who was pregnant with Ramesses's eldest child now. *I* was the one he'd wanted to bring to Nubia. And what if someone had denied my mother in her time of need because they'd thought *she* was a heretic?

Ahmoses reached a mottled hand into his robes, and produced a scroll. The guards retreated to their positions near the doors, but watched the old man with deep suspicion. As the Habiru moved slowly across the chamber, I saw that the carved staff he held close was not just a means of protection, but an aid to help him walk. Rahotep turned fully in his chair to stare across the chamber at me, and I wondered if I had made a grave mistake.

The old man stopped before the dais, but unlike every other peti-

tioner, he did not extend his arms in obeisance. My back straightened against my throne. "Tell me," I demanded. "Why am I the only
one who can read your petition?"

"Because it was your grandfather who brought my people into
Egypt," he replied in Canaanite, "and forced them to become soldiers in his army."

I glanced at the viziers to see if any of them had understood.
"How did you know I speak the language of Canaan?"

"All of Thebes knows of your skill at languages, my lady." We
watched each other in silence for a moment, then he held out his petition. "For the princess Nefertari, daughter of Queen Mutnodjmet
and General Nakhtmin." The harpists strummed softly while the old
men in the back of the chamber returned to their games, laughing
when somebody threw the knucklebones to their advantage. I un-
rolled the Habiru's scroll and felt the blood drain slowly from my
face. I glanced up to see if Rahotep was watching and saw his red eye
focused on me still.

"You want *what?*" I whispered under the babble of petitioners.

"I want Pharaoh to release the Habiru from his service," he
replied, "so that my people may return to the land of Canaan."

"And in what way are they yours and not Pharaoh's?" I demanded.

"Because I am their leader. Among the Habiru of Thebes, I am the
one who brings them closer to their god."

"So you *are* heretics."

"If that means we do not worship as the Egyptians do."

"It means you do not worship Amun," I said harshly, and I looked
over the top of the scroll at the rest of the court. But new petitioners
were distracting Rahotep and Paser.

"We worship a single god," he explained, "and we wish to return
to the land of Canaan."

"Canaan is *Egyptian* land," I said, raising my voice only loud enough to show the old man my displeasure. "Why would the Habiru want to leave Thebes for an unsettled land that Egypt's already conquered?"

Ahmoses regarded me with piercing eyes. I wondered if Paser had found them as unsettling as I did. "Because you know what it is to be treated like a heretic and threatened in the streets. This is why only you can grant this petition. In Canaan there are no Egyptian temples, and we may worship as we wish."

I realized in that instant that I would never escape my *akhu*. I looked down at the scroll and felt a sudden rage at the old man. "Did Henuttawy send you to remind me that my *akhu* were heretics?" I demanded.

"Your *akhu* were not heretics," Ahmoses replied. "They were shown a vision of the truth and they corrupted it by greed."

"*What* vision of the truth?" I challenged.

"The truth of one god. Pharaoh Akhenaten called him Aten—"

"And you believe in Aten?"

"The Habiru worship by a different name. It was only Pharaoh who called him Aten, and covetousness led to his ruin."

"*Heresy* led to his ruin," I said scathingly. But Ahmoses would not be dissuaded by my anger. His eyes were like the still waters of a lake on a windless afternoon, and there was nothing I said that disturbed them. "You said he was shown a vision of the truth," I said. There was no reason for me to be entertaining his petition further, but his certainty disturbed me. "So who showed him that vision?"

Ahmoses bowed his head. "I did," he said quietly. "I was Pharaoh Akhenaten's tutor when he was a young boy in the city of Memphis."

If Ahmoses had said that he had been an acrobat in his earlier life, I would have been less shocked. Here was the man who had planted the seeds of my family's ruin, asking me to do him a favor! Without him, the Heretic King would never have happened on the idea of a single god, or convinced Nefertiti to join him in ridding Egypt of

Amun. She would never have been murdered by the priests of Aten, who grew angry when she wished to return to the old gods . . . And if my father's life hadn't been taken in those flames, who knew what might have happened at my birth? Perhaps my mother's will to live might have been stronger. I looked down at him. "You *ruined* my family," I whispered harshly.

The old man clearly understood the impact of his words. "The truth that there is one god can be used for healing or for harm. It was your *akhu* who chose harm, starving the land of Egypt to feed their own glory."

"It was Akhenaten who betrayed Egypt, not my mother! Not my father!" The Audience Chamber had ceased to exist for me. While the business of the day carried on, it was as if only Ahmoses and I existed in that room. "Why are you telling me this?" I hissed, and it was a struggle to control my voice. "You could have come with your petition without telling me anything."

"But I wish to tell you who I am. More important, I wish to tell you who I am not. I am not a worshipper of gold, like the Pharaoh Akhenaten." When I flinched at my uncle's name spoken aloud, Ahmoses raised his brows. "He was sent to me in Memphis when all of Egypt believed it was his brother who would take the crown. He was a second son, a younger prince sent away to become a priest. A bitter child. Angry and resentful of his older brother's fortune. I thought the god of the Habiru could save him," he admitted.

"And now you would have me dismiss every Habiru from Pharaoh's service?"

Ahmoses met my gaze, and he was firm. "From the tombs, from the temples, from this palace where women work as body servants . . ."

"They are already free to go!"

"And the Habiru in Pharaoh's army?" Ahmoses challenged. "Every able-bodied man who was captured in Canaan was made to fight for

Egypt, and under Pharaoh Akhenaten when the army was used to build cities in the desert, the Habiru toiled like beasts. He promised our people freedom once the city of Amarna was built, but three kings have since taken the throne of Egypt. The Habiru soldiers have still not been given permission to leave Pharaoh's army."

"They are paid like every other soldier."

"But unlike every other soldier the Habiru cannot leave until they are too old to carry a weapon. If that is not slavery, then what are we?"

"You are Egyptians," I said hotly.

Ahmoses shook his head firmly. "No. We are Habiru and we want our freedom."

I sat back and regarded Ahmoses in shock. "My reputation is in danger simply by speaking with you. *You*, who brought a curse onto all of my *akhu*. The people already believe I am a heretic like my aunt!"

"Because there are men in this room who would have them believe that." Ahmoses's eyes traveled to the High Priest Rahotep.

"No." But even as I said the word I understood he was speaking the truth. I had always thought Henuttawy had bribed the market vendors to chant against me on the day of my marriage. But the anger in the streets had been too real. Those women with eyes as hard as onyx had not been paid; someone with words more persuasive than deben had spoken to them, someone with more power over their souls than even Henuttawy. I had been a fool not to see it before.

Ahmoses used his staff to lean across the dais. "I have seen him in the streets," he said quietly, casting a glance behind him. But Rahotep was still berating his petitioner. "He was rousing the men to rebellion even before your marriage. The people revere him as the mouth of Amun. But you can convince them of his lies by setting the

Habiru free. By telling the people that you are expelling the remaining heretics from Egypt. You wish to appear as a follower of Amun, and I wish to return my people to Canaan. So banish the heretical Habiru from Thebes and we both may profit."

For a moment, I thought of nothing but myself, imagining how the people would react to the final banishment of all heretics from Egypt. They would cheer me in the streets, shaking sistrums as I walked. Ramesses's face would fill with pride as he declared me queen. Then I thought of my husband's army, and how a sixth of the men were Habiru. "You and I may profit," I told him, "but how will Pharaoh profit? To our north the Hittites are waiting, to the east the Assyrians threaten to invade. You think I am willing to win my reputation at the expense of my husband?" I leaned forward on my throne. "Then you have petitioned the wrong wife."

Only then did Ahmoses's eyes blaze. "You know what persecution is! You know what it's like to be called a heretic. Imagine how the Habiru feel, worshipping for a hundred years in private, wondering if we'll be slaughtered like the followers of Aten for what we believe! All we ask for is the freedom to move from Thebes to Egypt's lands in the north—"

"And I cannot grant that without Pharaoh's consent," I said just as hotly.

"Then when he returns victorious from Nubia, I will come back with my petition." His eyes traveled to my thickening waist. "The Habiru's wishes are the same as yours. All we desire is a future for our children."

He turned away, but his words lingered with me like an upsetting dream.

⚏ ⚏ ⚏

I FOUND Merit in my chamber, folding my linens neatly into piles and placing them in chests. She looked up in surprise when she heard me arrive.

"Merit," I said sternly. She knew from the sound of my voice that something was wrong. I shut the door behind me, checking to see that it was locked, then advanced across the chamber. "Merit," I repeated, "what do you know about the High Priest Rahotep?"

She stood, searching my face to measure the strength of my demand.

"You knew him when Nefertiti was Pharaoh. You said he was against my being raised in this palace and that you convinced him to keep me here. But I spoke to a man in the Audience Chamber today. A Habiru who says he was Akhenaten's tutor."

Some of the color drained from Merit's face.

"He said the High Priest has been turning the people against me. Not Iset. Not Henuttawy. *Rahotep!* So how did you convince him to keep me here? He hates my *akhu*. He hates *me*." My voice rose. "What do you know about him, Merit? He wouldn't have allowed Horemheb to keep me at court unless you knew something. What is it?" I demanded.

Merit crossed to a chair next to the brazier. She sat, took a small fan from the nearest table, and began to cool herself vigorously. "My lady—"

"I want to know!" I shouted, and perhaps the anger in my voice broke the spell of silence she had kept for so many years.

"He was the High Priest of Aten," she whispered. "When your aunt saw that she must either return the gods to Egypt or face rebellion, she began to rebuild the temples of Amun. The priests of Aten were stripped of their power."

"Including Rahotep?"

"Especially him. He lost everything to her."

"The priests of Aten were given the chance to join the priesthood of Amun," I challenged. "He could have saved his position."

"Perhaps he didn't believe we would return so eagerly to our true gods. But he lived embittered and in poverty for many years. Your *akhu* were not interested in helping him. He reminded your grandfather of heresy and ruin."

"Do you think it was he who set the fire?" I asked. "Is *that* what you know?"

Merit looked down at the fan in her lap, and the strength to keep hidden what she had concealed for so long seeped out of her like water from a cracked bowl. "It may have been him. I would not be surprised. He is the Aten priest who helped to kill Pharaoh Nefertiti and her daughter." She raised her eyes. "Before their murders, I saw him enter the passageway leading to the Window of Appearances."

"Where she was killed?" I whispered.

"Yes. He was with another priest. I thought she had summoned them. She was always feeling sorry for the priests . . ."

"*Nefertiti?*"

Merit nodded sadly. "She was not always cruel. I know this is what they taught you in the edduba, but there were many times when she was kind."

"Were you there when they killed her?"

"I wasn't far away," Merit admitted. "I heard her screams and saw the priests walking calmly through the hall. Rahotep looked at me, and his hand was covering one eye."

"Because she fought back!"

"Yes, but I didn't know it then."

"So you didn't say anything?"

"Of course I did! I told your father! He searched for both of them, but they had disappeared. There are many places to hide in Egypt. When your mother died, Rahotep returned to court searching for a new position."

"Giving up his belief in Aten?" I was shocked.

"He is a believer in gold." Merit snorted. "And, of course, I recognized him. I would have turned him over to the army for murder, but when the viziers wanted to send you from this court, I warned Rahotep that if he spoke against you as well, all of Egypt would know how he came by that eye. So when Pharaoh Horemheb asked for his advice, he swore that you were of no harm to anyone. This bargain is why you remained here."

I studied Merit's face and marveled that she had kept such a heavy secret to herself for so long. For more than twenty years she had kept the memory inside. "Why did you never tell me this?" I asked quietly.

"What would be the purpose?"

"I would know my enemies!"

"*I* know your enemies, my lady, and that is enough. There's no reason to let the corruption of the court make you as old as I am."

I realized she was not talking about the wrinkles on her face. She meant a different kind of old, the kind that had made Iset bitter because she had lost Ashai and learned that love is not easy. She was speaking about an aging of the soul, when a person's *ka* is a thousand years older than her body. "Does Woserit know all of this?" I asked softly.

"Yes. Otherwise, if something happened to me," she explained, "these secrets would be buried. And in a tomb, there's nothing I could do to protect you, my lady."

"Then if Woserit knows, Paser must know as well."

"You are safe from Rahotep," she promised. "He will not speak openly against you in the temple, and I will not tell Egypt that he is the murderer of a Pharaoh."

"And probably two!" I cried, but Merit sat back in her chair.

"We don't know that."

"If he could murder Nefertiti," I said heatedly, "then he could have started the fire that killed my family. Why shouldn't I tell Ramesses what he's done? What power does he have?"

Merit laughed, sharp and full of warning. "The kind of power you have not yet seen because he's never used it against you. Thanks to his friend Horemheb, he is the mouth of Amun. The people trust him the way they trust Pharaoh."

"Not if he is a *murderer*."

"And would the people believe that? Or would they believe him when he says that the niece of heretics is spreading lies?"

"I don't know."

"Neither does he. So we are silent, and he is silent, and the arrangement holds."

"No, it doesn't! He is still turning the people of Thebes against me."

"And you are winning them back with every petitioner and foreign emissary."

I remained standing, looking down at Merit, and something occurred to me. "When Henuttawy lets him into her bed at night, she thinks she is convincing him to stand against me. But he already is!"

"Snakes can deceive snakes. But they also slither into unexpected places," she warned.

🜂 🜂 🜂

IN THE Great Hall that evening, Iset arranged Nubian dancers for the court's entertainment. Beneath papyrus bud columns twined with blossoms, perfumed women fluttered between tables, laughing behind their heavy golden cups as the generals told stories of their adventures abroad. Sermet beer flowed from open barrels, and bowls were filled with roasted goose in rich pomegranate paste and wine.

"While Ramesses is marching toward rebellion," I seethed under my breath to Woserit, "they are drinking and dancing!"

On the dais, Henuttawy raised a cup of wine. "To Iset," she announced cheerfully. "And to her second child who will one day rule Thebes!" The table raised their cups to Iset, and the few women who hadn't heard the pregnancy rumors now squealed in delight. When I refused to raise my cup, Henuttawy asked, "What's the matter, Nefertari? Not enjoying the feast?"

The viziers looked at me, studying my carefully hennaed breasts and the wide silver belt around my waist. Merit had taken extra care with my kohl, extending the line out to my temples and shading my eyelids with malachite. But all of the paint in Egypt could not cover my disgust.

"Does she look as if she's enjoying the feast?" Rahotep asked. "Everyone at court abandoned her today to be with Iset."

Henuttawy gave an exaggerated gasp. "*Everyone?*" she repeated. "I'm sure it wasn't everyone."

"You're right," Rahotep corrected himself. "There were a few courtiers who wished to play Senet." The emissaries around the table laughed. "But the princess wasn't idle," he revealed. "While Iset was preparing for the Feast of Wag, Nefertiti was listening to a petition from the greatest heretic in Thebes. He asked for her by name."

There was a shocked murmur around the table, and Woserit darted a questioning look at me. But Henuttawy clapped her hands with delight. "Well, you know what they say. Ravens will flock with ravens."

"And scorpions will nest with scorpions," I replied, looking between her and the High Priest of Amun. I stood from my throne, and Woserit stood with me.

"Leaving so early?" Henuttawy called, but Woserit and I ignored her taunt.

Outside the Great Hall, Woserit turned to me. "What happened in the Audience Chamber?" she demanded. But the doors of the Great Hall swung open, and Paser joined us in the courtyard. Woserit hissed at him, "You allowed *a heretic* to see Nefertari?"

I rested my hand on the swell of my stomach and tried to fight back a sudden nausea. "He wouldn't give his petition to anyone else," I explained. "His name was Ahmoses; he was a Habiru."

"But tell her what he wanted." Paser's look was riotous.

I realized he had heard more than I'd thought in the Audience Chamber. "For me to free the Habiru from the military."

"*Every* Habiru?" Woserit exclaimed.

"Yes. He calls himself the leader of his people. He wishes to take the Habiru back to Canaan where they may worship as they please."

"Canaan is still Egyptian land," Woserit said angrily.

Paser shook his head. "Only in name. There are no temples to Amun or shrines to Isis. He clearly thinks that the Habiru would be free to worship whom they wish in the land of Sargon."

I recalled the ancient myth Paser had taught us in the edduba, about the high priestess in the east who secretly gave birth to a son despite her vow of chastity. She had placed her newborn infant in a basket made tight with reeds and set it adrift in the River Euphrates where the child was found by Aqqi, the water bearer. The boy was given the name of Sargon, and he grew up to be a powerful king, conquering the lands of Gutium and Canaan. And now, Ahmoses wished to return to the land that Sargon had made fruitful.

Woserit exchanged a look with Paser. "Why did he request to see Nefertari, and not Iset?" she asked suspiciously.

"Because Princess Nefertari has a reason to grant his request,"

Paser guessed. "He knows that she could win favor with the people by telling them she is expelling the heretics from Thebes."

Woserit looked at me. "It *could* turn the people in your favor. There would never again be any question of your faith in Amun."

"You can't seriously consider it!" I exclaimed.

"A *sixth* of Egypt's army is Habiru," Paser warned. "Someday, the Hittites—"

But the seed had been planted in Woserit's mind. "She could finally win over the people, Paser . . ."

"I'll win them some other way," I said. "Ramesses can't risk Egypt's safety for me."

"He could increase the army's pay," she protested. "More men would join."

"With what gold?" Paser asked wryly.

"He could increase taxes on the land."

"And have the people resent *him* instead? Think of what you are saying," Paser said. He placed a tender hand on her shoulder. "There are other ways for her to win the people's love."

"And Rahotep?" she asked. "Did he hear all of this?"

"No. He was listening to petitioners. But Merit has told me what he did," I said darkly.

Woserit sighed heavily. "I know it was a terrible thing to learn. Especially the fire—"

"You knew he set the fire?" I cried.

"No one knows for certain," Paser said quietly.

"But everyone believes it?"

Neither Paser nor Woserit denied it.

"You must never speak a word of this to anyone," Woserit cautioned. "No matter how your heart bleeds, let only the gods hear its cries. Do not weep on anyone's shoulder. Not even Ramesses's."

I pressed my lips together, and Paser added emphatically, *"Especially* not Ramesses."

"The truth does not stay buried forever," Woserit promised. "Eventually the winds blow away the sand and expose what's beneath. But don't think of this now," she advised. "The most important thing is the child. You don't want him to feed off bitterness and anger. Have Merit send for food and heat you a bath."

I nodded my consent, but how could I stop myself from being angry? I watched Woserit and Paser leave, then listened to them as they whispered in the dark corridors of the palace, their silhouettes bent together like two sycamore trees, and I felt a deep longing to speak with Ramesses. If he had been in Thebes, we would be lying in my bed, talking about the Habiru Ahmoses, and I would have told him the painful story of how my uncle had come upon the idea of a single god. But out there in the darkness to the south, Ramesses was traveling on toward Nubia.

Instead of returning to Merit, I kept walking through the halls. The palace was silent. Every servant who wasn't in the Great Hall with Iset had gone to bed, and I made my way through the corridors to a door that no one ever opened. Once, that door had been guarded by four men in polished breastplates, and my family had used it to reach the royal courtyard. But that courtyard and all of its chambers had burned. I had not seen the charred remains since Merit had taken me as a little girl. There had been nothing to see then except weeds and ashes, but now I wanted to see with a woman's eyes the destruction that Rahotep had brought on my family.

I stepped through the door, and in the moonlight the scene looked like a shipwreck that had been washed onto a black and desolate shore. Charred timbers lay where they had fallen, surrounded by rocks and thickly growing vines. I moved through the courtyard, swatting at an insect that had made the devastation its home. I could see where a bed would have stood once, although all that was left was part of its frame. It might have been the one my mother shared with my father, but of course, there was no way of knowing. Smudged tiles supported its blackened legs, and I used the edge of my sandal to scrape away a few layers of dirt, uncovering more burnt tiles. No one had thought to take them away. The damage was so complete that Horemheb had left the chambers for nature to reclaim.

I picked up one of the broken tiles and smoothed away the ash with my palm. Although Merit would be furious, I used the sleeve of my robe to reveal the image, then held up the tile to the silvery light. It was nothing like what Asha had brought back from Amarna. Just a blue glaze where the fire hadn't melted the paint. But my mother's foot had probably touched it once. I pressed my hand to the cool surface and thought of how much Rahotep had taken from me. And yet the power of rebellion rested in his hands. My heart felt sick knowing I would have to keep his secret from Ramesses. I wanted to tell all of Egypt what the High Priest had done to my *akhu*. I wanted him to suffer the way I had suffered. I wanted him to know loneliness, and fear, and despair. Without Ramesses and Merit, whom did I have in the palace of Malkata? I looked down at my swelling stomach and thought that at least I would always have my children, and I was aware of the irony—that I was standing in a place of ruin and death while inside of me, new life was growing. I wrapped the tile in a fold of my robe, then cast a last glance across the shipwreck that had swallowed my family, pitching me alone into the waves of palace life. Merit would say that they were still watching me; that your *akhu* never leave you except in body. I hoped that this was true. I wanted to imagine my mother looking down at me from the realm of Aaru, the starry sky that separates the land of the living from the land of the dead. And I hoped that in Aaru she was sitting at Ma'at's table, whispering into the goddess's ear all the terrible things that needed to be set right on earth.

CHAPTER SIXTEEN

AMUN WAS
WATCHING US

IN THE WORST heat of Mesore, a messenger ran ahead of the army and declared that Ramesses had been victorious. "An uprising in Nubia has been averted and the rebels have been crushed!" the herald exclaimed. "The army is already approaching Thebes!"

There was elation in the Audience Chamber, and I shouted over the noise from my throne. "The dead! Where is the list of the dead?"

"There is no list!" The messenger was jubilant. He knew this news would bring him a dozen deben. "Pharaoh Ramesses has been completely triumphant."

I fought my way through the crush of bodies hurrying to leave the Audience Chamber, and Merit found me in the hall. "Hurry, my lady, or we'll be late! There's a ship already waiting."

"But did you hear? Not a single officer killed!"

"And all of it accomplished in only a month! The gods have protected him." She touched the ankh at her neck and murmured a quick prayer of thanks. Then she took my arm and pressed forward. "Move for the princess Nefertari!" she shouted. "Move aside!" Dozens of courtiers stepped back, as we emerged onto the quay, where Iset was already waiting aboard *Amun's Blessing,* shielded from the sun by a canopy of painted linen.

I settled into a shaded chair next to Merit, and when I put my fingers to my lips in excitement, Merit pushed them down.

"You're not a child!"

"But I feel like one." I giggled. "It feels like the first time I saw Ramesses, after being hidden away at the Temple of Hathor."

When the ship reached the eastern bank, armed guards led us down the Avenue of Sphinxes so we could greet Ramesses beneath the freshly raised columns of Luxor. Thousands of Thebans swelled in the streets, so filled with joy that the women even shouted blessings to me. Then they began chanting Ramesses's name and breaking off palm branches to shade him as his army went by. Heat billowed up in a shimmering haze from the sandy streets, and as we passed through the market I could taste the scent of cumin in the air. When we reached the gates of Luxor, I was amazed once more by the towering statues of Ramesses. Woserit took my hand and led me to the steps of the temple, beside Iset in her best sheath and crown. She looked stunningly beautiful, carrying the weight of her coming child in her swelling breasts and rounded hips. *What if Ramesses gives her his sword?* I worried.

There was a loud call of trumpets as the army appeared on the Avenue of Sphinxes with Ramesses at its head. He was wearing the *khepresh* crown of war, and his hair streamed behind him like wisps of fire. He was the tallest of any of the men and bronzed from the sun. In his kilt, with the golden pectoral of Sekhmet, there was no more beautiful man in Egypt. He met my gaze and slowly withdrew his sword. I could feel the rush of blood in my ears. Then Iset stepped forward, and Ramesses lowered the blade back into its sheath.

"Ramesses!" She rushed down the temple steps and flung herself gracefully into his arms. A deafening cheer went up around the temple, and she placed his hand on her slightly swelling stomach so that everyone might see him blessing her child.

Merit nudged me painfully in the side. "*Go!* Don't let her steal this chance," she hissed.

I moved carefully down the steps, and Ramesses let go of Iset. Immediately, the cheers of the people faltered. "Nefertari," he breathed. He swept me into his embrace and inhaled the scent of my perfume, my hair, the warm sun on my skin. "Nefertari, look at you!" he exclaimed. My profile was like a willow stick attached to a heavy ball.

"Five months," I told him. I didn't add that for the past month I had been sick every night.

"Gods, how I missed you in Nubia," he admitted. Then he reached for his sword and Iset immediately stepped closer to us.

"The entire court has been waiting for you," she said quickly. "There is a magnificent feast planned for the Great Hall tonight."

Ramesses smiled. "I am looking forward to it."

"Are you looking forward to visiting my chamber as well?"

He glanced at me, and when she realized where he meant to spend the night, her voice became urgent. "But I have something for you. A gift in celebration of your triumph."

At last, Ramesses let go of his sword, and I knew that he wouldn't present it to either one of us. I could feel the anger darkening my cheeks as Ramesses promised, "I'll come to see you before the feast."

Then the High Priest of Amun walked down the temple's steps. I felt my stomach turn. From his position on the lowest step, he smiled at Iset before announcing, "Night after night we have spent our time at the feet of Amun, praying for Pharaoh's safe and triumphant return."

I sucked in my breath at his lie. Night after night he had been in the Audience Chamber, drinking and eating and plotting with Henuttawy.

"Now it is Mesore," Rahotep went on, raising his arms like two hollow reeds. "And in this last month of the Season of Harvest, Amun has granted Pharaoh a harvest of his own. A victory over rebellious Nubia!"

The courtiers cheered, and the priestesses shook their long bronze sistrums. Then the army sailed to the palace in a spectacle of blue and gold pennants. While Ramesses shared a ship with his men, I sat next to Merit on the deck of *Amun's Blessing* and was too angry even to speak.

"He was going to present you with the sword," Merit swore. "I saw him reach for it."

"And, as always, Iset was there to stop it! And now he's going to her chamber before the feast so that she can give him a gift."

Merit sat back on the cushion chair and fumed. "And she will tell him she prayed for his safety every night when *you* were the one lighting incense at Amun's feet. I will let Pharaoh know what really happened!"

I sat forward. "No! He will think I have sent you out of jealousy. He won't believe you."

"Then he can confirm it with someone else."

"*Who?* Who will be brave enough to tell him the truth?"

The feast in the Great Hall lasted all night, but when the food had been served and the musicians began a victory song, Ramesses found me out on the balcony.

"Nefertari." He had grown dark after long marches in the sun. The white of his sheath shone against the bronze of his skin and the blue of his eyes was like turquoise. "I have been waiting to find you alone." He took me in his arms, and when I saw the new golden bangle on his wrist, I wanted to be angry with him. What kind of a fool couldn't see the game that Iset was playing? But his kisses were urgent and I felt a need beneath his kilt. He pressed his hand to my belly. "I thought of you every day," he whispered. "There were a thousand times when I wanted to send back a message to you, but I was afraid it might be intercepted," he admitted. "I want to know everything. Tell me *everything*."

We went to my chamber, leaving the feast and the musicians behind, but it was a long time before we spoke. We fell into the bed and Ramesses took me in his arms, slipping the sheath from my shoulders. We were gentle together, so we wouldn't hurt the child, but that night our embraces grew more urgent until finally Ramesses swore, "I never want to leave this bed again, Nefer. I never want to go on a campaign without you."

As the music echoed in the courtyard, we shared our secrets together. Every night I had lit incense at the feet of Amun, praying for his safety, and now I wondered how I could have feared he wouldn't come home. He was tall and strong, with hands that were capable of anything.

"While you were gone, I was so worried," I admitted.

Ramesses laughed, then saw the trembling of my lip and hesitated. "Oh, Nefer." He held me against his chest. "You and I are bronze and gold," he promised. "We will last for eternity."

"In name," I said. "Not in body. Not like this."

"It will always be like this," Ramesses swore. I wondered if victory had made him more rash. How could he be so certain? "We will live together in the Afterlife," he added, "and eat with the gods. They have heard all of our prayers. Amun was with me in Nubia. You should have seen how easy it was to surround the palace and find the men who were plotting rebellion. We slaughtered them like cattle."

When I shuddered, Ramesses said forcefully, "They were disloyal to Egypt. They betrayed us, after we built *everything* for them! A clean city, a citadel taller than any in Nubia, protection from the Assyrians." There was a conviction in Ramesses's eyes that I had never seen before, and I wondered what he would do if he knew how Iset had truly acted in his absence. "But Amun was watching us," he said seriously. "How else could it have gone so well? Next time, you will come with me, Nefer. When our son is born—"

"What if it's a daughter?"

"It will be a son," he said confidently. "Amun has heard my prayers and he will give us an heir."

My heartbeat quickened, and the fear of childbirth welled up inside of me again. What if I didn't bring him a son, or worse, didn't survive to see my child grow?

"But tell me about Thebes," he said gently. "Tell me what's happened while I've been away. Paser says a Habiru came to visit you."

"Yes, Ahmoses of Chaldea," I said, and Ramesses heard the hesitation in my voice when I added, "He came to the Audience Chamber with a petition for me."

Ramesses frowned. "Specifically for you? And what did he want?"

"For me to release the Habiru from your army."

He sat up in the bed. "All of the Habiru?" he exclaimed. "And what did you tell him?"

"That his petition must go to you, of course!"

"The Habiru cannot be released! Every year there is talk of a Hittite invasion from the north, and someday it will happen. Why did he think you would grant such a thing?"

"Because it was my grandfather who brought his people to Egypt. And under the Heretic King," I explained, "the Habiru were used as slaves."

"The *entire* army was used as slaves."

"But it was the Habiru that the Heretic King promised to set free. He lied."

"So this Ahmoses of Chaldea came hoping that you would honor the promise of your *akhu*?"

I looked across my chamber to the burned tile I had placed next to the painting from Meryra's tomb. Though the edges were blackened, the center was still a vivid blue. I thought of the fires that had destroyed my family and marveled at how destiny had brought back the man who had first kindled them. Why was I telling Ramesses his story? Why did I care what Ahmoses wanted when he had risked my reputation by approaching me? But I looked across the bed into Ramesses's eyes and replied, "Yes, that was his hope."

Ramesses laughed. "And where does he think so many people would go?"

"North. To make the land of Canaan their own."

"Canaan is Egyptian land!" His curiosity turned to anger. "Who *is* this man?"

I twisted the bed linens in my hands. "The same man who taught the Heretic King that there is only one god. The leader of the Habiru."

Ramesses sat up on the pillows, shocked. "His *teacher*?"

"And he didn't come simply because he thought I would honor the vows of my *akhu*," I admitted slowly. "He came with the idea that there was profit in it for me as well. That if I released the Habiru from the army, I could tell the people I was expelling the heretics from Thebes and win their approval."

"So he is clever."

"I would never have said yes. Not at the expense of Egypt."

Ramesses took my hand, pulling me toward him. "Enough of this Habiru from Chaldea. Let Paser deal with him."

"So there isn't anything we can do?"

"For the Habiru?" Ramesses was genuinely surprised. "Not when they're a sixth of my father's army. Why? Do you think we should risk—"

"No," I said quickly. "When he comes, you will have to refuse him as well."

CHAPTER SEVENTEEN

FOR WHOM
DO YOU WAIT?

Thebes, 1281 BC

WHEN THE NEW year arrived, so did Seti's court from Avaris, and although it was supposed to be the solemn Feast of Wag, Iset had planned a merry celebration to welcome him back. All of Thebes came to see the royal flotilla of ships sail into Malkata's lake. The masts were festooned with blue and gold pennants, and trumpets blared as Seti and Tuya stepped onto the quay. The courtyard in front of the palace was filled with drinking courtiers, and the doors were decorated with swaths of gold cloth and rich blue linen.

"The princess must think she's planning a marriage, not the Feast of Wag," Merit snapped from where we stood on the quayside. "What if there's another war?" she demanded. "Where will the deben come from to pay the army if it's all been spent on acrobats, wine, and musicians?" She turned to me. "What does Pharaoh say about this?"

I looked at Ramesses, who was greeting his father at the end of the quay. They both wore the blue and gold *nemes* crown, but no two men could have been more different. One was young and bronzed from his time in the south, the other was old, and thin, and weary.

But neither of them seemed to mind that the somber Feast of Wag had been turned into a festival. "Ramesses indulges her," I replied. "He wants to make her happy."

"Little Nefertari!" Pharaoh Seti called out. He crossed the quay, and courtiers parted to make a path for him. The queen pointedly remained with Iset. But when Adjo caught sight of me, his lips curled back in a threatening growl. "Oh, be quiet," Pharaoh Seti demanded, and when he reached me, he took me proudly in his arms. "Even with a child you're as slight as a reed! So tell me, when does the little prince come?"

"Only two months left."

He glanced behind him to where Iset and Henuttawy were watching us. "And the other one?" he whispered.

"Not too long after."

"So this must be a son."

"Yes. I've been praying to Bes every night, and Nurse Merit has prepared a special offering for my *akhu*."

"And the people?"

"I am trying."

"Because there is always danger in the north. If Ramesses ever takes the army to face Emperor Muwatallis, he cannot leave a foolish queen behind to sit on his throne. He needs a partner in the Audience Chamber whom he can trust. And that the people will accept . . ."

"Then Paser will have to watch the Audience Chamber. If Ramesses goes to war, I want to go with him. I want to be a partner to him wherever he is, even if that's in battle."

Pharaoh Seti stared at me, then a smile started at the edges of his lips. "Tonight, when you visit your *akhu*," he said quietly, "thank them for bringing you to my son."

That evening, I entered Horemheb's mortuary temple in Djamet and knelt in front of my mother's image. I lit a cone of *kyphi* that Merit had procured in the markets at great expense, and as the smoke made a shroud across my mother's face, I traced the scar that Henuttawy had cut across her cheek.

"*Mawat*," I said heavily, and already felt the burning in my eyes. "You don't know how sick I've been this past month. Merit gives me mint but it never helps. She says it's a sign that I'm carrying a son, but what if it's not? What if I never stop feeling ill?" My hand lingered on her cheek, and I wondered what her real skin had felt like. Had it been soft, the way I imagined it to be? "If you were here, you would know what to do," I whispered. Her image flickered in the lamplight. I heard a rustle of sandals and tensed.

"You miss her," a voice said softly.

I nodded, and Woserit stood at my shoulder.

"When the gods return, she will be resurrected and you will walk hand in hand with her in Egypt."

I glanced at Woserit and reminded myself of the further truth she was withholding. Without the status of Chief Wife, my mother would never return to Egypt. As Chief Wife, my lineage would be written on every temple from Memphis to Thebes, and the gods would remember my *akhu* until eternity. But without that title my ancestors would remain erased from history. It wasn't just for me that I had to become queen. It was for my mother. And her mother. And now my child. I looked down at my belly. "But what if it's not a son?"

"I have placed an offering to Hathor every evening in your name."

And if Iset has a prince as well? Without the crown, my child would become a second prince, sent away to Memphis to become a priest the way Akhenaten had been spurned as a child. I stood and, looking up at my mother's damaged face, felt a deep inner rage. "Egypt knows she never worshipped Aten. It was *Akhenaten* who was the

Heretic King. It was *Akhenaten* who wanted to erase Egypt's gods, not my mother. So why couldn't they just destroy him?"

"Because people are easy to convince." Woserit sighed. "And Horemheb convinced them that all of your family was corrupted."

"But he married my mother!"

"Because he knew that she never worshipped Aten. No amount of royal blood would have convinced him to marry her if he'd thought otherwise. And although she may not have wanted that marriage, it saved her from the same fate as your aunt. The fate of being completely erased from Egypt, your name chipped from all the monuments of Thebes as if you had never lived. At least you can come to see her here."

"In one painting?" I asked. "*One?*" I watched the cone of incense burn itself into ashes. "I miss her." My eyes blurred with tears, and the embers became a smear of red in my vision.

"I know," she said softly. "We all wait for someone to return."

I heard the gravity in Woserit's voice and looked up. Her eyes seemed nearly transparent in the lamplight, and her long blue robe hung almost black. "Who are you waiting for?"

"I lost a mother, too. And a father, who was very kind to me. I was blessed that they both saw me grow. They both knew that I was to become the High Priestess of Hathor."

I blinked away my tears and felt my resolution harden. "I will make my mother proud. I will follow Ramesses into every battle. No one will ever say I'm like the Heretic Queen, only interested in my palace and my gold. And I will become Chief Wife, Woserit. Whether this is a daughter or a son, I will become Chief Wife."

      🜚 🜚 🜚

A MONTH after the Feast of Wag, Pharaoh Seti returned with Queen Tuya to Avaris. Although there was a lavish farewell in the Great

Hall, I was too sick to attend. My stomach felt too large for my body, and even walking from my bed to the robing room felt dangerous.

On the eleventh of Choiak I awoke from my sleep in a sweat. Although it was only morning, my hair was wet and clung to my neck. As soon as Ramesses saw my face, he sprang from the bed in search of Merit.

Merit rushed into the room and tore back the covers. The bed beneath me was wet. "It's happening, my lady! You're having the child!"

I looked at Ramesses. Merit hurried into the hall and the entire palace was awakened by her loud instructions. Messengers were sent north to Avaris to tell Pharaoh Seti that his grandchild was coming, and half a dozen servants rushed to take me to the birthing pavilion.

"Is there anything you need?" Ramesses pressed. "How are you feeling?"

"Well," I told him from my litter, but I was lying. The fear in my mouth tasted like an iron blade. By tomorrow, I could be dead in childbirth like my mother. I might never live to hear my baby cry or see the expression on Ramesses's face when he held our first child. And I was afraid of what might follow if I lived, and it wasn't a son.

The bearers rushed me through the halls, and Merit held open the door of the birthing pavilion. I glimpsed its blue tiled floor before a dozen hands eased me onto the bed. The dwarf god Bes grimaced down at me from the wall, and from the wooden post hung silver amulets that would help to bring an easy birth. A statue of Hathor stared benevolently from the ledge of a window, but when the midwives brought in the birthing chair, I felt a rising terror. I stared at the high leather back, then at the hole in the middle of the seat where the child would drop into the arms of a waiting nurse. The carved wooden sides had been painted with scenes of every protective goddess, but I had never thought to ask whether I would be using the same chair that had failed to protect my mother. I looked across the room and saw that Ramesses was gone.

"Where's Ramesses?" I asked fearfully. "Where did he go?"

"Shh." Merit wiped the hair from my face. "He is waiting outside—he's not allowed into the pavilion until you've given birth. These women will watch over you, my lady."

I looked up at the midwives. Their breasts were hennaed and their hands had been washed in sacred oil. But how much did they really know about birthing? My mother had attended dozens of births too, yet she had died giving life to me.

"Calm yourself," Merit said soothingly. "The baby will come easier if you're calm."

My pains lasted throughout the day, and in the afternoon armed guards allowed Woserit into the birthing pavilion. Immediately, she ordered the reed mats to be lowered and more fan bearers to be brought. "This is a princess of Egypt!" she barked. "Someone bring a wet linen for her forehead and find her some *shedeh*."

The midwife's apprentice scurried out, and when the door opened, I glimpsed Ramesses's face in the hall. He looked sick with worry. I felt a tightness in my belly and cried out. I saw him rush to the door before Merit blocked his entry.

"Your Highness, this is a *birthing pavilion!*" she exclaimed.

Ramesses pushed past her, and the midwives gasped at this breach of tradition. But Woserit nodded solemnly, and Ramesses pulled up a stool to sit at my side. He took my hand and didn't flinch at my complexion.

"Nefer, you're going to do well today. The gods are watching over us."

I felt a strain in my back and my breath came in gasps. "It hurts," I told him.

He squeezed my hand. "What have they given you?"

"*Kheper-wer*, water of carob, and honey."

"To speed the delivery," Woserit explained.

"But what for the pain?"

I smiled grimly. "They've put saffron and beer on my stomach." The paste glistened in the low light of the room. All I was wearing was a simple kilt, without paint or even a necklace, but Ramesses didn't look away. Instead, he held my hand tighter.

"If the pain is too much, just look at me," he made me promise. "Squeeze my arm."

A sharp pain wracked my body and I arched my back. The midwives rushed to the bed and one of them cried, "It's coming!" They eased me onto the birthing chair, and my terror grew so strong I could barely contain it. The child would drop through the hole into Merit's waiting arms. If it was a son, the priestesses would do for me what they had done for Iset. They would ring their bells three times throughout Thebes to tell the people that I had given Ramesses an heir. If it was a girl, they would only ring the bells twice.

A bowl of steaming water was placed under the chair to ease the delivery, and while Merit crouched, Woserit and Ramesses stood at my side. I held Ramesses's hand, and it was in this moment that I loved his rashness most. It didn't matter that a Pharaoh had never before witnessed a royal birth. If something should happen to me, he wanted his face to be the last one I saw, and he knew that this is what I would want as well. We looked into each other's eyes as the midwives chanted, "Push, my lady! Push!"

I strained against the chair and felt the hard wood press into my back. Then my body shuddered and one of the women cried, "It's coming!" Merit opened her arms and I felt my body relieve itself of its burden. In a rush of blood the child appeared. Merit held it in the air to inspect its hands and feet, and I heard Ramesses cry, "A son! A prince of Egypt!"

But I was in too much pain to celebrate my triumph. I gripped the arms of the chair and felt a tremendous pressure between my legs. Then Woserit pointed beneath me and cried sharply. She took my son from Merit's arms, and my nurse held out her hands as another head appeared, then a body. There was an intake of breath in the birthing chamber, then the sharp piercing cry of another living child.

"Twin sons!" Merit cried, and the entire chamber rejoiced. I am sure that the courtiers who pressed outside the doors could hear the cries of the midwives as they thanked Hathor and Bes for twin princes. "Sons!" they repeated. "*Two* sons!"

The message was passed through the windows of the pavilion, and I heard a woman shout, "The princess Nefertari is beloved by the gods."

I looked at my sons in the arms of their nurses. Even with blood still covering their heads they were incredibly beautiful. My knees felt weak, and there was a pulsing ache between my thighs, but I was alive. I had survived the birth of not one, but two sons, and now I was a mother. I wanted to hold my princes in my arms, and stroke their heads, and learn the color of their eyes and the soft contours of their bodies. I wanted to press them to my chest and never let them go where harm might come to them. These children carried the blood of all of my *akhu* and Ramesses's *akhu* with them.

I was helped through the back door to the baths. While Merit washed and perfumed me with jasmine, she hummed an elated hymn to Hathor. Then she guided me to a long stone bench where she packed my womb with linen. I shut my eyes tightly against the pain, and Merit said softly, "These next few days are vital, my lady. You will need to be kept completely dry and rested." Many women survived childbirth only to succumb to disease a few days later. And my sons would have to be kept tightly wrapped, so that not even their little arms could move, in case they should accidentally reach out and beckon the shadow of Anubis.

I sat while Merit brushed my hair, and a servant brought me tea. Then I returned to the birthing pavilion. I could hear the priestesses in the courtyard ringing their bells six times each, and I imagined the people's confusion. Thrice for a son, twice for a daughter. When they learned what six meant . . .

Ramesses sat on a leather stool at my side and held my hand again. "How do you feel?"

I smiled, and for the first time I looked with a mother's eyes at the images of children painted across the wide walls of the pavilion. It was a large chamber, with long windows that faced the rising sun and soft linen curtains that blew gently with every breeze. It had been built to make a new mother feel at ease, for in every scene a woman sat smiling while her children were at play, at work, or asleep. I took Ramesses's hand and squeezed it tenderly. "I am feeling well."

His eyes filled with tears, and he moved from the stool to my bed. "I was frightened for you, Nefer. When I saw all the blood, I was scared of what I had done to you."

"Ramesses," I said softly, "you gave me a son. *Two* sons." I looked at my children suckling at their milk nurses' breasts. They had been bathed in lavender water and their small heads had been rubbed with oil. Without the oil, I was sure that their hair would be as red-gold as their father's, and I felt the overwhelming need to hold them and look into their eyes.

"And just as Ahmoses predicted," Ramesses whispered.

I looked up in astonishment. "What do you mean?"

"He came this morning to the Audience Chamber. After Paser told him that the Habiru would remain with the army, he wished you well in the birth of our two sons."

I sat straighter in my bed. "He said *two sons*?"

"He said twins."

"But how could he have known?"

"Perhaps he guessed. Or perhaps he thought . . ."

"Of Nefertiti?" In my joy, I hadn't considered this, but now I could see how the people could view my sons as a link to the Heretic Queen, who had also borne twins. Was every blessing destined to be seen as a curse? I clutched my stomach, and the pain between my legs suddenly sharpened.

"What is it?" Ramesses worried. "Is there something you need?"

I winced, and Merit was at my side at once.

"I will bring my lady some ginger and tea. It will ease the pain in her womb, Your Highness."

I sat back on my cushions, and Ramesses's eyes were dark and full of worry.

"I'll be fine," I promised. "But I can't bear to think—"

"Then don't. You are the mother to the first princes of Egypt, Nefer." He kissed my hand gently. "So what shall we name them?"

I looked at our children, wrapped in the very finest linen, and their little chests moved up and down with small, contented breaths. "I want to hold them first."

Merit disturbed their feeding to bring them to me, and Woserit and Ramesses stood back as my sons were placed in my arms. Their bodies fit snugly against mine, and I nuzzled their soft cheeks and downy heads. It was true. Both of my children had thin wisps of auburn hair and eyes the color of turquoise. In fourteen days they would be taken to the Temple of Amun and introduced to the gods. But before then I would have to announce their names.

I studied their small features; both of them had delicate faces, with hands so small they could barely fit around a river reed. They were tiny gifts from Amun, a sign from the gods that was undeniable. "Our first will be Amunher," I announced, and the midwives who were cleansing the chamber murmured happily, for *Amunher* meant "Amun is with him." "And the second . . ." I looked at Amunher's brother. His gaze was as curious and bright as Re. "And our second son shall be Prehir."

"Re watches over him," Ramesses repeated, and the women in the chamber sighed. "Woserit, tell the priestesses to make a special offering. Then let the people know that Nefertari is as healthy and strong as ever. Tonight, there will be a feast in the Great Hall."

Merit returned my sons to the pair of young milk nurses who sat in the pavilion's only private chamber. Although the pavilion was wide, the chamber door had been left open so that I could see my sons resting in the young women's arms. For most of the afternoon I slept, and as the sun dropped lower in the sky, Woserit bowed politely and left. As she parted, I could hear the excited chatter in the hall as courtiers peered inside to catch a glimpse of the princes. Then Henuttawy entered the pavilion. She wore the *seshed* circlet on her brow, and the cobra's golden hood gleamed from her dark hair as though it were ready to strike. Behind her was Iset, her eyes wide with fear. She hadn't been inside the birthing pavilion since her own son had died, and I knew it was Henuttawy who'd insisted she come.

"We have all heard the wonderful news," Henuttawy announced grandly. "Not one child, but twins, just like Nefertiti." She looked at me, and her eyes were as cold and hard as granite. "Congratulations, Nefertari. Although it's hard to imagine that a girl of your size could produce two children at once." I felt the pain between my legs increase, and she glanced up from under her lashes at Ramesses. "Are you sure they are hers?" she asked teasingly.

"Of course," Ramesses said sharply.

Henuttawy dismissed the remark with a laugh, as if she hadn't meant anything by it. "So what has our little princess named them?" she asked.

"Amunher and Prehir," I answered. I noticed that Ramesses was watching his aunt with a curious expression.

"Iset is thinking of Ramessu for her son. Ramessu the Great, just like his father."

"And if it's a girl?" I asked from my bed.

Iset put her hand over her large belly. "Why should it be a girl?" she whispered. "Ramesses has given his wives only sons."

"That's right," Henuttawy said brightly, then hooked Ramesses's arm in hers. And before I could protest, she led him away from me and into the midwives' chamber. Merit quickly took a bundle of linens and began folding them near Henuttawy.

But Iset remained next to my bed, and she looked across the chamber at my newborn sons with longing. They were nestled into their milk nurses' bosoms. I told her softly, "Henuttawy should not have brought you here. She doesn't care about you."

"Then who does?" she hissed. Her arm was wrapped around her belly, and I knew it was to protect it from the evil eye. "Do you think that Ramesses cares?" she demanded.

I was stunned. "Of course."

She smiled bitterly. "The way he cares about you?"

"There is nothing you owe Henuttawy. No payment—"

"And what would *you* know about payment? A princess by birth who never had to pay for anything in her life."

Ramesses emerged from the chamber ahead of Henuttawy, and his expression was taut, like leather stretched too tightly over a drum.

"Shall we prepare a feast for tonight?" Iset asked eagerly. She offered Ramesses her arm, but he turned his strained expression to me and asked, "Nefertari, what would you like?"

The smile froze on Iset's face.

"I'd like to summon Penre to tell him what to paint on the Wall of Proclamation," I said. "I want to let Amun know that two princes of Egypt have been born."

"And the feast?" Iset repeated. "Shall we go and plan the feast?"

But Ramesses walked back toward the milk nurses' chamber. "Why don't you plan the feast with Henuttawy?" he said.

Iset blinked away tears but didn't refuse his request. "Of course." She took Henuttawy's arm, and on their way out of the pavilion they met Woserit, who was returning.

"Such a happy day," Woserit said cheerfully. "Don't you think?"

Neither Henuttawy nor Iset replied. Woserit came to my bed, and I glanced at Ramesses, who was humming softly to his sons. He had taken off his *nemes* crown so that his auburn hair curled about his neck, and the little princes looked like miniature versions of their father. "Henuttawy was talking to him," I whispered. "Alone. But Merit might have overheard."

Woserit stood and went straight to Merit. I watched the pair of them speak in the alcove by the window. When Woserit came back to me, her look was grave. "Someone has spread the word in Thebes that your sons are not really yours, that they were born to a palace servant."

"*Someone?*" I hissed, nearly choking on my rage. "*Someone?* Who could it be but Henuttawy and Rahotep? Ammit will devour their souls," I vowed. "They will never pass into the Afterlife! When the time comes for their hearts to be weighed against the truth, the scales will sink to the ground and Ammit will destroy them!" Woserit put her hand on mine. I wouldn't be calmed, but I lowered my voice. "So what does this mean?" I demanded. "In fourteen days when my sons are brought before the altar of Amun, will I be declared Chief Wife?"

"The viziers will all tell Ramesses to wait and see what the people believe."

"You mean wait and see if Iset has a son." I could barely contain my rage. Across the wide birthing pavilion, Ramesses still hummed softly to the princes. I closed my eyes. "And Paser?"

"Of course Paser will speak for you! And Ramesses himself witnessed the birth. When the people see two red-haired princes with the same bright eyes and dimpled cheeks as Pharaoh, who do you think they will believe?" Woserit asked. "Though we must leave nothing to chance," she quickly amended. "Henuttawy's name is respected in Thebes. The people don't know what she really is."

"A *viper*," I said.

Ramesses smiled at us from the corner of the pavilion where he was watching our sons, and Woserit added quickly, "Iset doesn't know yet that it was Henuttawy who chased Ashai away. The moment has come," she said firmly. "You have kept my sister's secret long enough."

"And Rahotep?" I asked, imagining the High Priest's sickening grin as he helped spread Henuttawy's lie among the people.

"Kill the viper first. Snakes may be immune to their own kind's venom, but you have become something more powerful than a snake today."

I followed her eyes to the image of a queen painted above the door. The golden wings of the woman's vulture crown swept down her hair. As Chief Wife, I would wear a similar headdress, for the vulture is the most powerful symbol in Egypt. It is more powerful even than the cobra, for its flight brings it closer to the gods.

"Enjoy these next few days, Nefertari. There will be a Birth Feast tomorrow," Woserit said. "But when the right time comes . . ."

When the right times comes, I thought, *then the viper will see what a vulture can do.*

CHAPTER EIGHTEEN

A TRUTH MADE WHOLE

I TOOK WOSERIT'S advice and waited, savoring the days I had with my sons before I would have to return to the Audience Chamber and be parted from them. After the Birth Feast, I lay in the pavilion for fourteen days, reading to Amunher and Prehir, and singing to them the hymns of Amun that my mother would have sung to me if she had lived. There was nothing in the world so beautiful as watching them sleep, studying the steady rise and fall of their little chests, and listening to the small noises they made when they were hungry, or tired, or in need of being held in their own mother's arms. Of course, I was not allowed to suckle them, so Merit bound my breasts with linen and I watched while my sons fed from their milk nurses, cheerful women who had recently given birth themselves.

As my fourteen days passed, Ramesses came to me every afternoon to tell me the news of the Audience Chamber, bringing me presents of honeyed dates and pomegranate wine. At night, when the nurses had wrapped our sons in blankets and placed them in the pavilion's private chamber, Ramesses lit the oil lamps and climbed into my bed. And there, surrounded by gifts from foreign kingdoms, we studied the day's petitions together.

For a short while, I knew the perfect life. I wasn't in the Great Hall to hear the gossip about me, and I didn't have to see Rahotep's frightening grin. But the world could not be kept at bay forever, and the news that came into our happy pavilion and disturbed me the most was not about myself, but about Egypt's security.

"I won't let this go on!" Ramesses raged on my last night in the birthing pavilion. He pointed to the pile of growing petitions from Memphis. "Sherden pirates attacking our ships along the River Nile. Sherden pirates attacking our ships in Kadesh!"

"The same pirates who overtook the Mycenaean King's ship and stole the gifts that were meant for little Amunher and Prehir," I reminded, and Ramesses's face reddened.

"We won't let it continue. We will wait until Tybi," he said decisively. He wouldn't risk leaving Iset before she delivered her child, not knowing whether she lived or died. "And if these Sherden attack another Egyptian ship, or even a ship that's bound for Egypt, they'll be humbled by what will be waiting for them."

In the Audience Chamber the next day, the viziers crowded around the base of the dais, greeting me with unusually low bows as I took my seat. But when Rahotep smiled strangely at me, I felt the sudden urge to hold my sons. I knew that they were safe, yet as Ramesses struck his crook on the floor of the dais, and as the viziers took their seats, I had to remind myself that there was no better nurse in Egypt than Merit.

"Bring forth the petitioners," Ramesses announced. The doors swung open, and a figure crossed the tiles of the chamber. I recognized Ahmoses and his shepherd's staff at once. He didn't stop at the table where the viziers were waiting but came straight toward me. When the soldiers stepped forward to pull him back, I raised my hand to let them know that the Habiru should come forth.

"Princess Nefertari." Unlike our previous meeting, Ahmoses bowed briefly before my throne. I wondered if this was because Ramesses was present. No one in Egypt would dare to come before a Pharaoh without bowing. I didn't wait for him to rise. "How did you know I would have twin sons?"

"Because Queen Nefertiti gave Pharaoh Akhenaten twins," he replied, meeting my gaze. "I said nothing about sons."

Though we were speaking in Canaanite, I still glanced at Ramesses. He was watching us with a peculiar expression. "You are *never* to mention the names of the Heretic Rulers in Thebes," I said harshly.

"The Heretic *Rulers?*" Ahmoses frowned. "Akhenaten, yes. But your aunt . . ." He shook his head.

"Are you saying," I demanded, "that she didn't worship Aten?"

"She only worshipped Aten while her husband still lived. Otherwise, she allowed shrines to be built to the gods that her husband had abandoned."

Now both Ramesses and Iset had stopped listening to petitions. Both of them were watching me. "What are you saying?" I grew flustered.

"I am saying that Queen Nefertiti never stopping praying to Amun. She was not a heretic, as Pharaoh Horemheb called her."

"How do you know this?"

"Because I saw her shrines, and I watched your mother accompany the queen to the hidden temples of Tawaret. There was great danger in what your aunt was doing. If her husband had discovered it, he would have cast her off and taken Princess Kiya as Chief Wife instead."

I was aware that even though we were speaking Canaanite, the entire chamber had become my audience. "You have been to the palace of Malkata three times," I said angrily. "What is your purpose?"

"To remind you that your aunt suffered in the name of her gods. She wasn't free to worship as she wished. Instead, she had to bow to Aten, and your mother—"

"My mother never bowed to Aten!"

"But there were times when she wondered if she should, when the pressure was so great she would have done anything to escape it. Your family suffered like the Habiru are suffering—"

"Pharaoh will not set the Habiru free!" I swore. "They are a part of his army."

Ahmoses searched my face, to see if I might change my mind, and when he saw that I wouldn't, he shook his head and turned away. I watched him make his way across the chamber. When he reached the guards, I heard myself exclaim, "Wait!"

He turned slowly to face me, and I stood from my throne.

"What are you doing?" Ramesses asked. But I walked beyond the viziers' tables and met Ahmoses at the heavy bronze doors. The courtiers had stopped playing Senet to listen, but even if they could understand Canaanite, I lowered my voice so that only Ahmoses would hear. "Come again in Thoth," I told him.

"Will the Habiru be set free with the next new year?"

I hesitated. Because Ramesses trusted me, it was possible that I could persuade him. But was I willing to risk the safety of Egypt because one Habiru had revealed to me the truth about my ancestors? "I . . . I don't know. In eight months, a great deal can change."

"You mean perhaps, by then, you will be queen?"

I felt the eyes of the entire court boring into my back and whispered, "Have you heard what the people are saying about my sons?"

Ahmoses didn't flinch or look away. And he didn't lie, as one of the courtiers might have. "Your mother was known for her honesty at court, and I believe the same of her daughter," he said. "I have told the Habiru that Prince Amunher and Prince Prehir are royal sons."

I closed my eyes briefly. "My husband thinks he can threaten gossip away. He swears that anyone speaking such things will be sent to the quarries, but you and I know . . . Will you tell the rest of the people?" I asked, and I was aware of how desperate I had become that I was asking a favor from a heretic. "Will you spread the word in eastern Thebes?" I repeated.

Ahmoses regarded me for a moment, and instead of naming a price, as I thought he might, simply nodded his assent.

☖ ☖ ☖

LATER THAT evening, before Ramesses visited my chamber, I told Merit what had happened. "He told me she never worshipped Aten."

Merit stood from the brazier where she was setting aloe wood to flame. Poorer households used cow dung and river reeds for their fires, but the scent of aloe has a calming effect, and through the open door to Merit's chamber I could see that my sons were already asleep. Her brows drew together until they formed a dark line.

"Well, you were there!" I said passionately. "Is it *true?*"

Merit sat on the edge of the bed with me. "I saw her worship Aten, my lady."

"Because she had to?"

Merit spread her palms. "Perhaps."

"But did you see her go to other shrines as well? Did she secretly worship Tawaret, or Amun?"

"Yes, when it pleased her," she admitted.

"And when was that?"

"When she wasn't worshipping herself," Merit said with brutal honesty.

It was as though a heavy stone had been lifted from my chest. Perhaps she had been selfish, and greedy, and vain. Perhaps these things all went against the laws of Ma'at. But there was nothing worse than heresy. And she had not been a heretic.

The door of my chamber opened. Ramesses came inside and Merit stood to bow. As soon as she left, I joined Ramesses on the long leather bench near the fire and told him what Ahmoses had said. For several moments he was silent, then he placed the scrolls he had brought with him on a low table next to the brazier, and said, "I *knew* that what they taught in the edduba wasn't true. How could anyone related to you be a heretic, Nefer? Look at your mother; look at *you!*" His voice rose in excitement. "And what does Merit say?"

"The same as Ahmoses. She had seen my aunt worshipping at Tawaret's shrine." I held my breath, wondering if this was the moment he would decide to make me Chief Wife. If I could have silently willed the decision into his heart, I would have then.

He took my hands and swore, "The people may not know the truth, Nefertari, but we do. And someday, I will resurrect the names of your *akhu* in Egypt."

I was disappointed. "Until then?"

Color tinged Ramesses's cheeks. Surely he knew what I'd been hoping for. "Until then, we will try to change the people's hearts."

CHAPTER NINETEEN

SEKHMET'S CLAWS

IN THE DAYS after Ahmoses's visit, I thought a great deal about my family and wished for things that could never be. I wished I could have gone with Asha to Amarna and seen the crumbling walls and abandoned remains of the city that Nefertiti had built. I longed to tear down every statue to Horemheb the way he tore down the statues of Ay and Tutankhamun, or wipe his name from the scrolls just as he tried to wipe away theirs. To avoid being consumed with vengeance, I spent my time thinking about my sons. I tried not to love them as much as I did; I knew that half of all children born never reached the age of three. But every day with my sons was an adventure, and neither Ramesses nor I could help but take them into our arms whenever our time in the Audience Chamber was finished. We laughed over the new faces they made when they were happy, or tired, or frustrated, or sad. By Tybi, they had their own little personalities, so that at night when I heard them crying from Merit's chamber, I could tell their cries apart. Even after a long day of petitioners, I would sit up, and Ramesses would follow me to Merit's door. "Go to sleep," I'd tell him, but he wanted to be awake with me. So he would take Prehir, and I would take Amunher, and we would rock them by the light of the moon and smile at each other on those clear late-autumn nights.

"Can you imagine the day they're old enough to hunt with us?" Ramesses asked one evening.

I laughed. *"Hunting?* Merit probably won't even allow them to go swimming!"

Ramesses grinned. "She's a good nurse, isn't she?"

I looked down at Prehir's contented face in my arms, and nodded. During the day, I doubted if our sons even noticed we were gone. They ate and slept under Merit's supervision, and she was the perfect *mawat,* watching over them with a lioness's ferocity.

"In a month, Iset will be going into the birthing pavilion," Ramesses said quietly. "I'm going to take the army north before she gives birth."

"To fight the pirates?"

"Yes. And I've been thinking, Nefer. What if you came with me?" My heart raced in my chest, and when I didn't say anything Ramesses added, "What better way to convince the people that you're beloved of Amun than to let them see you at my side when I defeat the Sherden? You would remain in the cabin surrounded by guards. There would be no danger—"

"Yes."

Ramesses peered through the darkness at me. "Yes . . ."

"I will go with you. To the north . . . to the south . . . to the far-thest ends of the desert."

ON THE fifteenth of Tybi, good news came to Ramesses with the bad. Iset had been taken early to the birthing pavilion, and in the Northern Sea the Sherden pirates had attacked another Egyptian ship carrying five thousand deben worth of palace oil to Mycenae. Ramesses dismissed the day's petitioners, shouting that the Audience Chamber must be cleared at once. Even Woserit and Henuttawy couldn't calm him.

"There is nothing you can do today," Henuttawy reminded, but Ramesses ignored her.

"Guards!" he demanded, as the viziers gathered nervously around the steps of the dais. "Summon Asha and his father, General Anhuri. Bring General Kofu in as well!"

"What will you do?" Henuttawy asked. "The army isn't supposed to leave for ten days."

"I'll prepare a small fleet of ships tonight, and we will leave as soon as Iset has given birth."

"But what if it's a son?" Henuttawy asked. "How will Amun know that an heir has been born if no Birth Feast has been held?" Rahotep spread his hands in question, and the viziers looked at one another, waiting for Ramesses to make a decision.

"I will stay for the feast," Ramesses conceded. "But only so that Amun knows this child. I won't sit in Thebes while a band of thieving Sherden make *fools* of Egypt!"

I picked up the list that Paser had made, reading off the number of goods that Egypt had lost to the pirates. "A grove of potted myrrh trees for ointment, three golden collars from Crete, leather armor from Mycenae, chariots plated in gold and electrum, fifty barrels of olive oil, and twenty barrels of wine from Troy. The sooner we leave the better," I said cunningly.

Henuttawy and Rahotep turned. "*We?*" Henuttawy said, and her eyes grew so narrow they looked like they had been painted on with the thinnest stroke of a reed brush. "Where do you think you're going, Princess?"

"With me," Ramesses said firmly.

"You are taking the mother of your sons," Henuttawy asked calmly, "to war with the Sherden?"

"I wouldn't call it war." Ramesses glanced at me. "More like a battle."

But Henuttawy wasn't concerned about me; she was concerned that while Iset was recovering in the birthing pavilion, I would be riding into battle at Ramesses's side, like the lion goddess Sekhmet, who avenged men's evil deeds through war.

"It is kind of you to be concerned, Henuttawy," I said, noting silently how much she resembled the viper she wore on her brow. "But I have no fear when I am with Ramesses. I know he'll protect me."

The doors to the Audience Chamber swung open and Asha arrived with his father, General Anhuri, and a second officer. The viziers stepped back to allow them through. "Your Majesty." The men bowed.

"Have you heard?" Ramesses demanded.

"Sherden," Anhuri replied. He was tall, like Asha, but with darker skin and harder eyes. I thought, as I often had, that he looked like he had spent many days in the desert without water or shade, and that neither had bothered him. "We have waited long enough to deal with these pirates," Anhuri said. "Every day they'll grow bolder until ships no longer come to Egypt from the Northern Sea."

"We will wait until my wife has given birth," Ramesses said. "But make ready a fleet."

"Of how many ships?" General Kofu asked. "The Sherden use two ships to attack. Both ships work together."

"Then ready ten. We'll send one ship to lie in wait for them," Ramesses plotted. "And we'll stock it to look like a merchant ship. The soldiers will dress as sailors, and when the Sherden come to attack—"

"They'll become prey themselves!" Asha finished. His eyes were bright with expectation. A baited merchant ship could dock at a bend in the river, while around the bend, nine of Pharaoh's best ships could be waiting. When both of the pirate ships were lured in, Pharaoh's ships would surround them. "But the Sherden are no fools," he said cautiously. "They will be wary now of a ship moving slowly on the river."

"Then we can dock and pretend to be unloading barrels," Ramesses said.

"They have grown fat on their thievery," General Anhuri warned. "They will want something more than barrels of oil. Perhaps a ship they believe is carrying gold . . ."

"What if we sail the ship with Pharaoh's pennant?" General Kofu suggested.

"No. They may not trust that," Anhuri said.

"Then what if it's a princess's ship, sailing for Mycenae?" I asked.

"They may still be suspicious," Anhuri warned.

"And what if the princess was on board, wearing gold that would reflect far enough for them to see? I could walk the decks and there would be no doubt of it being a royal barge."

The generals looked at Ramesses.

"We're not using you as bait," he said. "It's too great a risk."

"But the idea is good," Anhuri admitted. "And we could just as easily dress up a boy. It might lure in the Sherden."

A messenger entered the chamber and bowed before the dais. Henuttawy demanded, "Has she given birth yet?"

I flinched at her callousness and wondered who was sitting with Iset while we clustered in the Audience Chamber.

"Not yet, my lady. But she will deliver His Majesty's next heir at any moment."

Ramesses stood from his throne. "Have the proper midwives been summoned?"

"Yes, Your Highness." The messenger bowed. "They are ready."

We rushed through the palace, and I wondered what Ramesses was hoping for. I never dared to discuss it with him at night, but if it was a son, the will of the gods would be unclear. However, if it was a daughter . . .

We reached the birthing pavilion, and behind us the courtiers halted to wait at the chamber's entrance. I hesitated in front of the doors. "I . . . I shouldn't. She already thinks I stole the *ka* of her last child!"

Ramesses scowled. "Then she will have to get over such superstitious nonsense."

I passed a look to Woserit, who followed us across the threshold of the pavilion. Inside the chamber, the wall hangings and reed mats had all been changed. Even the color of the linens was different. I heard the sharp intake of breath as Iset saw Ramesses cross the room, and I knew she was afraid that his presence might incur the wrath of Tawaret. From her bed, she cried out in pain, and the midwives lifted her up, a woman under each arm, until she was seated on the birthing chair. Her lap was covered by a wide strip of linen and her hair had been pulled back in elaborate braids. She was perfectly beautiful even in childbirth. I knew I had not looked so well kempt during my own time in the pavilion.

I went to the statue of Tawaret and lit one of the cones of incense. Most had been burned by the midwives, and a pile of ashes smoldered at the feet of the hippopotamus goddess. I closed my eyes and whispered obediently, "May you bless Iset with the strength of a lioness. May you give her an easy birth . . ."

Iset shrieked; Henuttawy pointed to me and cried, "Nefertari, take back that terrible prayer!"

I blanched. Even the midwives turned.

"I heard what she prayed for," Woserit said. "She was praying for Iset's health."

"Get her out!" Iset cried, gripping the arms of her chair.

"Nefertari is my wife," Ramesses said sharply. "She has prayed for your health—"

"She stole the *ka* of my son and now she wants another!"

I turned from the shrine. When Ramesses reached out his hand to stop me, I shook my head firmly. *"No!"* I pushed the door open with Woserit following close behind, as the waiting crowd shifted to catch a glimpse inside. Paser separated himself from the group of viziers expectantly. "Has she given birth?"

"No." Woserit scowled. "But she ordered us from the pavilion. Henuttawy accused Nefertari of praying for Iset's death."

Moments later, the heavy wooden doors opened again, and this time it was a midwife. The entire hall went silent, and I found myself holding my breath. I tried to read the woman's face, but she was keeping her own counsel to heighten the suspense. Finally, someone shouted, "What is it?" and the midwife let herself grin. "A healthy son!" she cried jubilantly. "Prince Ramessu!"

My heart fell like a stone in my chest. Woserit squeezed my hand and said quickly, "He's still younger, and she hasn't given him two."

Ramesses emerged from the birthing pavilion, and his eyes sought mine in the cheering crowds. He motioned to me and Woserit, and when we joined him on the steps of the pavilion, he took my arm. "Go back in to see her. Please don't take offense at what she said. She was in pain—"

"Was my sister in pain, too?" Woserit asked sharply. "She accused your wife of praying for your own child's death."

"She is punishing Nefertari for being your friend, and I have spoken to her about this."

"And what did she say?" I demanded.

Ramesses appeared tired, as if the conversation had taken a great deal out of him. "I'm sure you can imagine. But she's my father's sister."

We went into the pavilion, and in the milk nurse's private chamber, a crowd of midwives were gathered around Prince Ramessu. As the women parted, I felt a selfish thrill that his hair was as dark as his mother's. This child was bigger than the last, and he was feeding greedily from his milk nurse's breast. She carried him to a chair nearest the windows, so he could rest in the healthy light of the sun, and Ramesses stroked the downy curve of his head. Noblewomen fussed over the color of Ramessu's skin, his eyes, his little mouth, while across the pavilion, Iset sat in her bed, waiting for the traditional line of well-wishers. When I approached, she shrank into the pillows.

"Congratulations on a healthy son," I said.

"What are you doing back here?" she hissed.

"Enough of your peasant's superstitions," Woserit snapped, appearing at my side. "Even my nephew is tired of them."

"There are amulets all over this chamber," Iset warned us. "The milk nurse used to be a priestess of Isis."

"You are a fool if you think I can perform magic," I told her.

"Then who killed my son?" she whispered harshly. Her eyes brimmed with tears as Woserit stepped forward. "You are a young and foolish girl. Nefertari cannot conjure magic any more than you can. Learn to accept that the gods asked Akori to return from this world. If you're looking to blame someone, then blame Henuttawy."

"And why should I do that?"

Woserit looked at me, and I understood what she wanted me to say.

"Because if Henuttawy hadn't threatened Ashai to stay away, he might have been Ramessu's father instead," I replied.

Iset started. "Who told you this?" When I glanced away, her whisper became bitter. "You don't know what you're saying! Ashai left me to care for his father in Memphis."

"Is that what Henuttawy told you?" Woserit raised her brows. "No, Ashai is an artist in Thebes. He works on the Ramesseum, and he married a pretty Habiru girl. Of course, now that you have a son, perhaps you don't care about any of this."

But even as Woserit said the words, we both saw it wasn't true.

Iset's face had fallen like a heavy sail deprived of wind.

"We will light a cone of incense at the temple," Woserit said, "and thank Amun for a safe delivery."

Once we were outside the birthing pavilion, I turned to Woserit. "We shouldn't have told her that right after she gave birth," I worried.

"It was the right time for the truth. While Ramesses is gone, Iset will confront Henuttawy. My sister knew that Iset was a poor match for Ramesses, yet she still pushed her toward the dais. She has condemned her to a life of loneliness. But don't feel sorry for her," Woserit warned. "She chose this path. Just as you are choosing yours tomorrow."

ロ ロ ロ

THAT EVENING, I sat at the mirror while Merit painted my eyes. She placed a turquoise pectoral around my neck, and when she fitted a golden diadem on my brow, I stood so that I could admire the way the cobra reared up, its garnet eyes like twin flames against the blackness of my hair.

"You are in a good mood," Merit remarked, "given what's happened."

"I am about to set sail for the greatest adventure of my life, Merit." My heart ached at the thought of leaving Amunher and Prehir, but I knew that this journey would be recorded on the monuments of Thebes. The gods would see my dedication to Egypt, and the people would recognize my importance to their Pharaoh. "We are going to crush the Sherden pirates and remind the north that Egypt will *never* bow to thievery!"

"A battle is not an adventure!" Merit scolded. "You have no idea what might happen."

"Whatever happens, I will be with Ramesses. And Iset is not going to be made Chief Wife."

Merit put down a perfume jar to study me. "Did Pharaoh say something?" she asked eagerly. "Has he told you this?"

"No. He will attend the Birth Feast tonight, and he will pay Iset every respect. But we are *leaving*, Merit. He's going into battle a day after she's given birth."

Merit realized what this meant. "He spent every one of your four teen nights in the birthing pavilion with you."

Merit followed me into her chamber and we stood, watching my sons sleeping. Amulets hung from their cradles to keep away Anubis, and protective spells had been written on small scraps of papyrus and placed around their necks in silver pendants. When I journeyed north with Ramesses, I would feel safe knowing that both Merit and the gods were watching my sons.

The two milk nurses watched me from their chairs, feeding their own daughters while Amunher and Prehir slept. I had told the women to move their daughters' cradles next to Merit's chamber. Merit had snapped that the children of milk nurses should not be allowed to sleep beside princes. But Ramesses didn't mind, and I could imagine my own heartache if my job was to feed other children all day, while someone else watched over my own. After the first year, they would stop feeding them milk from their breasts and begin to use the clay bottles that potters make in the markets. I suspected that Merit's complaint had less to do with lowly birth than with having four children crying in the next chamber.

凸 凸 凸

BY THE time we reached the Great Hall, the singing and feasting had begun. Dancers, naked except for silver belts around their slender waists, moved their hips to the high trills of flutes, invoking the presence of the dwarf god Bes, who would look over Malkata and protect Prince Ramessu. Normally, Ramesses would watch these girls with rapt attention, and later in the night he would take me in his arms and his love would be even more passionate than usual. But that night, all we could think about was the Sherden. What if they had added more ships to their fleet? Or if they didn't fall for our ruse? The Birth Feast was to go on until morning, and when Ramesses and I both stood to leave, Iset reached for him from her throne.

"We must rest before we sail north tomorrow," he said. He kissed her hand, but Iset withdrew it in a fury.

"We?" Iset turned an accusatory look at me. "Nefertari is going with you?"

"She speaks the language of the Sherden."

"And doesn't Paser?"

"Yes, but if he comes, who will be watching my kingdom?"

Iset stood shakily from her throne, and her face was desperate. "But when will I see you? How will you know how Prince Ramessu is doing? What if something happens to your ship?"

I could see Ramesses softening under Iset's need. "Nothing will happen to my ship," he promised. "And Ramessu has the best nurses in Egypt."

"On your way to the Northern Sea, you will be sailing past Avaris," Henuttawy pointed out. "Will you stop to see your father?"

"Yes. On our return."

"Then why not have us meet you there? We can greet your triumphant return together, with my brother."

I wondered what Henuttawy was playing at, but Ramesses warmed to the idea at once.

"Yes," he said eagerly, "come to Avaris." Iset hesitated, but Ramesses took her hand and squeezed it lightly. "Sail for Avaris as soon as you can. Henuttawy will go with you."

He waited until the tears cleared from her eyes and she assented. Then we descended the dais, and the court stood from their chairs as we walked the length of the Great Hall together. Courtiers bowed at the neck, sweeping their arms before them in obeisance. A pair of guards opened the heavy wooden doors into the hall, and I thought, *they know that I am the future of Egypt now.*

In Merit's chamber, Ramesses stood with me over our sons' cradles. I felt my eyes burn, and Ramesses put his arm across my shoulders.

"I will care for them like my own sons," Merit swore, and I knew that she would. She would guard them with her life. But I also knew that all the spells in Egypt couldn't protect my princes from Anubis if the jackal-headed god of death set his sights on them. When sons live to see five years of age, it is a cause for rejoicing, and their heads are shaved but for a single forelock that is tightly braided and curled at the end. We have a saying in Thebes that a son is his father's staff in old age. Amunher and Prehir would be more than that; they would be the heirs to their father's throne if I were made queen. They would be the jewels in his crown.

Merit said solemnly, "You don't have to worry about them, Your Majesty. I raised Nefertari—"

"That's what I'm worried about." Ramesses laughed.

Merit crossed her arms over her chest and raised her chin. "I raised Nefertari, who was never sick and never in want of anything.

She may have turned out wild"—her lower lip trembled—"but that is no doing of mine."

"And you did very well, *mawat*." I embraced Merit and her sharp gaze softened.

"I would like to think so, Your Highness."

CHAPTER TWENTY

ON THE
NORTHERN SEA

IN THE GOLDEN mist of early morning, ten ships lay at anchor, clustered around the stone steps of the quay that abutted the palace. The largest was *Amun's Blessing*, and fifty soldiers who were dressed as merchants heaved and rolled barrels filled with sand up its gangplank. The ship looked like its sisters, except that from the masts, the blue and gold pennants of royalty moved quietly in the breeze. A young boy had been found to dress as a princess and walk the deck. He stood with Asha, examining a jeweled knife that he had been given. When the fighting began, he would be secured in the ship's cabin.

Senior members of the court stood on the quay, waiting for the ships to finally set sail so that they could return to the warmth of the palace and eat their morning meal. As the last barrel was loaded, Iset flung herself at Ramesses once more.

"She's wasting time," I said reproachfully.

But Woserit smiled. "Let the viziers see her making a fool of herself while you stand here, ready for battle."

Iset wept on Ramesses's shoulder, and kohl streaked down her cheeks in thick black lines. For the first time in all of the years I had known her, she looked neither alluring nor beautiful, and the stiffness of her walk told me she was suffering from yesterday's birth. "What if something happens to Ramessu?" she cried. "How will you know?"

"I will see you in Avaris," Ramesses promised gently. He pried Iset from his shoulder and glanced uneasily at Asha.

"But what if something happens to you?" Her voice rose, and Ramesses was about to smile kindly until she made the error of asking, "What would Ramessu's place be in the palace?" At once, she saw she had made a mistake. "I . . . I mean how would Ramessu know his place without a father to guide him?"

But it was too late. Iset had given herself away, and Ramesses's voice was cold when he replied, "Then it's a good thing the gods watch over kings, and our son will never have to be raised fatherless."

I strode ahead, meeting Ramesses at the edge of the quay, and in front of the viziers he asked, "Is the Warrior Queen of Egypt ready?"

I lifted my head with its heavy diadem. "Ready to show the Sherden pirates that Egypt will never suffer thieves to steal her riches."

Long clouds trailed across the sky, and ibis birds called to one another in the growing light. It was a good day for sailing. We boarded *Amun's Blessing*, and from the deck of the ship I saw Henuttawy whisper something into Iset's ear. But whatever plan Henuttawy was hatching, Woserit and Paser would be there to stop it. I waved to Woserit until the fleet slipped from the lagoon on its journey to the sea, and all I could see were her turquoise robes and dark head leaning against Paser.

Ramesses stood at my side while *Amun's Blessing* moved swiftly down the River Nile, its blue and gold pennants unfurling behind her like a woman's hair. "Woserit has been in love with Paser for as long as I can remember," he remarked. "Do you ever wonder why they haven't married?"

I wrapped a cloak tighter against the mist, choosing my words carefully. "Probably because she's afraid of angering Henuttawy."

"Henuttawy can have any man," Ramesses said dismissively. "Surely she wouldn't object if Woserit marries first."

"She would if Woserit is marrying the man that Henuttawy wants."

Ramesses stared at me. *"Paser?"*

I nodded.

"How long have you known this?" he exclaimed.

"Woserit told me." I walked with him into the ship's royal cabin. A bed had been placed beneath painted images of Sekhmet slashing her enemies.

"What else did she tell you?"

I searched Ramesses's face and determined to roll the knuckle-bones. "Woserit believes that Henuttawy wants Paser because he's the one man who won't have her."

We took chairs that had been arranged around a Senet board. "I am wary of Henuttawy," Ramesses confided. "She's beautiful, but under that beauty is something dark. Don't you think?"

I had to stop myself from telling him everything I knew about Henuttawy's darkness, from reaching across the table and shaking him awake, imploring him to see what his aunt truly was. Instead I replied, "I would be very careful before trusting her advice."

☖ ☖ ☖

WE SAILED along the river for three days, stopping at night to cook on the shore and drink barrels of *shedeh* from Malkata's winery. I was the only woman in the fleet, and if not for the boy who would play the role of princess when we reached the Northern Sea, I would have been the youngest as well. We sang and ate roasted duck in bowls from the palace, and the fat from the meat dripped off the soldiers' fingers as they sat around the fires.

On the fourth night, Ramesses announced, "We have asked the locals and there is word that the Sherden were here a few nights ago. They have raided a ship bound for my father's palace in Avaris."

The men around the fires began to grumble their indignation.

"Tomorrow, we will send a scout," Asha said. In the silvery light of the moon, he looked older than his nineteen years. When we were students in the edduba, he had broken the hearts of all the girls; I wondered now if he had met anyone yet, and whether he would marry. "The scout will go by land," he went on, "and when the Sherden have been spotted, we will send out *Amun's Blessing* and follow close behind. The fleet will wait at the bend in the river, and the scout will go out a second time. When he signals that the Sherden have approached our merchant ship, we will sail and attack!" Asha sprang to his feet for emphasis, and the cheers of the men rang out along the deserted stretch of riverbank.

Later that night, Ramesses stood behind me in our cabin and caressed my shoulders. We breathed together in the darkness, naked except for my long kilt. He removed the linen slowly, letting it fall in a pool at my feet. I shivered from his touch and he took me in his arms, carrying me to the ebony bed. He pressed his body against mine, inhaling the oil of jasmine from my skin. Over the sound of the ship groaning against its moorings, there was no one who could hear us, and when we finally fell asleep, it was in each other's arms.

☖ ☖ ☖

A shriek pierced the morning's stillness. Ramesses and I sat up in our bed, shaken from deepest sleep. I couldn't tell what it was. A child, an animal?

When it sounded again, we rushed to find our sheaths, and on the shore we saw the boy, who was dressed in a woman's wig and heavy bangles, weeping into his hands. A large soldier was shaking him by the shoulders.

"Leave him!" I cried, and the boy gaped up at me as if I had saved him from a tutor's merciless beating. When I reached the shore, he ran and clung to my leg, refusing to let go.

"He won't do it, Your Majesty!" the soldier shouted. "He is too afraid. We promised his father, the Stable Master, seven gold deben for his son to walk the decks, and he swore to us that his child was no coward!"

The boy began to cry loudly again, pathetic wails, and I pressed my hand softly to his cheek. "Shh, nothing terrible will happen to you."

"But what of *us*, Your Majesty!" the soldier protested. "What will we do with the Sherden so close? A young girl may not have any breasts, but if we use a man, how will we explain . . ."

"Maybe a soldier can wear the disguise," I suggested, "and he can stand with his back to the ship's railing?"

The man snorted. "And if the spies glimpse the muscles in his shoulders? We need someone who can pass for a woman. We need a princess's dowry ship that will lure them out!" He turned in supplication to Ramesses. "Please, tell me. What shall we do, Your Highness?"

I wondered if fatherhood had changed Ramesses, for instead of growing impatient with the child, he was watching him with pity. When the boy began to whimper again, I pried him from my kilt and said firmly, "I should go."

Ramesses looked at me, and concern was etched upon his face. "You understand this is dangerous, Nefer. You would need to carry a weapon."

"I can strap a knife to my thigh."

The soldier fumbled for his words. "But . . . but you're a *woman!*" he exclaimed. "You're a *princess.* Your life would be at risk—"

"And what is our alternative?" I demanded. "To waste days and let these Sherden slip away?"

His cheeks flared like a cobra's. "For this child to put on a wig and do as he's told! You realize, boy, that your father will be expecting his gold deben?" The little boy looked up with wide, frightened eyes and began to tremble. "He will be angry when you return without it!"

"Then I will give him the deben," I said. "And walk the decks instead. Then, when the Sherden arrive, I will lock myself in the cabin just as he was going to."

The soldier looked at Ramesses. "Your Highness, this is your wife!"

"And that's why I trust her to act responsibly. We shall keep her close."

The soldier stared at us, shocked beyond words, as we returned to the ship. Then the scout who had left in the night appeared with news. The Sherden had been spotted only a short distance away, in the channels and passages leading to the Northern Sea. Immediately, *Amun's Blessing* weighed anchor, and I sat in the cabin watching the soldiers in their merchants' clothes, laughing at one another and relishing their new roles.

"I want you to use the crossbar when we arrive." Ramesses indicated the lock on the cabin's door and added, "I'll post soldiers outside and two within. No matter what happens, Nefer, whatever you think you hear outside, you're not to come out."

"We don't even know that we will find them today—"

"We don't have to worry about finding them," he said darkly. "Their spies along the shore will find us once we dock in Tamiat and unload the barrels."

"How do you think they will send word to their ships?"

"Polished bronze mirrors . . . light signals," he guessed, and stood. "As I said before—do not come out of this cabin. Not even if you think I've been wounded. This isn't a game. These are men who haven't seen a woman in a very long time. They live on the water and eat what they catch. A glimpse of you and they will be beating down this door."

Listening to the seriousness in his voice, I felt real fear. "But if you're wounded, you will take shelter in this cabin. You won't fight if you're wounded."

"I will fight until the Sherden have been defeated!" he swore, and I was afraid of where his rashness might lead. He cupped my chin in his hand. "You are the bravest woman I have ever known. But if something were to happen to you—"

"It won't. I won't open the door. I'll lock myself in, and the guards will protect me."

For the rest of the morning, we prepared. Ramesses watched me dress first, telling me which wig he preferred, and which bangles— though I had brought them for the boy—would catch the light best. I took extra care in applying my paint, making the lines both dark and bold so that even from far away it was clear that my lips had been reddened. When I was finished, only my throat remained bare, and as Ramesses fastened my golden pectoral, I could feel his breath warm and fast on my neck. I turned, and though I wanted to run my hands over his chest, I slowly fastened his leather armor. He had strapped a hidden dagger to his thigh, and when he knelt to do the same for me, I realized, "Your hair. Merchants wear their hair in single braids, not loops."

Though we hadn't washed properly in several days, his hair still smelled of lavender from the baths of Malkata, and when I stepped back to look at him, I sighed. "I wonder if there has ever been a Pharaoh who has looked this beautiful before battle?"

Ramesses laughed. "I'll need a steady arm far more than beauty before these days are over."

⛫ ⛫ ⛫

AT MIDDAY, we emerged from the soil-laden channels of the Nile, and an endless expanse of blue stretched before us. The Northern Sea.

Our ship arrived at the port of Tamiat that afternoon, and Ramesses took my hand. "We're here. The soldiers will start unloading the barrels on the quay." He smiled at me, but I could see apprehension in his eyes. "Are you ready?"

I checked my image in the polished brass. My breasts were still heavy from childbirth, and my Nubian wig fell across my shoulders in small, perfect braids. My earrings were turquoise, and even my sandals were encrusted with precious stones. There was no one who would mistake me for a commoner, and certainly not for a man.

I followed Ramesses onto the deck, and Asha teased him. "That kilt becomes you, Ramesses!" It was threadbare and worn, taken from a merchant outside Malkata, and he looked like he belonged washing the decks. Only his sandals, which were thick heeled and well made, gave him away.

"Laugh," Ramesses rejoined, "but I'm not the one who smells of fish."

Asha smelled himself; the cloak he was wearing was repugnant, and I wondered who he had taken it from. Then both men turned to me, and Ramesses asked, "You know what to do?"

I nodded. Seven soldiers disguised as merchants had tethered us to the quay and began unloading the sand-filled barrels. I stood on the prow, letting the pale sunlight reflect from my jewels, and inhaled the scent of sea air and brine. The ocean was nothing like the waters of the Nile. Frothy waves spilled onto the beach, surging shoreward, then back again as though they'd been caught in a fisherman's net and hauled out to sea.

Then a pair of tall ships appeared to windward, and the men working around me grew tense. I looked at Ramesses, who was waiting on the prow with a polished mirror, and from the stern a soldier cried eagerly, "It's the Sherden! I can see it from their pennants, Your Highness!"

Ramesses held the polished mirror above his head, and the three scouts who waited in the distance to give word to the other ships disappeared.

Asha turned to me. "Get yourself into the cabin. Lock the door!"

When Ramesses rushed to my side, I made him promise, "Don't worry about me. Just remind the Sherden that Egypt will never tolerate thieves!"

I locked the door of my cabin and sat on my bed. Though guards stood on either side of the Senet board, armed with swords and javelins, the taste of fear was bitter in my mouth. I couldn't stop my hands from giving me away. I tucked them beneath my legs to keep them from shaking. After all, servants weren't the only ones who gossiped.

There was the thump of another vessel pulling up to the quay, then shouting as strangers began to board our ship. A scuffle resounded outside my door, then it seemed as if Anubis himself had been unleashed on the deck of *Amun's Blessing*. Men shouted in foreign voices, and I imagined the moment that Ramesses's soldiers must have torn off their cloaks and revealed their weapons. I heard the clash of metal on metal, and when a heavy object crashed against the door I cried out. But neither of my two guards moved. The gray-haired one said calmly to me, "They won't come in."

My voice came out in a gasp. "How do you know?"

"Because this was once a treasury ship," the soldier replied. "There isn't a door in the navy that's stronger than this one."

The shouting grew louder and more intense. Then a voice cried exultantly, "The ships have arrived!" I heard the panic of the Sherden as they realized that their own two ships had been surrounded, but even then the fighting continued.

The sun was still high when Ramesses called to me, his voice filled with triumph. I flung open the cabin door, and he spun me in his arms.

"More than a hundred Sherden are our prisoners," he declared. "There will be no more pirates haunting the quays of Tamiat. No more Sherden pillaging from Egypt or Crete or Mycenae. Come!"

He led me from the cabin onto the prow, and I became aware of the blood on his kilt as the soldiers cheered, holding up their swords in honor of our victory. "To Ramesses the Great and his Warrior Queen," one man shouted and hundreds joined in the chant. The words echoed over the waters and from the encircling warships, where the Sherden were being bound in chains. Ramesses led me to the quay, where chests filled with precious metals and ivory gleamed in the sun. In a happy reversal, our soldiers were unloading the Sherden ships, it appeared that the stolen treasures were endless: turquoise amulets and silver bowls from ships that had once been bound for Crete. There was red leather armor and alabaster jars engraved with strange scenes of a horse from a battle at Troy. Next emerged a golden litter adorned with carnelian and blue glass beads.

Ramesses put his arm around my waist. "The soldiers are all talking about you. It was incredibly brave . . ."

I waved away his compliment. "What? To walk the deck of a ship?"

"So many captives!" Asha interrupted. "We've had to place them on two separate ships. What do you want to do with them?" he asked. "They're shouting for something, but I can't understand what they're saying."

I separated myself from Ramesses. "What language do they speak?"

"Something I've never heard," Asha admitted. "But one man was speaking Hittite."

"They probably all speak some Hittite," I guessed. "They may have learned it in Troy, along with Greek. What do you want me to tell them?"

"That they are prisoners of Egypt," Ramesses said, then repeated what I had told him. "And that Egypt will *never* tolerate thieves."

I smiled.

"And will you show yourself to them?" Asha asked.

It was a risk. Ramesses wouldn't want the Sherden to think they were so important that the Pharaoh of Egypt himself had come to dispose of them. But if Ramesses appeared in his *nemes* crown with his crook and flail, they would be reminded of whom they had dared to anger, and that none could cross Pharaoh and remain unpunished.

Ramesses looked around the quay with its piles of looted treasure, and I saw his cheeks redden. "Yes, I will come."

A soldier ran to fetch Ramesses's crown, and Asha, forever cautious, said to me, "These men are pirates. Be careful. They are vicious, and if one of them should break loose—"

"Then I will have you and Ramesses there to protect me."

We boarded the first ship where the captives were being held, and almost at once I was overwhelmed by the stench. Blood and urine soaked the decks, and I put the sleeve of my cloak to my nose. I prepared myself for the sight of men in chains, bleeding and angry. But the wounded had been taken to a separate ship, and the fifty men who sat blinking into the sun were unbowed. They didn't wear beards on their chins like the Hittites, and their long yellow hair was a sight to behold. I paused to stare at them, and when they recognized Ramesses's crown, they shook their chains and shouted. I commanded in Hittite, "Calm yourselves!"

Many of the men passed looks between one another. Some leered so that I would know what they were thinking, but I refused to be unsettled. "I am Princess Nefertari," I addressed them, "daughter of Queen Mutnodjmet and wife of Pharaoh Ramesses. You have looted Pharaoh's ships, taken Pharaoh's goods, and murdered Pharaoh's soldiers. You will now repay your debt to Pharaoh by serving in his army." The men raised their voices, and next to me, Ramesses and Asha tensed. I saw Ramesses reach for the hilt of his sword, and I shouted over the outburst, "You may serve in Pharaoh's army where you will be given training, outfitted with clothes, perhaps earn a command as an officer. Or you may rebel, and be sent to a certain grave toiling in Pharaoh's quarries."

There was a sudden silence, as the men realized that they were not to be put to death but trained and fed.

Ramesses looked at me. "You know that their leaders will have to be executed."

I nodded solemnly. "But the rest of them—"

"May serve a better purpose."

CHAPTER TWENTY-ONE

PI-RAMESSES

Avaris

NEWS OF THE Sherden conquest traveled quickly up the River Nile. As we sailed toward the city of Avaris, people along the shore chanted triumphantly, "PHARAOH! PHARAOH!" Then the soldiers in the fleet took up the cry of, "WARRIOR QUEEN," which the people on the shore returned without knowing why. And yet, I felt unease—for I wondered what Henuttawy would do when she heard that chant repeated.

Three days after the Sherden were defeated, we stood on the deck of *Amun's Blessing* as the ship sailed into port. Because war and rebellion had stolen recent summers, the court in Thebes had not made its progress to Avaris since Ramesses had been crowned, and I was shocked by how much the city had changed. In the years I had been away, it was as if someone had taken a painting and left it out in the sun, allowing it to fade, then crack, and finally peel. I turned to Asha.

"What happened?" he gasped.

We both looked at Ramesses, and although he should have been basking in the adoration of the people who crowded the shore shouting his name, his face was stricken. "Look at the quay! Half of it's falling to pieces!" Entire boards were rotten, and there appeared to be no system for washing away the grime, which clung to the women's robes and feet. Merchants had dropped fish heads to rot where they lay, not bothering to kick them back into the river. "And the litters!" He pointed to the faded canopies resting atop chipped carrying poles.

"It's like Pharaoh Seti hasn't stepped outside of his palace in years," Asha murmured.

"But he came to Thebes for the Feast of Wag. He must know about this! He *had* to have seen . . ."

We disembarked with twenty soldiers who would accompany us to the palace of Pi-Ramesses, and the clapping mobs were too happy to notice Ramesses's distress. They ran before the litter he was sharing with me, throwing lotus petals into the air and passing the soldiers tall cups of barley beer. And even though he waved, I knew what Ramesses was thinking. Large holes in the main road had gone ignored, when all they would have required was dirt and stone to fill them in. The streets were littered with half-eaten pomegranates, sewage, and discarded papyrus. There was the unmistakable look of abandonment in Avaris, as if the city had been left to rule itself and no one much cared what happened to it.

When we reached the palace, heavily armed guards opened the gates. As Ramesses descended from the litter, he shook his head fearfully. "Something has happened. Something terrible has happened in there."

The gardens had been allowed to grow untended, and on a carpet of weeds the towering statues of Amun stood cracked and dirtied. Every house in Egypt kept a courtyard of tile or dirt at its front where no snakes would be able to hide, but weeds and grass had been allowed to grow right up to the steps of Pi-Ramesses. We reached the heavy wooden doors, and when Ramesses saw how worn they had become, he snapped angrily, "Is this my father's palace or the ruins of Amarna?" Even the tiles underfoot were cracked and broken. He turned to me. "I don't understand this—what could be more important than maintaining this palace? My grandfather built Pi-Ramesses. If it's crumbling now, what will happen in a hundred years? What will be left for our family to be remembered by?"

The doors swung open, and when there was no one in the hall to greet our arrival, the soldiers escorting us grew nervous. A figure emerged from the shadows, and as it grew closer I could hear a dozen swords being drawn from their sheaths. Then the light fell across Woserit's face, and she was weeping.

"Ramesses, your father has taken ill. He's lying in his chamber, waiting for you."

The color drained from Ramesses's cheeks. "When?" he cried. "When did this happen?"

"After we arrived. Just yesterday."

Ramesses dismissed his soldiers with a wave of his hand, and Asha knew to settle them in the Great Hall with food and drink. I followed behind Ramesses and Woserit, and because I had never seen her cry, the sound frightened me. Her turquoise cloak trailed before me, and I tried to concentrate on its beaded hem rather than allow myself to feel the horror of what was happening. Seti was ill, but that didn't explain why the city had been allowed to deteriorate, or why the palace, besides the few servants peering nervously between the columns, seemed to be an empty husk.

When we entered Seti's chamber, several guards parted their spears to allow us through. But the man in the bed was not the same man I had seen during the Feast of Wag. Not even the linens they had covered him with could conceal how slight he was, or how pale he had grown since I'd last seen him.

"Father!" Ramesses cried.

Queen Tuya, Iset, and Henuttawy already stood in a circle around him. Paser sat on a wooden stool nearby, and Woserit joined him. Pharaoh Seti opened his eyes, but he seemed to know his son more by his voice than by sight. "Ramesses," he whispered, and coughed.

"Iset will find you more juice," Henuttawy said. "Is that what you'd like?"

Seti nodded painfully, and she took Iset and quickly left the chamber.

Ramesses knelt at his father's bed. "What is it, *abi?*" He used the intimate word for *father.* I had never heard him use it before. There was heartbreak in his voice.

Pharaoh Seti let out a heavy sigh, and Queen Tuya began weeping. Her *iwiw* lay with his muzzle between his paws, looking almost as sick at heart as his mistress. He didn't even raise his head to offer me his customary growl. "I have been sick for many months now, Ramesses. Anubis is following me."

"No, *abi*. Please, not yet!"

Seti coughed again and bent his finger for Ramesses to come closer. "I want you to repair Pi-Ramesses for me. She has fallen into ruin." Seti groaned, grasping the heavy linen covers in his hands. "For a hundred years, the Hittites have threatened to invade. They think to rule Egypt when I am gone. All of the treasury's gold has gone to the stables. To my charioteers. Now the Hittites will become your problem . . ."

"We have just tasted victory over the Sherden! We have brought them here as prisoners to train with your army—"

Pharaoh Seti struggled to sit up. It was difficult for me to believe that this was the same man who had picked me up and sat me on his knee when I was a child. Eyes, voice, flesh: everything about him appeared shrunken, as if he was turning into the mummified Osiris before us. "I am past care, Ramesses. The physicians say it is a condition of the heart. The heart is weak," he wheezed.

Ramesses opened his mouth to argue, but Seti raised his hand. "There's not enough time. Bring me the maps." His watery eyes fell on a low-lying table. "My projects." Pharaoh Seti breathed heavily. "These are what you must finish for me."

That very morning, we had been celebrating our triumph. Now I realized we might be mourning Seti's death before the day ended. It occurred to me that the gods held life on Ma'at's silver scales. Great happiness must be balanced by great sorrow.

"There is my tomb in the Valley," Seti said. "The paintings are done. All that is left is to carry my sarcophagus into its chamber." A violent sob escaped from Tuya, and I pressed my lips together so that I wouldn't sob as well. But Pharaoh Seti carried on. "And this palace." His breathing became labored. "Be certain to restore this palace, Ramesses. Make it your capital so that you can be closer to Hatti. If you can defend the city of Avaris, Egypt will never fall."

"Egypt will *never* be conquered while I am Pharaoh—"

"Then you must not let the Hittites take back Kadesh. Without her, our lands are vulnerable." Pharaoh Seti sighed. "And Nefer."

Ramesses glanced at me. "Do you want to speak with her?"

"*No!*"

He was vehement, and I pressed my back to the door.

"Let her remember me as I was. Nefer—" His voice began to fail. "Nefertari is the mother of your eldest sons. A clever princess . . . but the people still don't want her."

"Who told you this?" Ramesses demanded. Woserit looked across the chamber at me, and we both knew at once: Henuttawy.

"It doesn't matter who told me this. I have heard. The people are what's important, Ramesses. You know what happened to Nefertiti. The people killed her—"

"The *priests* killed her," Ramesses argued.

"And the priests are the mouths of the people. Akhenaten—" Pharaoh Seti grasped the covers, and I imagined that I could hear his heart rattling in his shrunken chest. "Wait at least another year before you choose your Chief Wife."

"*Abi*," Ramesses protested. "It's already been a year."

"Do not risk what this family has built! Wait at least another year. Promise me."

I held my breath and waited for Ramesses to make the promise. But Ramesses didn't speak.

"Promise!" Pharaoh Seti exclaimed, and Ramesses whispered, "I promise."

I closed my eyes and slipped quietly out the door, shutting it behind me. The pain in my chest felt as if it burned with flame, and I ran to the Audience Chamber to be alone. The door was slightly ajar. As I stepped inside I almost cried out, but for the sound of voices from behind a pillar. I crept along the wall toward the front of the chamber, listening.

"I have bought you a year, and you will wipe that ugly scowl from your face and look me in the eye," whispered Henuttawy.

"The gods will see what you've done—" Iset swore.

"What *we've* done." Henuttawy's voice was calm. "Every servant in Avaris saw you with that cup last night."

"Because *you* gave it to me!"

"And who was there to see that? And anyway, all we did was speed his interminable passing. The longer we wait, the stronger Nefertari will grow. No one may ever question this," she said, "but if I should remind them—" Henuttawy glanced over her shoulder at the empty chamber before continuing in a harsh whisper. "You *shall* find a way to repay me, or as I am bound to Isis, I will take back everything I have ever given you! If he makes that girl queen, she'll have him banish us to Mi-Wer, and don't think I won't sacrifice you to save—"

There was noise outside the Audience Chamber, and their conversation fell silent. I escaped through the door and steadied myself with several deep breaths in case they should see me. Woserit appeared in the hall with Paser, followed by Ramesses and Queen Tuya.

Ramesses looked as pale as alabaster. "He's gone, Nefer." He shook his head and was not ashamed to weep. "Gone to Osiris."

I took him in my arms as Henuttawy and Iset appeared with cups of *shedeh*.

Seeing our tears, Henuttawy cried out, and Iset placed her hand across her mouth.

I buried my face in Ramesses's chest so that no one could see how sick the sight of them made me. Ramesses removed himself from my embrace. "Letters will have to be drafted . . ."

"With Your Highness's permission, I will take care of the letters," Paser said.

Your Highness.

The words struck Ramesses a visible blow. There would only be one Pharaoh of Egypt now.

"And what would you like me to do?" Henuttawy asked.

I wanted to shout that murdering the King of Egypt was sufficient, but the words stuck in my mouth and the burning in my chest increased.

"Go with Iset and Woserit," Ramesses said. "They will take my mother to the Temple of Amun where she will let the gods know . . ." He hesitated, since the truth was too terrible to speak. "She will let the gods know that my father is coming."

When everyone turned to leave, I motioned for Paser, and he saw me hovering near the door to the Audience Chamber.

"Nefertari, what are you doing?" he demanded.

"He should never have died!" I whispered fiercely.

Paser looked behind him, but the hall had cleared.

"When I left the chamber I heard Henuttawy speaking with Iset. They were talking about a cup," I said frantically. "Henuttawy told Iset that she had bought another year. *Another year*," I repeated.

"We all saw Iset pass Pharaoh a cup last night . . ." Paser replied.

"But it was Henuttawy who gave it to her! And now she has a secret she can use to ruin Iset if Iset won't give her whatever she wants. And what she wants is to banish Woserit to the farthest temple in the Fayyum, then rebuild the Temple of Isis so that she'll control the largest treasury in Egypt."

"This only comes to pass if Iset becomes queen—"

"And now she has another year to try! You heard Ramesses's promise, and even if he doesn't honor it . . . if Henuttawy could kill her own brother . . ."

For the first time, I saw fear in Paser's eyes. "The physicians said it was Pharaoh's heart. No one suspected poison." He looked at me. "Who else has heard this?"

"No one," I promised.

"Then keep your own counsel. I will tell Woserit—"

"And Ramesses? Pharaoh Seti was his *father!*"

But Paser shook his head. "And there is no proof of what you've heard."

"A physician can determine if it was poison."

"Or he might determine that it was his heart, and you will have wrongly accused the High Priestess of Isis. Keep your silence. Ramesses may believe you; he may even summon a physician, but how will we know he's not in the pay of Henuttawy? There are politics in everything, Nefertari."

"So Seti's death will go unpunished?" I clenched my fists to keep the rage from shaking my whole body.

"No evil deed ever goes unpunished." He raised his eyes to a mural of the goddess Ma'at, who was weighing a heart against the feather of truth. Because the heart had been honest in life, it was equal in weight to the feather, and in the painting, the man was smiling. His *ka* would not be devoured by the crocodile god. His soul would go on to live for eternity.

"Henuttawy's heart will outweigh the feather," I swore.

Paser looked suddenly sad when he replied, "Yes. It probably will. Eat nothing that Merit hasn't prepared for you, Nefertari."

Paser left me standing alone in the hall. I had birthed two sons, I had gone with Ramesses into battle against the Sherden, and I thought selfishly of how all of those triumphs would be forgotten now that Pharaoh Seti was dead. The words that the soldiers had chanted this very morning would become songs of mourning by tomorrow. In the nearby Temple of Amun, Henuttawy and Iset were already weeping false tears with the queen, tears for my truest protector at court. It was as if everything I touched turned into ash.

That evening, dinner in the Great Hall was solemn, and Ramesses left his father's chair empty on the dais. When Iset suggested that he take his place in it, he asked sharply, "Why?"

The court knew enough to be silent after that.

Later that night, in the privacy of my chamber, I bit my lip to keep from telling Ramesses what I'd heard. He sat on the gold and ebony bed I had slept in during every childhood summer in Avaris. Raised on a platform in the middle of the room, it overlooked the gardens that Seti had let grow untended. Layers of scum stretched unbroken over the pools, and I wondered if the fish had survived such neglect.

"Have you seen my father's stables?" he asked quietly. He didn't want to speak about his father's death. *He will carry it with him like a heavy chain around a prisoner's waist,* I thought. "They are massive," he said, though his voice was distant. "Five thousand warhorses in all."

I pressed the covers to my chest. Even the fires in the braziers did nothing to warm me. "That's more than all of Thebes."

"And they are well kept," he said, a flicker of life in his eyes. "He had weaponry for more than ten thousand men, and four thousand chariots are polished and ready. He was serious about war with the Hittites, Nefer."

"The Hittites have threatened war for generations—"

"Not like this. Look around. Do you see the disrepair? *All* of the treasury's gold has gone to preparation for this! Since the Hittite emperor conquered Mitanni, there remains no buffer between ourselves and Hatti. My father recognized how dangerous that was. He knew it was only a matter of time. Paser says that Muwatallis will move as soon as he hears of my father's death."

"Another battle?" We had just returned from victory over the Sherden. There was a funeral to plan. Too much sorrow had fallen on us.

Ramesses gazed into the brazier ruefully. "No, not another battle, Nefer. A war."

古 古 古

ON THE deck of *Amun's Blessing* the next morning, Pharaoh Seti's body was wrapped in linen and placed on a small dais surrounded by myrrh. His lips were curved in a gentle smile, released now from his watch on Egypt's northern wall. In twenty days we would arrive in Thebes, and after seventy days of mummification, Seti would sleep in the tomb he had chosen, among Egypt's greatest kings.

Ramesses stood at the prow, and a single flag painted with an image of the mummified Osiris flapped solemnly in the breeze.

Women lined the quay dressed in their long white robes of mourning. They floated lotus blossoms ahead of the ship and beat their chests with their hands so the gods would know of our plight. All along our passage south, I watched villagers and fishermen kneel on the shore in honor of their Pharaoh. *If only they knew the truth of his passing, how many of them would be content to quietly bow and weep?*

When we reached the palace of Malkata, Woserit warned, "Do not let your sons from your sight. Not even to bathe."

"And Merit?"

"You may tell her what you heard." There were deep half-moons beneath Woserit's eyes, and I wondered if Paser had comforted her through the nights the way I had tried to comfort Ramesses.

Inside my chamber, Merit greeted me. I felt guilty over the pleasure I took in seeing my children while the rest of Egypt was in mourning. The milk nurses stood and watched as my sons raised their hands to me. "Look how they've grown!" I cried. We had been gone for a month, and my sons were nearly unrecognizable. They smiled when I called each of them by name, and I marveled at how clever they already were. "And their hair!" My sons' heads were like crowns of the finest gold.

"Like the king himself," Merit replied, but as soon as she said his name, she thought of Seti's death and her voice dropped to a whisper. "I was sorry to hear of Pharaoh, my lady."

"It happened as soon as we arrived in Avaris."

"We heard that the Sherden had been conquered, then news came that Pharaoh was ill, but no one could believe it. They said it was his heart—"

"It was poison," I said harshly.

Merit covered her mouth. She waved the milk nurses back into their chamber, and when they had shut the doors, I told Merit the full story.

"I can't understand . . ." Merit cried. "What happened to his tasters?"

"He dismissed almost all the palace servants," I said. "To pay for war with the Hittites, and to buy armor from Crete."

Merit pressed her fingers to her lips. "Henuttawy has given up her *ka* to make Iset queen. She will come for you," she said with certainty. "You must hire a taster of your own."

I recoiled from the idea, but Merit persisted.

"Ramesses has tasters."

"Because he is Pharaoh."

"And you will be queen! If you use a taster, Henuttawy will know, and she will never risk poison. Think of your sons! What would become of them if something were to happen to you? Do you think that Iset would keep me in this palace to watch over them? I would be sent with Woserit to the farthest temple in Egypt, while they lay here, defenseless."

I felt my limbs grow cold. It was true. I looked at my children, beautiful princes of Egypt who might someday be kings. "Hire a taster," I said.

"And if Pharaoh asks?"

"I will tell him . . ."

"That you are afraid of Hittite spies?" Merit said helpfully.

Henuttawy and Iset were liars. I didn't want to lie to Ramesses as well. *I should tell him the truth,* I thought: *that I am afraid his own aunt will kill me with a cup of wine or sip of shedeh.*

There was a knock at the door, and before Merit received it, she turned to me. "Another year, my lady . . . Do you think he will keep his promise?" she asked.

I tried to ignore the hurt of Pharaoh Seti's request. "He has never broken a promise," I said.

"Even when Pharaoh Ramesses knows he made it to honor a lie?

The people in Thebes heard from the messengers what happened to the pirates. They are starting to call you the Warrior Queen. They are saying that you risked your life for Egypt."

But I repeated, "Ramesses has never broken a promise."

Her shoulders sagged and she answered the door. "Your Highness!" She was startled in the doorway, quickly straightening her wig. "You have never knocked before . . ."

"I heard voices and thought Nefer might be telling you what happened in Avaris." Ramesses entered my chamber and saw me with our sons. "I didn't want to interrupt."

"I am sorry for what happened to your father. He was like a father to my lady as well. Always kind, always gentle."

"Thank you, Merit. We will all be moving down to my father's court at Avaris as soon as his funeral has been held."

"The entire palace?" she cried.

"Even Tefer." Ramesses looked down, and Tefer responded with a plaintive cry. The cat had been sleeping beneath our sons' cradles and appeared in no hurry to abandon his post. "It will take seventy days to prepare my father's body. But once he is buried in the Valley of the Sleeping Kings, the court will move with us to Pi-Ramesses."

I could already see Merit cataloguing the work that would have to be done. She excused herself with a bow, and Ramesses stood next to me.

"My father loved you, Nefer."

"I'd like to believe that," I said softly.

"You *must* believe that. I know you heard what he made me promise. He feared for my crown. He wanted to see you made queen, but someone misguided him."

"I don't think he was misguided," I said carefully. "I think he was lied to."

Ramesses watched me, and I wondered whether he was thinking

of Iset and Henuttawy. I could not be the one to tell him the truth. It would have to be something he came to on his own. At last, his look of concentration faded, and he put his arm around my waist. "I will protect you. I will always protect you, Nefer."

I closed my eyes and prayed to Amun, *Just let him discover whom to protect me from.*

CHAPTER TWENTY-TWO

IN THE VALLEY OF THE SLEEPING KINGS

Thebes

WHEN THE SEVENTY days of mummification were complete, Pharaoh Seti's body was placed in a golden bark and carried on the shoulders of twenty priests into the Western Valley. Assuming that his heart was as light as Ma'at's feather of truth and he was allowed to pass into the fields of Aaru, he would need this boat to travel with the sun on its daily journey around the world. Thousands of Thebans had crossed the River Nile to follow the winding funerary procession, and as the sun began to sink beneath the hills, the scent of sage baked all day by the sun was carried down on the cool evening wind. Adjo raised his muzzle to sniff at the air, and though I walked next to him with the rest of Seti's closest family, the *iwiw* remained strangely subdued. *I wonder if he knows that his mistress's life has been changed forever?* Now Tuya had become a Dowager Queen, and although she'd remain in Avaris when we arrived, she would probably retire to a quiet room in the palace, leaving the court's politics and festivities to Ramesses. I had never seen her smile at children or laugh at their antics when they scampered through the halls. Some widows settled into contented lives as grandmothers, but I imagined

Tuya's days would be spent alone with Adjo, and that pampering him would become the sole purpose of her remaining years. She leaned heavily on Ramesses's arm as she walked. In front of them the High Priest of Amun strode purposefully across the sands, following Penre and a small group of viziers whose job was to guide Seti's golden bark to its rest.

I looked behind us at the priestesses of Isis, and even from a distance I could see the red figure of Henuttawy. She had chosen to walk among her priestesses instead of accompanying her family at the front, and she took no pains to preserve a solemn silence.

"She's enjoying the attention," I whispered harshly.

"And Amun will punish her," Merit vowed. "Her heart will tell its tale."

"When it's too late, and she has destroyed everyone we love." I thought of Amunher and Prehir, sleeping in the palace. I'd warned the milk nurses not to leave their side.

Merit read my look and promised, "I trust them. They will not leave the chamber, or I would not have left it myself." She looked beyond the dunes to where the hills rose steep and jagged in the fading light. "Do you think his tomb is far?"

"Yes. I think it is high in the cliffs," I said, then added bravely, "but there's nothing to fear."

"Only jackals," Merit whispered.

"And the High Priest of Amun." I glanced ahead at Rahotep, who lingered near Seti's body like an animal hovering over one of its kills. With his hunched shoulders and his mirthless grin, he looked as remorseful as a hyena that has chased a lioness from her prey. This night belonged to him. He was the one leading the royal family into the Valley, and he would be the one to seal Seti in his innermost chamber, with everything Pharaoh would need in the Afterlife.

I had last been inside a tomb for the burial of Princess Pili. I was six then, but I still remember the walls inside, covered with directions for navigating the Afterlife. Questions that the gods ask of the dead would be answered, so that when Seti's *ka* traveled down the final corridors of this world, it would be able to memorize the answers for passage into the next. Assuming he was able to pass these tests, he would need everything he had once used in this life. This was why Seti would need a mask, so that his soul would have a face in the land of Aaru. Surrounding his sarcophagus would be hundreds of *ushabti*, small statues of servants that would come to life in the next world to toil for their master. And so that none of these important things were besmirched, servants would place pinches of salt in their lamps, preventing any black smoke from rising.

I watched Iset and the High Priest of Amun – in profile they were the very image of two hyenas, sniffing about to see what they might scavenge. In the sharp light of sunset, with half of Rahotep's frightening grin cast in shadow, I was suddenly struck by the resemblance between them. They walked side by side, and it seemed strange that I had missed how similar they were – not just in the animal grace of their movements, but in the way their noses grew straight and their cheekbones sat high on their narrow faces, as they squinted into the sun's last rays. Iset's mother could have married whomever she wished yet no one seemed to know who had fathered Iset. What if Rahotep's interest in making Iset queen wasn't solely out of hatred for my *akhu*? With Iset as Chief Wife, would he be grandfather to the future Pharaoh? The High Priest looked in my direction, and when Iset saw that I was watching them, she quickly moved from his side.

I guarded my thoughts, for now we entered the Valley and the road narrowed. The thousands of mourners remained behind. Only the highest-ranking members of the court were allowed to know the location of Seti's tomb. Everyone else would wait for our return, holding their oil lamps on the rim of the cliffs to light our way back to the river. The sun had already passed the horizon, and the deep burning color of the sky silhouetted the hills. Each night, the sun god would leave his position in the sky completely and pass through the Underworld to defeat the snake god of darkness, Apep. When the snake was crushed, Ra would emerge in the east, the revealer of all things, riding on his solar barge to bring light back to the earth. Pharaoh Seti would never see the sun again, and if the order of things could be so upset in Egypt, I wondered, why couldn't it be upset in the Underworld, too? What if tonight Ra was overcome, and tomorrow there rose no more sun? I banished such thoughts, and reminded myself that the sun had *always* risen. Ra had *always* been victorious. *Just as I will be.*

We began to climb the limestone cliffs, and even over the grunting of the priests who carried Seti's barge on their backs, I could hear Iset's breathing grow ragged. She was afraid of the darkness, and once, when a jackal sounded in the distance, she let out a frightened cry.

"Anubis," I said. "The jackal-headed god of death. Perhaps he's coming for the guilty."

"Don't listen to her," Rahotep said sharply.

But I challenged the High Priest, "How do you know it's not Anubis? Where else would he be if not in this Valley?"

"Be silent!" Henuttawy snapped. Her voice echoed over the cliffs, and from the front of the procession, near the sarcophagus, Ramesses turned to see the cause of the commotion. Henuttawy lowered her voice. "Be *silent*," she threatened.

"Does the idea of Anubis stalking through these hills *frighten* you? I'm not afraid of death. When he comes for me, there is nothing I have to hide."

Behind me, Merit sucked in her breath.

Henuttawy hissed, "Have respect for the dead."

"By dancing and gossiping?"

We reached the mouth of the tomb, and Ramesses dropped back to walk at my side. "What is this whispering?"

"Henuttawy has said she wants to lead us into the tomb," I invented. "She wants to be the first to see her brother's sarcophagus placed inside its burial chamber."

Ramesses looked at Henuttawy. Even in the low light of the flickering torches I could see that she had lost the color in her cheeks. "That's very loyal," he said. "You may go after Penre. He will show you the way."

Henuttawy turned her dark eyes on me, but she didn't argue. She raised her chin and stepped after Penre, leading the procession into total darkness. Woserit dug her nails into my arm, warning me to be careful. But what was there to lose? Important courtiers followed after us, and armed guards stood watch at the mouth of the chamber to see that no one else was let inside. We descended the stairs into the belly of the earth, taking care not to touch the walls where images of Seti's life had been painted. Penre had told us that there was no other tomb in Egypt as long or deep as this, and when the air grew dank, I wrapped my cloak tighter around my waist. We moved through the first and second corridors by torchlight, and when we reached a four-pillared hall, the procession paused. I marveled at the shrine to Osiris and the scenes from the Book of Gates. "It's beautiful," I whispered, and Ramesses held my shoulder. "Your father would be proud."

"Doesn't this frighten you?" Iset whispered. Ramesses let go of my shoulder and took Iset's arm "As a child, I watched my father build this tomb," he said. We moved into another passage, deeper still. When the High Priest removed the ebony adze that hung from his neck, to begin the Opening of the Mouth Ceremony, Iset began to shake. The ceremony would give Seti his breath in the Afterlife.

Rahotep placed the adze against Seti's mouth, and I watched as Henuttawy stood as still as a figure carved in stone. After all, what words might Seti say if he again drew earthly breath?

"Awake!" The High Priest's voice resounded in the chamber. Queen Tuya stifled a sob. Ramesses held her while I stood close to Merit. "May you be alive and breathing as a living one, healthy and rejuvenated every day. May the gods protect you where you are now, giving you food to eat and fresh water to drink. If there are any words you wish to say, speak them now, that all of Egypt may hear."

The viziers shifted uncomfortably with their torches, and the courtiers held their breath to listen. When there was silence, I imagined that I saw Henuttawy smile thinly at Iset. Then the sarcophagus was lifted through the narrow corridor into its final chamber. The small party turned to Henuttawy, who would be the first to kiss the Canopic jars and see the sarcophagus lowered into the black void of the shaft below. We watched her step forward. Then she knelt in the dirt and quickly kissed the jars that would carry Seti's poisoned organs into the Afterlife.

Rahotep, raising the adze in his hands, repeated a solemn passage from the Book of the Dead. "My breath is returned to me by the gods. The bonds that gag my mouth have been loosened and now I am free. Those who have done me harm in my life, I kindly forgive, for the gods will punish you, not me."

Henuttawy stood, wiping the dirt from her sheath.

꒐ ꒐ ꒐

SITTING IN my chamber around the warmth of the brazier, I told Woserit and Paser what I suspected about Iset. Woserit gazed at the flames in silence, while Paser cradled a cup of warm Sermet beer in his hands. But neither was as surprised as I had thought they would be.

"She had to be someone's daughter," Paser said at length. "Everyone assumed it was some nobleman at court."

"But she's the child of the man who killed my family!" I cried. "He's the murderer of Nefertiti. And if he set the fire . . ." My throat began to close with emotion. "Then he is the murderer of two generations. Do you think he would hesitate to commit another?"

But neither Woserit nor Paser seemed to see the danger I did in the prospect. They were more concerned about the coronation, and Woserit asked sternly, "Is there any chance he will crown you queen?"

I shook my head. "He will never break his promise to his father. But as for Iset, Merit reported seeing a man near her rooms last night."

Both Woserit and Paser sat forward. This news, at least, appeared to shock them as much as it had me.

"Who was it?" Paser demanded.

I turned up my palms. "She couldn't see."

"It might have been the Habiru Ashai," Woserit guessed immediately.

"No. I'm sure she's not *that* foolish," I replied.

But Woserit shook her head. "I wouldn't be surprised if she paid a servant to go in search of him."

"She's desperate," Paser added. "Who does she have to turn to? Not Pharaoh. Not Henuttawy. She already owes the High Priestess of Isis more than she may ever be able to give."

Woserit rested a hand on my knee. "Rahotep can do *nothing* more for her. He can't speak too loudly against you because his past is still his prison. Iset may not know this yet, but we do."

CHAPTER TWENTY-THREE

FOR THE KING IS RA

RAMESSES'S WIDE PECTORAL caught the morning sun, and the blue faience tiles across the dais made it seem as though he was walking on water as he approached his new throne. It was seven days after Pharaoh Seti's burial, and thousands of noblemen filled the Temple of Amun at Karnak from cities as far away as Memphis. I wondered what they thought of crowning a king without his queen. From my place beside Iset on the third step of the dais, I looked down at my sons in their milk nurses' arms. They were such bright, happy babies. I felt the burning need to know that they would always be safe, that they would never be subjected to Iset's whims if I were to die and she were made queen.

A trumpet pierced the crisp air of Pharmuthi, silencing the courtiers in their fur-lined sandals and heavy cloaks. And though I hadn't been chosen for Chief Wife, Ramesses glanced at me as Rahotep placed the red and white *pschent* crown on his brow. Several of the viziers did the same, and of those who were gathered on the dais, only Queen Tuya with her ill-tempered *iwiw* avoided my gaze.

"For the King is Ra," Rahotep declared. "He is the creator of all things, the begetter of the begotten. He is Bastet who protects the Two Lands, and the one who praises him will be protected by his arm. He is Sekhmet against those who disobey his orders, and Lord-south-of-his-wall. And now he is Pharaoh of all of Egypt, Ramesses the Second and Ramesses the Great."

Cheers erupted throughout the temple. When Ramesses descended the dais, the chanting was so loud no one could hear him when he held my chin and swore, "If not for my promise . . ."

But no one in the chamber missed his kiss on Amunher's head, and when he took our son in his arms, Ramesses's meaning was clear. Amunher was the future of Egypt. Queen Tuya's glare could not stop Ramesses from raising our son above the crowds. While young dancing girls beat their ivory clappers together, Rahotep passed Henuttawy a meaningful look.

I grasped Merit's hand; she had seen it, too. My sons could not leave her sight for a moment; every dish brought to the milk nurses' chamber must be sampled by palace tasters first. Though Ramesses held out his arm for me to take, I remained where I stood.

"Go with Pharaoh," Merit prompted in my ear. "Nothing will happen."

"But Rahotep—"

Merit pushed me forward. "I'll be watching."

In the courtyard outside of Karnak's temple, Thebans waited to see who Ramesses would take into his chariot. He had kissed Amunher before the court, and now, before the cheering crowds of Egypt, he offered me his hand. I held my breath, dreading that the people should fall silent, but instead, their cries became thunderous. As we rode through the streets in a procession of soldiers and golden chariots, Ramesses turned to me and smiled.

"You are conquering their hearts. You really are a Warrior Queen, Nefertari."

CHAPTER TWENTY-FOUR

TO THE RIGHT
OF THE KING

IN THE AUDIENCE Chamber, Ramesses still wore his *nemes* crown. He appeared no different to me than three months earlier, when only Thebes had been his to govern. But the palace of Malkata had certainly changed since his coronation. The walls had been stripped of their vermillion rugs, and from every niche the statues had been taken and placed in wooden chests bound for the palace of Pi-Ramesses. Wherever I went in the halls of the palace, servants were carrying heavy reed baskets, filling them with every conceivable luxury that the city of Avaris might lack. Few petitioners ventured into the Audience Chamber with the palace in such a state, so when Ahmoses appeared and demanded to see me, Paser waved him by, already knowing what my answer to the Habiru's request would be.

"You've come at a bad time, Ahmoses. The court is leaving tomorrow," I said.

"Then this would be a good time for the Habiru to leave as well," he offered. "Why make them suffer the move to Avaris?"

"The army does not suffer." I laughed. "They'll be sailing the Nile in the same ships as Pharaoh."

"Not every Habiru is in Pharaoh's army. Some must sell their stores of grain to hire boats."

"And they will have to hire boats to reach the shores of Canaan."

"Not if we walk."

"The Habiru cannot leave!" I exclaimed, more sharply than I intended. "Reports have come from the north of advancing Hittite troops. If the Hittites take Kadesh, there will be war. Every soldier is needed. Wait until Thoth."

"I want to know when Pharaoh will set my people free!" His eyes were blazing. He brought his staff crashing down on the tiles, and armed guards moved forward, but I raised my hand to stop them.

Ramesses turned from his business with Paser. "My wife has told you the truth. Every soldier in Thebes will be coming to Avaris," he said with a sharp dismissal. Then he turned to me. "Why do you entertain him?" he asked quietly.

As Merit and I made our way to the baths that night, she repeated Ramesses's question.

"Because my mother suffered the way the Habiru do. But if Emperor Muwatallis moves for Kadesh, every soldier in Egypt may not be enough to stop him. And if Kadesh falls, Avaris will be next. Then Memphis. Then Thebes . . ."

The dark silhouette of Merit's head shook as we walked the tiled path leading to the bathhouse. "If Pharaoh knew that you were considering this," she began, but I held up my arm to stop her.

"*Listen!*"

There was the sound of weeping. I glanced at Merit.

"It's coming from in there," she whispered.

We slipped quietly through the columned entrance to the royal courtyard. Standing behind the girth of a sycamore tree was the shape of Iset and with her was a young man. From any other entrance, they would have been hidden from view. Her back was to us.

"You could come every morning," she pleaded. "You're a sculptor, Ashai. We could tell the court you're sculpting my bust. No one would know—"

"I should never have come to you." The Habiru moved away. "I loved you once, but I've learned to love my wife. She's given me two children . . . But inviting me here—you're putting my life in jeopardy!" He must have caught a glimpse of our movement, for in a moment he had fled.

Iset turned, and when she saw me standing with Merit, she covered her mouth in horror. She sank to her knees among the belt of flowers bordering the path to her chamber. "Are you going to tell Ramesses?" she whispered, her head bowed.

"No. Your secret is safe from him," I said quietly.

Merit looked at me in shock. "My *lady!*"

Iset looked up at me, eyes narrowed in calculation. "And what will I have to pay for this silence?"

"It is only people like Henuttawy who expect payment," I replied.

LATER, IN my chamber, I told Woserit and Paser what had happened. "They were hidden beneath the branches of a sycamore," I finished. "If we hadn't been on our way to the baths, we would never have seen them."

"A wife of Pharaoh must be beyond suspicion," Woserit said darkly. "When Ramesses discovers this—"

"He won't discover it. I told Iset that her secret was safe." Though Woserit and Paser both stared at me in astonishment, I shook my head firmly. "Henuttawy has already made her life miserable enough. And Ashai swore that he would never return. How would knowing this make Ramesses happy?"

"But Iset is betraying him!"

"For love. My mother betrayed her family for love. I wouldn't be here if my mother hadn't chosen the general Nakhtmin over duty to her sister."

"But your mother wasn't married to your sister!" Woserit cried. "They hadn't sworn an oath before Amun."

It was true. The situation wasn't the same, but now that the time had finally come, and it was in my power to destroy Iset, I didn't have the heart.

ᴛʜᴇ ɴᴇxᴛ morning, every Theban who depended on Pharaoh for their employment was on the road. I shaded my eyes with my hand, and from my balcony, I could see the thousands of wagons, loaded with grain, chests, and weapons of war, beginning the long journey to Avaris. Those who could afford it hired barges, packing their belongings into simple chests. Beyond the city, farmers carried their last baskets of threshed grain to the whitewashed silos, where scribes paid them from the treasury. The fortunate used these copper deben to purchase a place for their families on ships.

I embraced Ramesses tightly as we stood together looking out over the sea of people.

"It's not like Nefertiti and Akhenaten," Ramesses promised. "We aren't building a city in the desert to glorify ourselves. We're moving to Avaris to protect our kingdom." Ramesses looked down at me and smiled. "Do you know what I instructed the builders to see to first? Your chamber," he said. "I've had them build you one next to mine, painted with all the scenes from Malkata."

No one had ever done something so considerate for me. I put my hand to my heart, and when he saw that he had left me speechless, he kissed my lips, my cheeks, my neck. "Your *akhu* built Malkata, Nefer. Your mother lived here. I don't want you to feel sad when you leave it today."

I pressed my hands against the hardness of his chest, then down to his waist, and even farther. He swept me into his arms, carrying me from the balcony, but the servants had already packed my bed.

Next to the brazier was a sheepskin, deep and white and soft. "Like you," he whispered when he laid me against it. He knelt to kiss my shoulders, then my breasts, then the soft inside of my thighs. He inhaled the scent of jasmine I always wore between my legs. We lay on the warm rug in my empty chamber and made love until Merit's knocking had become too loud to ignore.

Still, I wanted to look out over the fruit trees in the garden one last time. Their branches were supported on painted trellises, and some nights I imagined that it was my mother who'd planted them. She had been a great gardener, but there was no one to tell me which flowers she had left to me in Thebes. I'd told Ramesses that I wouldn't be sad to leave Malkata, but now I realized that I had lied. In four months, during the Feast of Wag, there would be nowhere for me to go to in Avaris to light incense for my mother's *ka*. She would sit untended in Horemheb's temple, her face enshrouded by darkness, forgotten.

"We'll return." Ramesses came up behind me.

"My mother walked these halls," I said. "Sometimes, I stand on this balcony and wonder if she saw what I am seeing."

"We will build her a temple," Ramesses promised. "We will not let her be forgotten. I am Pharaoh of all of Egypt now."

"Akhenaten was once Pharaoh of all of Egypt—"

He took me by the shoulders. "You are related to *me* now. To Amunher and Prehir. The people have seen my victories in Nubia and Kadesh. They've seen our conquest of the Sherden. The gods are watching us now. They *know* us."

That afternoon, we sailed with a flotilla of more than a hundred ships, and I stood on the stern watching Malkata disappear. Ramesses's finest ship was filled to bursting, piled with chests and heavy furniture from the palace. Ebony statues of the gods peeked from the cabin, seemingly as anxious as I was to arrive. There was little room to stand, and the courtiers who'd come with us sat beneath a sunshade, unable to move. So much would change, and I sighed wistfully. "I wonder what it will be like to live in Avaris permanently?"

As always, Merit's reply was sensible. "The same as it was when you were a child and the court spent every summer there. Now don't let Iset decide which chamber she will have."

"Ramesses has already chosen my chamber. He built me a new one next to his," I told her, "and there are two rooms next to it. One for you, and one for Amunher and Prehir. You won't have to share with the milk nurses anymore. It will be the largest room in Avaris."

Merit put her hands to her heart gleefully. "And does Iset know this?"

⸙ ⸙ ⸙

WE ARRIVED in Pi-Ramesses in the middle of Pachons, and it was a different palace from the one we'd seen in the chilled month of Tybi. In the months that had passed, thick clusters of flowers had bloomed from newly painted urns and hanging vases. From the lofty heights of the sandstone columns, fragrant garlands of lotus blossoms had been twined with branches painted in gold. The sweet scent of lilies filled the halls, and in the tiled courtyards water splashed musically from alabaster fountains onto blooming jasmine. An army of servants must have worked every day since Seti's death. I imagined them buzzing about the palace like bees, darting into the chambers to clean, and polish, and prepare for our arrival. The freshly painted walls gleamed in the sun, and a thousand bronze lanterns waited for nightfall to reflect in the newly tiled floors. Everything was rich, and new, and glittering.

I turned to Ramesses in shock. "How can the treasury of Avaris afford this?"

He lowered his voice so only I could hear. "It can't. You can thank the Sherden pirates for this."

Hundreds of courtiers assembled in the Audience Chamber with its colossal statues of King Seti and Queen Tuya, and Paser read out the locations of every chamber. When he came to my name, the court seemed to hold its breath.

"The princess Nefertari," he announced, "to the right of Pharaoh Ramesses the Great."

A murmur of surprise passed through the room, and I saw Henuttawy glance at Iset. To be placed at the right of the king meant that Ramesses had made me Chief Wife in all but name. It wasn't a public declaration engraved on the temples of Egypt, but the entire court of Avaris knew his preference now.

"Shall I show you the chamber?" Ramesses asked. He led me to a wooden door, inlaid with tortoiseshell and polished ivory, and then placed his hand over my eyes.

I laughed. "What are you doing?"

"When you go inside, I want you to tell me what it reminds you of."

I heard him open the door, and as soon as he withdrew his hand, I gasped. It was exactly like home. On the farthest wall were the leaping red calves from the palace of Malkata. On another was a large image of the goddess Mut, passing the ankh of life to my mother. I stared at the painting, remembering the mural that Henuttawy had destroyed, and tears coursed down my cheeks.

🜖 🜖 🜖

OVER THE next month, the Audience Chamber of Pi-Ramesses was never silent. Our days were spent in work, touring Avaris, overseeing repairs, meeting with emissaries and viziers from foreign courts. But at night, there were endless distractions. The deben in Seti's treasury had gone to prepare for war and provide him with entertainment, so even while all around him the palace lay crumbling, he had never been without Egypt's most beautiful dancers. They crowded the Great Hall in numbers, seeking support from the new Pharaoh of Egypt, and the entire court felt alive and merry. Amunher and Prehir could now sit upright on Woserit's lap and clap in time with the rattle of the sistrums. But no one was allowed to hold Ramessu except his own mother or his nurse. Iset kept her watchful eye over him, and if Amunher and Prehir crawled too close, she gathered him in her arms and whisked him away. From his mother's grasp, poor Ramessu listened to the delighted squeals of my sons, crawling together on the dais. *He will grow to be a very lonely child,* I thought.

But no one else in Avaris seemed lonely. In the grand villas beyond Pi-Ramesses, there were nightly feasts as new relatives arrived on the road from Thebes. The aroma of roasted duck wafted into the corridors of the palace, and in the mornings the scent of pomegranate paste was so strong I would awake to the sound of my growling stomach. From the balcony of my chamber, I watched the farmers harvest the amber-hued myrrh, and at night their wives would take their small children and stroll the city's tree-lined avenues. The fear of devastating famine was gone, and though the people believed that it was Penre's invention that had changed their lives, I knew better. I wondered what my *akhu* would think, knowing that not everything from Amarna had been destroyed.

Then came the message that we knew would arrive. We had been in Avaris for only a month, and our days of touring and feasting were soon ended. Paser came to us in our chamber and closed the door. Ramesses took the scroll and unfurled it.

"Ten thousand Hittite soldiers have taken Kadesh," Paser reported. "The city has already changed its allegiance."

"Does anyone else know?"

"Only the messenger, Your Highness."

I read the report over Ramesses's shoulder. Ten thousand men had marched on the city at dawn, and the people of Kadesh were so afraid of war they had surrendered by afternoon. Ramesses crushed the papyrus in his hand. "He thinks I am too young to challenge him! Muwatallis thinks he's a hawk swooping in on the nest of a chick!" He flung the crumpled scroll across the room. "He greatly mistakes me."

"Emperor Muwatallis is a veteran of war," Paser warned. "He's seen battle in every kingdom in the east."

"And now he will taste war with Egypt."

CHAPTER TWENTY-FIVE

BEFORE THE WALLS
OF KADESH

Avaris

"YOU'RE GOING ALL the way to *Kadesh?*" Merit shrieked. She stood over Amunher and Prehir, who looked up at me beneath their fringes of red-gold hair and flapped their arms, wanting to be held. "It's enough that you went to the north, my lady, a *princess* of Egypt on a ship with pirates—"

"And you saw how the people reacted," I argued. "It was worth the risk."

"Because there were only a hundred men!" Merit cried. "Not ten thousand Hittites prepared for war. Does Pharaoh understand the danger—"

"Of course he does." I only had one day to prepare, but Merit was standing in the way of my traveling chest. "He's stayed up nights thinking about it. We both have, *mawat*. And last night he decided."

"But think of all the ways there are to die in war," she begged. "Please." Her voice rose in desperation. "What will happen when Pharaoh is in battle? You'll be completely alone."

I drew a steady breath. "No. I will have Amunher and Prehir." I saw the look on her face and added quickly, "Ramesses first went on campaign at eleven months old. Iset is going as well. With Ramessu."

Merit's hands fell from her hips, her defiance melting into astonishment. "To *Kadesh?*"

"It's Henuttawy's suggestion. She wants to be sure that Ramesses spends as much time with Iset as he does with me. We will be with the camp outside the city," I explained, "in the hills. We'll watch the battle from afar."

Merit threw up her hands in horror. "Well, then, if you can join the camp, I can, too!" She stood with her fat little legs apart, and when she placed her hands back on her hips, I knew that there would be no arguing with her. "What do I prepare?"

"Linens and sandals," I said swiftly.

"And for the princes?"

I kissed each of my sons on their soft cheeks. They were the brightest babies, always wanting to touch, and grab, and explore. "All they truly need is each other," I told her. They had recently stopped nursing, and now they drank their milk from clay bottles and ate chicken from my bowl when it was cut small enough. They ate together, played together, and now they would see their first battle together, watching from the hills. I laid my sons back on their linen, and felt the thrill of knowing that by Epiphi the gods would recognize them. It might only be a small thing, and their names might not echo in Amun's ears just yet, but to share in Egypt's conquests was certainly a beginning.

In the Audience Chamber that morning, petitioners had been forbidden, and from a dozen polished tables, generals and viziers debated the strategy that Egypt would use to take back Kadesh. I sat listening to Asha and his father as they described the Hittite army.

"They have allies from eighteen kingdoms," Anhuri warned. "Nearly

two thousand chariots and thirty thousand soldiers. They have men
from Aleppo, Ugarit, Dardany, Keshkesh, Arzawa, Shasu . . ."

"Aradus, Mese, Pedes, and many more," Asha finished. "There is
no doubt we will need all our twenty thousand soldiers."

"Then we will break the army into five divisions," Ramesses decided. We had stayed up for nights looking at maps, translating
cuneiform messages that spies had intercepted. "There will be the
division of Amun, which I will lead. The division of Ra, with Kofu at
its head. General Anhuri will take the division of Ptah and name a
general to the division of Set. Each division will march a day apart,
so that if Hittite spies should see Amun's division, they will think we
are only five thousand strong. Then Asha will take a final, smaller
army by river. If we can surround the Hittites and cut off their supplies, they will face starvation and will surrender within a month."

The viziers frowned at one another. "You are going to divide the
army, Your Highness?" Paser was wary. "No Pharaoh in my memory
has done this."

Around the tables, men shifted in their seats. It was either a brilliant plan or madness.

"I think it can work," General Kofu spoke up.

"*Can* work, or *will* work?" Paser challenged.

"*Will* work," Ramesses said fearlessly.

Rahotep remained silent, his bloody eye fixed on Ramesses's
throne. But Paser was braver. "If there is any chance of success in
this, there will need to be excellent communication between the
divisions."

"And I have grave reservations," General Anhuri admitted.

Ramesses hadn't expected dissent from Asha's father. "Tell me
why."

"You will lead four divisions up through Canaan, then on through the woods of Labwi. It will be a month's march. If the Hittites should turn and surprise Amun's division, how quickly can a runner be sent to Ra, Set, or Ptah? This has never been done—"

"Which is why we must try," Ramesses said passionately. "Akhenaten lost Kadesh along with the Eleutheros Valley. Since then Pharaohs have tried to regain it and failed. It belongs to Egypt! How long was it in my father's possession before the Hittites took it back? Without the Valley, we will never regain our land in Syria. If we allow the Hittites to hold Kadesh, they will keep Egypt's territory along the Arnath River forever! Akhenaten let our empire crumble, but we will rebuild. We will reconquer. And to do that, we must crush the Hittites. We cannot simply use a huge blocking force, as before. It's not enough to push them back— we must surround them, starve them, and force them to surrender completely!"

Ramesses's speech roused his generals. They understood that if something different wasn't tried, there might be battle after battle against Hatti without end. The Hittites had to be engulfed and destroyed once and for all.

⊔ ⊔ ⊔

THAT EVENING, I looked at Ramesses in the low light of the oil lamps. He sat on our bed, perched tensely like a bird of prey, a nineteen-year-old Pharaoh of the most powerful kingdom in the world. In a month, he would show the Hittite emperor that Egypt should never be mistaken for a gosling.

"Since the reign of Tuthmosis," he said, "only my father and I have led armies into battle. And only a few pharaohs in history have ever taken their wives."

"We will be fine," I promised him.

"It's not you who concerns me. It's Iset. The march will be long, and she isn't meant for such things." I wanted to ask him what he thought Iset *was* meant for, but he went on. "I could send her on by ship in Asha's galley," he considered, "but they will be far ahead of the army, and that could prove more dangerous."

"She has chosen to come," I reminded. "She will do well."

But I could see that Ramesses wasn't convinced.

The next morning the court assembled on the small bluff outside Avaris. Viziers, wives, priestesses, and noblemen had come to see the awesome sight of twenty thousand soldiers readied for battle in the fields below. Helmets and axes gleamed in the sun, and from each division flew the standards of Amun, Ra, Set, and Ptah. Among the thousands of soldiers were Nubians, Assyrians, the new Sherden re-cruits, and the Habiru. They carried leather shields to be quick and agile, where the Hittite armor would be cumbersome and heavy.

"You see how fast our chariots are?" Paser pointed a driver out to me who charged across the floodplains, then reined in his horses with the slightest tug of his hand. "The Hittite chariots are much heavier than ours, because they carry three men."

"A driver, a shield bearer, and an archer," I guessed.

Paser nodded. A slight wind rustled his kilt, and in the morning sun his eyes looked tired. "Be careful, Nefertari. The Hittites will not hesitate to kill a woman. They aren't Egyptians, and they may not take you alive . . ." He left his words unfinished, then stepped back so Woserit could embrace me.

"You are braver than I."

"Or more foolish," I answered. "But I've promised Ramesses that wherever he goes, I'll be with him. And if he should meet with disas-ter, all Egypt would fall to the Hittites anyway. How could I stay here? I must have a hand in my own fate."

We both looked to Henuttawy and Iset. Although they were standing close to each other, a wide river might as well have been flowing between them. Neither spoke, and the women Iset had grown up with since childhood shifted nervously. They had never known anything but life in the harem, and now Iset would be riding a chariot between desert cities while the army marched. They had no advice to give her, and Iset's face was as white as her diaphanous sheath.

Woserit shook her head. "She will never survive. She'll want to ride in the litter with the children all the way to Kadesh."

Ramesses appeared in his golden pectoral, his courtiers chatting excitedly. The early morning sun reflected from his breastplate: His bronze armor was cinched with an azure sash, and from his *khepresh* crown of war the uraeus bared its fangs at the enemy.

"Like Montu," I told him, the male god of war.

"And you are my Sekhmet," he replied.

Iset came up beside him; her broad inlaid belt was so thick that it weighed her down as she walked. Up close I could see her nails had been hennaed. She was perfectly beautiful, like a freshly painted doll from the palace workshops. "We're marching through the desert," Ramesses exclaimed. "Not hosting a feast!" He looked at my linen kilt and simple sandals, then hesitated. "You are simply too beautiful for the battlefield, Iset. Perhaps you should—"

But she wouldn't listen to him. "I am coming with you," she said. "I want to be by your side. Battle doesn't frighten me."

Yet even the courtiers from the palace, who wanted to believe everything of her, could see through this. One of her women, the daughter of a scribe, suggested kindly, "You could remain with Vizier Paser in the Audience Chamber, Iset. Pharaoh needs loyal eyes to look after his kingdom."

"Pharaoh needs someone to look after him in *war!*" she snapped, and then she turned her gaze in my direction. "And if it means I have to look like a boy, I'll do it."

"Then go and get dressed," Ramesses said, and I detected a note of impatience in his voice. "When you return, you can take the litter. It will protect you from the dirt and the sun."

⸆ ⸆ ⸆

THE MARCH was as long as General Anhuri had predicted in the Audience Chamber, and Iset rode for a month in her covered litter, borne on the shoulders of eight men. She never dared to complain about the oppressive heat or lack of places to bathe. When Ramessu cried, we could hear her shouting at him to be quiet, that if he didn't behave she would leave him by the side of the road.

The poor thing will learn to hate her, I thought. *She should allow him to ride with Amunher and Prehir.* I looked across at the second litter, and from the squeals of delight behind the linen I imagined that my sons thought this was a great adventure. Merit rode with them, and I could see her shadow as she moved back and forth, keeping them from trouble. Although there was room for me in the litter too, I steered my own chariot next to Asha and Ramesses. And at night, when the army made camp where it could, Ramesses crept into my pavilion and we listened as Merit told stories of the gods in the pavilion next to ours. Some nights we could hear that Amunher and Prehir had gone to sleep at once. But most of the time, they had slept throughout the day and were no longer interested in settling down. Then Ramesses would call them over to us, and the three of them would crawl among the cushions, delighting in each other, while I stayed up translating messages our spies had captured.

"Emperor Muwatallis knows nothing of this march," I said with certainty. We had passed through Canaan and traveled down toward the Bekaa Valley. We were steadily approaching Kadesh from the south, and I held up the latest scroll. "He is sending missives home that his wives must be there to greet him, and that a victory feast should be prepared for Epiphi. He has no idea we are coming. Though I don't know about this." I pointed to a line of ancient cuneiform. It was written in a Hittite that only priests used. I squinted, trying to recall what I had learned from Paser. "It's something about the woods of Labwi." I hesitated. "Something about . . . woodsmen perhaps?"

"Scouts!" Ramesses shouted, frightening Amunher and Prehir. They held their breaths to see if he was shouting at them, and when he failed to look in their direction, they carried on playing. "There will be scouts in the woods of Labwi!" he exclaimed.

I continued to study the scroll. "Yes." I nodded quickly. "That must be it." Though I had never seen some of the words before, *Labwi* and *woodsmen* were clear enough.

"Tomorrow, we will pass through Labwi," Ramesses said. "And whatever Hittite scouts they've left behind, we will encircle them to cut off any warning." He smiled at me. "We are going to take back Kadesh before Muwatallis has a chance to sit down at his next feast!"

The four divisions of the army on foot were assembled the next morning. Twenty thousand men listened to their orders as the sun rose beyond the hills, gilding their helmets and reflecting from their swords. Seti had amassed ten thousand leather shields, stretched taut on strong wooden frames that could deflect even the strongest arrow point, and now, after a month's march, they would finally be used.

"The divisions of Amun and Ra will make camp across the River Arnath on the highest point," Ramesses instructed his generals. "Set and Ptah will remain at the base of the hill. We've intercepted a message that indicates that there will be Hittite spies in Labwi. When we reach the woods this evening, I want them captured!"

There was a nervous excitement as the divisions marched. We were nearing Kadesh, and when the camp passed through the cedar forests of Labwi, this nervousness only heightened. But there were no sightings of Hittites anywhere in the tall, flat-topped groves, and when the divisions of Amun and Ra made camp on the hill above Kadesh, there were murmurs of shock as the men looked below them. The walled city appeared completely silent, and the Hittite army seemed to have disappeared. Ramesses stood on the crest as the cool of evening settled over Kadesh, and Egypt's generals stared out in amazement.

"Perhaps they have retreated," Kofu suggested.

"An army of ten thousand men does not capture the most important city in the north only to abandon it a month later. Perhaps they're hiding within the city," Anhuri offered.

"Either way, we must send a scout," Kofu said. "Even if the Hittites have already left the city, word of us will reach them and they'll return in force. You can be sure of it."

The four divisions of Egypt's army waited for news around thousands of campfires that dotted the hillside and filled the air with the scent of burning timber. Some of the men played Senet and rolled knucklebones. But once the sun set there was a tense expectation among the soldiers; the silence of the city below was more disturbing than seeing any Hittite army. Around our fire, Iset was the first to break the uneasy quiet.

"Where can they be?" she demanded shrilly. "We have marched for a month! And now we've come and there isn't any war!"

Anhuri smiled warily. "You will get your war. In one day or ten, the Hittites will return."

The hood of Iset's cloak fell back around her shoulders, revealing her exasperated look. "With how many men?"

Anhuri glanced behind him. There was a commotion in the camp, but he answered her quickly. "As many as we've brought from

Egypt. Likely more." He stood as a young boy came running toward him, dressed in the printed kilt of a messenger. At once, we were all on our feet.

"What is the news?"

The boy paused to catch his breath. "Nothing!" he cried. "The Hittites left two nights ago. They have installed their own governor in charge of the city, but the army is gone!"

Ramesses glanced between his generals, and all of them wore guarded expressions. "It could be a trap."

But the messenger boy was confident. "It's not a trap, Your Highness. I've been through the city. There's not a curly beard or striped kilt among them. Only in the governor's house . . ."

"*Two* days ago?" Anhuri challenged. Asha's father was incredulous. "It's too convenient," he dismissed, and I wanted to agree with him. But the other generals wondered if perhaps the emperor was so confident of his conquest he felt no need to remain in Kadesh.

"It's possible they waited a month to see if an army would come from Egypt by river, and when none came, they decamped," Kofu suggested.

"We'll wait," Ramesses decided. "If there is no sign of their army by tomorrow evening, we'll take back the city."

The generals returned to their fires, and the young scout was given two gold deben for his trouble. But in my pavilion, Ramesses couldn't sleep. I kissed his shoulders, then his chest, but I could see that he was in no mood for me to undress him.

"If the Hittites have truly left," he said, "we can take Kadesh tomorrow evening before the Hittite army has a chance to return. We can shut the gates and defend the city from within. You will remain on this hill with the provisions. I have given the Master of the Guards, Ibenre, instructions that only you may move this camp. If a division that doesn't carry a banner of Amun, Ra, Ptah, or Set approaches this hill, I want you to leave for the south, for the city of Damascus."

I placed my fingers on my lower lip, and gently, Ramesses brushed them away.

"There is nothing to fear. The gods are watching, and we shall be victorious."

🜚 🜚 🜚

THERE WAS whispering outside my pavilion. A dark shape moved against the moonlight, and Ramesses sat up with his hand on his sword.

"Your Highness!"

"It's General Anhuri," I said. I felt a selfish pleasure that he had known to look for Ramesses with me. Ramesses rushed to the opening and pulled aside the linen. Next to his guards, the general stood with Kofu and two bound prisoners.

"Two Hittite soldiers, Your Highness," said Anhuri. "Found lurking in the hills beneath the camp."

I dressed myself quickly and joined Ramesses outside. The spies had been bound with rope, and a large gash cut the taller man's cheek. Both wore the long kilts of the Hittites, with their hair braided away from their faces.

"What story have they given you?" Ramesses demanded.

"They speak little Egyptian," Kofu replied. "But the taller one says they deserted the army."

"What are your names?"

"They call themselves Anittas and Teshub." Anhuri raised his brows. "Whether those are their real names is anyone's guess."

Ramesses peered down into the faces of his captives, and even the tallest one only came to his chest. "Why would you leave Emperor Muwatallis?"

Both men shook with fear, but it was Teshub, the fatter one, who replied, "We understand very little Egyptian."

"Then you may use the little Egyptian you have," Ramesses roared, "and explain yourselves to me, or you will be explaining yourselves to Osiris!"

Teshub glanced in my direction, and his gaze lingered on me. "We left the army of Emperor Muwatallis," he said quickly. "We did not want to fight for such a coward."

Anhuri prodded the fat man with the edge of his sword. "What do you mean coward?"

"Emperor Muwatallis has fled!" Teshub said. "He heard that the great Pharaoh Ramesses was coming with an army that could fill the horizon!"

Ramesses looked at me, then at his generals. A wide grin spread across his face, and he stepped closer to the deserters. "Muwatallis heard that I was coming and fled? In which direction?" he asked eagerly.

Teshub pointed to the north.

"Aleppo?" Kofu demanded.

"Yes." Teshub nodded swiftly. "To find more soldiers."

Ramesses's eyes glowed. "We will take Kadesh tomorrow!" he vowed. "I will lead Amun's army north to the city before Muwatallis brings reinforcements. Instruct my men to get up. They are done sleeping tonight."

"And the other divisions?" Kofu asked.

"They shall follow at first light."

Even before the gray of dawn brightened the sky, the division of Amun assembled on the hill. They would reach the gates of Kadesh before nightfall, and I wondered how long it would be before the Hittite army returned. In the privacy of my pavilion, Ramesses encircled my waist with his arms. They had been bronzed by the harsh summer's sun and were corded with muscle from his years of training. I felt them tighten protectively around me and wished they would never let go. But he still had to make his farewell to Iset, and to Merit, who was dressing our sons.

"Capturing the governor will be quick," he said eagerly. "When Muwatallis returns, he will see that Kadesh has been retaken. Then Asha and the fifth division will appear! It's over for him."

"And what will stop him from taking this hill?"

"Because Muwatallis has fled north, Nefer! He will have to get by us first. You are well protected here."

☗ ☗ ☗

WE WATCHED the Amun soldiers move out, and by afternoon, the men had disappeared and all we could see was a dusty marching column in the distance. Merit held tightly to Prehir, wiping away his tears as he gestured toward the horizon. But Amunher squirmed in my arms, feistier than his brother, and he didn't shed any tears.

"He would crawl after Pharaoh if he could," Merit remarked.

"He will be a little warrior. Won't you, Amunher?"

"He will be a *crown prince*," Merit said firmly. "As soon as this year has passed."

"Rahotep would sooner give up his leopard robes and go naked than crown Amunher."

"Then I hope he enjoys the cold," Merit snapped.

We both looked to the tent where armed soldiers guarded the Hittite deserters. Even from the edge of the hill, I could hear the two men arguing inside. One of the guards called to me, "They are speaking in tongues, Princess. Their captivity has made them lose their minds."

I listened, then quickly handed Amunher to Merit and moved closer to the tent. One of the guards opened his mouth, but I shook my head fiercely, putting my fingers to my lips. When I had heard enough, I stepped back. "They are speaking in Shasu. And they're fretting about what Egypt will do to *spies!*"

There was silence inside the tent. The guards looked at me with terror as I shouted for someone to bring General Anhuri. The cry of *spies* echoed over the hill, and even Iset emerged from her pavilion where she had spent the day chastising Ramessu.

When General Anhuri came running, he had his hand on the hilt of his sword.

"They are spies!" I said. "These men are not Hittite deserters! They were speaking Shasu!" My voice rose with terror. "They were arguing over what will happen to them once Ramesses discovers the Hittite army hiding behind the hills of Kadesh!"

General Anhuri and his bodyguard entered the tent, armed with canes. I winced at the sounds of the men being beaten within. The nearby soldiers had heard what I was saying, and news was already spreading among the ranks that Pharaoh was marching into a trap. The division of Ra was already mobilized, and the men of the other divisions took up their spears, and axes, and shields. When Anhuri emerged from the prisoners' tent, fresh blood stained his kilt. His grim nod confirmed what I had feared. "The three divisions are moving!" he shouted. "The princess Nefertari is placed in charge of the supplies and the three hundred guards who will be left behind."

🝘 🝘 🝘

MERIT AND I watched from the top of the hill as three divisions disappeared down the slope into the valley below. They wouldn't reach Kadesh until morning, and although there were hundreds of guards to keep watch, that evening I refused to sleep. "I want to wait here and see it," I told Merit.

"See what?" she cried, shivering in her cloak.

"I want to see Amun's pennant flying triumphantly from the city's walls," I said stubbornly.

But even in the gilded light of the moon, it was difficult to make out what was happening below. Campfires blazed before the walls of Kadesh, and though I knew that three divisions were making their way toward Ramesses, only their torches were visible from above. I listened to the night sounds of crickets, and sometimes I could make out small animals scampering through the brush, but it wasn't until the sun rose that I could clearly see what was happening. And then I covered my mouth in shock.

When Merit joined me at the rim of the hill, she followed my gaze into the distance and saw for herself what I had been watching since dawn. Although Amun's division had taken Kadesh, the heavy walls of the city had been breached. Columns of our troops trod the northern road toward the city, still short of the river. Then she saw the encircling wings of Hittite troops coming toward us, only a single day's march away, and panicked. "They're coming! The Hittite army is coming!"

Her sharp cry summoned women from their tents, and when Iset saw how close the Hittites were, her voice rose to a hysterical pitch. "We must leave! We must leave now before they reach us and murder us all!"

But I knew that Ramesses would fight back. Three divisions had come to his aid, and surely Asha would arrive by river at the head of the fifth division to crush the soldiers now marching toward us. If we fled now . . .

A boy clambered up the hill into our field of vision, wearing the kilt of a messenger. Ibenre took his news.

"What is it?" I asked swiftly.

Ibenre's look was grave. "The division of Ra has been ambushed. At least two thousand soldiers have been killed."

"We must go!" Iset pleaded. "We must go before they kill us all!" She turned to run back to her pavilion, but Ibenre put out a hand to stop her.

"If you leave alone, you will be captured. We go when Princess Nefertari says we go."

"But look!" Iset pointed wildly to the plains below.

"Those columns are still a distance away," I told her. "Once we leave for Damascus we can't turn around. It's a two-day journey." I saw Iset blanch, and I added calmly, "Asha may yet come. We cannot abandon Ramesses here, his supply lines cut and surrounded."

We waited as the sun rose higher in the sky, hoping to see Ramesses's victory banner flying alongside the pennant of Amun. But as the Hittite division grew closer, Iset began to pace the hill, and then finally she screamed, "He's going to lose! Don't you see? He was fooled by a pair of Shasu. He will die, and now we will all die with him! Forget Asha! *Please.*"

I looked to Ibenre. "Do we have more time?"

"Until noon."

Iset's eyes were pleading, for even if Asha arrived, there would no longer be time to cut off the Hittite division now fast closing upon us. "Then we should move," I told him. "We have waited as long as we can."

Iset closed her eyes in deep relief, and Ibenre nodded briefly. "Move out!" he shouted, and in a chaos of armed guards, grain wagons, and horses, we fled down the hill for the Egyptian city of Damascus.

CHAPTER TWENTY-SIX

THE HEAVY SHROUD
OF THE GOD PTAH

Damascus

THE GOVERNOR OF Damascus had been instructed to accommodate me in his largest chamber, and it was a testament to Iset's overwhelming fear of being killed that she didn't complain about this slight. Instead, she wandered the halls for two days, wringing her hands over what would happen to her if Ramesses should die. On the third day, I seated myself next to her in the Great Hall, and though she shrank from me the way a rat shrinks from a hawk, I placed my hand on hers and said softly, "Even if the Hittites come, Iset, which of the women do you think they'll save? Look around. Who here is more beautiful than you?" She cast her eyes timidly about the room, and I withdrew my hand. "But Ramesses isn't going to die," I said firmly. "He isn't going to be defeated by the Hittites."

"How can you be so certain?" The light of the Great Hall illuminated her face, and though her eyes were red and weary, I hadn't lied. She was still the most beautiful woman in Damascus.

"Because the gods are watching over him," I said. "Amun, Ra, Osiris, Sekhmet."

I pretended to have no doubts about our victory, acting as if I knew it were only a matter of time. Yet every day without news had been unbearable. At night, dusty desert heat hung over the palace, and I imagined it looking like the heavy shroud of the god Ptah, wrapping the entire city in its embrace like the mummified husband of Sekhmet. It was impossible to sleep, impossible to eat, almost impossible to breathe not knowing what was happening to Ramesses at the walls of Kadesh.

For five days we waited like hungry cats for scraps of news, and every rider who approached the city was met by Ibenre, impatient for word. At last, a messenger came with a report from the front, and immediately the governor sent word to my chamber.

"My lady!" Merit cried. "A messenger!"

I didn't care that it was unseemly for a woman to run, or that I hadn't put on my Nubian wig. Ramesses had taken twenty thousand men into an ambush. If they'd been defeated, it would mean not only the loss of Kadesh, but likely the loss of Egypt itself. He had gambled, risking everything for this.

I entered the Audience Chamber, and the governor took my arm and led me to one of the four thrones on the dais, three of which always remained empty for Pharaoh and his two most important wives. I took my seat next to Iset, but neither of us fooled anyone with our brave faces.

The boy looked between us. "A truce has been declared!" he exclaimed. "A truce between Hatti and Egypt!"

I glanced at Ibenre at the bottom of the steps.

"A *truce?*" he demanded. "What are you saying?"

"The Hittites have retreated to the hills," the boy replied. "And Pharaoh's army is marching in victory toward Damascus."

Iset slumped against her chair. "We have won," she whispered. "Egypt is saved."

"Egypt may not be lost," I said, "but Pharaoh hasn't won. A truce is not a victory." I thought of how foolish Ramesses had been to believe a pair of Hittite spies. He had risked everything because his father had asked him to, taking twenty thousand men north to Kadesh where he imagined an easy victory over the Hittite emperor. And when spies had hidden themselves in the hills, he had been more than eager to believe that a veteran king of war had fled from his path in fear. "Who will keep Kadesh?" I demanded.

"The Hittites, my lady. But the generals say it could have been much worse. They say that Pharaoh was saved because of you."

The governor of Damascus and all of his courtiers turned to look at me. "I didn't do anything," I demurred.

"But you did, Princess. The three divisions you sent after Amun gave Pharaoh enough time to prepare a counterattack."

"They were already preparing to march—"

The boy shook his head as if that didn't matter. "They are calling you the *Warrior Queen*, my lady. Even the Hittites know your name!"

We followed the boy to the Window of Appearances, where the governor stood whenever he wished to address his people. And beyond the city walls, the battle cry of "RAMESSES" could be heard. Then came the unmistakable second chant, a cry of "WARRIOR QUEEN."

"How many are there?" I whispered.

"Twelve thousand men," the boy revealed.

I turned. "A *third* of the army has been killed?"

The boy lowered his gaze. "Yes, my lady. But look at them all."

He was too young to understand the gravity of it. The army had approached the palace gates, thousands of weapons gleaming like burnished gold beneath the sun. Iset and I pressed together in the narrow window, close enough to smell the lavender oil on her skin, and the scent of jasmine from her hair. "He is back," I cried to her. "He's returned."

When Ramesses appeared in the courtyard below, he raised his iron sword to us in triumph. His leather shield was stained with blood, and he had removed the *nemes* crown so that his hair streamed loose behind him. He climbed the stairs to the Window of Appearances, and though Iset held back, the guards parted for me and I rushed into his arms.

"Nefertari!" he exclaimed. "Oh, *Nefertari*."

He greeted Iset with a firm embrace, and she wept in his arms the way she had wept daily since we left Avaris.

"How did you survive it?" I whispered. I searched his body for any sign of wounds.

"Only by the grace of Amun," he admitted, but when he turned to greet the people of Damascus, he raised his arm triumphantly and declared, "We have returned!"

A magnificent cheer rose through the courtyard, echoing beyond the open gates into the city's streets. Then Ramesses promised the people peace. He promised them trade in the rich Aegean Sea through the hostile territories of the Hittites, and he swore that although Kadesh had been lost, Egypt would endure.

"We have taught the emperor a powerful lesson," Asha declared, his voice carrying over the thousands assembled. "The Hittites will never again rush to invade the kingdom of a Pharaoh as brave as Ramesses the Great."

While the city feasted, Ramesses found me in my chamber.

"Tell me what happened," I said. "Tell me how Egypt can be victorious if a truce has been declared and we have lost Kadesh for good."

Ramesses sat on the edge of the bed and placed his head between his hands. "We were victorious because my soldiers weren't slaughtered. We were victorious because although I lost Kadesh, I didn't lose Egypt." His eyes brimmed with tears. "And I didn't lose you." He took me in his arms. "Nefertari," he whispered. "Nefertari, my pride almost killed you. It killed so many men. Good soldiers who *trusted* me to lead them."

"You couldn't have known that they were spies," I said, but he was right. His pride had cost thousands of men. When we returned to Avaris, their mothers would wait at the gates to greet their sons, searching the faces of every soldier until the entire army had passed and they realized their children weren't coming home. His pride had done this. His rashness. His belief that the gods were with him and that Sekhmet would prevail over reason. That a divided army could confront the Hittite power. He should have waited for the rest of his army to take Kadesh. But how could I tell him this? I looked at Ramesses in his short white kilt and golden pectoral, and even in his *nemes* crown he looked like a frightened child, like the one who had begged Amun for Pili's life in the temple. I repeated, "You couldn't have known."

"What would have happened if you didn't speak Shasu? What would have happened if the Ne'arin hadn't come to our rescue after six thousand Egyptians already lay dead?"

Ne'arin meant *young men*, but I didn't understand. "Who are the Ne'arin?"

Ramesses fixed me with his gaze. "Habiru mercenaries from Canaan."

I gasped. *"Ahmoses?"*

"Who else could have summoned them? They appeared out of nowhere with the division of Ptah. They fought like they were possessed by Montu. But how could Ahmoses have known?"

"The Habiru must have been willing to fight for a chance at what they want," I told him.

Ramesses was quiet, surely thinking about the Habiru in Canaan.

"They will rebel," he said with certainty. "If they settle with their brothers in Canaan. Their army of Ne'arin were well trained."

"But they came to fight for you."

"Because under the Hittites there would be no chance of being set free. In helping me, they are helping themselves. If I don't set them free, the Ne'arin will rebel. I could crush it. They're not so many men . . ."

"Enough to save your army."

Ramesses nodded. "I saw more blood before the walls of Kadesh," he admitted, "than my father saw in all his years. I vowed to give them victory, but I should not have made that promise. There are many promises I should not have made. I thought I could make the gods listen to me. I thought a victory in Kadesh would write my name in their halls. But the old priestess was wrong. The gods were already listening," he went on. "They've always been listening."

The Ne'arin were proof of that, I thought.

CHAPTER TWENTY-SEVEN

TO DIE BY THE BLADE

Avaris

.WHEN WE RETURNED to the city of Avaris and the Dowager Queen saw that Ramesses was safe, she crushed her son in her large embrace, and even took Amunher in her arms, marveling at how big he and his brother had grown.

"In two months they've become different children," she exclaimed, and I wondered if her newfound interest was sparked by the cries of "Warrior Queen" that filled the streets. "Tell me about the battle," she implored, "and how you helped to crush the Hittites!"

I told her the story, and that evening in the Great Hall, there was a celebration surpassing anything ever seen in Seti's time. Dancing girls with bracelets on their wrists flitted from one room to the next, laughing and singing with the elated men. Asha presided over a group of noblewomen, recounting for them the story of how he arrived just in time as the Hittites broke down the gates of Kadesh. I noticed them leaning forward to listen, but he seemed to be speaking to one red-haired woman in particular, and I saw with a start that it was the priestess Aloli.

The feasting was to continue for seven days, and each evening when the oil lamps were lit, women emerged from the shadows of the palace with their eyes rimmed in kohl and their cheeks rouged with ochre. Each evening I marveled over the quantities the cooks of Pi-Ramesses unveiled. There were the common servings of olives and dates, but in larger bowls there was goose with honeyed lotus, glazed in heavy pomegranate wine. The scent of slowly roasting meat woke me in the mornings, and by the fifth night in the Great Hall, Ramesses said jokingly, "I think that Amunher and Prehir have doubled in size since returning to Avaris."

The courtiers around our table laughed, their voices like polished bells, and Iset added eagerly, "Ramessu has grown so big that his hand can fit around a spear. He'll be hunting hippo before he's two." She smiled at Ramesses, but Paser had approached the dais with a scroll, and Ramesses's attention was diverted.

"There is a message from Kadesh," Paser announced.

Henuttawy sighed. "Is it always work with you?"

"Yes. Just like for some it is always play."

Ramesses frowned over the courtiers' guffaws, taking the scroll from Paser. "This isn't the seal of Emperor Muwatallis."

"No. It is the seal of his son, Prince Urhi."

Ramesses glanced around him. Everything was bright and happy. Women in jeweled collars and linen tunics laughed with young soldiers, who described the Hittites fleeing from the division of Ptah and the Ne'arin. The women never asked how it could be a victory if Egypt had not regained Kadesh; the soldiers saw the battle as a warning to the Hittite king that Egypt would be taken seriously. We had won Emperor Muwatallis's respect. But then why was his son writing to us, and not the emperor himself? "If it's bad news," he whispered to Paser, "I don't want to read it here. Come into the Per Medjat." He looked at me, and it was clear that I was invited as well.

I had only been inside Seti's Per Medjat once before. Seeing it again I realized how much larger it was than the library in Thebes. Scrolls filled the polished wooden shelves, reaching to the top of a chamber painted with images of Thoth, the ibis god of scribes who first invented language. On every wall his beaked head was painted or raised in relief, and scenes from his sacred book were depicted around him. Of course, it is forbidden to read the Book of Thoth, for it is filled with powerful spells. But I wondered if somewhere within Pharaoh Seti's great library the dangerous book still existed.

We sat at the farthest table, and when Ramesses broke the seal on the prince's message, I wondered aloud, "Why isn't Muwatallis himself writing?"

Ramesses looked up from the papyrus. "Because Emperor Muwatallis is dead."

He handed me the scroll and Paser read it over my shoulder, both of us squinting in the candlelight. "It doesn't say how he died!"

"But Prince Urhi is writing for confirmation," Paser replied. "He is telling the kingdoms of the south of his ascension, before his uncle can make a claim for the throne."

"Muwatallis's brother," Ramesses said darkly. "He's the general who ambushed the division of Ra. General Hattusili."

And now Hattusili wanted his nephew's throne. The young prince was writing to Ramesses, asking for his support. Hatti had never asked for aid from Egypt before. "And what about the truce?" I asked fearfully.

Paser was firm. "Prince Urhi will want peace. He will have enough to do in keeping his uncle at bay."

"Prince Urhi might want peace," I said, "but if Hattusili takes the throne, how do we know he won't rise against Egypt?"

"Because he's already seen war with Pharaoh," Paser said, "and he didn't much like it. If there had been a chance of defeating Egypt, he would have convinced his brother to carry on."

"Then what will Egypt do?" I asked. "There are two contenders for the throne of Hatti. If we pledge support to Urhi, but Hattusili takes the crown . . ."

"We will wait." Ramesses gave the scroll back to Paser. "Wait until there is a certain victor, and pledge our support to him."

I glanced up at Paser, who appeared equally impressed that Ramesses was choosing the safest thing to do.

"Shall I draft a message?" Paser wanted to know.

There was the loud creak of the door, then the sound of several sandaled feet making their way across the tiles. The three of us turned, and Henuttawy stepped into the light. I could smell that she had been drinking.

"Ramesses! What are you doing here?"

"There is business to attend to," Ramesses said severely.

"With Nefertari?" She laughed, and Iset appeared behind her in a netted dress of beads. "The entire feast is waiting for you. Come." Henuttawy stretched out her bangled hand, and to my surprise, Ramesses refused to take it.

"There is new trouble in Kadesh. This is no time for feasting."

A messenger burst into the Per Medjat, startling Iset. The young boy straightened his shoulders, trying to appear taller than his height.

"What is the news?" Paser demanded.

"The Emperor of Hatti," he piped in reply. "He is here, Your Highness, in the Audience Chamber!"

We stood from our table and followed the messenger through the corridors of Pi-Ramesses. Courtiers still danced in the Great Hall, singing and laughing, and Ramesses turned to a passing servant and said, "Send for the Master of my Charioteers, the generals, and every vizier in this palace."

The messenger opened the doors to the Audience Chamber, and

while laughter filled the halls outside, within there was silence. A lone figure stood near the dais, covered from head to foot in a cloak, and I saw Ramesses tense. But the messenger boy approached the cloaked figure in the darkness. "Your Highness?" he said tentatively.

The man turned, lowering his hood, and I was shocked to see how beautiful he was. He did not have the angular jaw or handsome cheekbones of Paser, nor did he have the same bronze beauty as Ramesses with his sapphire eyes and bright red hair. He had a soft, youthful beauty, and I couldn't imagine him as the Emperor of Hatti.

"I am Urhi-Teshub," the cloaked man said in flawless Egyptian.

"And what are you doing in Avaris?" Ramesses demanded. "Is there an army with you?"

"If there were an army with me," the prince replied bitterly, "I would be using it to defend my crown. Didn't my message arrive?"

Paser held up the scroll. "It came tonight."

"Then it came too late," the Hittite said. "My father died in his sleep and now my uncle has seized the throne. The kingdom that my father left to me has been stolen by his brother. I have come to Egypt seeking the help of the Pharaoh they are calling Ramesses the Brave. I have heard extraordinary things about you—that you are a leader in battle unlike any other. I have heard of your ferocity, how you fought off a hundred of our chariots when your divisions were scattered and fleeing around you. If you will help me regain my throne, I will offer you the cities that your predecessor Akhenaten lost. All of the cities he gave away. They shall be yours, forever, ceded in exchange for your support," he promised.

I glanced at Ramesses. He had not told me of any personal victories in battle, yet in the streets the people hailed him as a hero. The Hittite prince held out his hand. I wondered if Ramesses would take it.

"This is not something I will decide now," he said. I heard Paser exhale. "I must summon my generals and my viziers. But you may stay with us until I have determined what to do."

"And if my uncle demands my return?"

"You will find safe refuge here."

"He will know I am here," Prince Urhi warned. "He will ask that you send me back to Hatti so that he can receive me with *open arms*." His tone was caustic.

"Then he will have to content himself with receiving your letters instead." Ramesses turned to Paser. "Give the prince the largest guest chamber in Pi-Ramesses. Have someone escort him to the feast."

"I will take him," Henuttawy said quickly. "Let me show the Hittite emperor how we Egyptians celebrate." She held out her arm, and as Urhi took it his dark eyes grew luminous.

When she led him away, Ramesses remarked smugly, "He may not want to return to Hatti after this."

I wondered if the prince would be so radiant if he knew what Henuttawy really was.

We moved ourselves to the longest table in the room, and as the generals and viziers arrived, Asha glanced at Iset. "Wouldn't you rather be in the Great Hall, Princess?"

"Would *Nefertari* rather be in the Great Hall?" she snapped.

"Yes," I said curtly, "but the business of Egypt is more important."

When the heavy doors to the chamber were shut, Ramesses saw that Iset had stayed and said kindly, "You may rejoin the feast."

"Is Nefertari going as well?"

"No, Nefertari is remaining here," he said calmly. "She can contribute to this meeting in a dozen different ways. Is there anything you would like to contribute?"

Iset looked between the viziers for their support, yet their faces were all set against her.

"Then I think your skills are best used in the Great Hall," Ramesses said, and although he was not purposely slighting her, she turned on her heel and stormed from the chamber. The doors swung shut behind her with a crash that echoed through the room. The generals avoided Ramesses's gaze. Ramesses looked at me, and even I looked away so he would know how shameful Iset's behavior had become.

Paser cleared his throat tactfully. "Prince Urhi," he began, "is the son of Emperor Muwatallis. He brings news that the emperor has died in his sleep."

There was startled conversation around the table, and Paser waited while the generals speculated what could have been the cause. Rahotep said it must have been poison. General Kofu thought it might have been the stress of war.

"Whatever it was," Paser went on, "the throne has passed to his son, Prince Urhi. But Urhi is seventeen and has never led an army. He is not Pharaoh Ramesses and the people don't trust him. They have accepted his uncle, General Hattusili, on the throne in his stead."

"So what does this prince want Egypt to do?" Anhuri's voice was suspicious.

"He wants us to place him back on the throne," Ramesses replied. "And he has arrived in Avaris with a very attractive offer."

Paser spoke up. "Prince Urhi has offered a return of the lands that the Heretic lost."

"*All* of them?" Asha challenged.

"All," Ramesses replied.

"And how do we know he won't change his mind?" Asha shook his head. "Look at Kadesh! No Hittite can be trusted."

Ramesses agreed. "We could march into Hatti and discover a trap. We might discover that Urhi hasn't been displaced from his throne at all. We could be ambushed, and all of Egypt would be lost."

"I don't think Urhi is that cunning," I said. "He has never led an army into battle. Listen to what the Hittite servants in this palace have all said about him. They take their gossip from travelers who come by, and they call him pretty, they call him a prince, but never an emperor. Who among us would dare to call Ramesses a prince?"

None of the men at the table spoke up.

"If Ramesses were to follow him into Hatti, Egypt would profit, and Urhi wouldn't dare to go back on his word. He's not a fighter. But he may be a fool, and if that is the case, how can such a man be expected to keep a crown?"

The viziers nodded in agreement with me. Egypt could help return Urhi's throne, but if he lost it a second time, then what was the purpose?

"And the truce?" Asha asked. "If the prince remains here, what will Hattusili do?"

"He may go back on his brother's truce," Vizier Nebamun predicted.

"But Hatti is not as strong as she was," Paser argued. "While she was busy stealing our land in the north after the Heretic's death, Assyria conquered the kingdom of Mitanni."

"And now the Assyrians won't be satisfied with Mitanni alone," Ramesses mused.

Paser agreed. "They will move west to the cities that belong to Hatti. With the Assyrians at his throat, Hattusili can no longer afford to make an enemy of Egypt."

Ramesses sat back in his chair, and the generals watched while he closed his eyes to think. "We will send Hattusili a treaty," he said, haltingly. "A signed gesture of peace between Hatti and Egypt. The promise to send military aid to each other if the Assyrians attack. Hatti may be our rival, but Assyria has become the greater threat."

"If Hattusili signs the treaty," Paser added, "we could promise them aid in time of famine."

"And in exchange for that," Ramesses said with growing excitement, "they must give us access to their ports. And to Kadesh."

But Vizier Nebamun's look was wary. "No kingdom in the world has ever made such an agreement with their enemies."

Ramesses sat straighter in his chair. "We can be the first."

We stayed in the Audience Chamber until the early hours of morning, discussing the terms of this treaty, and by dawn only Paser remained with Ramesses and me. Once the temple's morning rituals were finished, Woserit came to bring us fresh fruit.

"Tell me about the treaty," she asked, but Ramesses was too tired to speak.

"It will give Hattusili the chance at peace and to consolidate his throne," I said. "But if he doesn't want it, then he can risk a war with both Egypt and Assyria. And we still have the prince . . ."

Paser smiled wearily. "Pharaoh Ramesses is forging a new way of living among nations. If Hattusili won't sign, then we will make the same offer to Assyria."

"And we are offering more than just military aid," I said. "If a criminal dares to run and hide in Hatti, they will have to send him back. And if a Hittite tries to do the same, we will send him to Hatti."

Woserit saw my name at the bottom of the papyrus and glanced at me. My signature was now on official correspondence. In deed, if not in name, I had been made Queen of Egypt. I wanted to dance across the palace and shout the news from every window, but I knew enough to keep my silence. Unless Hattusili approved it, the treaty would remain a secret. But if he agreed, the entire court would know that I had signed it.

"You should get some sleep," Woserit said with real pleasure in her voice. "This has been a long, though very rewarding night."

"*If* the Hittites agree." Ramesses sighed. He squinted against the early light of dawn, and we took her advice and retired to my room.

As we settled into my bed, the linen sheets felt deliciously cool against the rising heat of morning. When I asked him if we should go instead to the Audience Chamber, he said, "Unless it's a messenger with news from Hatti, there's no one in Egypt I wish to see right now. Except you." He reached out tenderly to caress my cheek, but a knock resounded throughout the chamber and he withdrew his hand.

"Nefertari?" A voice came through the door. I glanced at Ramesses, and the pounding came again. "Nefertari, open up!" someone shrieked. I recognized the voice as Iset's.

"What is she doing?" Ramesses exclaimed.

"I don't know." I crossed the chamber and swung open the door. The rage in Iset's eyes was so blinding, she didn't seem to recognize Ramesses behind me.

"Is it true?" she demanded. At once, I knew that Rahotep must have told her. "Did Ramesses put your name on the message that's being sent to Hatti?"

I opened my mouth, but it was Ramesses who came to my side and spoke. "Yes."

Iset staggered backward. "You *promised,*" she whispered.

"Iset—" Ramesses reached out to stop her from leaving, but she shook her head angrily.

"No! You made a promise to me, and I should have known you would break it for her!"

"I have *never* betrayed a promise!" Ramesses swore.

"You have!" she insisted, and now wouldn't move. A small crowd was gathering in the hall. Courtiers stopped to stare, and servants pressed themselves against the wall in fear. "On our wedding night, you promised to love me above all other women. You promised it!" she screamed, and there was a wildness in her eyes. "You took me in your arms—"

"Iset!"

"And swore there could never be a woman as beautiful or charming as me. You said the people loved me!" she cried. "But it's not my name on that scroll. It's Nefertari's!"

Ramesses glanced at me to see my expression. The entire palace would know of it now.

"Go to your chamber," Ramesses commanded. "Go to Ramessu and calm yourself."

"How can I be calm," she shrieked, "when you have slighted me in front of the entire court?" She looked around, and for the first time saw that it was true. Rahotep had come to see the commotion. Now he stepped forward to take her away. "Don't touch me!" she shouted. "*You* are the one who convinced him to do this! *You* are the one who's pretended to be my ally while speaking for Nefertari!"

"No one speaks for Nefertari," Ramesses said sternly. "She speaks for herself. And that is why she will be queen when the feasts of Kadesh are finished."

Rahotep stopped where he was in the hall, and Iset grew very still.

"You say you've never broken a promise," she whispered. "Then what of your promise to your father to wait a year before choosing a Chief Wife?"

I held my breath. Then Ramesses said quietly, "It is the first and last promise I intend to break."

There was nothing Iset could do or say. Rahotep led her away, and Ramesses closed the door. "She is not the same woman I took to wife," he whispered.

I wanted to tell him that she was, that she hadn't changed at all, but instead had grown desperate, knowing she would never be able to give Henuttawy what she wanted. Instead, I said cryptically, "Sometimes, we misjudge who people are."

"Like the Shasu spies?" he asked miserably. "Perhaps I should leave the judging to you." He took my hand and led me back to our bed. "You know, it's true."

"What's true?"

"I have never broken a promise. This is the first promise I intend to break, and in a few days, Egypt will have another cause for celebration. A magnificent queen for its throne."

⊐ ⊐ ⊐

BY EVENING, the entire palace of Pi-Ramesses had learned that I would be made queen. As I entered the Great Hall, where Henuttawy sat drinking with the prince of Hatti, I was flocked by courtiers wishing to congratulate me.

"It's not done yet," I told them demurely, but Aloli was among the women, and she exclaimed loudly, "Not done yet? All that's left is to fit the crown!"

Woserit and Paser appeared arm in arm, and when they came to offer me their best wishes, Woserit squeezed my hand and I knew, at last, that our long struggle was over. For the first time in my life no one would look at me as the Heretic's niece. In the streets, on the dais, in the Audience Chamber, I would be treated with the respect due to a queen. And in the temples, the images of my *akhu* would never be erased. Their names would be carved with mine until eternity, and the gods would remember them when they returned to walk among the living.

Woserit smiled. "It's done."

"There's still the coronation," I worried.

"And what do you think will go wrong by then?" She laughed with real joy, and I realized it was a sound I had heard very rarely from her.

Merit appeared with Amunher and Prehir on each hip, while

about her servants rushed to light the hundreds of candelabra that would burn deep into the night. I looked to the dais and wondered what my reception there was going to be. Henuttawy was sitting with the Hittite prince, passing him wine and sipping from his cup.

Merit saw the line of my gaze and whispered, "She'll still expect payment from Iset. And who knows what she promised to Rahotep to ruin your name."

"I should think her body has been payment enough."

"For Rahotep?" Merit's upper lip curled. "She doesn't know his history, then."

I looked for the High Priest of Amun, but he was missing from his place at the dais.

Ramesses joined me in the doorway, dressed in a kilt striped with gold, and his smile was brilliant. "Ready?" he asked. He took my arm in his, and through a crowd of courtiers offering us their blessings, we approached the dais. For the first time, small wooden seats had been arranged for my sons, and because they were too young to behave themselves, there was an armed chair for Merit where she could sit and watch over them as they ate.

I took the throne to the right of Ramesses. The viziers stood, and Henuttawy announced with a sneer, "The princess who will be queen. Come. A toast to Nefertari!" She raised her cup and everyone at the table did the same.

"To Nefertari!" they echoed merrily.

"Of course, I don't want to celebrate too long," Henuttawy said, and her words were slurred from too much wine. "After all, I have to make *obeisance* in the morning." She stood up and, as she looked at Iset, added bitterly, "Are you coming?"

Iset glanced at Ramesses. "Of course not. My . . . my place is here."

Henuttawy narrowed her eyes. "Then I will see you all in the morning." She smiled intimately at Uhri. "Good luck with your petition."

Her scarlet robes disappeared through the double doors, and for the rest of the night, the Hittite prince sat alone, watching Ramesses anxiously. Finally, when the feast was nearly over, he asked, "Has Egypt made its decision?"

"I'm sorry, but we must consider it further."

"Your Majesty," Prince Uhri said passionately. "My throne has been taken. There is no chance I can raise an army on my own, but with you at my side, think of the triumph we would know! I would cede you all the lands that Pharaoh Akhenaten lost. Every last one in our empire."

Though I could see that Ramesses was desperately tempted, peace was more important now. "I understand your proposal," he began, then the doors of the Great Hall suddenly swung open and a servant cried, "The High Priestess of Isis has been murdered!"

There was a moment of stunned silence in the hall, and then the entire chamber was thrown into confusion. The courtiers rose, and Ramesses rushed from the dais, as I followed close behind. General Anhuri reached the boy first and took a bloodied knife from his hand.

"Move!" Ramesses shouted. "Move!" He grasped my arm, and as we approached Anhuri and the stained blade, Ramesses's face became ashen. "Who did this?"

The young stable boy looked fearful. "Your Highness, I heard a scream coming from the quay. I took the other boys to see what it was, and the High Priest of Amun rushed into a boat. His robes were covered in *blood*, Your Highness. I called for the guards. They've already captured him!"

I tightened my hold on Ramesses's arm as seven soldiers escorted the High Priest of Amun into the Great Hall. Bright smears of fresh blood stained Rahotep's kilt, and when Ramesses stepped forward, his voice became enraged. "What have you done?"

There was a moment when I thought that Rahotep would deny it. But he caught sight of the servant who had seen him, and his shoulders tensed. "I have avenged Pharaoh Seti's death, Your Highness," he swore, and when he saw the baffled look on Ramesses's face, he added, "Your father was poisoned!"

A murmur of shock spread through the Great Hall, and as Ramesses tried to comprehend this statement, Rahotep said bitterly, "If that news is so shocking to you, perhaps you should question the other viziers. Or your future queen, the *princess* Nefertari."

Ramesses turned to me. "Is it true? Did you suspect—" He followed my gaze to Paser, and then shouted, "Did Henuttawy murder my father?"

His voice echoed through the Great Hall, and a fearful silence fell over the room.

Paser stepped forward in the crowd. "No one knows," he said quietly. "A conversation was overheard in the Audience Chamber."

"Between *who?*" Color bloomed on Ramesses's cheeks.

"Between Henuttawy and Iset," Paser replied. "It's possible that Henuttawy gave your father poison."

"And no one knows the truth?" Ramesses shouted. Rage and heartache broke his voice, and I realized how deeply we had all betrayed him.

"What could we have said?" I cried, but even as I spoke the words, I knew that I should have told him the truth. "To accuse a High Priestess and have her deny it . . ." I tried to comfort him, but he shook off my touch.

"No!" he shouted, and he looked at Rahotep. "*You* know," he challenged. "What did she tell you?"

"That she murdered her brother with antimony in his wine."

Ramesses's rage seemed to crumble, and he looked around him. "Iset. She heard it from Henuttawy *herself* and never told me."

"How could she have told you," Rahotep demanded, "when your aunt would have blamed her for Pharaoh's death? Henuttawy poured your father's wine out of sight. She gave innocent Iset the cup. Your High Priestess was cunning."

I saw what was happening. If no one challenged his story, Ramesses might pardon him for Henuttawy's murder. But he had killed Nefertiti. He'd still set the fire that destroyed my family.

"She was a snake," Rahotep went on proudly, "and now she's dead."

"But that's not why he killed her." The entire court turned to me. "He may tell you that he murdered her in your father's name, but that is a lie. He killed Henuttawy to silence her. Henuttawy had no reason left not to accuse his daughter of murder. And she had every reason to try and save herself."

"And who is his daughter?" Ramesses whispered.

I closed my eyes briefly, so I wouldn't have to see the betrayal on his face, and when I opened them again, she was standing beside us. I nodded. "Iset."

Ramesses turned to her in bewilderment. "The High Priest Rahotep is your father?" he demanded.

"How can I be certain?" she exclaimed.

Rahotep stepped forward, and this time, the guards didn't pull him back. "Henuttawy wanted things my daughter could never give her. Gold, deben, promises of power. I killed her not just in the name of your father, but in the name of Iset."

"Don't believe him," I swore. "He murdered your aunt just as he murdered mine. For vengeance." I turned to face Rahotep. "I know that you murdered Nefertiti. Twenty years ago, Merit saw you at her chambers, just as this boy saw you bloodied tonight. But when you returned to Thebes as the High Priest of Amun, you threatened to tell the court that I was cursed by Amun as a heretic's child. You threatened to have me banished from Thebes, and Merit kept her silence. But no one can keep me from the palace now." I looked at Ramesses. "Ask him about the fire in Malkata. Ask him who killed my father, and my cousins, and what he did it for!"

The guards tightened their circle around him again, and this time, Rahotep's voice shook with fear. "Remember what Henuttawy did to your father. She was a *murderess!*"

"Did you murder Nefertiti and set that fire?" Ramesses demanded, and when Rahotep saw he was defeated, he simply looked at me with loathing. "Strip him of his cloak," Ramesses commanded.

Iset covered her mouth in horror, and Rahotep shouted, "I saved you from a murderess! I saved you from a lifetime of ignorance!" Two guards held Rahotep's arms behind his back; his nostrils flared, reminding me of a bull that had been penned for the slaughter. He had escaped punishment for the murder of a queen, and now it was a lowly stable boy who'd brought him down.

"Why did she kill my father?" Ramesses asked. Rahotep's red eye darted in every direction. "You can die by the blade or slowly of starvation."

When I saw that Rahotep wasn't going to answer, I said, "Because she wanted power over Iset. Henuttawy promised to put Iset on the throne, but she wanted to make sure Iset would never forget their bargain once becoming queen."

"And what bargain was this?"

"To rebuild the Temple of Isis into something so vast that every pilgrim in Egypt would leave their deben at its gates."

"Making her treasurer of the greatest fortune in Egypt," he said slowly. He had awakened from blissful ignorance to a nightmare of intrigue he'd never known existed. He looked at Rahotep and drew himself up to his fullest height. "General Anhuri, escort Rahotep to the prisons. Give him death in whatever manner you think he deserves."

Iset shrieked as her father was taken away, as her ladies fluttered helplessly around her. I pressed Ramesses's arm firmly in mine and steered him through the commotion into the privacy of my chamber. When I had locked the door behind us, we sat together on the edge of the bed.

"I wanted to tell you," I whispered. "It has haunted me for months, but everyone cautioned me to keep my word. Paser, Woserit . . . even Merit swore that if I ever spoke out, Henuttawy would find a way to make me look like a liar."

"So everyone knew?" Ramesses cried.

"Yes, but there was no way to prove it! After the coronation, once you knew that I had no reason to lie, I was going to tell you about Henuttawy and Rahotep. And they must have sensed that my queenship would spell their ruin. For so long they had worked together—until the time came to save themselves. But I couldn't tell you—they would have done anything in their power to keep you from believing me! You have to understand—"

But I could see that he didn't.

"I should have told you sooner," I said. "I should never have kept anything from you, Ramesses. I'm sorry."

"Why didn't Iset tell me about her father?"

"Perhaps she was ashamed."

"Of the High Priest of Amun?"

"Of a *murderer* and a man they call *the jackal!*" I cried, and though I knew I should have been trying to defend myself, I was tired of calculating every move and weighing every word before I said it. "This palace has been a web of secrets," I told him. "Every night, I've gone to bed wondering what Henuttawy might do. Or Rahotep. It doesn't pardon what I've done," I said desperately, "but don't be harsh with Woserit and Paser. Even Iset must have had her reasons."

Ramesses buried his head in his hands. "But I *trusted* Henuttawy and Rahotep," he said, "just like I trusted the Hittite spies in Kadesh. Why?" His voice rose with his anger. "*Why?*"

If there had ever been a time to tell him about Iset and Ashai, it would have been then. But I was a coward. I was afraid he would wonder how many other secrets I had hoarded in the chambers of my heart, and I hoped it could lie hidden in Ashai's quiet village.

"Everything feels like darkness," he whispered, and I caressed his cheek.

"You are Pharaoh of the greatest kingdom in the world. And you have princes. Three handsome princes."

He looked through the open door of the milk nurses' chamber, and when he smiled, I knew he was going to forgive me. But I didn't deserve his kindness. I had kept from him things that a better woman would have revealed without worrying over her status. Still, I felt a sudden lightness in my heart as if a long and terrible journey had finally come to an end.

CHAPTER TWENTY-EIGHT

FOR THE KING IS
PTAH-SOUTH-OF-HIS-WALL

THE NEXT MORNING, the palace lay subdued. Men quietly offered their petitions in the Audience Chamber, unwilling to break the uneasy silence. But when Woserit appeared in her blue robes of Hathor, a ripple of whispers passed among the courtiers.

"Woserit." Ramesses stood to embrace her, and the viziers rose to offer sympathy. I searched her face for any trace of sadness, but when she turned to me, I could only see immense relief in her eyes.

"Nefertari." She embraced me, and when I encircled her in my arms, I heard her whisper, "It's over." There was an unsteadiness in her voice, as if she had never really believed that her sister was mortal. The courtiers of the chamber surrounded her, wanting to express their own sympathy and shock. That evening as I prepared for the Great Hall, I asked Merit quietly, "What do you think will happen to Henuttawy?"

"What does it matter?" She placed Amunher with his brother on the bed and returned to fasten a pectoral around my neck. "She will probably be buried in an unmarked grave, placed inside the earth without even an amulet for the gods to identify her with."

I thought of Henuttawy's final moments, and I shivered to imagine how she must have felt knowing that Rahotep's blade was meant for her. I walked to the bed and kissed Amunher softly on his cheek. "There will never be a question anymore," I whispered. "When you learn to walk, when you learn to speak, all of Pi-Ramesses will pay attention and know that you are the heir to your father's throne." He reached out and pulled at my earring, giggling as if he understood what I was telling him. But the rest of Pi-Ramesses was not so merry.

For ten days, we waited for news from the Hittites, and though only two thrones of polished ivory and gold now rested on the tiled dais of the Audience Chamber, it felt as though I had been robbed of my triumph. In the month of Thoth I would become Ramesses's queen, but it wasn't until a message arrived from Hattusili that I felt it was complete.

Ramesses took the scroll, and when he'd finished reading, he looked up with amazement.

"What is it?" I asked.

"Peace," he said, triumphantly. "With the Empire of Hatti."

Cheers erupted in the Audience Chamber, breaking the silence that had hung like a heavy pall over the palace of Pi-Ramesses. He handed the scroll to me and watched as I read. There was agreement that the Hittites would retain Kadesh, and in the case of war with Assyria, neither country would use the advantage to encroach on the other's kingdom. For the second time, I read over Paser's flawless Hittite and thought, *It is a pact for the ages. In a thousand years this treaty will remain as a testament to our reign.*

"Is there anything you would change?" Ramesses asked.

"No." I smiled triumphantly. "I would seal this treaty and dispatch it before sunset."

"Bring me the wax," Ramesses commanded. A tablet with heated wax was brought, and when Ramesses was finished, I took my ring and pressed it deep enough to make an impression. Two sphinxes with the ankh of life appeared, the symbol that had belonged to my *akhu* since the scrolls of Egypt had first recorded history. My family would live on; even when the sands buried Amarna and my mother's face disappeared from the mortuary temple in Thebes, the cartouche that belonged to our family would endure.

"Our kingdoms are now at peace!" Ramesses declared.

"And the blessing of the treaty?" Paser asked. "Shall we consider the replacement for High Priestess now?"

Asha spoke up from the table beneath the dais. "I would like to suggest Aloli of Thebes," he offered.

Ramesses looked to me. "I think she would make a fine High Priestess. But the decision to release her must be Woserit's."

Woserit was summoned, and when she arrived, I again searched her face for any trace of sadness. Her sister was condemned to be forgotten by the gods for eternity. But she smiled at Paser as she approached the dais. When Ramesses asked her about Aloli, she looked to Asha.

"Aloli would make an excellent replacement," she pronounced. "If she would like, she may start with morning prayers."

Asha settled back in his chair, red-faced from his brow to his neck. "And the High Priest of Amun?" Ramesses asked his viziers. "By the first of next month, there must be another High Priest. I have waited two years to crown my queen, and I will wait no longer."

☩ ☩ ☩

I CAN remember very little of my coronation in that month of Thoth. For all the anticipation, when the moment came, I felt a strange calm settle over my chamber. Although Merit was rushing from chest to chest, and servants were tearing through boxes to find

my best leather sandals and lotus perfume, I sat in front of the polished bronze mirror and thought of the events that had brought me
to this day. My bitterest enemies in the palace were gone, and
though they say that snakes can't kill each other with their poison, I
saw it happen.

When Rahotep was executed and the news was brought into the
Great Hall, the court looked to Iset, but she didn't cry. Perhaps the
shock of her father's death weighed equally against the murder of
Henuttawy. But aside from these thoughts, I remember very little,
and in my memory the day seems like an artist's palette, with colors
and scents running into each other.

I know that Merit dressed me in Pi-Ramesses's finest linen, and
that the Dowager Queen gifted me her collar of lapis beads and polished gold. I can recall Aloli coming into my chamber with Woserit,
and that both of them had never looked so happy or talked so much.
Aloli thanked me for what I had done for her in the Audience Chamber. I told her that it was Asha who had first spoken her name.

"I think he is very much in love," I said. "Perhaps like someone else
I know."

We both looked to Woserit, who bowed her head like a young
bride.

"Will you marry after Nefertari's coronation?" Aloli pressed.

"Yes." Woserit blushed. "I believe we will."

"But as High Priestess—"

Woserit nodded at me. "I'll have to give up my chambers in the
temple and move into the palace. Someone else will perform the
morning rites. Then someday, if there are ever any children, perhaps
I will have to leave altogether. But . . . but not yet."

"And Henuttawy?" I whispered. "Do you know what will be
done—"

"She is to receive a burial without recognition. But I will place an amulet in her mouth," she promised. "So the gods will know who she is."

I nodded quietly, and I understood that even though they had never been friends in life, they had still been sisters, and Woserit would do what was right.

In the Temple of Amun in Avaris, the new High Priest, Nebwenenef, poured the sacred oil over my wig. I closed my eyes, knowing that somewhere below the dais Iset was watching. I imagined her face holding the same bitter expression Henuttawy used to wear. If she had sent Rahotep after Henuttawy, I didn't want to know. Then came the words. "Princess Nefertari, daughter of General Nakhtmin and Queen Mutnodjmet, granddaughter of Pharaoh Ay and his wife, Queen Tey, in the name of Amun I crown you Queen."

There was a deafening sound of cheers from all around me. Amunher and Prehir were bouncing and clapping as well, caught up in the jubilation of the crowd. My wig was removed and the vulture crown of queenship placed on my head. The wings of the vulture swept from the diadem over my hair. I would never wear the *seshed* circlet of a princess again. On the steps of the altar, Ramesses took my hand.

"You are queen," he said, marveling at the beauty of the vulture headdress that framed my face in lapis and gold. "The Queen of Egypt!"

A thousand courtiers celebrated behind us, and when I looked beyond the Temple of Amun, the faces of the people were filled with joy. The morning had dawned cloudless and brilliant, and the sound of sistrums filled the temple and echoed far beyond the banks of the River Nile. Children held palm branches above their heads, and the women who had come in their finest wigs laughed beneath their white linen sunshades. For as far as the eye could see, there was smiling and celebration, and the scent of roasted duck with barley beer and wine filled the streets. Thousands of people pressed into the roads, wanting to share in the joy of the day. I was their queen. Not the Heretic Queen, but a Warrior Queen, beloved of Ramesses the Great.

"So what will you do first?" Ramesses asked me.

I thought of the Ne'arin who had come to Egypt's rescue in Kadesh, and when I turned to Ramesses, he knew my request before I said the words.

☩ ☩ ☩

THAT EVENING, Ramesses announced to the Great Hall that I had expelled the heretics from Egypt. The people rejoiced as if the army had just taken back Kadesh. But across from me, Iset's face grew pale. "Will every Habiru be leaving?" she asked desperately.

"Only the ones who want to go," I replied in a low voice.

Iset excused herself early, and though I knew where she was going, I kept my silence.

The next morning, Merit reported that a painter named Ashai would be keeping his family in Avaris while the Habiru journeyed north.

CHAPTER TWENTY-NINE

YOUR AKHU WILL
STAND WITH MINE

Nubia, 1278 BC

BEFORE DAWN, IN the third month of Akhet, the court sailed in a flotilla of ships up the River Nile. Gold pennants snapped from the mast of *Amun's Blessing*, and on the deck of the ship Ramesses pointed to the west. He had waited two years to show us this. "Do you see them?" he asked, and as the sky brightened behind the eastern hills, light fell across a pair of temples carved into the face of two mountains.

Courtiers flocked to the sides of the ships, awed by the grandeur we had traveled so far south to see. Asha asked the architect Penre, "You created these?"

But Penre shook his head. "They were Pharaoh's design, from beginning to end."

When the ships reached the quay, Ramesses took my hand. He led me to the entrance of the smaller temple while the astonished court of Pi-Ramesses followed behind. At that moment I knew what it must feel like to be a beetle in a human's world. Everything around us made me feel small. Two images of Ramesses and two of myself gazed across the Nile, our colossal legs taller than anything the gods had yet created, and when we stood beneath the entrance, Ramesses indicated the words that had been carved into the stone.

For my queen Nefertari, beloved of Mut, for whose sake the sun shines in Nubia every day.

"For you," Ramesses said.

After nineteen years I could lay down libations in my own mortuary temple to my *akhu*. It was a temple that would last until eternity, and as we entered the cool recesses of the hall, I was too overcome to speak. On every wall the artists had depicted me smiling, raising my arms to the goddess Hathor, and offering incense to the goddess Mut. Statues of my ancestors were carved in granite, and when Ramesses explained how long men had toiled in the desert for this, I let tears roll down my cheeks and ruin my kohl. I touched the limestone statue of my mother, Queen Mutnodjmet, together with my father, General Nakhtmin, and felt for the first time that I had come home. Only Nefertiti had ever possessed her own temple as queen. When I looked across the hall and saw her eyes gazing back into mine, I realized then how much we were alike. "Ramesses," I whispered, "where did you get—"

"I sent Penre to Amarna to search for their likenesses."

The ache in my throat made it painful to swallow. "But what will the people think?"

"This temple belongs to you. Not to the courtiers of Avaris or the viziers of Pi-Ramesses. And for as long as there is an Egypt," he promised, "your *akhu* will stand with mine." He led Amunher and Prehir by the hand into the second temple's innermost chamber, and Penre instructed the courtiers to step back.

Ramesses grinned at me. "This will only ever happen twice a year. Are you ready?"

I didn't know what to be ready for. Then, through the cool shadows of the early morning, shafts of light crept slowly across the floor of the inner sanctum, and the statues of Ramesses, Ra, and Amun shone in sudden illumination. Only the statue of Ptah, the god of the Underworld, remained in darkness, and cries of wonder echoed through the halls.

"It's *magnificent*," Merit murmured.

Ramesses searched my face for my reaction. These were our mortuary temples, side by side, together for eternity. On every wall in Ramesses's temple, my image was as tall as his own. There were scenes of us hunting in the marshes with Asha, images of us using throwsticks to catch waterfowl on the river, and on the largest wall, artisans had re-created the Battle of Kadesh.

"The gods will never forget this," I told him.

"But does it please you?"

I smiled through my tears. "More than you'll ever know. And someday, when our children are old enough to understand, we will bring them back here to meet their *akhu* and they will know that they have never been alone in Egypt."

"Neither have you," he said, and when he held me in his arms, and I looked from Merit to Woserit and my beautiful sons, I knew that it was so.

HISTORICAL NOTE

RAMESSES II is one of the most well-known and widely written-about kings of ancient Egypt. A copy of his Treaty of Kadesh, written in cuneiform and discovered in the village of Hattusas, hangs in the United Nations building in New York as the world's earliest example of an international peace treaty. It is also believed that Ramesses is the Pharaoh responsible for some of the most visited sites in Egypt: Nefertari's tomb, the Ramesseum, much of Pi-Ramesses, Luxor, the Hypostyle Hall at Karnak, and the stunning mortuary temples in Nubia (or modern-day Abu Simbel). Because he outlasted most of his children and lived into his nineties, entire generations grew up and died never having known a different Pharaoh. To them, Ramesses must have seemed like the eternal king. When his mummy was recovered in 1881, Egyptologists were able to determine that he had once stood five feet seven inches tall, had flaming red hair, and a prominent nose that his sons would also inherit. Yet many holes exist in the available knowledge of Egypt's Nineteenth Dynasty, and while I tried to adhere to known family trees, events, and personalities, I bridged those many gaps in history in the most creative way I knew how, which makes this book, first and foremost, a work of fiction. I regret that not every important person from Ramesses's life could make an appearance in this novel, but the characters of Seti, Tuya, Rahotep, Paser, and many others are all based on historical personages, and to them I have tried to remain faithful.

Historically, Ramesses is remembered as a great warrior and prolific builder, although his most famous battle—the Battle of Kadesh—ended not in victory, but in a truce. Yet in images from his temple in Abu Simbel, he can be seen racing into this war on his chariot, his horse's reins tied around him as he lays waste to the Hittites in what he depicted as a glorious triumph. Ramesses was a master at public relations, and on his frequently updated Walls of Proclamation he would depict his latest conquest, whether or not it was technically a success. Nefertari is thought to have accompanied him to this famous battle, and at sixteen years old she was made Chief Wife over Iset.

Like Nefertiti, it is unknown whether Nefertari ever produced twins, but I used this plot element to forge a link between Nefertari and the infamous Heretic Queen. Historically, it is unknown exactly how Nefertari was related to Nefertiti. In order for Nefertari to have been the daughter of Mutnodjmet, Horemheb's time as Pharaoh would had to have been much shorter than the improbable fifty-nine years that he claimed. After destroying Nefertiti's city of Amarna and usurping Ay's mortuary temple at Medinet Habu, Horemheb erased Nefertiti and her family from the walls of Egypt, then added their years of rule onto his own. The Egyptian historian Manetho records Horemheb's real reign as being only a few short years. If this was the case, then Nefertari could indeed have been the daughter of Mutnodjmet. But all of this is simply conjecture.

What is known for certain about Nefertari, however, is that she and Ramesses were a love match. Buildings and poetry remain today as testaments to this, and in one of Ramesses's more famous poems he calls Nefertari "the one for whom the sun shines." His poetry to her can be found from Luxor to Abu Simbel. On a letter to Queen Puduhepa of the Hittites, Nefertari's name appears at the bottom, and it is clear that she played a distinctive role in Egypt's foreign affairs. She bore Ramesses at least six children, yet none of them lived long enough to become Pharaoh after him. In fact, it was Iset's son Merenptah who succeeded Ramesses on the throne. But even though the novel depicts Iset as a disloyal princess, as with so much else, it is impossible to know who she really was in life. Liberties were taken in ascribing Pharaoh Seti's death to poison, given that he died from unknown causes at around forty years of age. And while many of the Eighteenth Dynasty's mummies have never been positively identified, including the mummies of Pharaoh Ay and Queen Ankhesenamun, I chose to ascribe their sudden disappearance from the records to fire.

Readers familiar with ancient Egypt will also notice that some of the historical names have been changed. For example, Luxor and Thebes are both modern appellations, but are far more recognizable than their ancient names of *Ipet resyt* and *Waset*. And for reasons of simplicity, I chose to use Iset rather than Isetnofret, as well as Amunher instead of the long and much more unwieldy Amunhirkhepeshef. Of course, the most obvious change of all is from Moses to Ahmoses. Readers looking for the biblical Moses within this story will be disappointed. Outside of the Old Testament, there is no archaeological evidence that supports Ahmoses's existence in Egypt. What is known for certain is that a group of people called the Habiru existed in Egypt at that time, although whether they were related to the Hebrews of the Bible has never been proven. With such scant historical evidence, and given that I was attempting to portray events as they might have been, I chose to create the character of Ahmoses. I mention in the novel the myth of Sargon, in which a high priestess places her forbidden child in a basket, then leaves him on the river to be discovered by a water bearer to the king. This myth predates the biblical Moses by a thousand years, just as Hammurabi's Code, a set of laws supposedly given to the Babylonian king by the sun god Shamash on the top of a mountain, predates Moses by half a millennium. I wanted these myths to be a part of the novel because the Egyptians would have been familiar with them, just as the Babylonians would have been familiar with Egypt's most important legends.

Yet for every historical gap I had to bridge, there were many facts that I included that might otherwise seem fictional. For instance, Ramesses really did fight the Sherden pirates, and the Trojan War is thought to have taken place during Egypt's Nineteenth Dynasty. During the famous Battle of Kadesh, spies were captured who gave information about the waiting Hittite army, and the subsequent death of Emperor Muwatallis really did result in his son's flight to Ramesses's court in search of aid. If the world of the ancient Egyptians seems shockingly contemporary in some ways, that's because they used a variety of things most of us would consider quite modern: cradles, beds, linens, perfume, face cream, and stools that folded to save space. And although the invention that Penre discovers in Meryra's tomb seems unlikely, it is the first recorded instance of a shaduf anywhere in Egypt.

As for Queen Nefertari herself, she enjoyed at least twenty-five years of rule at Ramesses's side. In Abu Simbel, Ramesses built her a mortuary temple next to his, and twice a year the rising sun illuminates the statues just as it does in the novel. When Nefertari died, she was buried in QV66 in the Valley of the Queens, and her tomb is the largest and most spectacular of any ever found in the necropolis. On a wall of her burial chamber, Ramesses summed up his love for her as such: "My love is unique and none can rival her . . . Just by passing, she has stolen away my heart."

GLOSSARY

Aaru: After death, it was believed that a person's soul entered into the underworld (Duat), where their heart was weighed against Ma'at's feather of truth. If the heart weighed the same as the feather, the soul was allowed to pass into Aaru, eternal reed fields located somewhere in the eastern sky.

Abi: An affectionate term for father.

Adze: A tool composed of a long wooden handle and blade. A miniature version of the adze was used in the Opening of the Mouth Ceremony, which was supposed to give mummified Pharaohs back their five senses.

Akhu: A person's ancestors; an immortal soul.

Alabaster: A hard, white marblelike mineral mined in Alabastron, a village in Egypt.

Ammit: The god of karmic retribution who was often depicted with the body of a lion and the head of a crocodile. During passage through the Afterlife, if a person's heart weighed more than Ma'at's feather of truth, Ammit would eat their soul and condemn them to oblivion.

Glossary

Amun: King of the gods and the creator of all things.

Ankh: A symbol of life, resembling a looped cross.

Anubis: The guardian of the dead, who weighed deceased hearts on the scales of justice to determine whether they should continue their journey. He was often depicted as having the head of a jackal, since jackals were seen to lurk near the Valley of the Kings, where the dead resided.

Apep: An evil demon in the form of a snake.

Aten: A sun disc worshipped during the reign of Akhenaten.

Bastet (or Bast): The goddess of the sun and moon. She was also a war goddess, depicted as a lion or a cat.

Bes: The dwarf-god of fertility and childbirth.

Canopic jars: Four burials jars in which a person's most important organs (liver, lungs, stomach, intestines) were kept for the Afterlife. Each jar was carved with one of the heads of Horus's four sons.

Cartouche: A circular symbol with a horizontal bar at the bottom in which a royal name was written.

Crook and flail: Pharaoh held these implements as a symbol of royalty, and to remind the people of his role as shepherd (crook) and provider (flail, used for threshing grain).

Cuneiform: A pictographic language inscribed on clay tablets. First used by the Sumerians, it was later adopted by the Hittites.

Deben: Rings of gold, silver, or copper that had fixed weights and were used as units of currency.

Des: An ancient Egyptian measure of volume that is roughly equivalent to 1 pint or 0.5 liters.

***Deshret* crown**: A red crown symbolizing Lower Egypt. The tall, white crown that symbolized Upper Egypt was the *hedjet*.

Duat: The Underworld where the sun god Ra travels every night in order to do battle with the snake Apep. Ra's victory and subsequent return to the skies each morning brings about the return of daylight.

Glossary

Faience: A glazed blue or green ceramic used in small beads or amulets.

Feast of Wag: On the eighteenth day of Thoth, it was believed that a person's ancestors returned in spirit form to their mortuary temples on earth. This day was used to honor one's ancestors by bringing them food and incense.

Habiru: A little-known tribe living in the Fertile Crescent, whose existence was recorded by Egyptians, Hittites, and Sumerians.

Hammurabi's Code: One of the earliest known examples of written laws, dating back to 1750 BC. They were written in cuneiform on a stele that depicted the Babylonian sun god Shamash. The stele was discovered in 1901 and can now be viewed in the Louvre Museum. Hammurabi, a Babylonian king, believed that the gods had chosen him to deliver these laws to his people.

Hathor: The goddess of joy, motherhood, and love. She was often depicted as a cow.

Horus: The falcon-headed god of the sun and sky.

Ibis: A wading bird with a long, curved bill.

Isis: The goddess of beauty and magic, she was also revered as a wife and mother.

Ka: A person's spirit or soul, which was created at the time of one's birth.

Khepresh crown: A blue ceremonial crown of war.

Khnum: A god who was often depicted as a ram-headed man sitting at a potter's wheel. It was believed that Khnum would take his clay creations and place them in a mother's womb, thereby creating life.

Kohl: A mascara and eye shadow made from mixing soot and oil.

Ma'at: The goddess of justice and truth, Ma'at was often depicted as a woman with wings (or a woman wearing a crown with one feather). During the Afterlife, a person's heart would be weighed against one of her feathers to determine whether they were worthy of passing into the Blessed Land. The word *Ma'at* came to stand for the principles of justice, order, and propriety that every Egyptian was responsible for upholding.

Mawat: Mother.

Menat: A necklace associated with the goddess Hathor. The *menat* consisted of a beaded string to which a small pectoral was attached. This pectoral was worn on the chest, while a decorative counterweight dangled on the wearer's back.

Min: The god of fertility and harvest thought to be responsible for the flooding of the Nile. Depicted as a man holding an erect phallus in one hand and a flail in the other, his black skin was supposed to reflect the dark sediment common during the Nile's inundation.

Miw: Cat.

Montu: The hawk-headed god of war.

Mortuary temple: A temple that was often separate from the tomb of the deceased and built to commemorate a person's life.

Mut: The goddess of motherhood and female partner of Amun. She was often depicted with the head of a cat.

Naos: An ancient Greek term used by Egyptologists when referring to a type of shrine containing the image of a god or goddess.

Ne'arin: A tribe whose existence was recorded by the Egyptians and who were given credit for helping Ramesses during the Battle of Kadesh.

Nemes **crown:** A royal crown made of a headcloth that was striped blue and gold. It is the crown depicted on Tutankhamun's sarcophagus.

Opet Festival: The largest festival in Thebes. During this celebration, a statue of Amun was carried by boat from the Temple of Amun in Karnak to the Temple of Amun in Luxor.

Osiris: The husband of the goddess Isis and the judge of the dead. He was murdered by his brother, Set, who scattered pieces of his body across Egypt. When Isis gathered his body parts together, she resurrected him, and he became the symbol of eternal life. Osiris was often depicted as a bearded man dressed in mummy wrappings.

Papyrus: A type of reed plentiful on the Nile that could be dried and smoothed, then used for writing.

Per Medjat: Library.

Pschent **crown:** The red and white double crown symbolizing both Upper and Lower Egypt.

Ptah: The god of builders and artists.

Pylon: A stone gate or entryway often accompanied by statues on either side.

Ra: The god of the sun, often depicted as a hawk.

Renpet: An entire year, according to the Egyptian calendar, which comprised 365 days (twelve months of thirty days each, with an extra five days added to the end).

Sarcophagus: A stone tomb or coffin, often covered in gold.

Sekhmet: The lion-headed goddess of war and destruction.

Senet: Considered to be the world's first board game, Senet later became a religious symbol and was often depicted in tombs.

Senit: Little girl.

Seshed: A circlet crown with a single uraeus.

Set: The god of storms, chaos, and evil who killed his brother Osiris. When he was not depicted with the head of an unknown animal, he was depicted as having red hair.

Shamash: The Babylonian and Assyrian sun god.

Shasu: Nomads who appeared in Egypt as early as 1400 BC.

Shedeh: A favorite Egyptian drink made from either pomegranates or grapes.

Shen: A symbol of eternity in the form of a looped rope. The cartouche is an elongated version of a shen ring.

Sistrum: A small bronze (or brass) instrument made from a handle and a U-shaped frame on which small discs were placed. When shaken, the instrument made a loud, tinny noise.

Tawaret: The goddess of childbirth, who was often depicted as a hippopotamus.

Thoth: The god of scribes and the author of the famous Book of the Dead. He was credited with inventing both writing and speech and was often depicted as an ibis-headed god.

Uraeus: The cobra crown that symbolized kingship. The cobra was depicted with its hood flared and was thought to be able to spit fire into the eyes of the wearer's enemies.

Ushabti: Small figurines placed in tombs as servants, which could be called upon in the Afterlife to do manual labor for the deceased.

Vizier: An adviser to the royal family.

CALENDAR

Season	Month	Festival	Dates
AKHET AUTUMN	Thoth	Wag Festival	July 19th–August 17th
	Phaophi	Opet Festival	August 18th–September 16th
	Aythyr	Festival of Hathor	September 17th–October 16th
	Choiak		October 17th–November 15th
PERET WINTER	Tybi		November 16th–December 15th
	Mechyr	Festival of Isis	December 16th –January 14th
	Phamenoth		January 15th–February 13th
	Pharmuthi		February 14th–March 15th
SHEMU SUMMER	Pachons		March 16th–April 14th
	Payni	Feast of the Valley	April 15th–May 14th
	Epiphi		May 15th–June 13th
	Mesore		June 14th–July 13th
THE EPAGOMENAL DAYS	1st day		July 14th
	2nd day		July 15th
	3rd day		July 16th
	4th day		July 17th
	5th day		July 18th

ACKNOWLEDGMENTS

HAVING ALREADY PUBLISHED my first novel in which I thanked everyone from my seventh-grade teacher to my next-door neighbor, I am going to use these acknowledgments for the people who contributed specifically to the creation of *The Heretic Queen*. As always, I am deeply indebted to my mother, Carol Moran, who has supported me in every meaning of the word with her generosity and incredible spirit. My husband has been my champion from the very beginning, editing my work from first to last, and with his red hair I like to think of him as my very own Ramesses (minus the rashness and harem, of course). And without the hard work of New York's finest editor Allison McCabe, who insisted that there be an *iwiw* somewhere in the book, *The Heretic Queen* as it is written would never exist. To Danny Baror, Dyana Messina, Donna Passannante, Heather Proulx, my copy editor Laurie McGee, and Cindy Berman, thank you for being part of *The Heretic Queen*'s journey to publication. And to my wonderful agent, Anna Ghosh, who made sure my third novel, *Cleopatra's Daughter*, had a home with Crown, thank you very, very much.